D0278543

THE HOUSE OF MARVELLOUS BOOKS

FIONA VIGO MARSHALL

Fairlight Books

First published by Fairlight Books 2022

Fairlight Books
Summertown Pavilion, 18–24 Middle Way, Oxford, OX2 7LG

A CIP catalogue record for this book is available from the British Library

1 2 3 4 5 6 7 8 9 10

ISBN 978-1-914148-09-5

www.fairlightbooks.com

Printed and bound in Great Britain

Designed by Nathan Burton

To my friends in publishing

IT IS SAID that those who go against the way end up being called unlucky. And as luck would have it, I, Mortimer Blakeley-Smith, have been charged to tell the tale of our last ill-fated voyage. Now, I have reached the land of detachment, from which there is no return. There remains only this record. A logbook if you like from a sinking ship, though for centuries we never touched shore.

Where to begin, how introduce this navigatio? *Our great Ship of Fools has always been there, sailing the seas without a rudder, weighted by its cargo of magical books that bristled with spells and secret words so potent that many times they imploded, ripping apart our keel and knocking us overboard. So many times we abandoned ourselves to the mercy of the waves; so many rescues, so many miracles. Like the mariner saint, Brendan of Clonfert, who sailed in circles for seven years before realising his destination was inner as well as outer, we travelled from book to book as if from one magical island to the next, always believing the next would be the one, always cast again on the ocean, garments stained with salt water, faces burning in the air and heads dizzy with the rocking, glinting waves. Setting forth again and again on our unknown journey, welcoming the sea as the sacred landscape of estrangement; throwing our oars overboard as a gesture of faith, ever-questing, never losing hope of finding the blessed isle. People of the way, they called us; the way being simply the infinite sea...*

Wednesday 2 January

Back to work. Snow driving sparsely over London. Steely smell of London on the air. The dark flakes flying in my face as I left the tube; snowflakes peppering the sleeping bags of the homeless. Snow dashed away by the windscreen wipers of the ambulances turning impatiently into the hospital down the road. Snow half-settling on the steps up to our great, ancient building, set back from the London traffic like a grounded ark. Welcome to HQ. Place of study, offices, shelter for the dispossessed: a portal into many different worlds.

I trotted up the steps and past the foundation stone with its motto, *Nisi Dominus ædificaverit domum, Unless the Lord build the house* (Psalm 127). Don't suppose the Psalmist was thinking of a publishing house, but it fits all too well. With £1 million debt and a slit in the roof, things look bleak.

For now, the gold lettering above the grand twin doors still proclaims our identity with all the untrammelled confidence of this enduring medieval institution: *The House of Marvellous Books.* I went through into reception and an illusion of quiet, swiftly broken by a yodelling of hymns from the post room on the right, where Ursula was at work flinging letters and parcels about. Cries of 'Drat!' and 'Bother!' punctuated the untuneful recital. I crept past. A willing editorial factotum is a necessity in our trade, of course, and Ursula's been with us a long time, twenty-seven years; but it can't be denied that her singing makes a poor impression on visiting hermits and naturalists from the British countryside, who stand in reception clutching their manuscripts with something akin to growing dismay in their hearts. Doesn't really fit with corporate London.

The off-key notes of *Abide with Me* faded as I crossed reception with its shabby armchairs and opened the door in the wood panelling into the silence of the library. The aroma of antiquarian books came to meet me, nut and wood, wafting up two galleries to an arched criss-crossing of beams like some vast ship. A gallery of shadows on the first floor hinted at where our offices were, encircling the library like watchtowers. The armchairs were empty in the alcoves, and a large antique globe sat in its wooden base, patently untouched for decades. A long table down the middle, dotted with reading lamps, was the only reminder of our origins as one of the London coffee houses of the 1650s, with their bubbling political discourse and vigorous outcrops of early print. What was once a bustling core of intellectual life is now a huge, largely unused asset, visited by around thirty visitors a year, who mainly come to study the calligraphy of the seventeenth-century books.

I wandered down through the body of the library to the grand window above the librarian's desk at the far end, where the stained glass of gorgeous colours showed Chaucer with his hat and his horse and his pilgrims: *The Lyf so short, the craft so long to Lerne.* In the chill morning silence, broken only by the muffled exclamations from the post room, it smote me to the core. My epitaph? Would I, too, have enough time to do all I was meant to do? Before the sacred light of learning was extinguished for ever, before the library shelves were torn out and their contents carried away? New year foreboding and gloom laid a cold finger on my heart.

The ghosts of the past and future gathered about me. I am thirty-eight, single; somehow Lady Right never came along. I have a history of being made redundant from small charities. Here, in this beached ark, I had found shelter. And now? In this ephemeral, quicksilver time, tyrannised by an ephemeral media, would the Dark Ages return, libraries close, books dwindle and die? Then Lucifer, Son of the Morning, would come bounding in with wings spread and take up his abode, spinning eternally in self-jouissance and anguish.

From somewhere, I sensed danger. I looked up to where the crack in the roof might leave us vulnerable to invasion by strange entities that could enter and descend into our midst. For a moment

I thought I caught a glimpse of a vast shape in the shadows of the library, crouched there with its great wings gathered about it.

I was a tad the worse for wear, admittedly. Probably a push too far to have had another lads' night out with my unfortunate friend Hugo. I mean, I'm sure Chaucer, too, was a bit of lad at times, but even so. The Schubert on New Year's Eve was probably enough. The glorious last quartet, the D887 in G major, at the South Bank, accompanied by a bottle of champagne and snow falling on the river. So yes, I guess it was maybe a touch greedy to have indulged in the Bach cello sonatas at the Barbican last night as well. It will be the last of the dissipations, however, as Hugo goes back inside today. Odd to think of his transition from evening dress and white tie to grey pyjamas. Hugo says he fails to see why he is in prison for theft and fraud when so many pillars of society are successfully practising both outside. Quite a relief in a way, though. What with trying to steer him out of mischief and keeping the ship afloat at work, I have my hands full.

For now, all was quiet. I went back to reception and up the side stairs, through corridors smelling faintly of toast to where the empty offices waited. I felt a presence, something soft that brushed against my trousers: Moriarty, ship's cat, a huge, fluffy tortoiseshell of mixed Persian ancestry and boundless self-will. No problems of good or evil for this feline, no troubles about fulfilling divine destiny. Just pure, ancient selfishness, which we exploit to keep the mice down – you could say, the way we exploit the selfishness and vanity of authors to keep ourselves in work.

'Happy new year, Moriarty,' I said.

A quiet day, most people still away. Sat in my office with Moriarty on my lap, he unperturbed by the occasional scuttle and swish of the mice behind the wainscot, and read Henry James's *A Little Tour in France*. About 3pm it occurred to me I could be doing this just as easily at home in Wimbledon. Left early.

Thursday 3 January

The silence of the library, which was beginning to get to me a little, was broken today. I was mooching round the bookcases, perusing the Diaries of John Dee, 1583–1608, magus, alchemist, last royal diviner and adviser to Queen Elizabeth I, looking for any evidence for Hugo's theory that he was our founder, when I heard a sound like the dragging of a suitcase in reception and peeped out to see that was exactly what it was. Drusilla Foat, senior editor, *grande dame* of publishing, in a long fur coat and imposing fur turban, was heading purposefully towards me, pulling her distinctly battered luggage. Step definite, eyes suspicious, she brought what was lacking into the place: authority. No Satans would risk bounding and flirting before her.

'Mortimer, it's you!' she said crossly in her high, elegant drawl, setting her case firmly against the reception desk. 'Leaping out of the shadows like a leprechaun. What are you doing?'

'Oh – er – just browsing. Happy new year, ma'am! It's good to see you.'

'Happy new year,' she conceded, but that, too, sounded like a warning. She removed her hat and a silver curtain of hair fell obediently into place and made her look younger. 'Everything okay?'

'Not too bad, thanks. How was Georgia?'

'Hard work.'

'Oh? Were the princesses difficult?'

'Countesses. They were both fine. I mean that times are hard. It made me realise I have it relatively easy, being an affluent seventy-four-year-old here in London, as opposed to a poverty-stricken countess of similar age in Russia. Anna and Natalia have it rough. They live in a vast castle in the middle of nowhere with no money, and we got drunk every night, sitting round the fire telling stories, because there was nothing to eat except mouldy yellow apples, and nothing to drink but vodka. Three old ladies all squiffy in a castle in the middle of the snow. They fell on the Mars bars in my luggage, poor things.'

'Oh dear. Did you starve?'

'I had a square meal just now at Gatwick. I consider McDonald's a square meal, anyway. Cheeseburger – protein; bread and fries – carbohydrate; vanilla milkshake – calcium. It all tasted like ambrosia.'

'Was it very cold out there?'

'Oh, brass monkeys. Every day we had to go round the castle grounds gathering sticks for the fire. They were frozen to the earth so we had to pry them loose. No hot water, of course; just a big kettle heated over the fire in the mornings. Makes my little East End terrace look like a luxury hotel. How was your Christmas?'

'Oh – quiet.'

'Did you go to your father's in France?'

'No. He couldn't accommodate me in the end. That might have been something to do with my *belle-mère* Jacqueline and her family. Anyway, I don't think the French have quite the same attitude to Christmas as we do.'

'Don't tell me you spent it alone?'

'Oh well… various plans with friends fell through…'

'Oh, Mortimer. You should have said. You could have come to Georgia with me. Goodness knows there was enough room in the castle.'

I was touched. Behind her stern exterior, Drusilla has a heart of gold.

'Thank you. Very kind of you. I do have a standing invitation to my Uncle Albany's on the east coast, but…'

'Yes, quite. Ah well. Next time. Any news?'

'Not that I've heard.'

Drusilla paused. 'Nothing from the governing body?'

'Not a word.'

'Oh dear. That sounds ominous. What about Molly? Did I hear on the news that she'd had some sort of accident?'

We both turned to look at the poster of Bishop Molly Roper in the author display. With her black bob, noble nose and set lips, she looked just like Holbein's portrait of Thomas More, gazing with burning intensity towards the martyrdom coming to meet him, a terrifying remnant from a sombre, savage age. You could almost see the hair shirt peeping out from beneath the purple blouse. Nothing could have been more misleading. Her former reckless life as an international yachtswoman, her dramatic conversion mid-ocean, her innate sympathy with the storms of life, made her one of our best-loved authors. *Wild Seas, Wild Heart* had topped the bestseller list for many a month, followed by a flow of books salty and sparkling as the ocean itself. She looked ready to leap down from the photo and join us in belated new year jollifications, her merry laugh ringing out over the library.

'Broken her ankle and wrist, I'm afraid.'

'Oh, Lord. How did she do that? Drunk?'

'She slipped on the steps here, after a meeting with Sales and Marketing. Quite a nasty tumble. We did bring her out some of the governing body's sherry. I think it cheered her a little, poor Molly.'

'It's her own fault. Too much fast living!'

'Oh, let's not be too harsh. Think of the good she does.'

'Molly has to learn she can't be all things to all people,' continued Drusilla severely. 'Sailing to Norway with a women's refuge one moment, then running off to a green spirituality meeting in the East End the next. Too flighty by far. When is she going to write that book for us? She knows how much we're depending on it.'

I couldn't help but agree it was worrying. Molly had promised so faithfully to write us a new bestseller to extricate us from our present grim circumstances. So far *Sailing with the Angels: Reflections on a solitary voyage to Alaska* was four months late.

'Well, she's going to be housebound for a while. The perfect opportunity.'

'It's a disaster having just one big author,' went on Drusilla. 'How many times have I told the governing body about having all your eggs in one basket? It's just not good business practice to have most of your revenue dependent on one person's sales,' shaking her head, 'but do they listen? Only two years before we run dry. The next few months are crucial. If only we didn't have the library to maintain. Those ancient statutes don't give the publisher a chance. Those wretched restrictions tie us hand and foot.'

'Yes, if only we were allowed to sell the library,' I said. 'A plague on those ancient statutes!'

For these, alas, expressly forbid the sale of any of our assets, and dictate that we, the publisher, must always remain as guardian to the library and its books, ensuring that the original collection never leaves the site, lest it be damaged or lost.

'I don't know what we're going to do if Molly doesn't produce. If we could only...'

For the first time a quaver entered her voice.

'Find the Book?'

Somewhere on these premises it was rumoured to exist. The marvellous book. The Daybreak Manuscript. This long-lost medieval masterpiece, with its bold strokes of script and lavish illustrations, full of *prisca sapientia*, or ancient wisdom, decorated with gold leaf, mystic shapes, ornate trees, rare botanical plants, unicorns, salamander and other mythical beasts. Said to be worth more than all our debts and this library put together, it has haunted us for centuries. Just as Ireland's Book of Kells defines a nation, so a book we have never seen shapes our identity. Rumours of it have maintained our shares in the stock market, keeping us afloat like one of those mythical islands which feature on ancient maps but which can never be found by those at sea.

'Sometimes I think I'm the only one who believes it exists,' said Drusilla.

'It may turn up yet,' I said.

'Mortimer, I've been combing this place for twenty years. It could be anywhere; hidden in the library, like Borges' *Book of*

Sand, buried beneath the foundation stone, or, most likely, already sold or traded by the governing body. If it wasn't for the fragment…'

She extracted her passport from her money belt and opened it carefully to reveal a scrap of vellum about the size of her hand. Found a few years back in a secret drawer in the librarian's desk, it showed a line of golden letters torn across, clearly the bottom line of a title. An apple tree laden with golden fruit showed a decorated capital M for *mālum*, apple, intermingled with the boughs of the tree, along with peacocks and other birds, in intricate patterns and swirls. Ragged though it was, it seemed to glow with the brightness of a summer far from this world, fresh and timeless. For an instant I fancied I could almost smell the apples. We both drew a deep breath.

'Fabulous,' I said.

'And worth a fabulous amount,' Drusilla reminded me. The value of the Daybreak Manuscript was estimated to be somewhere between the St Cuthbert Gospel, acquired by the British Library for £9 million, and the Book of Kells – 'which is literally priceless,' Drusilla said briskly, putting the vellum away again. 'Enough to get us out of trouble and to spare, for sure. Oh dear, what a treasure to have lost.'

Our spirits, momentarily cheered, fell again. From somewhere upstairs came the faint sound of unsteady plainchant.

'Well, you've got Ursula on the case, helping you look.'

Drusilla sighed. 'Yes. I know…'

We gazed despondently down the line of author posters that enlivened the rest of reception, arranged roughly in descending order of vanity. The druids and church dignitaries, the historians and storytellers, the mystics and mythicists, the wise women and wise men, the educated derelicts and simple lifers, the mavericks. We draw the line at witches, unlike some of our competitors such as Calling Crane, but we have psychologists; ecopsychologists, of course, to cater to our own particular blend of ecology, myth and spirituality.

'And Sister Evangeline?' said Drusilla. 'Still set to overtake Molly as our up-and-coming next lead author?'

We looked at the poster of the nation's favourite nun, beaming out at us with a copy of *Sister Shepherdess* in one hand, and her crook in the other, a lamb tucked into a fold of her habit and her headdress streaming in the wind. Since her tale of a small colony of farming nuns on the east coast had become a surprise hit, this rustic sister's meteoric rise from household and linens sister in the Convent of Small Mercies to urban celebrity had established her as an authority on silence and solitude. This unlikely bestseller told of old pink flannel sheets mended again, of sloes and damsons gleaned from the wind-bent trees of the hedgerows, of a small field or two where a handful of ageing sisters struggled valiantly with the lambing beneath the frosty stars of the long February nights.

'As high maintenance as ever, I gather.'

So much for the authors. Drusilla glanced up the stairs to the right of reception.

'And Gerard?'

'Not sight nor sound. His office door is still locked from before Christmas.'

'I see. Nothing like having your publishing director abscond in an emergency. Typical.'

There was a silence. As usual, Drusilla had gone to the heart of the matter. She continued:

'I mean, I appreciate it's difficult to run a publishing business when you also have a home farm to manage, but even so. What's he doing, culling deer?'

'No, that's March, I think. Although I understand that deer management is quite a serious issue in Gloucestershire.'

'The good news is of course that it gives us a free hand for a while before he comes back and carries on selling us all down the river with his useless schemes. Well, that's what you get when you appoint people for their conservationist activities rather than their publishing experience.

'Quite apart from the fact that we're teetering on the brink of ruin, supposing we needed access to one of the contracts he's been sitting on for the past six months? Honestly! You and I are the only ones who keep the ship going! —Well, I'm dying for a hot bath, but I thought as the most senior member of staff who isn't bedbound or insane at the moment I'd better look in. Make sure the place is still standing.'

She looked round. The crack in the roof wasn't visible from where we stood of course, but a wind seemed to whistle through from somewhere and I became aware of the library's vast spaces and the warren of our offices upstairs. Drusilla sighed again, then fumbled in her hand luggage, a big, carpet bag with the contents spilling out.

'Have a chocolate. Filled with Georgian brandy, Chacha. That'll get you cha-chaing round the place, young Mortimer. Grape vodka, sixty-five percent alcohol. Some call it the Devil's brandy. The country people start the day with a dram to get them going. Remember, the kid editor soon becomes the next king.'

Most unlikely. Drusilla, rather like a kindly teacher, I think regards me as a promising student about to do rather well in his A levels and Oxbridge entry exams. I can't seem to convince her that I am somewhat older than I look. One of the Devil's gifts at my birth was a *puer eternus* face reflecting my Irish ancestry, trim and blue-eyed, and somehow even now those first grey hairs above my ears don't really show against the black. Or maybe it's just the dim lighting in here.

I took a chocolate the size of a small egg, reluctantly, and the gush of strong spirits filled my mouth; but Drusilla wouldn't be satisfied without me trying one of each flavour, seven in total, and insisted I take the bag to choose.

'Different, eh? Give me a handful,' said Drusilla. 'A chaser to my junk food of earlier. Well, onward. The Lord gives, and the Lord takes away, but the slush pile is always with us.'

'Yes, ma'am!'

She popped a few chocolates into her mouth and we proceeded up the draughty stairwell to the right of reception that leads up to the offices. Almost before I had time to regret the chocolates, the place began to rock slightly like a ship putting off to sea and I went along the corridor at an almost imperceptible roll, like a sailor still trying to get his sea legs. Alas, Drusilla has no head for alcohol either and it soon made her sing. It was highly audible as her office and mine, overlooking the library side by side like boxes at the opera, are kind of roofless shacks all too clearly rigged up for the temporary accommodation of an expendable staff, so that everything one says – or sings – resounds all over the library. It was something of a trial to hear her attacking Monteverdi's Vespers all morning. The acoustics in this library are rather good.

Text from Hugo saying he is not liking the adjustment to the prison routine. Thought you couldn't have mobile phones inside?

Friday 4 January

Drusilla spent the morning, with the occasional chuckle, working on her proposal for *The Bible for Gluttons and Drunkards: A History of sacred food and drink* to add to her formidable history list, *Darwin Lives!* At intervals she called over to me: 'The ideal book, don't you think?... No problems with the Author... No advance, no royalties... No tiresome lunches to stroke the ego, no squabbles about the cover... No expensive changes at proof stage, because *quod scripsi scripsi*... Don't you think?'

'Oh, definitely... barring a thunderbolt or flood to express divine displeasure, of course!'

'Well, that would liven the place up a bit, at least!'

All this enthusiasm from our senior editor should have had an energising effect on me, but I personally found it hard to imagine that I could ever commission a book again. My own little *Earth* list, the junior and most unimportant list, is hardly going to save the planet. When I voiced as much aloud, Drusilla called over, 'Oh, don't say that. From little acorns...'

Regarded without enthusiasm the manuscript of *The Natural Kindness Manual*, latest offering from environmental science professor Ivan Skrulewski, mainstay of the list and the least kind person I know. Chased up *Wilderness Therapy for Wellbeing* by Eileen Fallon, which is seven months late. Tried to check sales figures for my January title *Trunk Call: Trees, burial myths and mourning in the deep wild,* but the warehouse hadn't updated since before Christmas, which meant we had just twenty-nine early sales. Not promising. The entire *Earth* list seemed a completely heartless jest on the part of the Almighty. Who really cares about nature therapy and wellbeing at such a time of year? However, the green ink brigade had been busy over the Christmas break, so I broke the ice by writing rejection letters all morning.

Got depressed by the gloom of my office in the afternoon, so went and sat in Gerard's at the far end of the corridor, a proper office with a door that closes and plenty of daylight, which vastly improved my mood. An enormous window looked onto the bare plane trees in the park, their bristly seed balls dangling motionless on the wintry air. Within, Gerard's huge *ficus benjamina*, shedding leaves from the ceiling downwards, seemed to embody his benign presence, while the pell-mell of books and letters on the desk looked as if he had just popped out for a sandwich, or, more likely, a nice long lunch with an author. A copy of *Shooter's World* lay open atop the melée, *The role of shooting in landscape management: a conservation-based ecosystem service.* In a corner, Gerard's walking sticks stood propped in their box, twelve of them, one for each month, while his Norfolk jacket was slung across the chair, a faint aroma of tobacco emanating from the pipe stuck in the top pocket.

Sat down at his desk and imagined myself doing his job. I'm sure I couldn't do any worse. Read Jorge Luis Borges on the laborious madness of composing vast books. Moriarty appeared and leapt onto my lap. Fed him a bit of leftover cake from the kitchen, which he seemed to enjoy.

Took advantage of a more private office to make a few phone calls. Tried to call my father in France to wish him a happy new year, but no joy. Perhaps he is still out celebrating. Got through to Hugo. Asked him about having mobile phones in prison, and he said something about earning privileges and having an obliging warder called Sam. Then a not so obliging warder truncated the conversation.

Watered the plant carefully, then sat and read a book of Cavafy's poems which I found on the desk. It was nice to refresh my memory – I haven't looked at Cavafy for years. After all, I am a bit of a *poietes historikos* – a historical poet or poet-historian – myself.

Ithaca particularly struck me, with its longing advice not to hurry the voyage, to spin out the journeying years, so that you only reach the island when you are old.

At a loss for anything to do after that, so turned with relief to my own writing: *On the Wave with St Brendan*, about the mariner saint's obsessive quest for his island. Destined – though no one knows it yet – for our own award-winning nature list, *Wayfarers and Wilderness*. It draws somewhat heavily on the original accounts of his *navigatio* in the *Navigatio Sancti Brendani Abbatis (Voyage of St Brendan the Abbot)*, composed maybe in the eighth century, and the slightly later *Vita Brendani* (Life of Brendan), it yet has, I flatter myself, a flair and panache all of its own. Diary, I confess, once I hoped this book might be the one to save the list, might even make some small amends for the loss of the Daybreak Manuscript, presumptuous though that sounds. Now, alas, I'm not so sure. Oh, the long, choppy whale-road to publication!

How easy the old tales make it sound. Brendan the Navigator set off from the coast of Ireland in a boat made of twigs and greased leather to shoot the buffeting waves. Well, willow boughs and forty-nine oxhides, to be precise, a curragh boat, with provisions for forty days, some time between AD 512 and

530. Although my own Irish ancestry is far in the past – some eight or nine generations, in fact – I like to think of myself as a latter-day voyager querant, launched on the inhospitable waves of modern urban life. Can I compare my journey to those legendary *immrama?* Sea quests made by the *peregrini* of old, those early Celtic pilgrims who sailed the Atlantic in their thousands in search of the otherworld. Drawn by the *terra repromissionis sanctorum*, ancient stories of a land far beyond the sea, they left the shores of the familiar in droves to explore the vast, forbidding wilderness of that northern sea. Our soul journey—

At this point the phone rang. It was our author Melissa Todd wanting to know how *Rewild Your Body*, published in November, had done over Christmas. I told her that the warehouse was still shut and I didn't have up-to-date figures. Thought it best to suppress the fact that I do have first month sales of thirty-seven.

Lost my flow after this, so updated my Twitter account, @floatmyboat. Purportedly written by Brendan himself, it is of course not long, but thought-consuming. Couldn't think of anything so in the end I just put, 'Occian yced overe so no rowynge todaye by the mercie of Godde. Staye warme, folkes!' Hopefully that'll reach a few more people than my current four followers.

Saturday 5 January

Stayed in bed and read Parson Woodforde. I'm sure his detailing of meals is due to innate love of list-making rather than to gluttony. Very cold still – though, luckily the chamber pots didn't freeze as they did in Woodforde's time! (25 Jan 1795). Got lonely around 3pm, so went for a walk. Absolutely nothing in Wimbledon to entice one out, except possibly the spectacle of the birds landing on the frozen lake in the park, surprised each time to find themselves skidding, accompanied by their reflections in the greeny ice. Wonder if Brendan and his men had ever had to chop their way out of an icy sea…

Sunday 6 January
Epiphany
Took down the decorations, to wit, the mini tree that stands on the mantelpiece. Was tempted to recycle it as space is so tight in my flat, but finally managed to tuck it away on the top of the cupboard. Cleaned and hoovered the flat. Even for one room this seemed to take an inordinate amount of time as the tree, just eighteen inches tall as it was, and stationary for three weeks, had yet managed to shed silver threads all over the place.

Tried to call my father again, in vain. Called Uncle Albany on the faraway east coast instead, with more luck. He waxed lyrical about the Gallhampton Gap new year gathering on the beach where the community had assembled for Prosecco and the morning dip.

I said, 'Did you get in?'

'No fear. At seventy-nine, I don't feel the need to prove myself. Patti did. She can still take liberties at her age, only fifty-four. In her fancy dress, black evening gloves and all, brave girl.'

'Oh, what did she go as?'

Uncle Albany hesitated. 'Queen of the Night. Or was it Lady Macbeth? Not sure now. The costume is the same for both, anyway.'

'Oh, splendid. I hope she didn't suffer from exposure afterwards.'

'Patti? Good Lord, no. Take more than an ocean wave to keep that girl down.'

'Did you go as anything?' I asked.

'Yeah, a pirate. Strictly on dry land, though. How about you, Mortimer? Were you living it up with a lady friend?'

'Sadly, no.'

Told him about Hugo and his last night of freedom and he tut-tutted and said, 'We have to do better than that. Getting a bit old for the carefree bachelor life, aren't you? Or maybe you like it that way? I shouldn't be talking about a gay bachelor life, should I?'

'No, no. You know how needy Hugo is, and he's latched onto me more than ever since his conviction. I've had a terrible year, seeing him through all the court hearings. He's been a wreck.'

'Serve him right for being such a little tea-leaf. I thought the whole point of libraries was that they were free. What does he want to go round nicking books off them for? All over Europe, wasn't it?'

'Well, yes. They've got his picture up behind the desk in every academic library from Dublin to Munich. A lot of librarians were relieved when Hugo went inside. No, Hugo's not an emotional contender. I'd willingly swap him for a nice girl. It's just I can't be the last one to abandon him, after all our other university friends have dropped off. You can't possibly be more frustrated about it all than I am.'

Albany sounded relieved. 'You really should come down here for some of our gatherings, Mortimer. I can introduce you to people. You'd love it, a ladykiller like you.'

Albany said New Year itself had been disappointing as the council had cancelled the fireworks because the wind was in the wrong direction.

'Got to jet now, geezer,' he said. 'No peace for the wicked. Hamlet and Dolly Parton we are tonight, for a Twelfth Night party. Listen, Mortimer, what are you doing tonight? It's an open invite for this party, you know. No need to be lonely. Why don't you hop on a train and come on down? You could come as you are, as an Edwardian gent. It's not too late. That's our motto down here, you know. Never too late.'

'That's very kind of you.'

I thought for a moment of the bleak, windswept peninsula where he lives, once an island before time silted it up; of its bony, off-white cliffs, stretches of desolate green grass along the promenade, and wind whistling through the railings. I thought of Brendan's dream isle as he and his little crew ploughed on through the salt blue, to their impossible quest of balmy airs, youth, happiness. I said, 'Next time.'

So what if you're old by the time you reach the island?

Got a bit of Sundaynightitis after thinking about all this, so had a glass of wine and sat making notes far into the night for *On the Wave with St Brendan.*

*

The quest for Paradise. Monks with chunky calves and calloused hands, wet robes roped up round their waists, shoving the boat out: Heave to, lads. Clouds of soft charcoal and a castle edged with pink standing out ahead above the waves. I think of Avalon, Brendan's journey to the edge of the world, a long roll of waves in the grey sunlight. I think of the three extra monks who arrived late for the voyage and were thus marked as unlucky. Their late arrival upset the balance of the magical numbers; Brendan led a boat of fourteen, seven at each side. The latecomers did not complete the voyage but were lost along the way. I think of Fang Feng, one of the lords of the Xia dynasty, summoned to a meeting of the spirits on sacred Guiji Mountain by Yu the Great, conqueror of the floods in ancient China. Fang Feng arrived late. Yu had him executed. The Way closes for the one who is late...

*

Monday 7 January

From: Ursula Woodrow Sent: 7 January 10.47 To: ALL@HQ
Subject: Weekly *Please be kind* list

Hullo everybody,

Happy new year! Here's hoping it'll be a better one than last year!

This week, **please be kind** to:

- Our lead author Bishop Molly Roper, recovering at home from a broken wrist and ankle after an unfortunate fall.
- Mortimer Blakeley-Smith's unfortunate friend Hugo Castle, currently starting a six-year jail term for aggravated theft and fraud.
- All of us here at the House in its current difficulties after the unfortunate downturn in nature publishing of the past year. Frankly, we need all the kind thoughts we can get, folks!

Ursula

Ursula Woodrow, editorial assistant
The House of Marvellous Books
Wayfarers and Wilderness, our award-winning nature list

Please send any kind thoughts for next week to Ursula Woodrow by Friday.

Tuesday 8 January
Back to it with the first editorial board of the year. The table in the cold, draughty Fisher Room strewn with post-Xmas offerings, as if to the *genius loci* of this daunting space: mince pies, fruit cake, Yule logs, stollen, panettone, shortcake, etc. The mood distinctly subdued. Thanks to Ursula, word had got round about Bishop Molly's latest disaster and without her ebullient presence to convince us otherwise, we sank into the natural gloom and despair that our case merits. Drusilla, game old trooper that she is, tried to break the depression by handing round her horrible chocolate liqueurs. Most people shuddered slightly and refused.

Drusilla herself too tough after a lifetime in publishing to be affected by such things. The light of battle in her eyes, she sat waiting impatiently for everyone to take their seats so she could present her proposal: *The Bible for Gluttons and Drunkards: A history of sacred food and drink*. She was all ready for the attack with Matthew 11:19 ('The Son of man came eating and drinking, and they say, Behold a man gluttonous, and a winebibber, a friend of publicans and sinners. But wisdom is justified of her children'); and Luke 7:34 ('The Son of man is come eating and drinking; and ye say, Behold a gluttonous man, and a winebibber, a friend of publicans and sinners!') but such was the new year depression that there was not a murmur of objection, not even from her sister editor Fay Meredith, always ready to challenge a proposal of Drusilla's. I suppose even Fay can't quarrel with a proposal where we don't have to pay the author anything.

Fay said, 'I can't see it being a blockbuster, but it does at least fit with our new initiative to publish more mainstream commercial titles, as mooted by Gerard before Christmas,' and everyone automatically turned to the empty chair that represented Gerard, before establishing that no one knew where our esteemed publishing director was or when he might be back. However, there's no doubt that meetings run more smoothly in his absence than in his presence, so we quickly passed the proposal.

Odd about Fay really. With her tumbling black curls, comely figure, and long dresses swishing neatly to her person as she walks, I sometimes wonder that I don't find her more appealing. The dark wisps of hair against her pale, creamy skin, her otherworldly green eyes with flecks of navy blue, her *princesse lointaine* beauty, give her the air of some orthorexic, austere faery – one of the more dangerous kind, who haunt the wild, desolate hinterlands of reality with their permeable barriers between the actual and the beyond, and who might appear suddenly in the wilderness as woman or as worm. It's not that I don't admire Fay, it's more that she doesn't admire me! Actually, she doesn't really admire any of us much, viewing us all as a naturally inferior race to her own elven kind.

Fay herself in her capacity as senior editor for her great *Wayfarers and Wilderness* nature list then proposed a major new book as the one to save our fortunes, with a working title of *Heaven is A Clear Blue Sky* (*Heaven* for short) by Trevor Trefnant-Jones, and a great follow-up to his last year's *Releasing Wolves Back into London.*

'Something a bit more cosmic,' said Fay. 'London was admittedly a bit niche. Good for a first book, but we don't want to be too parochial. We in London do tend to live in a bit of a bubble.'

This, too, went through smoothly, though someone did ask what it was about.

'The main feature of Heaven is that it's unimaginable in advance,' said Drusilla dryly before Fay could respond. 'Eye hath not seen, nor ear heard, remember. We just have to take it on faith. Although I take it that doesn't extend to the logical absurdity of blank pages, does it, Fay?'

I guess Fay was grateful even for this measure of support, heavily laced with irony though it was.

'The pages,' Fay assured her, 'will be written on.'

In Gerard's absence, Fay also took the opportunity to push through *Lays from a Shepherd's Hut* for her nature poetry list, *Antler Bones*, by the peripatetic poet Dafydd ap Dafydd, who is currently residing in just such a hut somewhere in Clwyd, appropriately smocked and bearded, which Gerard had opposed before Christmas on the grounds that the only poetry on the list should be by himself. Drusilla now opposed it too, on the grounds that Fay is neglecting her initiative to commission more women authors – she only has two on her entire list – and is overly prejudiced in favour of male Welsh authors, but this is such an old bone of contention that not even Sales and Marketing responded. Hunched along their row at the table like so many baleful crows, there was little spirit in them. Even beaky sales director Roland Meath, self-styled king of hyperbole, displayed uncharacteristic disinterest. He sat listening to the meeting with head bent, like a Knight Templar of old resting between crusades, with black beard, black hair touched with silver and black shirt. He's not usually with us as he spends most of his time on the road, on his lonely mission to sell books in the far north. His sales area includes the whole of Scotland and Ireland, and he is expert at penetrating remote places where eccentric and crusty booksellers may have hidden themselves. He usually calls us (if he can get reception) while standing on the deck of a ferry watching the quay of some remote little harbour recede as he makes his way from island to island. Like a modern-day St Brendan in a way. Perhaps so much solitary travelling in the remote reaches of the UK has given him this rather sombre, slightly forsaken air of quest, as if he were perpetually in search of some mythical, unattainable book.

The ever-changing sales team – Harold Cuxton, Oupie Hoo, and Noreen Snodland for now – were ranged alongside him, staring glazedly at Fay as if hypnotised by an exceptionally clever and agile snake. Drusilla, probably mindful that Fay had not opposed her *Glutton's Bible*, also sank into resigned silence and acceptance as the proposal was passed.

Our two redoubtable senior editors did have words just after the meeting, but that was about the heating, which was still off from before Christmas as Ursula hadn't remembered to turn it on.

'The heating is hardly my responsibility, Fay. No one can convince the governing body that it's a false economy to turn it off for the break. Besides, it feels quite balmy to me after Georgia. Why didn't you turn it on yourself if you find it that chilly? Unless of course you, too, don't feel the cold after rural Wales?'

'Honestly, Drusilla. I may have spent Christmas in the wilds of Tremeirchion, but that doesn't mean I'm inured to low temperatures. They managed to turn on the heating for midnight mass in St Asaph Cathedral, I'll have you know. And my parents do stretch to a coal fire. We even have stone hot water bottles. They're very comforting!'

The two ladies parted in appropriate glacial *froideur.* The Fisher Room not conducive to high spirits at the best of times. Today it was like an icebox – or maybe I should say like an icy ocean, tossed about by the stormy emotions of the commissioning editors. It will take at least another two weeks to warm up.

In any case, I've long thought there's something inimical in the Fisher Room's atmosphere, with its vast spaces, massive boat-shaped oak table, fourteen chairs with their tall, wrought-iron backs and red velvet seats, and the throne at the head, always left empty for Sophia or Wisdom. A window or two would surely be more conducive to inspiration, but naturally a secret room via the library (the door is disguised as an antique bookcase) militates against that. Any light has to be inner light.

Wednesday 9 January

Still ploughing through the submissions, most of which are unexpurgated autobiography in some form or another. To wit:

- The straight autobiography:

> Dear Editor,
>
> *Me, Myself and I*: I am writing with regard to an autobiographical account of my life I'm looking to have published after finding your email details in the *Writer's Market*. The finished material is over 170,000 words in length and took the last four months to compile.

NO.

- The unexpurgated autobiography disguised as cute medical book:

  Ileostomy Revealed: 'Hello, my name is Craig. I have a friend who is a frog. I have just completed a 450-page humorous novel.'

NO.

- The unexpurgated autobiography disguised as motivational book:

  Over the Hill: How to be happy in your 40s, by Elinor Moony.

Sorry, NO.

How any of these relate to ecological concerns is hard to see. In desperation, amended the submission guidelines on the web page to state: NO life coaching proposals and absolutely NO personal stories or autobiography in any form whatsoever. Don't suppose it will make much difference.

Thursday 10 January

Tried to commission a writer in Cork called Proinséas O'Cheevers to do a book on *Ecotherapy for the Shy and Socially Isolated* but couldn't get through because his phone doesn't accept incoming calls from strange numbers. A good start.

Messaged Hugo commiserations for his life in jail but he was incredibly patronising in his reply. 'I don't see how my situation is any different to yours, you, too, have no freedom, serving time at the House, trying to make an impossible situation work. No way are you ever going to get out. You're just commodifying nature with all your books on ecology and myth. It's a facile form of self-help & self-help is fascist, conservative and capitalist, an offshoot of a brand of evangelism pushed in 1930s America.' This depressed me inordinately, not so much for its truth, which is indubitable, as the element of betrayal in it from Hugo. After all I've done for him. Surely it's rather ignoble of him to attack me in this way, on the assumption that I'm in exactly the same position as he is? After all, I *can* just walk out if I want. Was relieved to hear he is not allowed visitors for the rest of January after he told one of the warders he had no poetry in his soul.

Friday 11 January
Drusilla and I both in early. I could hear her over the partition, grilling Ursula first thing about her progress in searching for the Daybreak Manuscript, and the sad descent of Urusla's loud and happy new year hopes, to perplexity and tears.

'It doesn't really matter whether it exists or not,' Drusilla was saying, in response to some confused protest of Ursula's. 'Its actual existence is irrelevant. Belief in it is all that really matters.'

More protest from Ursula.

'It's the same with any book,' Drusilla continued. 'You have to take a publisher's gamble on a manuscript that may or may not ever exist and trust your editor's instinct that it will materialise at some point. When you commission a work, you're placing faith in something that isn't there, pulling it out of nowhere, like Prospero.'

And finally, in response to another wail of incomprehension, 'Well, *go* and read *The Tempest*, then, if you don't understand!'

Saturday 12 January
Took my Christmas cards to the recycling bin at the supermarket. Took care to fish out the annual £100 Xmas cheque from my father first. I kept Molly's card – a spray of mistletoe, holly and a bottle, saying, *Let's get merry together.* I know she sends one to everyone in the building, but even so. It fills a certain emotional vacuum. I wonder should I have kept Hugo's card, too? Not out of

emotional investment, but his signature might be worth something in time to come, especially as he signed himself in full, Hugo Castle, rather than the catchy nom de plume he's taken to using recently, Hu Cass; or his online Twitter alter ego, @kleptobook (something of a mistake, in my opinion, if he wants to be taken seriously as a literary figure). Of course he's rather dropped out of sight with some of the more narrow-minded literary mags but quite a few have stayed faithful, even eager to support him, taking a certain defiant pride in publishing him, for which he mustn't get paid, according to prison regulations. No problem with that as far as most literary magazines are concerned, I'd have thought. Indeed, as usual, he's his own worst enemy as the only thing that really stops him publishing is his convoluted inner attitude to writing. Why he abandoned short stories for a life of crime is beyond me, though hopefully it may provide material for the future. All very Dostoevsky – or that's my best hope, anyway.

Don't want to complain, but, thinking about it as I went round the supermarket and collected assorted tins and fresh produce to feed the inner Mortimer, there's no doubt that an invite to the Vendée from my father and Jacqueline would have fleshed Christmas out. With an entire campsite at their disposal and that massive house, it's not as if they don't have the space. I suppose they don't have the psychic or emotional space. Sometimes I can't help thinking it's a shame my father ran off with the family nanny.

Deep in such musings, I didn't pay too much attention to what I was buying and the bill came as a considerable shock. I do believe the corner shop, Ahmed's, is not much more expensive. May transfer my attentions there for a while.

Sunday 13 January

Hugo messaged in the evening to say I should have donated my Christmas cards to the prison, as they are useful for the arts and crafts programme. I said I would certainly bear it in mind if he was still inside next year (as seems probable). He then asked would I go back to the supermarket and get as many cards out of the recycling bin as I could when no one was looking and send them on to him. I told him it was too late. Hugo always will push an idea too far.

Monday 14 January

Problems already. Fay's star book, *Heaven*, has gone into the system as *Heave*. Gone through onto the warehouse and Amazon overnight. No mean feat considering how long it usually takes. Drusilla says – not, I am afraid, without all satisfaction – it will be the Devil's own job to get it changed now, though I still think that even he would quail before Drusilla in one of her more chipper moods. We've managed to keep it a secret so far from the author, Trevor Trefnant-Jones. Luckily he tends not to look at the internet much, as he works on one of the smaller Welsh islands as a marine biologist and doesn't get much signal. Fay highly displeased all the same. As usual, no one is sure who's to blame but fingers are being pointed at the usual scapegoat, Ursula, whose failing sight has been a matter of concern for some time. Among other concerns, of course.

Drusilla a bit more cheerful today, possibly as a result of Fay's contretemps; in fact, she passed on two key pieces of advice for publishing. We all listened up over our coffee and walnut cake in the kitchen, hoping to hear the magic words that might save the house from extinction. Drusilla smiled graciously, waiting for our full attention. When we were all quiet she lifted a forefinger.

'One: never let the author choose the restaurant.

'Two: never let them get there first, especially if they're from the BBC, or by the time you arrive, they'll have run up a huge tab.'

Then she started preparing for her annual trip to New York, to visit the legendary Tip (an affectionate shortening of Tippex), the great editorial manager who first trained the young Drusilla and honed her eagle eye, making her what she is today and earning her undying loyalty in the process. Now in her nineties, Tip lives in a small Manhattan apartment crammed from floor to ceiling with her own paintings, fruits of a long retirement. Drusilla worries a lot about what will happen to them all when Tip 'goes'. Tip won't sell them as each one represents a period of her youth. I'm sure I'd feel exactly the same in her place.

Drusilla said, 'Of course, had I known Tip was going to live for ever when I first started going, I'd have thought a lot harder about taking the commitment on.'

I personally dread the day I live to hear of Tip turning 100. It may happen. Hugo may be right. I may never get out of here. This isn't really how I planned for my life to turn out, whereas Drusilla seems to have everything taped. I sat at my desk and gazed down into the darkness of the library, where the floor lights muted it into a place of shadows and ghosts. The sound of Drusilla on the phone bullying travel agents about her ticket to the States only added to the gloom. I called over, 'I wonder could we sue the governing body for dysthymia caused by lack of natural daylight,' but a cry came back of, 'Just off to collect the grandchildren from school and take them swimming!' – she gets in as well of course – and by the time I went to say goodbye, two minutes later, she'd gone.

Tuesday 15 January

Gathered my forces and went round to House Editorial at the end of the corridor to greet Ethel as a politic post-holiday move. It's always wise for a commissioning editor to be on best possible terms with the all-powerful editorial manager, who can hold up or speed up publication of one's books as she sees fit. Deep in work as usual, Ethel was slicing paper on the house guillotine and did not look best pleased to be interrupted. With her dark brown hair piled high, thick eyebrows and inscrutable gaze, she looks rather like Frida Kahlo in her more severe mode, but without the moustache and more plainly dressed, in an elegant orange roll-neck jumper, beige leggings and big, hoop gold earrings. Her skin is prettily blotched with freckles which stood out a little as she said, 'Happy new year, Mortimer,' which made me wonder how happy it was going to be, really. I asked her how her Christmas had been. Ethel said icily that she had gone home to Texas, seen her family, then taken a bus to Querétaro, Mexico, and done a pilgrimage to the shrine of the Virgin of Guadalupe, Mexico City, walking 186 miles. I said, 'I thought it was the Santiago de Compostela walk you were doing,' and she said, 'No, I've done that three times already.'

Then she softened a little and said, 'Not going to lie, Mortimer, I found it a stretch.'

A stretch! It would kill me!

Wednesday 16 January

Dire rumours going round about the Christmas sales. Impossible to check as, due to our canny, cutting-edge technology, Gerard is the only one who has access to the figures.

Thursday 17 January

Hah! Things getting going a bit! Commissioned a book on tree communication in the Blue Coat Boys café, from a rather keen lady called Mair Jones. *What Trees Talk About When They Talk About Love (Tree Talk* for short) is the last word on distress signals about drought, disease, insects and other communications exchanged by trees via mycorrhizal networks. Mair Jones seemed to be a pastoral author of the wounded healer type, being herself unable to speak in anything above a faltering whisper, I think due to throat disease rather than a cold, though, naturally this was not a subject for conversation over the Earl Grey and passion fruit cake. However, she seemed passionately devoted to tree speech as a subject, and moreover is content with the advance, so I suppose we could do worse. Even better, the book is already written as another publisher has let her down, and she promised to send it in at once.

Went back to work with my brolly held high against the squalls of wind and snow and shared the good news about my latest acquisition with Fay in her office, perforce as Drusilla was out. Fay was pretty scathing. Pulling her elbow-length, salmon-pink cardigan more closely round her (I believe she only wears pure wool), she said, '*Tree Talk* comes quite low down on my list of priorities at the moment, Mortimer. Right now I'm fairly preoccupied with my star book, *Heaven*.'

I said, 'We have to start somewhere,' but Fay snapped, 'We have to start, progress, finish and succeed, and we're much more likely to do it with *Heaven* than with *Tree Talk*.'

I looked round her sumptuous snuggery, resplendent with red cushions, armchairs and paintings, the burnished spines of books across one wall and the two huge windows onto the park, and could only agree. She's put up a new lot of watercolours of the lakes and mountains of Snowdonia, which look exactly the same as the last lot. She was not impressed when I remarked on this. I beat a hasty retreat.

Braved House Ed again to ask how they were getting on with the editing of Ivan Skrulewski's *Nature and the Golden Rule*. Ethel was fuming because – true to the good professor's style of communicating by one-word emails: 'Yes', or, more usually, 'No' – he had just sent her an email saying simply, 'I don't like it,' when she sent him the back cover copy for approval. 'He doesn't seem to be following his own golden rule,' she commented drily. Didn't like to remind her that Ivan's new book, *Planet Self-Sabotage*, would be hard on its heels any day now (he tends to have two or three books going through the system at any one time.) Beat another hasty retreat.

Friday 18 January

Submissions still ongoing. Rejected *A Tree My Therapist*, by one Evie Barrett-Browning, despite her excellent platform as a great-great-something or other of the poet of not dissimilar name, on the grounds that she has to learn that her personal experience needs to be mediated through *some* form of literary voice. Besides, I've got enough trees for the time being. Also, a parchment offering, *Earth Blood*, hand-scripted on the skins of roadkill by an author who lives in a shed on some allotments in Hampshire. Sent this back by recorded delivery to be on the safe side, as the return address was rather vague.

I told Drusilla that my motto was now '*Je responderay*,' 'I will answer,' from the family crest of Denys Finch-Hatton, as mentioned in Dinesen's *On Mottoes of My Life*. Not for me the cutting silence of editors so fashionable today. I answer every email, and reject every submission most punctiliously. Drusilla looked rather guilty and said, 'You're an example to us all, Mortimer.'

Saturday 19 January

Tried the experiment of doing my weekly shop at Ahmed's but left it rather late, and Ahmed and his brothers were having a bit of a party and kept offering me bottles of vodka and stale loaves from under the counter for a fraction of their original price. Not really what I had in mind, but by the time the party was over, I'd forgotten what that was.

Finally managed to get hold of my father this evening. He sounded slightly surprised to hear from me and we didn't talk long as he and Jacqueline were just off to dinner at *La Dune Les Loups*, but we exchanged happy new year wishes. Hopefully that's the last time I'll have to say it now.

Sunday 20 January

Back to the supermarket. Bought a family pack of carrots. I can have them grated or *rapées*, in salads, in soup, in carrot cake etc. Great value at 69p. Two tubs of frozen chicken livers (cheap and nourishing) and some knocked-down bread for 19p.

Not a bad haul.

Monday 21 January

From: Ethel Gutierrez Sent: 21 January 8.53 To: ALL@HQ:
Subject: Sellotape holder

Hullo

Desk Ed's Sellotape holder has gone missing. If you've borrowed it, please return it.

Sincerely,
Ethel

Ethel Tula Gutierrez, editorial manager
The House of Marvellous Books
Wayfarers & Wilderness – our award-winning nature list

Yikes! I wouldn't be in the borrower's shoes for anything.

A day of minor irritations, the telephone possessed of a demon of triviality, as G.K. Chesterton says (what would he have made of Twitter!) These were the callers:

Sister Evangeline, modern-day anchoress, currently on sabbatical from her coastal convent and roving the UK in her campervan in search of silence and solitude. She's actually Fay's author but Ursula, at the switchboard, put her through to me by mistake. The good Sister was absolutely furious at having been sent a marketing questionnaire, and said she wrote for a higher calling than to concern herself with low questions of publicity. I tried to explain it wasn't my doing but she said she was only allowed ten minutes speaking time today and wasn't wasting it on me and slammed the phone down after about thirty-five seconds.

Professor Ivan Skrulewski, complaining in high style that House Editorial had given him too tight a deadline (like too tight a corset) for the proofs of *Nature and the Golden Rule* – only a four-day turnaround. Does admittedly seem a wee bit cavalier of House Ed. Couldn't help being sneakily glad there is someone strong enough to stand up to them.

War doctor, healer and professional exorcist Dr Chauncey Rivers, wanting to talk about his Christmas, spent in a haunted monastery in Tibet with white-clad monks drifting down the cloisters etc. He said he had a book on demonic possession 'simmering'.

Tuesday 22 January

Editorial board. We discussed who was going to get back to Sister Evangeline after her call. It's plainly Fay's responsibility, but she said, 'Unless she's actually submitting a manuscript, I just haven't the time. I'm after this really promising new writer, Dr Troy Malone, who's doing some important work on wilderness initiation rites.'

I said, 'What form do they take, exactly?'

'Rites of passage, Mortimer. I'm surprised you haven't done any yourself, it's quite a big thing in male culture. So, Troy takes people into the wilds for a week with no provisions or anything and they all live off stream water and what they can forage. By the end of the week most of them are seeing visions. Very spiritually expansive, or even explosive, I might say.'

'Didn't I see some article about that?' said Drusilla. 'On the top of Box Hill in Sussex, though, I seem to remember things went slightly wrong last summer. Wasn't there some to-do about them all getting food poisoning from living off the land?'

'It was Chanctonbury Ring, actually,' said Fay. 'That spooky circle of beeches atop an Iron Age hill fort. Yes, unfortunately some of them had to go home early one session. Some unwise choices in mushrooms. However, Troy won't let a little thing like that hold him back.'

Drusilla said, 'You wonder what being Mrs Malone must be like, left behind with two small children in Worthing.'

I said, 'I imagine she hangs on for those weeks the way other wives hang on for fishing or golfing holidays.'

'Maybe there isn't a Mrs Malone,' said Fay, with emphasis.

Wednesday 23 January

Long chat with Uncle Albany on the phone. We went through my old flames: Claire, Cynthia, Tracey. Painful stuff.

'Is there really nobody at work?' he said. 'What about that Fay you talk about? Any chemistry there?'

'No,' I said. 'I am quite fond of Fay in a funny kind of way, but no, I'm afraid not.'

Thursday 24 January

Drusilla in high spirits, commissioning a book of prayers for her *Unheard Voices* list from a prisoner in HMP Wandsworth. She says some of them are very good.

Needless to say, I thought of Hugo. Thank goodness he's been lying low since Christmas, well, perforce as he can't really do otherwise now. Actually, prison seems to have had a calming influence on him, although of course there's no way he should be in Wandsworth. Ford Open Prison at most. It was purely because the police cottoned on to the tiny razor disguised as a tie-pin that he used to slice out plates and pictures from books, and because of this 'offensive weapon' deemed Hugo to be a danger to the public. Poor Hugo is really only a danger to himself. He used to go round telling people that he was a secret grandson of Borges and had inherited his library, and that an international conspiracy of librarians was trying to have him murdered so they could get their hands on it. The librarati, he called them, an unholy brotherhood of book guardians with huge amounts of money stashed away in a Swiss bank account and plans to seize control of the world's entire libraries. Something already foreseen by Borges, of course. I hope it's not too unkind to say that Hugo's fantasies tend to be tediously self-aggrandising. I'm sure Nabokov says something about most fantasy being bourgeois. Texted this to Hugo to see if it would shock him out of his self-centred view of life, but he texted back, 'Actually, Nabokov said that what is really banal and bourgeois is paranoia, which is much more relevant now even than when he first said it in 1957, now that paranoia is justified by the real and all-pervasive surveillance that characterises our society.'

Drusilla, however, was so pleased with herself that I didn't think it was worth mentioning any of this. She was bustling round all morning working up the inmate's sample prayers for the editorial board so she can get them through before she leaves for New York. Her voice rose high and animated over the partition.

'Any thoughts on the title, young Mortimer? *Prayers from a Prisoner*, do you think? Or *The Prisoner's Prayers*?'

'The latter, I think. Seems slightly snappier. *Prayers from Prison*? *Intimacies from an Inmate*? Or something a bit more academic? *De Profundis: Petitions from an Insider*'?

'No, don't think so. We want these to have widespread commercial appeal. I see this as very trade.'

'*Prayers and Porridge*?' I suggested.

'That might do. That might do.'

She came into my office and rather coyly showed me a handwritten letter from her new author. The writing was most peculiar, with tiny little heads for bs and ds, but great long curvilinear tails and arabesques for gs and ys, like a series of malignant spiders. Drusilla sighed fondly over this rather sinister epistle. I get the impression she has a wee *tendresse* for her prisoner.

Friday 25 January

Some excitement caused by Ursula bursting into Drusilla's office saying, 'Is this it?' but it was only a copy of *Praecaria Plantarum Historia*, *History of Wonderful Plants*, 1509, that she'd found on a shelf of medieval recipes in the library. Drusilla pointed out that it wasn't even one of our books, as it bore the stamp of the Kunsthistorisches Institut in Florence.

'I don't really see where the confusion comes in,' said Drusilla. 'You know what you're looking for. The provenance is quite clear – the intertwined initials and the little black boat. Should be on the last page or so. Provenance isn't rocket science, you know. You're lucky to have something so recognisable to look out for.'

'And there's the curse on thieves at the beginning,' agreed Ursula enthusiastically. 'Anathema Maranatha for anyone who steals this book.'

'Ah, but I'm not so sure that exists. Doesn't appear to have protected the Book that well so far,' said Drusilla drily.

Ursula was daunted for a moment, then rallied.

'Oh well, never say die. What did Captain James Lawrence say on the capture of his frigate the Chesapeake in 1813?' Her voice rose over the partition. 'Don't give up the ship.'

I couldn't resist calling back. 'Aye-aye, Captain! Fight till she sinks!'

Monday 28 January

Fay came visiting Drusilla – a most unusual event. Of course, I couldn't help hearing the reason for her visit, which instantly became clear.

'Drusilla, those prayers from your prisoner that you're intending to bring to the editorial board tomorrow – you do realise most of them are straight out of the Methodist prayer book?'

Swift investigation revealed that the prisoner had indeed pinched all the prayers off the prison chaplains, particularly the Methodist one. Poor Drusilla was very downcast. A mournful cry of, 'Did you hear that?' came over the partition as Fay's footsteps receded down the corridor.

'Never mind. Maybe it did him some good spiritually, just to get the prayers together. You never know.'

'Yes. That's true,' brightening slightly. 'You never can tell. God moves in mysterious ways sometimes.'

'What *is* he inside for, by the way?'

'I don't know.'

Most unwise not to check his credentials in advance, and very unlike Drusilla. The author bio is always the first thing we look at. She must indeed have been swept away by her feelings.

'Thank goodness I hadn't drawn up the contract,' she added gamely, 'though I suppose it would be invalidated anyway by infringement of copyright.'

Poor Drusilla. I bet she spends her free days visiting prisoners in the East End among her numerous other good works. She was rather quiet for the rest of the morning.

To cheer her up, I suggested that Hugo take over the project – with some trepidation, I must admit. He would hardly be an easy author. Nevertheless, especially with the coincidence of them both being at Wandsworth, it seems so obvious a transition I could hardly not suggest it, in fact I'm only surprised Drusilla didn't think of it herself. Drusilla leapt on the idea.

'Oh, that would be wonderful. I'm so short of books for my poor little *Unheard Voices* list. After all, one prisoner is pretty much like another, and he has the advantage that he can write. Do you really think you could ask him?'

'I'm sure he'd be delighted. His non-fiction writing is really rather good. He did get sidetracked by plays in his Joe Orton period. Rather a pernicious influence, in my opinion; in fact, I blame Orton for Hugo's whole obsession with libraries. It started, as many things start, in Islington, where those two literary grotesques Orton and his lover among other subversive activities stole seventy-two books from Islington library. Hugo got it into his head he had a certain literary heritage to uphold—'

'And we can still call it *Prayers and Porridge*,' said Drusilla, plainly not listening to a word of this.

Duly messaged Hugo. He replied that he was about to embark on a text campaign to get himself out of prison, and would be contacting the Queen, the Prime Minister, the Home Secretary, the *Daily Mail*, and various other august bodies to try and secure his release. Not sure whether my request got through to him. He does so live in a world of his own.

Tuesday 29 January

Editorial board cancelled due to Drusilla withdrawing her proposal, the only one on the agenda. A long morning in consequence. Went to visit Sales and Marketing on the other side of the library. You could hear the merry chatter all the way down the corridor, unlike us editors, who work in solipsistic silence punctuated by the occasional solipsistic, waspish remark. In Roland's absence (he's up north, selling books) Harold, Oupie and Noreen were all lolling back in their chairs talking and laughing and eating lemon puff biscuits – my favourite, so I purloined a couple to help fill the end of month gap. Very cheering. There's been too little laughter in this place lately.

Advance orders pouring in for *Heave*. I wittily said the author should be called Dr John Typo. We all roared.

Apparently Molly's been sending daily jokes to Sales and Marketing. Rather hurt at this. I haven't heard a word. And she's been summoning people to lunch in deepest Berkhamstead or Petersham or wherever she is while she's housebound, I hear. She says she can't survive without her lunches. Of course, it's entirely natural she shouldn't think of me.

Don't know why I'm bothered really, she's never done anything for me, and frankly should be doing more for the House, given how desperately we're hanging on for her long-awaited *Sailing with the Angels* as the book to save our fortunes. But I do have a soft spot for her. It's the way she drops in out of the blue, her gales of laughter, and how she stops for a chat and remembers everything about you. She comes and goes like the wind, blowing where it listeth. Never where she should be, always on the move, Molly has an exciting, unpredictable quality all too sadly lacking in my own life.

Wednesday 30 January

Gerard has been spotted in the building! An unmistakeable, stately figure in his gentleman farmer's tweeds, flat cap, and long, curly side whiskers of reddish pepper and salt, he approached me in the corridor like a dream, swinging his walking stick. His normally ruddy face pale, his far-seeing blue eyes fixed on the middle distance, as if pacing the skyline and regarding the weather on the hills, he was about to pass me by. It was only when I greeted him that, like a ghost which must be addressed first before it can speak, he stopped and came down in time as it were to the present moment and, finally recognising me, said, 'Oh – er, er – Mortimer! Did you have an enjoyable Christmas?'

I cast my mind back. It seemed a long time ago.

'Yes, thank you. And you?'

'Very pleasant, thank you. I'm sorry to be distrait just now. I've just come back from lunch with Bishop Molly at her house while she's wheelchair-bound... though hopefully she'll be progressing to crutches before too long...'

He tailed off, gripped by his constitutional inability to say directly what was going on. I noticed his normally rugged countenance was rather pale. The silver owl's head on his walking stick glared at me balefully.

I said, 'Not bad news I hope?'

He said, 'I wish I could reassure you on that point, Mortimer,' and went into his office and shut the door.

A slightly dispiriting encounter, but he may be referring to no more than a slighting remark of the good bishop's about some aspect of late nineteenth-century/early twentieth-century poetry. Gerard is so terribly protective of his period, and Molly may have dismissed Rupert Brooke as sentimental, or laughed at a late poem of Matthew Arnold's. Whether they discussed the real point – i.e. our dependence on Molly's earning power for us to survive, and the need for *Sailing with the Angels*' immediate delivery – is impossible to tell, though knowing Molly's forthright nature she's pretty sure to have brought it up, if only in the form of a request (demand) for more money on her advance. Well, at least he's back now and can sort all this out.

Thursday 31 January

From: Gerard Delamere Sent: 31 January 7.37 To: ALL@HQ
Subject: Speaking clock

Dear All

Can we please refrain from calling the speaking clock, unless there is a genuine business case? This appears on our itemised call list every month and as the World Clock is on the internet and free it seems an unnecessary expense.

Thank you.

Very kindly yours,

Gerard Delamere, Publisher
The House of Marvellous Books
Wayfarers & Wilderness – our award-winning nature list
Sailing through Storms – transcendence through crisis

Don't judge each day by the harvest you reap but by the seeds that you plant

—Robert Louis Stevenson

The smallest act of kindness is worth more than the grandest intention

—Oscar Wilde

Accounts say someone has run up a £400 bill on such reckless phone calls this quarter.

Drusilla has been nagging me about *Prayers from Prison* as she's off to New York tomorrow, so I texted Hugo again to see if I could engage his mind on the subject.

End of January – hoorah! Don't want to wish my life away, but there's no denying January is my least favourite month. Must get out of the UK next year and go to some sensible hot country that doesn't do winter.

Resolved to have a grateful February.

Friday 1 February

Drusilla has taken refuge in fantasy! She came in for her last morning before departing to New York, pulling her suitcase behind her, looked round, and exclaimed brightly, 'It's all the same! Nothing's changed!'

Tactful questioning revealed that she had been reading Harry Potter on the tube. I had never thought of Drusilla as easily influenced before. It was rather endearing. I told her she should read Diana Wynne Jones and Tolkien, as precursors of the Harry Potter brand, but apart from muttering something about Tolkien being so stuffy and all about war, Drusilla barely heeded this. She seemed quite happy about it, however, and when I went in with a coffee for her at 11am, she was beaming vaguely at far-off entities between plunges into work – these not always successful due to her ongoing battle with technology. At the best of times, she regards the computer as little short of some alien fantasy being itself, with a mind and works of its own. Today her work was punctuated with little cries for help. 'My inbox! It's all gone! How do I get it back?' At every cry I sprang from my chair and hastened into her office to help. My own technological skills are only a step or two ahead of hers, really.

Perhaps a fugue into fantasy is preferable to reality at this time. Fay told me she went into Gerard's office early this morning, before 8am, and found him with his head in his hands, crying. She said, 'If it was anyone else I'd have given them a great big hug, but Gerard! Somehow the braces and side whiskers keep you away.' I know what she means – they're just not conducive to familiarities. A toff in tears is hard to comfort.

Business must be very bad; not so much for Gerard to cry, as for Fay's heart to be touched. Fay wouldn't tell me exactly what was said as it was confidential, but she didn't contradict me when I put two and two together and guessed that it was something to do with Gerard's lunch meeting with Bishop Molly yesterday, and that he was deeply worried about our future. She just sighed, and looked into the distance with her misty, visionary stare.

Got a text back from Hugo's phone sent by a prison warder called Sam Mungo saying that Prisoner DW34M was not allowed private texts at the moment because of inappropriate use of his phone.

Hesitated to mention this to Drusilla but luckily she seemed to have forgotten about *Prayers from Prison* for now, and, instead, gave me a lecture about the importance of using charm in publishing.

'Given that we pay such small advances, we really need to make the balance up with good manners and good will,' etc etc. Made an extra effort to exude charm into emails and phone calls for the rest of the morning, until Drusilla left at noon, when it was a relief to lapse into what I suppose must be my natural sullenness and introversion.

Saturday 2 February

Hugo texted – evidently he's been given his phone back – would I go to his flat, of which I have the keys, and find his copies of James Frazer's *The Golden Bough*, David Foster Wallis' *Infinite Jest*, and any Thomas Pynchon I came across for an article he's writing, and bring them in my next visit. I texted back, 'Will do. And did you get my text about taking on a book potentially entitled *Prayers from Prison*'? He texted back, 'Oh, was that for me? Sam my warder thought you were asking him and he's working on it now. He says he's always wanted to be a writer.'

Knew it would be a mistake to get Hugo involved.

Sunday 3 February

Duly arrived at Hugo's flat, a dreary little abode in the more northerly reaches of Islington, to find it all still boarded up from when the police kicked in the door, so couldn't gain access to find the books he requested. Luckily, I've got my own copies of *The Golden Bough* et al I can take in for him. I won't tell him about the flat just now – don't want to upset him further.

On the cumbersome tube trek home, I reflected that, like a wayward St Brendan, there is no doubt that Hugo is embarked upon a journey. He desired to sail his craft into islets and creeks where few go, into foreign waters and to the ends of the earth. Such a quest has to be kept in bounds by the strictest discipline if we are not to be blown off course. Hugo is the perfect example of a spiritual quest gone astray.

Monday 4 February

Got in to hear a loud, clear quacking emanating from the kitchen. 'It's PERFECTLY all right, Ethel! Not really rank at all! YOU'D be bubbly if *you'd* been shaken, too!' and realised with a sinking heart that Ursula was there, defending her goat's milk again. By a series of cunning evasions, I've managed to avoid a face-to-face encounter all this year up to now. I'm sorry to be unkind. I know Ursula is one of the women in cardigans who keep the place going, usually described as a 'lynchpin' – receptionist, researcher and right hand of House Editorial – but I just don't feel myself when Ursula is nigh.

She was standing at the open fridge door, in her yellow sou'wester (hood up), wellington boots and mauve tweed skirt, her hand-knitted mustard and green scarf wound thrice about her neck, and her backpack sticking out, which meant that no one could get in or out of the kitchen. Her glasses were steamed up and her nose was red with cold. Like some uncombed, shaggy wilder-woman of the woods, a kind of wodo, half-woman, half-forest. What am I? asks the ancient Anglo-Saxon riddle, and Ursula might well ask the same.

In her lighter moments, Fay has a theory that Ursula is an escaped nun – with her thin, angular body, innate physical awkwardness, and ginger hair wound in a plait around her head, she might be of course, but let's face it, we don't really know anything definite about Ursula's past beyond the fact that she's been with the House for twenty-seven years. Apparently she's never had a birth certificate, so she doesn't know how old she is, or when her birthday is. I'd put her in her mid-fifties at least, with that slightly sheeny, ageless quality that comes from never having had children.

She was arguing with Ethel as usual, this time about whether angels drink milk and if so whether they would be more likely to prefer cow's, goat's, sheep's or camel's, or whether Heaven provided some special kind of lactasial ambrosia, just about recognisable as dairy to our earthly eyes. As soon as she saw me, Ursula broke off her argument and started urging me to try her goat's milk, with a long explanation about how nowadays the goats feed on wild herbs and fresh green grass, giving a bouquet of buttercups and other lovely things, as opposed to the bad old days when they were allowed to browse on rubber tyres, weeds and old socks which did admittedly impart an off-taste to the milk.

I said, 'It's very kind of you, but not today, thanks,' got my coffee and two chocolate biscuits, and fled. Fay almost jammed with me in the door as she, too, made her escape with her steaming mug of vanilla and violet infusion. We looked at each other in the sudden camaraderie that comes from encountering someone you both dislike even more than you dislike each other, although as Fay is impartially intolerant of all, it doesn't really say that much.

'Bang goes our morning peace and quiet,' grumbled Fay as we made our way back through the library and into reception to the stairs. 'What a shame her Christmas pilgrimage to Holy Island didn't extend a month or two longer!'

I said, 'Yes, one doesn't want to be uncharitable, but...'

Fay said, with some passion, 'If only she would wear deodorant!' and scurried up the stairs ahead of me and into her office, banging the door closed behind her.

Tuesday 5 February

Tiresome day. Nipped into Gerard's office for privacy while he was at lunch and called the police about Hugo's front door. I explained that for various reasons I needed to gain access quite urgently. Didn't mention Thomas Pynchon, David Foster Wallace and James Frazer, as I felt they might not understand, but did tell them how Hugo is under pressure to provide his own clothes as due to the growing prison population they are running short of jumpsuits, and he has no clothes beyond two pairs of trousers, poor fellow, and those are working increasingly loose with the prison regime. I've lent him a belt but obviously that's only an interim measure and I know he has several smaller pairs dating from his younger days stuffed in the back of a wardrobe somewhere. A long, inconclusive conversation. The police only half sympathetic. They said it was unlikely that Hugo would be allowed a belt in prison. Hadn't thought of that, but said the point was the door, not the belt. For people so quick off the mark in kicking the door in – surely unnecessary anyway with a shrimp like Hugo – they seem remarkably slow in redressing the damage. I pointed out that they could have knocked.

Then tried to book a visit to Hugo, to take in Thomas Pynchon et al, copies of which I did manage to find at home, but to my annoyance you can't book a visit online any more and now have to obtain a prison visiting order. Spoke to some complete oik who kept saying he didn't understand a word I said. I suppose that's my mumsy voice again. Did my best to adopt a Cockney accent and threw in a trial, 'Yes, mate,' to see if we could make better contact, but it's difficult to sound truly colloquial when one has inherited a natural Edwardian drawl.

But worse was to come. As I was absent-mindedly fiddling with the piles of paper on the desk while on the phone, I came across some poems of mine, *Travesties*, that I sent in anonymously some months ago for our nature poetry list, *Antler Bones*, using my pseudonym Oliver Todd. Gerard's firm italics were scrawled over the title page: *These look dire!* I was devastated. *And* he didn't even bother to send them back to me with a proper, formal rejection. That's the very last time I'm watering his *ficus benjamina*.

I don't know whether it's the ups and downs of the last few days or the remains of some seasonal depression, but I was ashamed to find tears in my eyes when I returned to my gloomy office. I sat quietly for a while in the soothing company of all the old tomes on the shelves around me, and it passed.

Remembered I'd used Hugo's address to send in *Travesties*, so Gerard may have sent a letter there. I suppose it's worth hanging on to that slender hope. Read through the first one, *Cavalier oh my chevalier*, and apart from the undeniable shades of Gerard Manley Hopkins, honestly didn't think it was too bad.

Wednesday 6 February

The roof started leaking again today owing to a slight thaw, so went up to the attic with Ursula to empty the buckets. This took up most of the morning. Ursula has a tic of making sudden movements and it pays not to be too close to her when she is moving around with a laden bucket.

Posted Hugo the books from work. Bit naughty I know, but they do weigh heavy in the old briefcase. They can look on it as part of the advance for the book of prison prayers.

Why doesn't Hugo get a Kindle? Texted him to this effect.

Must remember the gratitude. An undervalued quality in our society.

Thursday 7 February

Fay still fussing about *Heaven*. Her author is waiting for a sign from the angels before setting pen to paper, or rather fingers to keyboard (I don't think Fay's authors are quite as aged as Drusilla's). This naturally causes difficulties with the schedule. Maybe because of this, Fay had a row with Ursula. She told her to stop the singing and attend to her work on the index of *The Dangerous Path to Soul*. She says she can't bear to listen to *There is a Green Hill Far Away* crooned off-key one more time. She can hear it all along the corridor even with her office door closed and her William Morris draught excluder pushed up against the gap at the bottom of the door. Ursula took it very humbly; it was painful to hear her apologising, in her loud, clear, home-counties voice. Fay, however, was not charitable about Ursula at all, she said she can't bear her. Fay said that not only is Ursula totally incompetent as an editorial assistant, but she has a physical aversion to her.

She said, in her soft hiss, 'It's when she comes clumping into the office in her lace-up shoes, thick beige tights, beige wool waistcoat and blue polka dot pleated skirt with that backpack sticking out above her shoulders and starts telling you how she saw the frost rime sparkling on the fields, or a robin on an ash tree, as she was cycling to the station. She seems to take up far more than her fair share of space. And she can't do the simplest task. Gerard ought to sack her but he just won't face anything unpleasant. One small part of the reason why we're in the mess we're in now.'

Drusilla stuck up for Ursula and said that someone happy to be an editorial dogsbody was indispensable to any publishing office, and that at least she could help search for the Daybreak

Manuscript, but I think this was just to annoy Fay, as Drusilla wants Ursula sacked just as much as Fay does. They've both been in to see Gerard about it several times over the last few years.

Fees book lost. It always seems to go missing when Ursula gets upset, which means that the life of the entire place grinds to a halt while everyone hunts for it from office to office and all along the corridors and down to the basement and stacks. The Fees book is what keeps us going – without it all our authors would desert in a body, as it's the sole modus operandi of payments. I used to think that it was just my authors who were full of cupidity, but Drusilla says no, given a chance all the high-minded hermits and historians she knows would just take the money and run, it is only her relentless pursuit that actually results in any books at all. Fay finally found the Fees book downstairs in the Ladies, a big, immensely tattered red volume – why it isn't electronic, these days, God only knows – with a torn, faded notice sellotaped onto the front cover saying *Boys and Girls, please write CLEARLY.* This directive comes from Charlene in Accounts, who openly thinks she runs the place and that if it wasn't for her we would shut down in a week. Probably she is right.

Fancied a bit of a leg stretch after all this so threaded my way southward through the London streets and popped into Westminster Cathedral after work and lit a candle to St Anthony, begging him to get me out of the House. As the years keep on rolling by, so does my plight grow. I don't want to be one of the majority mentioned by Thoreau who live lives of quiet desperation. In my experience, a candle to the miracle-working saint always has an effect, even if not always exactly the one you've asked for. I'm sure I'll see *some* shift in my working life as a result.

Friday 8 February

What a day! Went for a job interview with the famed Rosie Beal, queen of Calling Crane, our arch-rivals. It's all happened so quickly, I hardly know where to start. I spotted a job in *The Bookseller* this morning as commissioning editor for their list *Wellbeing Witch* and emailed them on impulse, never dreaming they'd reply – lo and behold, a reply straight back asking me if I could come in this afternoon! Rosie herself came to the door of her offices on the Isle of Dogs to meet me, a familiar figure in her floor-length yellow Chinese robes and long grey plait, and bowed in welcome, hands tucked up her wide sleeves. (I bowed back, of course. Memories of dance lessons and soft black pumps, hah!) I was overcome with astonishment at her office. In quite some contrast to our own shabby cubicles, it was a riot of colour and *richesse*, filled with First Nation totem poles, Inuit carvings in whalebone, African masks, Chinese pottery, Mayan weavings and bright Mexican rugs, reflecting her famed travels. Their latest releases, *Sex, Spells and Seeds: Ancient fertility rites for health and harvest,* and *Wilderness Folk: Spotting and filming elves, fairies and other small woodland entities* were blazoned on gigantic posters on the wall. So this is where my unlived life got to! It made me feel I have been surviving in black and white while everyone else has been luxuriating in a riot of colour.

Rosie was most amenable. We had a jolly good chat and I told her all about our plans for the list for the next two years, and all the topics we're planning to cover such as natural kindness, wilderness therapy, ecological grief, the mythic imagination, tree communication and the mycorrhizal internet, and our latest book from acclaimed mythologist Drewie Knock, *Healing Stories and Hearth Smoke: Reading the flames in the wild fire.* She listened most attentively. It was so warming to talk to someone who really gives you her full attention. She asked what Fay and Drusilla were up to, so I told her about the blunder with Fay's book *Heave* and how difficult Sister Evangeline was, and Drusilla's despair at failing to get any of Bishop Molly's new book out of her, but how they were consoling themselves respectively with *Lays from a Shepherd's Hut* and *The Glutton's Bible*, while Fay was busy courting the emerging star Dr Troy Malone for his latest book on wilderness initiation rites, at which Rosie nodded in a satisfied manner.

Rosie asked me what kind of new list I'd be interested in forming. I seized my chance and said I thought it was time for a resurgence of Chinese poets of the Tang dynasty such as Li Bai and Du Fu, for too long the province only of enthusiasts. She asked me what I knew of Li Bai and I recited *Drinking Alone by Moonlight* to her, with appropriate gestures (my own interpretation, culled from various translations).

To be drunk in spring is a special thing...
Ah, drinking alone by moonlight,
the joy of raising a full glass to the full moon.
Alone under the trees, the moon shadow falling,
Who needs friends, when you have the moon?

I said I'd always thought of the moon as my oldest friend, so it was interesting to see such sentiments being expressed thirteen centuries ago.

Before spring flickers and goes out,
I must make the most of the fleeting time
To be drunk in spring is a special thing...

I said I preferred Arthur Waley's translation, Ezra Pound's being perhaps a little peremptory, although with more than seventy to choose from, one was really spoilt for choice. We talked about the legend that Li Bai drowned drunk while trying to embrace the moon's reflection in the Yangtze River. So warming. I haven't had a chat like that with anyone since Hugo went inside. I really feel I met a fellow soul and that we formed a real rapport. Rosie introduced me to her daughter, Lydia, who's taking over the business when she retires. Lydia, or Lyd, was a young woman in jeans with, I have to say, a much less accommodating vibe; in fact she looked at me rather challengingly and asked what I'd think of doing a wild witchcraft list. I said I was certainly willing to have a go. Lyd looked unconvinced. Whether due to this or not, I felt the mood was rather punctured, and an uneasy feeling stirred in me at the sight of a long line of desks stretching away outside Rosie's office as I left. They reminded me of something. It was very quiet out there, especially after all the laughing and talking in Rosie's office. Everyone was head down and working. At the front door Rosie said, 'By the way, how's the library, has Gerard managed to effect a sale yet?'

'Um... doesn't ring any bells, I'm afraid.'

She laughed and said, 'Don't worry, just me being nosey. I expect I got hold of the wrong end of the stick. Of course, you're subject to all those ancient restrictions anyway, aren't you, about keeping the library intact and only selling it as a whole, and all that. So if anyone wants to buy one old book off the library, they have to purchase the entire building, right?'

First glass, I merge with life and death
Second glass, I merge with Nature
Third glass, ah, I enter the Way...
But I cannot tell you about the Way,
What I see there, what I feel,
Unless you are drunk along with me

Returned to work feeling quite chipper and actually had a nice chat with the House Ed team tucked away in their den at the end of the corridor, about the dreaded use of 'it's' as a possessive instead of 'its', of which we've been seeing a worrisome recent increase lately. Ethel said it was the bane of her life. I said I couldn't agree more, it was like nails scraping on glass to me when I saw things like, 'It won't fit in it's case,' and Ethel gave a pitying half-smile. She added that she would put a reminder into the house style guide next time it was updated and thanked me most politely for drawing the matter to her attention again.

Stayed a little later to make up the time I was absent at Calling Crane, so that it was full Friday night rush hour when I left. Barely able to breathe on the tube, forced into the closest physical proximity with strangers, so close we could not vow as Elizabeth Barrett Browning says, I thought of the ocean solitude sought by hermits – of Brendan and his men rowing from island to island looking for one that was unoccupied. Even then it was difficult. Amazing how the remotest islands tended to be inhabited. Brendan earnestly prayed that God would give him a land 'secret, hidden, secure, delightful, separated from men.' Looking out over the mighty intolerable ocean, he seemed to see far off the island he had prayed for hovering over it. I looked over the heads of the many people in the carriage and dreamed likewise.

Saturday 9 February

Woke up and realised that the long line of desks at Rosie's reminded me of a line of sewing machines – a sweatshop, in fact. That explains the heartsink. I did like Rosie, though. That Rapunzel rope of golden grey, her wide, shimmering gold sleeves, and the merry twinkle in her eye. Must curb my weakness for sassy older women. It's just that they seem so sure of themselves. And think what working for Rosie would bring out in me; all sorts of opportunities for displaying talents that have hitherto lain dormant. By the time I'd woken up properly and had my coffee and almond croissant, however, it had all faded and become rather unreal. Something tells me that this is going to be a road not taken.

Sunday 10 February

Well, well – my father rang for once! Jacqueline says I may come out for a weekend soon, if I don't mind sleeping in one of the mobile homes again. I must say, it cheers the heart to think of seeing the Vendée and its wide skies, even at this time of year. Although it's rather a long way to go for just two days.

Uncle Albany called, inviting me down to Gallhampton Gap. I regretfully declined on account of going to France.

Monday 11 February

Sure enough, my fling with Calling Crane is over. A *coup de foudre*, brief as summer lightning, no more. Rosie's daughter Lyd rang me first thing and explained that while my knowledge of eighth-century Chinese literature is impressive, they really need someone with twenty-first century digital skills. I understand. Naturally they want a bright young thing.

Later Rosie herself rang. She sounded rather quelled. She said they'd decided to go for someone who would start a transgender list. We agreed we would go out for lunch one day.

I suppose I should be glad and grateful to have got two phone calls. These days the style is simply not to get back. Such poor manners, I think.

Met Fay in the kitchen opening a can of pilchards. She looked up and said, 'Going to jump ship, Mortimer?' Could she possibly suspect something? Maybe she has the second sight. I said, 'Not at the moment, no.'

Bit of a bad day all round. House Ed emailed Gerard and put in a formal complaint about the satanic content in the *Earth* list books. I was a bit puzzled about this as there is no satanic content. Rather mean of them, I thought. We had such a nice chat about English grammar on Friday. I thought Ethel had got over her Satan complex. It certainly slowed things down last year, when she insisted on vetting each book for demonic content. She's certainly been very grumpy lately about receiving the summer manuscripts, but honestly. After all that bonding over possessive pronouns. I wasn't even copied in on the email. I only heard about it via Fay though how she found out, the Lord knows. She must definitely be psychic.

Met Ursula blundering along the corridor, unable to find her office. She had left her glasses on her desk by mistake before going to the Ladies, the massive establishment at the bottom of the sweep of spiral stairs, like one of those grand Victorian public lavatories at the seaside. She confided to me that she was waiting for a cataract operation, and added that her eyesight had deteriorated even since Christmas (along with, apparently, her spatial awareness and geographical memory as really she ought to know the way blindfold after twenty-seven years in the place. Borges would have.) Worrying, considering how much access she has to our systems. She made a disturbing sight, hands outstretched in the corridor, with her untidy ginger-grey plait down her back and long, dark-green pleated skirt. I guided her back to her desk.

Tuesday 12 February

Sister Evangeline called – somehow she's latched onto my direct line and I couldn't work out how to transfer her to Fay. She said she had started *Columba and the Crane*, a book based on the legend that St Columba had cared for an injured crane, blown in and beaten about by the wind along the seashore. When I said I didn't think we'd commissioned it yet she said sharply, no, we hadn't, it had to be for Calling Crane because of the avian theme and the Godincidence of the title matching the company name, but she thought it best to be transparent and tell me in case we'd had thoughts of doing a similar book. I felt a dull pang at the mention of our rival's name and my lost opportunity there. All the same. Something tells me it would have been no picnic, working there.

Went round to Fay's office to tell her about Sister E's call. Thought she might also like to hear about my impending trip to the windswept, rain-soaked camp site in the wilds of the Vendée, where I would be sleeping in a primitive caravan listening to the hooting of the owls and the tapping of the bare boughs against the windows. Fay said she was off to Wales again herself for a long weekend of solitary meditation in a remote cottage on the Llyn Peninsula overlooking the rolling grey Irish Sea, accessible only by foot or 4x4. Trust her to go one better.

Then I tried to extract a spring catalogue from Ursula. This should have been done months ago, of course. She, too, was surprisingly unsympathetic considering I rescued her from a blind search for her office only yesterday, when she clung on to my arm most pathetically. What short memories people have.

'What do you want a catalogue FOR?' she demanded.

'Well, people ask for them,' I said, apologetically.

'Maybe I can hash something up online,' she said grudgingly. 'You only need the spring titles, don't you, not the backlist?'

Ursula said Gerard is taking the view that to have the books up on the website is enough and there's no need to send out catalogues to the trade or to anyone else. Worrying. Mustn't be paranoid – I'm sure he's not actually deliberately running the list down – but it does suggest a distressing lack of commitment to the *Earth* list. All the other editors have a catalogue for their lists.

I do see what Fay means about Ursula taking up a lot of space, by the way. I saw that she had made a kind of nest for herself at her desk, with piles of manuscripts, books, bright fluorescent yellow reflective coat (for cycling to the station in deepest Berks or wherever she comes in from), bike lamp, basket, tupperware boxes, and an entire loaf of sliced bread dumped inelegantly on its tail and standing slightly skewiff on the desk.

Wednesday 13 February

Gerard called me into his office and said there must be no mention of Satan in the books. An unlucky reference to this entity would appear to be what triggered Ethel's complaint. It slipped in to my November title *Mountain Meditations* when no one was looking. Gerard read me out Ethel's email. It said that invoking the Devil in this way posed an invitation to volatile entities and 'things that go about' to enter and reside there, presenting a highly dangerous situation.

'Moreover,' added Gerard, peeping at me atop his glasses without attending to my words, 'it trespasses on the province of our competitor Calling Crane who, it may safely be said, do cover this kind of theme.'

I blenched at the mention. Did he suspect something of my ill-fated visit to Rosie Beal's domain? However, I rallied and asked him how did that differ from *Alchemical Symbols in Atheistic Satanism* on his own alchemy list, *Grasping Gold*, but he just said, 'That's different.' I've noticed it time and again, you simply can't argue with people when they're in the grip of an ideological complex. Gerard asked me what I thought of starting a mindlessness list, to counter the splurging growth of mindfulness which we must deplore as a rogue Buddhist concept. Gerard said the governing body are quite keen on it. I said I thought it was a bad idea.

Annoyed with House Ed. Honestly, they are two-faced.

On reflection, bit peeved about Calling Crane, as well. Thought of ringing Rosie and Lyd back and explaining that actually my real speciality is English literature 1796 to 1930 (Jane Austen starts *First Impressions/Pride and Prejudice*, to the death of D. H. Lawrence.) I'm not really an expert in Chinese poetry of the Xian dynasty. Not that I'm precious – I just don't want to be turned down on false pretences.

Drusilla back from New York, lashing her tail. She bought a new fur coat (she sent her old one to her penniless countess friends in Georgia), hired a car and drove hundreds of miles up into the snowy mountains to visit all the US publishers she could. She had snapped up the rights of a book on the repentance of a serial killer called Beau S. Beauchamp, *Kill, Pray, Eat.* So that's all right.

I was glad to see her and told her the office had been dead without her, at which she looked pleased. I found all this new world-conquering energy hard to match, however, especially as I have commissioned nothing since she's been away apart from *What Trees Talk About When They Talk About Love*, so told her about the fracas with House Ed and the stray, unruly Devil. Drusilla was immediately sympathetic and said that Ethel was exceeding her station as editorial manager in censoring the content of the books after we commissioning editors had accepted them and should just be sending the manuscripts out to the copy-editors, not reading them through and marking up the passages of which she disapproves. No wonder we're always behind schedule. Fay passing in the corridor overheard, and came in and said that, as a sensitive, she introjects Ethel's negative moods and can't get rid of them, which must certainly make life very uncomfortable. I wonder why she doesn't introject my negative feelings, though?

'Oh,' added Drusilla suddenly. 'I ran into Rosie Beal of Calling Crane on the tube just now. I gather you had a bit of a chat with her the other day.'

Yikes! Of course these two *grandes dames* have known each other from time immemorial, queens at rival establishments.

'She says you're a brilliant young man, full of ideas; quite rightly so,' went on Drusilla, adding reflectively, 'Of course, Rosie is a bit of a tartar. You need to be a strong character to survive at Calling Crane. I know of at least five girls who went to work for her full of high hopes, only to leave in tatters after three months.'

My mind roamed uneasily over my conversation with Rosie. Only now did it strike me that I may have been a tad indiscreet in telling her our entire publishing schedule.

For a few moments, wished that I, too, could flee to New York. Booked France as next best thing – Eurostar to Paris, then TGV to Nantes, and local train to Les Sables d'Olonne, my father's nearest town. Felt immediately uplifted. Drusilla overhearing called over the partition to ask if I wanted to borrow her *À La Recherche du Temps Perdu* for the journey. I sprang up and went in to her office saying, 'That's very sweet of you,' and found myself confronted by all seven volumes, hardback, of a strange orange-brown colour unknown to book covers these days, with yellowed pages in small print, in French of course. I think Drusilla suddenly realised that they might be a tad cumbersome for a weekend trip because she added defensively, 'Everyone over thirty should have a go at Proust.' I said, '*Mais oui, certainement*, but I'm not sure I have room in my bag for all seven this time.' And she said, 'Well, they're here if you want them, feel free any time. Of course no one ever gets to the end of Proust.' I opened *Du côté de chez Swann*, and read aloud the immortal first sentence, '*Longtemps, je me suis couché de bonne heure*.' I said, 'What a wonderful fall it has to it. It seems to go echoing right down the past.'

Drusilla beamed and I retreated, clutching the volume, which smelled strongly of mildew. Well, I can now safely say I've made a start on Proust!

Hugo texted and asked me to cancel the milk at his flat. Oh dear. Surely that was done long ago. However, went round to his place after work to check there wasn't a long line of milk bottles outside, but if there ever had been, someone must have taken them all, perhaps the milkman himself in default of payment, as there was nothing, just the bleak boarded-up door and a pile of post outside, mostly junk mail and red bills. Texted Hugo about these but got a reply from warder Sam saying that Hugo was in solitary confinement for the day because he's been driving the other prisoners mad trying to make them all do Twitter poetry and lecturing them about the constraints of writing in 140 characters – worse than haiku. The prisoners flocked to Sam pointing out that social media is officially forbidden. Sam added, 'Guess I will need more than 140 characters myself to do this book hahaha! Looking forward to meeting my editor soon!! Cheers for now, Sam.'

Yikes! I sure will be glad to set foot on that Eurostar!!

Thursday 14 February

Drusilla got a Valentine's Day card! I recognised the handwriting instantly, the creepy scrawl of the prisoner she was courting for this wretched book of prayers. She showed me with a certain tremulous pride saying, 'I shan't take it any further. I'm old enough to recognise the danger signs.'

She added, 'Highly appropriate given that St Valentine initiated the card tradition by writing to his own beloved from prison the night before he was executed, don't you think?'

I said, 'Did you send any?'

She laughed and said, 'Ah, that would be telling, wouldn't it!'

I hoped her card wasn't the beginning of some stalking campaign and said so, probably more clumsily than intended, but Drusilla only laughed again and said, 'Oh, I've had all that. As an MP's wife living in the East End, you get used to everything. There used to be someone who rang me up every day at the same time – a quarter to eight in the morning – just as I was getting the children ready for school. He never said anything. We all got used to it. The children would pick up the phone and there'd be silence and they'd yell, "Mum, it's your stalker!" I had a good idea who it was – and you'd be very surprised if I told you – so I had a think as what to do, and in the end, I thought, if it's the person I think it is, I know just the phrase to send him off.'

She paused impressively.

'So what did you say?'

'Next time the phone rang, I picked it up. There was silence as usual. I said, "*Semper idem*." Latin, meaning, always the same. He never rang again.'

'Oh,' I said. 'That seems an extraordinarily refined way of getting rid of a stalker.'

Drusilla sighed. 'He was an extraordinarily refined being. But then, so was Satan. I grant you it wouldn't work with all stalkers; it was a special case. You see, not only was *semper idem*, or *eadem*, the motto of Elizabeth 1st, reflecting the royal stability and dependability, and may have evolved from the earlier *semper fidelis*, now the motto of the United States Marine Corps, and bearing in mind that the numerical value of *semper idem* in Chaldean numerology 5, and in Pythagorean, 8, but it also refers to divine eternity. Fortune, or *Fortuna*, is *semper variabilis*, always changing. In contrast, the feature of divine eternity is its unchangeability, and as stated in Hebrews 13:8, *semper idem* was a phrase much used by English Puritans in the seventeenth century to refer to the immutable mercy of—'

Just then my own phone rang and I had to spring back into my office. Alas, no cards in my pigeon hole. Not that I expected or wanted any, of course. But still. Even Drusilla at seventy-four has her admirers. And as for Uncle Albany! He received nine cards but had to hide eight of them from Patti. He asked how many I'd had so I told a white lie and said, 'Only three.' Told Fay all this and she snorted. 'Honestly, Mortimer, what century are you living in? You're hopelessly old-fashioned! No one gets Valentine's cards these days, it's all social media.'

Thought I'd treat my father and Jacqueline to dinner at *La Dune des Loups* one evening, and was just researching the menu online, when I got an odd text from Hugo saying, 'What's for dinner tonight then?' I had a rush of blood to the head and texted back, '*Huitres normandes no 2, Poisson de la pêche locale avec pommes sautées, Soufflé Glacé au Grand Marnier, accompagné de son café et de ses mignardises.* A fairly modest *idée du Chef*, hah!' He texted back by return, '???What happened to the chicken korma?' and then another text arrived hot on its heels, saying, 'Sorry, it's Sam the screw here, thought I was texting my wife, we always have a curry on a Thursday, was hoping for a Valentine's special.' I got quite annoyed. Texted back, 'Look here, I'm a private individual planning a private holiday and I consider you are taking a liberty in using my friend's phone to intrude upon my life.' Then turned my phone off for the night. That'll show him!

Looking forward to my jaunt. It will be nice to spend eight hours just sitting on a train. Kindle at the ready. Downloaded Proust!

Friday 15 February
Up bright and early for the Eurostar. Got dressed and turned on my phone to find a text from my father sent late last night saying it wasn't a convenient time for me to visit this weekend.

For a few wild moments I thought of going anyway and booking into a hotel. But common sense prevailed, and after some scrambling about I was able to access my booking online and defer my crossing.

Damn and blast. He always does this.

Decided to go into work and take my day off another time. Not great news. Calling Crane have poached *Wilderness Rites for the Uninitiated* by Dr Troy Malone.

Fay very upset. 'Troy and I were getting on so well. I can't think how Calling Crane even knew about it. Troy told me he was keeping it under his hat until it was done.'

Oh dear. More and more, it strikes me that it might have been a mistake to have confided so generously in Rosie.

Saturday 16 February
Got a bit of a cold. Just as well I didn't go to France, I suppose.

Stayed in bed. Couldn't quite face Proust. Read Trollope – *The Way We Live Now*. An interminable story of 100 chapters, mildly addictive. Its soothing trundle just what was required. At the same time, it seems to lack a certain *soupçon* of something which maybe only Proust provides.

Sunday 17 February
Bit of a long day. My father called in the evening. After a brief apology for putting me off, he said it was pretty icy over there in the Vendée. Glad I didn't go, really. Don't want this turning into pneumonia.

Monday 18 February

Bother! I'm in hot water for not bringing *What Trees Talk About When They Talk About Love* to the editorial board. I must admit, I was so pleased to get a workable book in, the usual procedures clean slipped my mind. It was made clear to me that I must not sidestep the formalities, as the books need to be properly presented and minuted in order to penetrate our (fairly impenetrable) system. 'Apart from anything else,' said Gerard quite kindly at the end of his wigging ('At this juncture we must do all we can,' etc etc,), 'the book won't get the publicity and marketing it needs if it isn't in the system. How are we to make *Tree Talk* known to the world if officially the book doesn't exist?'

Was tempted to say that it was an ontological question but held my peace. Sat down and did the paperwork there and then and sent it to Ursula, for when she collates the agenda. After ten years, the bureaucracy does get a trifle forgettable. Hopefully the tree experts – turns out there are two of them, Mair and Phoebe – should be less trouble than my more volatile authors.

Ursula said she contacted the Kunsthistorisches Institut in Florence about *Praecaria Plantarum Historia*, and they were very glad to hear from her as the book had long been missing, presumed stolen. My heart lurched a little. But surely not. When was Hugo even in our library?

Tuesday 19 February
Shrove Tuesday

To work again. I'd forgotten it was Shrove Tuesday. Almost unable to turn around in the kitchen for the amount of goodies brought in by people eager to clear their homes of sweet eatables by tomorrow, the start of Lent. At least half I suspect had been baked specially – how many people really have home-baked chocolate and orange cake and caraway seed muffins just hanging around in their freezer? And a twelve-pack of doughnuts from the governing body. Very kind of them, I'm sure. It was a successful exercise – by the end of the day I personally didn't want to lay eyes on anything cake-like again for at least six weeks, which is good as I am giving up cake for Lent in line with my Irish Catholic heritage. The rest of them of course, being Anglican, don't have to give anything up.

Drusilla welcomed me as I took my seat in the Fisher Room for the editorial board. 'How was France? Bit taxing? You're looking slightly haggard, if you don't mind me saying so. A long way to go for a weekend, and that Atlantic coast is freezing this time of year. How did you get on with Proust?'

'Ach, no one really reads Proust!' said Fay, joining us, before I could reply. She said she'd had a wonderful long weekend in her solitary cottage, meditating and listening to the wind and the cry of the curlews over the bay. I managed to interject and say I'd spent the weekend keeping warm in bed. Fay listened, frowning, and said, 'Sounds like it was wasted on you, Mortimer. An opportunity to commune with the wild in winter, and all you can do is bleat about hot water bottles. Where's the spiritual growth in that?'

I was just starting to explain further when Gerard came in and said, 'What's all this about Sister Evangeline writing for Calling Crane? We've already lost too many authors to that Machiavellian Rosie.' Goodness knows how he found out, especially given that normally he is too preoccupied with the cycles of the farming year to have much idea of what's going on. He does, however, have these alarming savant streaks which break through from time to time. I said, 'Oh – er yes, she's writing a rather niche book about St Columba and the crane. I hardly think it would be of any interest to us,' and Gerard shot out his lip, as the Bible has it (Psalm 22:7), saying, 'Nonsense, it's her name that sells the books, not the content, you should know that, Mortimer. You know we're trying to grow *The Roaming Nun* as our back-up brand for Molly and *The Sailing Bishop*. Any chance of making Sister Evangeline a counter offer?'

Susceptible as I am to father figures – though Gerard is only about seventeen years older than me – I quailed somewhat at this but said, 'I'm not sure it would be successful. You know what she's like when she's made up her mind. She feels quite strongly that her crane should go to Calling Crane, if you see what I mean.'

Drusilla said, 'I wonder what – or who – gave her that idea?'

I quailed in my boots. Why oh why did I ever go blabbing to Calling Crane? My heart smote me. Would I be the one to have driven the final nail into the coffin of the House?

Drusilla continued, 'Sister Evangeline should be careful, too. Promising though she is, she's only done one book with us. If she's got any sense, she should be consolidating her reputation here before branching out further afield.'

Gerard said, 'What can we tempt her with?'

Fay said, 'Could she do a swan?' and I thought, here we go. Too right. Forty minutes later we had exhausted all known varieties of birds and had moved on to dragons, salamanders and other beasts mythical. So tiring. I do wish people would mind their own business.

Then Gerard, who gave the impression of having something up his sleeve, cleared his throat and said, 'Let's not get sidetracked,' and announced he was pleased and proud to have acquired *Pure Water, Blue Ocean: Skimming the waves with Bishop Molly, a spiritual quest for the speedy*, by our own dear Bishop Molly Roper who was now off crutches and with her writing wrist healing well. Drusilla said, 'But what's happened to *Sailing with the Angels,* which should have been in nearly six months ago?' and Fay said, 'Yes, and what about *Ecological Grief: Mourning the loss of the natural world?* We've been waiting for that as well for two years now. Surely she shouldn't be starting a new book! All it means is that we keep on paying out hefty advances and never see anything for it!'

Gerard said, 'The governing body are keen on it,' and – after a fierce and bitter row between him, Drusilla and Fay, and sales director Roland, who requires six months to sell the books in to the trade and is much opposed to 'helicoptering titles in' – that was that. Gerard said that he and the governing body were heavily invested in Molly for the simple reason that her books outsold the rest of all our other authors put together (when they come in, that is) as well as her having a special hotline to the press by virtue of her position and personality both, of course. He certainly is fiercely loyal to Molly. Shame most of her books don't exist. Sometimes I wonder if the governing body, that elusive group of powerful City masons, is a real entity as well, or whether, like Dickens's Spenlow and Jorkins in *David Copperfield*, they are just a handy figment of Gerard's imagination, wheeled in at intervals to back-up his own plans and desires. I've never met any of them, anyway.

I was slightly shocked by Gerard's lack of proper editorial procedures, given all his recent fussing about following the letter of the law with regard to *What Trees Talk About When They Talk About Love*. He didn't even bring a draft proposal of Molly's new book to the meeting, and no sample material, let alone a costing from Production – just a title and concept, verbally presented. I would be shot if I did that. Still, I have my own modest concerns to worry about. *Tree Talk* didn't get through as Ursula had forgotten to include it in the agenda. To be honest, I thought we could have discussed it impromptu, or they could even have waited five minutes while I printed out copies of the proposal for everyone, but Gerard just said, 'No matter, we'll do it next time.' Relegated again.

Some 8,400 orders for *Heave* so far. Fay still quite unable to get through to the warehouse and Amazon on this one. She keeps saying, 'But I've cancelled all those dues,' as if that sorted everything out. I don't know why they don't simply change the title from *Heaven* to *Heave*. I suggested this, saying we'd been handed a bestseller on a plate, given all the orders pouring in for this rogue book. But, predictably, I was laughed to scorn. Well, they had their chance.

Told Drusilla about having a grateful February and she roared and said, 'But there's nothing to be grateful *for* in February!' That took the pressure off, I must say.

Wednesday 20 February
Ash Wednesday
Loki, trickster god of mischief, active today! An email marked high importance to ALL@HQ from Gerard, disclosing that Bishop Molly's advance is £60,000!!! Sixty thousand pounds!! I didn't think we had that much money in the kitty! Most people's advances here are between £300 and £800. This was immediately followed by another message re-calling the first email, explaining that it was a mistake and contained confidential and misleading information, and asking people to delete it unread. Too late. I expect Fay's already sent it on to *Private Eye*.

There seems to be a bit of a hex on money at the moment, as Gerard lost £335 cash, which turned up unharmed in the dishwasher, having been through an entire wash. Naturally jokes are flying round about the House and laundered money, but there is a funny kind of atmosphere around this cash. It's a lot to be carrying around, even for work-related purposes. People are sitting around with their noses quivering, but unable to say exactly where the smell is coming from, or what it is, and how the money even got into the dishwasher in the first place. Ursula suggested Gerard might have somehow picked it up along with his soup bowl and tucked it into the dishwasher unawares, but as Gerard goes out to lunch every single day without exception this is unlikely. It is Ursula who dines on a tin of Heinz and crackers – admittedly a very superior cracker from Marks & Sparks – while Gerard is whooping it up on oysters and steak at the Savoy.

Covers meeting. Ursula had forgotten *again*, and the door of the Fisher Room was firmly locked. We all gathered outside shivering until I went down to reception to extract the key from her.

Gerard, emerging up from the spiral staircase in time to hear this, all neat and tidy in his Sunday best – mustard tweeds with a thread of orange, ivory silk stock trimmed with gold, freshly oiled sideburns and walking stick with a deer's head handle – looked very angry indeed. And if it was possible for his visitor to bristle more, he did so. Ursula was, of course, totally unmoved by the two stony faces, and merely went back to answering the switchboard in her usual bright way. But while I have no idea what he was meeting Gerard about, I recognised the note in the visitor's voice; it was the chill sound of lost money if ever I heard it.

When they'd gone upstairs, Ursula turned to me and said in a stage whisper, 'The chairman of the governing body! In mufti today!' and I said, 'Oh, was it? Wish I'd had a closer look. It would be good to know some of them by sight.'

Ursula said, 'Yes. They're all in a bit of a two and eight today for some reason.'

'Oh, why?'

'Oh, I expect we haven't paid our two and a half pigs rent or something. Gerard's in a terrible old tizz.'

'And it's thrown out all the meetings,' said Drusilla, joining us. She added it was a strange thing, all the years she'd been here, she'd seen through several changes of governing body and the odd thing was that even though the individual members changed, the body itself seemed to remain exactly the same and to make all the same old clunky and incompetent and tactless decisions.

Hope Gerard is okay.

Was just turning away when my eye was caught by several satsumas loose on the desk in front of Ursula. I counted twelve of them. Why? I had to ask.

'Do they represent the twelve apostles, Ursula?'

'No, they were on offer at Waitrose. Very sweet, very fresh. Do have one. I find that everything tastes so much better when eaten *al desko*, don't you?'

I took one on the premise that I would be safely removing Judas and Ursula could enjoy the other eleven untrammelled by worries about their sanctity. Not sure she got it.

Covers meeting finally just before lunch. Another fine old row. Design, for reasons best known to themselves, wanted to use Michelangelo's David for the new edition of *When Earth Cracks: Dealing with Global Psychospiritual Crisis*. Gerard didn't like this. He said he felt a male adult nude was inappropriate for the *Earth* list. Design, in the person of Toya, a loud and plangent Catalan, extolled the virtues of nudity on a cover. She pointed out that the Catalan edition of *Great Soil Mother: Breath, bone and blood* had a bare female torso complete with nipples and pubic hair, and that in her book earth meant earth, and why were we publishing nature books if no one could face the natural body? No one likes to contradict Toya because, as well as being incredibly strong-minded and vocal, she's also in a wheelchair due to some horrible neurological condition and, I know, genuinely suffers at times. In this case, however, one thing led to another and before anyone knew it the editorial team was launched into its favourite pastime, a full-scale shouting match.

Drusilla tactfully tried to lighten the mood by saying that when she first joined publishing and went to her first jacket meeting, she dutifully donned a jacket, but her words were swept away by the increasingly heated discussion and in fact, as usual, nobody paid the slightest attention. Everyone seemed to have forgotten that the book was on my list, not theirs, so I slunk away and went back to my office to work in peace on the editing of *Wilderness Therapy for Wellbeing* by Eileen Fallon, which came in at last – a very lazily written book indeed, and very bald and tactless, but at least not controversial.

Was just writing the author a tactful critique saying I felt it needed another draft, and a more fundamental re-working than could be provided by in-house editing, as the language was unlikely to endear itself to the sensitive reader, when Fay appeared at the door to disparage Toya further as being 'sex-mad.' I'd love to ascertain on what grounds. I mean, how does she *know*? Fay also said that Gerard should have stood firm, but was weighted by some secret sorrow, some responsibility too heavy for a single man to bear. What on earth could it be? At any rate, Gerard left immediately after the meeting to give Sister Evangeline and her fellow nuns a hand with the lambing. It's not right, he says, that these older ladies should be getting up in the middle of the night to deal with birthing ewes, however picturesque.

Took the tube to Westminster Cathedral at lunchtime, away from the chill Anglican breezes that blow here. It was packed to the hilt. Seven priests in purple were distributing the ashes to seven lines of people stretching to the back of the cathedral. They seemed endless, as if all the penitents of the world were queuing up. Sunshine was billowing in and out of the horrible great Victorian windows around the altar, bringing a sudden memory of daffodils and lambs and the essence of spring itself. Suddenly all the grim greeny-maroon marble and its depressing swirls seemed softened to nothing, just warm golden sun-mites filling the air, gold dust. I stood entranced. The entire building seemed to have dissolved. I wonder if this is a spiritual experience. I came out with a great thumbful of dark ash on my forehead, a dramatic cross rather than the discreet grey fuzz I remembered from times gone by. I could see it mirrored on the foreheads of others around me. We looked a marked and branded crew to be sure. One young, suited man stood clutching the foot of the statue of St Antony, pressing his head to it in a silent agony of repentance. I felt he was a projection of myself, a curious sensation.

Thursday 21 February

Gerard has gone down with brain fever! – something I thought was extinct, like wasting disease and neurasthenia. Poor Gerard, he does seem to have the most dreadful bad luck. The lambing was clearly too much for him. I believe the nuns are looking after him, though.

The diagnosis did not go unchallenged. Fay said, 'No one has brain fever these days. Even in Victorian times, it didn't exist. I hope to God it's not meningitis or encephalitis.'

Drusilla said, 'What are the symptoms?'

'Fever, hallucinations and forgetfulness.'

'I see, standard states when it comes to running a publishing business. Treatment?'

'Leeches, blood-letting, wrapping in wet sheets and immersion in hot and cold baths,' said Fay with satisfaction. 'Speaking of which, Mortimer, do you have to splutter and sneeze all over us!'

'I am using a hanky.'

'Yes, you can't miss the hanky. Thought it was a bed-sheet!'

Drusilla said, 'Now, now, Fay, show Mortimer a little mercy. He's just gone trekking out to remote rural France in the most arduous conditions in order to visit his aged father.'

I tried to explain again that my trip had been cancelled, but Fay said, '*I* visit *both* my aged parents in remote rural Wales regularly and *I* don't come back with a cold. *And* I've just come back from an even more remote cottage without mishap! I took a rural bus as well on the way back and visited Dafydd ap Dafydd in his shepherd's hut, and *he* does all his writing there no matter what the weather, in fingerless gloves! Mortimer shouldn't undertake such trips if he finds them too much.'

'Yes he should!' said Drusilla crossly. 'He's free to do what he wants, without having to justify it to you!'

'I'm not asking him to justify anything to me. All I'm saying is, it's anti-social to come into work sniffing and blowing like that and he should stay home if he isn't in a fit condition to come to work!'

At this point I got tired of being discussed as if I wasn't there and went back to my office.

Design still having trouble making David respectable for *Global Psychospiritual Crisis*. On orders from Gerard, Toya put scaffolding around David, with one bar covering the strategic area, but was very unhappy about it. She summoned me to her large and airy ground floor studio, created specially for her needs in a former stock room beside the post room. She spent a good half hour miserably moving the scaffolding to the right or left to try for the most tactful and impressive effect, while I sat on the desk proffering what encouragement I could. Alas, it still all looked wrong in her eyes, so in the end, she said, 'The hell with it,' and framed him fair and square within the scaffolding with everything showing.

Drusilla, in the safety of our own offices, told me that Toya's penchant for male nudes is the real reason our house style forbids showing people on the covers. Long ago, it seems, Gerard issued an edict banishing the human form from our book designs because he couldn't face confronting Toya.

'Yes,' drawled Drusilla, 'Gerard took the easy way out.'

Something about the fall of these words made my heart sink a little.

Friday 22 February

Tried to research brain fever on the net. Not encouraging. It said, 'The best chance for a complete recovery is for treatment to be given before you lapse into a coma.'

Ursula sacked from arranging the author gratis because she makes such a hash of it each month. All she has to do is send each author the six copies of his or her book to which he or she is entitled by terms of the contract. And we only publish ten books each month. The maths of this not impossible. However, we are losing author good will left, right and centre – and sometimes the authors themselves – because they are not getting their free copies or, even worse, are getting copies of other people's books. It's worse still when they disagree with the politics or theology of the books they've been sent, as frequently happens. Apart from the several rows and feuds this has engendered, it's just bad practice. As Drusilla said, 'A basic knowledge of author psychology is the first requisite for working in publishing, rule number one being: never, ever deprive an author of a freebie.' Once again it was suggested to Ursula that she might like to consider having her cataract operation, as a major part of the problem is of course her inability to read the names and addresses correctly. It's not a question of a waiting list – she's been on that so long that even her GP is losing patience with her, as she keeps getting to the top of it and then chickening out of the op and sliding back down to the bottom again.

Ursula said that if she has a panic attack at the dentist's – which she does, regularly every six months – how on earth would she face an eye operation? Drusilla and Ethel offered to accompany her – one for each eye, as it were.

Dr Chauncey Rivers called with another Iraq ghost story. I don't really want to write it down here, due to the primitive fear of rousing and summoning something by writing about it. Chauncey does make my spine tingle. He said that inspiration had died for his book on demonic possession, *Enthralled*, but that he was working on a new one, *Encounters*, about haunted modern sites such as factories, housing estates, motorways and airports. I wonder could I pass him on to Fay. I have an editor's instinct that she might warm to him. After all, I seem to be fielding Sister Evangeline quite a bit.

Don't think I am going to finish the Trollope. Not often I abandon a book halfway through, but the prospect of ploughing through all 425,000 words, approx twenty-five hours reading time, doesn't exactly daunt me but does fail to entice. I read the plot on Wikipedia so it's not as if I'm losing anything. If I'm going to spend that long on a book I'd rather it really was Proust. *À la recherche* has an estimated word count of 1,267,069, although I think that's in French. No, Drusilla's right. It's a crying shame I haven't read Proust yet at my age.

Saturday 23 February

Started Proust in earnest (in English, relying on Scott-Moncrieff to guide me through this first time). Was pleasantly surprised to find that his egoism draws you in at once, making it quite readable.

Just as I was falling asleep, I remembered I'd forgotten to text Hugo about a visit. Hope I don't get Sam in reply. Why does Hugo have to lead such a complicated life?

Sunday 24 February

Can't visit Hugo as he is doing a reading skills course all week. Honestly, he is a demanding friend. It would have been so easy for all this simply not to have happened. When I think of all the time I spent trying to distract him by taking him to concerts and exhibitions and talking to him about Wagner in the kindest possible way, and he would insist on going ahead with what counsel called an audacious and arrogant plan to gut the libraries of Europe of some of their most valuable and valued treasures. Even so, he might have got away with it if he hadn't pushed it. As it was, it took the libraries a long time to get on to him. They called him *das Gespenst* on the German library circuit, the spectre, he was so elusive. He so looked the part of a harmless, down-at-heel academic, with the longish hair and the shirt hanging out.

Monday 25 February

Gerard on the *Please be kind* list – a bad sign.

A box arrived today for Drusilla, full of handwritten pages, from some Monsignor who retired about a century ago. (Drusilla's authors tend not to favour anything other than quill and ink.) When she came to examine the manuscript, *Wounded*, by Monsignor Philip Midwinter, ninety-four, Drusilla found the pages weren't numbered, possibly on the grounds that book pages were rarely numbered in the Middle Ages. There are about 400 pages. She has asked Ursula, unwisely in everyone's opinion, to number them for her. The smallest, simplest request brings the light of panic to Ursula's eyes, but Drusilla is fond of delegating and has a touching faith in people's potential, undeterred by the fact that Ursula has now spent about forty-six working hours so far this year looking for the Daybreak Manuscript.

A rare moment of harmony with Fay, who invited me to a lunchtime concert to which she had free tickets for some reason. Lovely Chopin as befits this fine winter day. We walked along, the London sky a clear pale blue overhead, and she told me all about her long-lost past as an athlete in her teens. She said, 'I was nearly a professional acrobat you know, Mortimer. I even had dreams of joining the Cirque du Soleil. I was just not quite good enough.'

I didn't know what to say. 'A miss is as good as a mile' was the only thing that came to mind, and that didn't seem quite right somehow. In the end I managed, 'The Cirque du Soleil's loss is our gain,' and she looked down her nose graciously. Relief.

Ursula, maybe picking up the musical vibes as well as the lost hopes, spent much of the afternoon choosing and singing through her funeral hymns. Strains of *Guide me Lord, the storm has ended*, floated through to us, punctuated by her comments. 'Oh that's a *beautiful* one!' to Ethel, with the low rumble of Ethel's reply, mercifully inaudible. I don't see why Ursula should be the only one to be in on the act, and, during the course of a long afternoon, decided that I would have the *Ave maris stella* from Monteverdi's Vespers played at my funeral. It is, without exception, the most beautiful piece of music I have ever heard. For me, there is life before Monteverdi, and life after Monteverdi. I suppose I must have been about seventeen when I discovered that.

Tuesday 26 February

Still no word from Gerard. Bit worrying. Should we all be preparing black bands for our arms in the best Victorian tradition?

I understand that in any case brain fever can be quite lingering in its effects.

Ursula has started numbering Monsignor Philip Midwinter's 400 pages so that wherever one is, one seems to hear her loud, clear voice counting slowly, 'One – two – three – oh bother!' I can't bear the suspense.

Wednesday 27 February

An extra editorial meeting organised by Fay in Gerard's continued absence. She had a dinky pencil with *I was once a plastic cup* written along its length. We spent forty minutes trying to work out exactly what kind of illness Gerard had but could only conclude that it sounded grave. Think I managed to unload Chauncey Rivers, though. We looked at his proposal for *Encounters*. A very spooky book, all about meeting extremely troubled entities in bleak suburban houses and beneath railway bridges and on new road routes being constructed atop ancient burial grounds. I watched Fay with bated breath while she read it through. She looked up at last saying, 'Why do you not want this, Mortimer? It's really good!'

Told her about the scary phone calls and she said, 'Put him through to me next time. I'll talk to him. In fact, I'll give him a ring this afternoon.' I was tremendously grateful and said so. Told her about Sister Evangeline as well while we were at it, and how abusive she was on the phone, and Fay tossed her head and said she wasn't afraid of anyone whose real name was Delilah Prunty.

Ursula still numbering Monsignor Philip's pages. I think she's got to page seventy-nine. Drusilla showing signs of impatience.

Thursday 28 February

A complete lack of health bulletins from Gerard. No one knows if he's a) in intensive care hovering between life and death; b) recovering quietly at home; c) anywhere between these.

Ursula has finished numbering Monsignor Philip Midwinter's pages but has muddled the first 200 with the second 200 in some odd way so that all sense is completely lost.

Friday 1 March

Drusilla arrived and tore Ursula to pieces. Tears from Ursula; wails of '*Perfect* sense!' Drusilla says she will now have to take the manuscript into deepest Cornwall and go through it with the good monsignor page by page, which will take about a week – provided he survives that long, of course. At ninety-four, one may be forgiven for feeling that life is slightly precarious.

Fay said again that Gerard should have got rid of Ursula years ago, but that he just hasn't got what it takes to bite the bullet and face any uncomfortable situation. 'Gerard's like that. He's the boy who always wants things to be nice.'

For once Drusilla agreed with Fay. 'No doubt about it, Ursula's a complete waste of time and money. She's also just run up a $400 bill on copyright after taking it upon herself to go ahead without deigning to consult me. For just two extracts! I hadn't even decided whether we were going to use them or not!'

'We certainly don't need a $400 bill right now.'

'And that's just the two I know about,' said Drusilla. She sounded quite worried. 'Anyway, I've asked her to start searching the attics for the Book, which I don't think has ever been done, so that should keep her tucked out of the way for a while.'

She tried seconding Fay into the search for the Daybreak Manuscript as well, but Fay takes the view that she is far too busy to look for a book when books are standing all around us.

Gerard reported as 'having turned the corner.' It then transpired that we should have had this report about five days ago. So we still don't know how he really is.

Saturday 2 March

No peace for the wicked, as Uncle Albany says. Hugo rang me five times today – he now has more freedom with the phone as he's been given a little job to do looking after the prison library (not unduly arduous as the library consists of seventy-three books, in some contrast, as Hugo pointed out, to Dr Dee's Mortlake library of 4,000 books), and access to a landline is one of the perks. Said he was writing, working away on something called *Lucifer Tumbling Upward* which he hopes we might publish. He's full of plans for when he comes out such as a) me to act as his literary agent and arrange a three-book deal for him; b) me to get a flat next to or near his; and c) me to move in outright. None of these are acceptable to me.

He didn't even thank me for sending him the books. Talk about ingratitude!

It all left me quite wound up. Found I was muttering to myself up and down the aisles when I went shopping, and people were looking at me strangely. Realised I had to take myself in hand so came home and called Uncle Albany. I was really grateful to hear from him and found myself telling him all about Hugo. He said, 'Mortimer, take advantage and steer well clear while he's inside. He'll find someone else to look after him, poor soul.'

In the heat of the moment I agreed to go down to Gallhampton Gap tomorrow. Albany sounded delighted and I felt rather guilty at having avoided the trip for so long. Then I looked at the temperatures for tomorrow and didn't feel so guilty. Minus 2 and a wind chill factor of minus 7!

Sunday 3 March

When I checked my phone this morning, rather hoping that Albany might have cancelled, there were eight missed calls and six texts from Hugo. I was shaving when he texted again and said he was cold and would I send him some socks when I gained access to his flat as the other prisoners had stolen all his. I texted back, 'Will do.

By the way what about *Prayers from Prison*, have you thought any more about it?' but got a reply from Sam Mungo his prison warder saying that Prisoner DW34M had exceeded his texting allowance for the weekend now, but not to worry about the book, it was all in hand. I'm pretending I haven't received this.

Was smitten to the heart by Hugo's sockless condition, however, so bundled up some of my own – fortunately quite new – into a jiffy bag, stuck two first class stamps on, and posted them on the way to the station.

Duly went down to Gallhampton Gap, with a mixture of qualms: qualms at not having gone before, qualms at having to go at all. Don't think I've been since we went night fishing on the rocks in September. Quite as chilly as forecast. A searing wind. Albany very spry in his parka and fur-lined cap, and was touchingly delighted to see me, indeed he had walked up to meet me. Hope I'm in as good shape when I'm seventy-nine. I hoped we'd be heading straight back to his nice warm Regency flat for a hot toddy, but first we did our obligatory four-mile perambulation along the cliff top and then, when I was ready to drop, Albany said, 'How about a spam sandwich? Nice little café just opened up, does wartime food. A sticky toffee pudding, too, I do believe. And how about you, young Mortimer? You're looking very sprightly. Have you met a girl?'

I said, 'No, not yet.'

'Oh well, keep looking. Puts a spring in your step, I've always found.'

He should know. Twice married and it would be thrice if Patti had her way. As my father says, 'Albany's never short of a woman or two to look after him.'

The Don Juan of Gallhampton Gap led the way to the café, where the waitresses edged past the table in enormous pinafores and seemed delighted to be chaffed by Albany. We duly consumed the spam and toffee and watched the world go by: youths in baseball caps; old hippies with grey ponytails, leather jackets, and drainpipe jeans; women in jackets of long fake fur; and a string of mobility scooters going past the café window.

Over this repast I learned that Auntie Juls was hard on my heels, driving down from London and bringing her partner Carol, along with one or two more of the gals and a few bottles of wine. I resolved to take my departure immediately. Juls is a big cheese in local government in Bromley and cares for Albany deeply but can be a little overwhelming at times and is best taken in small doses.

Albany showed me the crumpled roll of manuscript that was his autobiography as I was buttoning my overcoat, and said rather wistfully, 'If anything happens to me, will you take charge of this, Mortimer?'

'Of course.'

'Get it published and everything?'

'I'll do my best. Have you got an electronic version?'

He looked rather guilty. 'Somewhere.'

'Well, send it over to me, will you, so I have it safely.'

'I will do.'

'Today?'

I felt a slight sense of urgency.

'As soon as I can find it. It's on my laptop somewhere.'

He insisted on walking me to the station, saying it would serve as another little leg-stretch before Auntie Juls and her entourage arrived. Very windy. The streets had a weird dark grey light and seemed to be gusting with coal smoke and salt and wasted opportunities. Albany stood at the barrier and waved me out of sight. I felt a pang at my last view of his face, puckish and rather wistful beneath his parka hood.

Bought a packet of mints from the platform vending machine to take away the taste of the wartime food. Bit of a relief to get back on the train.

So glad to have saved Proust for later life. I felt his ironic, disdainful spirit hovering around me as we trundled through the wastes of eastern England on a Sunday afternoon a great comfort.

Monday 4 March

From: Ursula Woodrow Sent: 4 March 9.10 To: ALL@HQ
Subject: Weekly *Please be kind* list

Morning All,

This week, **please be kind** to:

- Our publishing director Gerard Delamere, still down with brain fever.
- Ursula Woodrow on a very important mission as she searches for something lost and precious.
- Bishop Molly who has an important birthday this week – her fiftieth.

Ursula

Ursula Woodrow, editorial assistant
The House of Marvellous Books
Wayfarers and Wilderness, our award-winning nature list

The fury of Molly at this is said to be beyond reason.

Got in to a fairly average inbox:

a) An email from a New Zealand author giving me her address as requested but ending it with The Earth, The Universe and a smiley face.

b) An email from someone called Paul Fagg addressed to my predecessor of ten years ago asking if he could send in a submission on *Pan and Panic: Healing with the wild god*.

c) A submission from someone saying she is the reincarnation of Vashti, Queen of Persia and the first wife of Persian King Ahasuerus in the Book of Esther, and would I like a book on *The Ancient Concubine – Dancing with Vashti – thoughts on gynaecology, complications and our culture*? I said no.

d) An email from the great environmental activist Sir Noah Singleton pleading to be released from his contract for *The Earth is Dreaming Us* on grounds of insanity, with a somewhat terse letter attached from his doctor backing this up.

e) An impertinent email from literary agent Jon Grisi of Batten & Leech pointing out that we have put 31 April deadline in our contract with Ivan Skrulewski and that we have omitted the agent's clause so that payments will go direct to the author instead of to them – *sacré bleu!* Jon feels very strongly about such things and can be a little excitable at times. Hope he doesn't ring up. Not sure I'm in the mood today.

Arranged the cancellation of the contract for *The Earth is Dreaming Us*. Gerard won't be best pleased, but some things we are powerless against.

Tuesday 5 March

Drusilla back from Cornwall, looking brisk and satisfied, and the *Wounded* MS all in due order. She said they got through it in record time, at which I couldn't help feeling a pang for poor Monsignor Philip. Although he is now insisting the book be called *Broken*, to great inconvenience as we've now done the catalogue and all the publicity as *Wounded*.

Drusilla had managed to miss all the furore about Molly's fiftieth as she never reads the *Please be kind* list – I rely on it as our leading source of gossip and information – and just deletes anything that comes from Ursula unread, so I told her about the birthday blunder and she laughed and said, 'I heard that Molly was furious about something. Hopefully she, too, will push for Ursula to be sacked now,' adding, 'the *Please be kind* list has always been a pretty cavalier affair. Ursula was going to do something similar for Fay a few months ago when she hit fifty, but Fay managed to find out and forestall her.'

I said, 'She would! Well, I wouldn't have put Fay at fifty, that's for sure – more like thirty-eight or even thirty-three!'

Drusilla said, 'You're too gallant, Mortimer,' and launched into a long spiel about how Fay is 'mutton dressed as lamb,' and that 'she can't keep it up for ever,' but you have to admit there is no one quite like Fay, with her tumbling black ringlets and ageless air of belonging to the fairy race.

Drusilla went on, 'There's no way I'd be fifty again, Mortimer, it's a time of great personal upheaval and confusion. The calm waters of the sixties are bliss compared to it. Menopause and empty nest syndrome all mixed up with regrets about what you have and haven't done. I dare say Fay has a few of those, more about what she hasn't done than what she has, of course. By the way, speaking of such things, what's the latest with your chum behind bars?'

'Well, he's pretty furious because he's been put on an anger management course.'

'Hard lines,' said Drusilla without undue sympathy. 'Have you put it to him that he might feel better if he channels his anger into writing that book?'

'Yes, several times. I understand a synopsis is in progress.'

Didn't say that I'm hopelessly confused about who is doing the synopsis, Hugo or Sam. Maybe Sam needs the therapy of writing more than Hugo does at the moment, who knows.

As I was pondering these perplexities, Ursula came thundering along the corridors and into my office, the desk shaking as she marched up to me, the light of purpose in her eyes. She said, 'Hello, Mortimer, where would I buy a man's hairbrush?' It was like one of those Anglo-Saxon riddles which you must answer correctly to get out of the cave or the barrow, or else spend the rest of your life dodging your enemy in the dark passages. I am not clever at riddles. I said, 'Any pharmacist or supermarket, I should think?'

There ensued one of those awful, long conversations that one invariably has with Ursula. Really, only Ethel can keep her in order, usually by being quite spectacularly firm with her, although I think Ursula quite enjoys it.

'Oh, I forgot,' said Ursula suddenly. 'I really came to call you to the editorial board. They're waiting for you to present your *Talking Trees*.'

Oh, Lord! I jumped up, my heart thudding, and made for the Fisher Room as fast as I could. Thirteen severe faces greeted me round the big oak table. What with being taken off guard and breathless from running through the library, it goes without saying that I could barely talk my way through the presentation but, thank goodness, the proposal got through, mainly on the strength of the author's platform in the forestry community, and the faces relaxed into benevolent neutrality.

Where *do* you buy a man's hairbrush?

Wednesday 6 March

Realised that the man's hairbrush is a trick question, like all riddles. There are no differences between male and female hairbrushes.

Hoorah! Well done, Mortimer! Ticked off the last of the new year rejections, ending with *The Ultimate Natural Sex Muffin*. The author said it was all about self-esteem and relationships in the natural world, but closer inspection revealed that it wouldn't do. Most of the others could easily be dealt with on the grounds that the governing body have forbidden the use of the word 'suffer' as being derogatory and patronising to readers. Alternatively, I fell back on our formula that 'we didn't think we'd be able to do the book justice in terms of sales.' The real problem is that no sane person will write for the advances we offer. This naturally limits the selection quite a bit. Shared all this with Fay who said she was still working through her own lot of, 'The editors were glad to see this,' as she takes such care over her rejection letters. She said, with a beam of pride, 'People say it's the nicest rejection letter they have ever had, that it's a pleasure to be rejected by me!' Drusilla needless to say favours a much blunter approach along the lines of, 'This is highly unlikely to go anywhere.'

I left until very last the submissions that began with, 'God told me to write this.' For all my years in publishing, went strangely brain-dead on this, until Ethel came to my rescue and supplied the second half of this antique chestnut. Overhearing me complaining to Fay in the kitchen, she rumbled, grasping the kettle, 'God may have told you to write it, but He hasn't told us to publish it.' She smiled grimly at me and raised her eyebrows. I said, 'Oh, thanks, Ethel, that's brilliant,' and she actually smiled again and said, 'All part of the House Ed service.'

Was the more grateful for this as I felt it made up the Satan row. It's a relief to feel I can now go back to visiting Desk Ed in person and walking down the corridor when I have a query, instead of emailing, and receiving punctilious replies of icy politeness.

A big bunch of red roses arrived today for Drusilla from Monsignor Philip Midwinter.

She told me all about their long past as fond friends, which goes right back to when she was at university.

'He was a history don… I was engaged to someone else, you see. And then, he was ordained…'

Her voice coming over the partition quavered with emotion. I sat there listening and invisible in my dark cubicle like a priest myself in the confessional. Maybe I really have missed my vocation. After all, isn't it the priest's job to hear the same sins over and over again? And what do we come to work for, but to tell and re-tell each other our stories?

Thursday 7 March

A pathetic text from Hugo thanking me for the socks.

Drusilla has hired a professional debt collector to collect £1 million owing us in foreign rights from the Vatican. She said, 'That would save our bacon for six months at least.' This debt is seven years old, and dates from an exceptionally successful book we did called *Beasts, Flowers and Other Natural Objects in the Vatican Library and Secret Archives*, (*Animali, fiori e altri oggetti naturali nella Biblioteca Vaticana e nell'Archivio Segreto*) of which they bought thousands of copies without ever actually paying the bill. Drusilla said she was prepared to forgo the interest out of good will and hopes to go to Rome soon to seal the deal. Let's hope the monsignors pay up!

Gerard reported to be on the mend. About time, too. It's been nice having this period of freedom but we could do with a bit more direction, in fact, any direction, as no one knows where we are heading at all. Our great Ship is on the loose, tacking lightly away with the winds, and listing badly.

Friday 8 March

Dear Sir/Madam,

Would you be interested in a personal memoir? *Shadows of the 70s: Rewyrding Britain, or, How the Devil Left his Footprint under our Village Bridge* was seven years in the writing and is a hundred and eighty-two thousand words long and eagerly awaited by my mates... In it I tell of my psychological demons and half memories from the 1970s... a time hungover from the sixties... a time which left many children haunted by a weird culture, weird TV programmes, weird teachers and weird adults generally... flares and sideburns... patterned carpets and growing motorways... a time of UFOs and sudden political violence... an uncanny and liminal era... I promise you the book is different. Contemporary. And will hopefully break the mould. Thank you for taking the time to read this whilst I know you are so busy.

Nigel Rookhope

Aaaaah! I do wish people wouldn't use 'whilst' for 'while'! Ethel refuses to have it in the house, saying it's old-fashioned, and indeed it's been officially barred in our style guide for some time.

On the positive side, Fay bit! She and Dr Chauncey Rivers are going out for lunch!

Day went downhill after that. Ivan Skrulewski rang up and gave me hell over an unpaid advance. He said, 'I know damn well that Gerard considers it a matter of honour to sit on the contracts for six months before signature, but if you want me to write this book for the execrable amount you pay, I have to have something solid today or the deal's off. It's my birthday on Sunday and I intend to go out and have a few drinks. The advance will just about stretch to that.'

No one could accuse us of tempting authors to write for money, it's true.

I said, 'I'll see what Accounts can do.'

Ventured accordingly downstairs into the basement to the underbelly of the business where Accounts live, six strong women who spend the day shouting across the desks about football, diets and their respective mothers-in-law. They are remarkable for being married and living in proper houses in the suburbs with gardens and garages, in contrast to the more refined race we represent upstairs, single almost to a man or woman, who dwell in small flats in obscure corners of London like a twee, threatened race from Beatrix Potter.

It's been a while since I faced Accounts and I'd forgotten how fearsome they were. The row of stalwart bodies round a central oblong of desks resolved itself into the persons of the two figureheads, Shannon and Charlene. With their grand fronts, swept-back hair and powerful arms, they are almost indistinguishable except that both are the sort of beings you'd be afraid to meet outside of Wagner.

'We don't do cheques any more,' they snapped in unison when I explained Dr Skrulewski's plight and pleaded for an emergency payment. This is untrue by the way – I've seen the paperwork

'Sorry,' she said, 'I've had rather a lot of people in off the street saying they're Jesus. It does get rather distracting, Mortimer. I do feel I have to listen to them. Supposing one of them happened to be true? How could I face the Lord on the Last Day? Imagine Him saying, "You didn't recognise Me."'

I agreed it was an unenviable part of her job. She sprang up and went dashing down into the basement to get the key. Why the keys are kept down there I really don't know – Ursula guards them in something called The Box, which she in turn keeps locked up in a safe in a secret location. Goodness knows what we'd do if she got knocked down by a bus.

The minutes ticked by. Questions about life went through my mind. Why is the Fisher Room kept locked anyway? What else is in The Box? Could it be any relation to the fabled Box of Joanna Southcott, with its secret prophecies sealed within, to be revealed only at a time of national crisis? And what *had* been in Joanna's Box in the end, when finally opened? A rusty pistol and a lottery ticket or two, I seemed to remember.

Meanwhile a sparse, severe looking man entered, spanking up the steps with the urgent air of one who bears bad news. His face was familiar to me, but I couldn't quite place him. This happens quite a lot with the dignitaries who pass through our doors; it might be the Bishop of London taking off his bicycle clips, or the latest delivery of egg sandwiches and cupcakes from M&S, you never know here. Without moving a muscle, this personage conveyed a considerable level of fussing and fretting at being kept waiting. I explained that Ursula was on her way, at which he seemed to suppress a gesture of impatience. Eventually Ursula re-appeared from the submerged regions, beaming at her own achievement. 'There you are,' she said, handing me the key, and to the visitor, 'Morning, my Lord! Have you come to see Gerard?'

'Yes, quite urgently,' he said.

'Well, he went down to the loo… he's been about seven minutes so he shouldn't be much longer.'

going out to overseas authors at royalties time in July, and the cheques are as big as the payments are small.

I said, 'He'll take cash.'

In the end, after much wrangling, they parted with a cheque for £400 which I posted first class, going out to the post box on the park gate and using one of my own stamps to avoid the vagaries of Ursula in the post room. I wondered was it worthwhile? Ivan could probably get that from a couple of sessions with his patients. I suppose it's the principle of the thing. It usually is with Ivan.

Saturday 9 March

Got a long and frantic message from Hugo saying he'd been transferred to Borstal for some reason and begging me to visit him if I valued his sanity and his life. Arranged to go to go down to Borstal tomorrow accordingly, after much wearisome faffing about.

For the rest, I do not remember, as Dorothy Wordsworth says.

Sunday 10 March

Went down to Kent to see Hugo in Borstal but the sniffer dogs took such an interest in me – they kept coming up and nosing at my pockets although I assured the warders I had no drugs on me – that Hugo and I weren't allowed to meet face to face, and had to converse through the glass, supervised. They're not the sort of dogs you can fraternise with, unfortunately. There were phones but these weren't working so we had to shout either side of the panel and hope for the best. Not a very satisfactory conversation, especially when trying to discuss authorial absenting in American literature (Pynchon disappearing into reclusiveness, Wallace into suicide.) The best I can take out of it is that at least I didn't meet Sam (who has I think been left behind at Wandsworth.)

Never mind *Infinite Jest*, infinite trek would be the best way of describing the journey to Borstal and back from Wimbledon. Still, at least I was able to make a little progress with Proust on the journey.

Monday 11 March

Ursula tried to explain how Easter is calculated and got herself into such a tangle with gibbous moons that she ended up in tears.

I felt more empathy than I might otherwise have done as I suffered what can only be called persecution all day at the hands of literary agent Jon Grisi of Batten & Leech, wanting me to take on a Chinese author who speaks no English and has written no book. I offered to consider the translation when it was done, but it turned out there was no book in Chinese either.

Ivan Skrulewski rang and said the cheque had bounced. Apparently it was unsigned.

Got a distraught phone call from Drusilla, working from home, begging me to switch on her computer and re-send her the last but one email, as she's expecting a vital communication from the Vatican, and when she logs onto the server from outside the office she can only access the first twelve emails in her inbox, and she estimated that the one from the Holy City would be number thirteen. Evidently no one has told her about the little cursor at the right-hand top of the page that lets you scroll down to the next lot of messages. When I turned on her machine I found 33,332 messages in total in her inbox. Evidently no one has ever suggested to her that she delete messages after a couple of years or so either.

Damn! I could have waited after all and visited Hugo in London! His 'long weekend' in the wilds of Kent is over and he is back in Wandsworth. But he says it will never feel like home.

Tuesday 12 March

The sunshine with Ethel didn't last. She had another row with Prof Skrulewski, who was very high-handed about going on holiday to Eastbourne and not doing the proofs of *Nature and the Golden Rule*. He got straight on the blower to me, of course. It's all right for Ethel to unleash her emotional frustrations on my authors, but it's me who has to pick up the pieces.

Editorial board. Title change from Fay, who now wants to change her bestseller from *Heaven*, to *God: Sky cleaner, star shiner.* The truth is that she's at the end of her tether with the persistence of *Heave*, which refuses be eradicated from either Amazon or the in-house system, but her official line was rather different. 'The author was going to do both books but I can now officially say that he won't be tackling both *God* and *Heaven* because there's too much overlap.'

Amid the sedate chuckles this produced, Drusilla said she thought that *Emails from Heaven* was a much better title, but this was rather impatiently rejected by Fay.

'It's nothing to do with that, Drusilla. There isn't an email in it.'

'It's just such a good, snappy title. Can't you produce an author for it? You young things are much more in touch with modern technology than an old dinosaur like me. What about *Emails on the Way to Heaven*?'

'I don't understand, Drusilla. What do you mean?'

'You know the kind of thing. When God messages you. What they call Godwinks. Messages. Signs. Hearing a special song on a radio or seeing a particular name on the side of a lorry. God is always online. Always replies, never blocks you. Etc.'

Fay thought about it a moment, then said it was too complicated theologically as well as technologically for her, too.

Showed the meeting *Rewyrding Britain* by Nigel Rookhope simply because I felt I lacked the moral strength to reject it without the support of my colleagues. However, they were unanimous in saying I should snap it up, the rage for 1970s nostalgia being what it is.

Fay was very enthusiastic. 'All this hauntology and urban weird – or wyrd - stuff is just what we need!'

I said, 'But it's barely coherent.'

'Make the author cut it by half first,' said Drusilla, handing me back her copy of the proposal. 'Then your job will be easier.'

Wednesday 13 March

Gerard is back! – in what could be called convalescent attire – knee-breeches duly buttoned at the knee, sage-green jumper, and a beige and black wool scarf, his hair close-cropped as if it had been shaved for his illness and his side whiskers trimmed down from their usual curly exuberance. He was rather grey and ashen about the eyes, but behaving as if nothing had happened, in the best tradition. Asked if he was better, he replied firmly, '*Much* better, thank you,' as if answering a query as to whether he'd had a nice holiday.

Fay incandescent with rage as the warehouse, due to a misunderstanding, have put her new bestseller, *GOD*, down as GOP – Going Out of Print. It's not even written yet, much less published! I suppose they are all too used to our books falling into this category. Last I heard, she was berating the good people of Middlesbrough on the phone, or rather, the single individual, Nicky, who appears to do all the work in the warehouse and must be either of infinite patience, or a robot.

Talking of overhearing, couldn't help blundering into a strange telephone conversation of Ethel's, as I went in to her office to find out how far along she was with the editing of the re-written *Wilderness Therapy for Wellbeing*. She was enunciating very distinctly and clearly, as if speaking to a foreign caller far away.

'No, the 400,000 is brilliant, I'm very happy with that, sir... yes, sir, when we finally conclude our business, I've promised myself a trip back home Texas-way... indeed, sir, I, too, hope we will meet... yes, sir, that's fine, the 400,000 can be transferred in the usual way...'

At this point Ethel looked up and saw me hovering and an expression of guilt crossed her face. I withdrew as swiftly as I could, not wishing to have the appearance of eavesdropping. All most mysterious.

Spent the afternoon reading *Rewyrding Britain* and it's actually really good. Very well-written and funny. Feel rather guilty for being so cavalier in my initial dismissal of it. That'll teach me to read the MS and not to judge a book by its cover letter.

Later: Called my father. He said he will come over to London when the lilacs are out. How will he know, I wonder. I will have to keep an eye out for him.

Thursday 14 March

True to form, Gerard has returned to make trouble it seems, as he at once summoned an emergency editorial board to make known his disapproval of Fay's book *God*, previously known as *Heaven*.

'*God*,' began Gerard, 'is *not* a good title. I'm getting complaints from the bookshops and the wholesalers because when they google the book about two million other things come up. They can't find it.'

'God *is* hard to find,' murmured Drusilla, who I think is still miffed that her suggestion of *Emails from Heaven* was so rudely rejected by Fay.

'Either that or *Heave*,' agreed Fay gloomily, slightly quelled for once. 'When people key in the ISBN, that is what comes up, I regret to say. I've tried every way I can to get it changed. Technology should be our servant, not our master, but I'm sorry to say that in this case at least, Amazon and the system appear to have got the upper hand.'

'The title is perceived as being frivolous,' concluded Gerard, 'especially in our current state. The bookshops don't like it. In short, the trade is miffed.'

Faced with this, Fay put up a good fight but in the end reluctantly conceded, saying she would ask the author for further thoughts on a new title.

Fay spent the rest of the meeting complaining about how noisy Accounts are, sitting there shouting across the desks to each other all day. Normally, Fay would be in there like a shot, telling them to shut up, but she says Accounts are in the unique position of having a hex on her. Accounts say that they, 'liven the place up,' and that, 'at least they're not stuck-up.' I said I'd never noticed the noise, given that they are two floors below us, but Fay, who is definitely the princess with the pea, said that with her acute sensitivity to sensory stimulus, she suffers dreadfully as, by some trick of the acoustics here, their relentless shouting penetrates all the way up the stairs, along the corridors, through her door and right up to her ears. How horrific she made it sound! Like an evil imp of noise was taking up residence, squat and black, on her desk. Anyway, she took advantage of Gerard's return to health by asking him to send out some kind of tactful email telling Accounts to be quieter. Drusilla said she would sort them out.

Gerard countered this by saying we all had to fill in personality test questionnaires, which among other things marked our level of sensory sensitivity to noise.

Went down into the basement later to witness this new version of Accounts as propagators of unearthly, hellish noise, but was merely met by the sound of laughter and the sight of Drusilla, sitting on their desk along with Moriarty, swinging her legs and eating a banana, which they were teasing her about in no uncertain terms. Drusilla, too, was laughing a lot. She was telling them all about her night work as a street pastor and all the stray teenage girls she takes in off the streets and allows to sleep on her sofa and floor, and how she taught this one to cook, and this one to write, and, with some pride, how they were all doing now.

When I got back to my office, there it was on my desk, a complete personality test questionnaire, all printed out, but there were so many pages to fill in that I lost interest in myself long before I got to the end and hid them under the piles on my desk. It's sinful how much paper we still use. No wonder the photocopier is buckling under the strain. The engineer from the printing company was in again today, at the photocopier's side like a doctor in his white overall anxiously assessing its chances. The machine was overheating and throbbing irregularly in a way that didn't bode well for its overall health. Long-term prognosis not good, I'd say.

Just before home-time, Gerard sent round a long memo to ALL@HQ asking people among other things not to make unnecessary journeys across the building. Any message to Accounts was completely and impenetrably veiled.

Friday 15 March

Gerard's birthday, so we all assembled in the kitchen at 3pm for cake as usual. Gerard smiled indulgently at our felicitations, as if the entire event – nay, his birth itself – had been arranged merely to give pleasure to us. As a special treat, we were allowed to look at his Book of Mementoes, laid out on display, photographs of a much younger Gerard meeting various dignitaries such as the Queen, the Pope, etc, though as Drusilla *sotto voce* suggested, it did sometimes look as though the Queen, the Pope etc were meeting Gerard.

The event was organised by Ursula, whose Marks & Sparks fetish was well in evidence with lemon drizzle cake (the UK's most popular, I understand), Victoria sponge (a close second), chocolate cake and Viennese whirls. Hard to resist and no one seriously tried, apart from Fay. As far as I know, she's the only one who disapproves of the cake culture here.

She unwrapped her usual two thin slices of rye bread and nut butter, biting into them with baleful nibbles, while the rest of us tucked into the delicacies. Talked to her about the history of the Battenberg cake, and how the pink and yellow chequerboard (also known as a church – or chapel-window cake) were unlikely to represent the four Battenberg princes of 1884, while consuming my own slice of said cake. Alas, she showed little interest.

Gerard read out a poem he had written, *Ode to Mr Kipling on Attaining Another Year.* I can't bear to reproduce it here but it all scanned nicely.

Ethel took me aside in the course of the celebrations and said that as I'd overheard so much of her conversation on the phone yesterday, she might as well tell me the truth, which is that she is descended from tycoons on both sides and is in fact an oil princess in Texas who has fled to London in search of a more refined life, living here incognito under her maternal grandmother's name. She said it was actually more of a burden than an honour as she has various trusts and other business that she has to administer, adding, with a sigh, that if one of them in particular could be sold – a big oilfield called El Chapo, I think – it would be 'life-changing,' but that there was little hope of that because the other trustees regard it as her duty to carry on her illustrious family's redoubtable work and refuse to release her. It's also a bore as it means flying out to Texas twice a year, which is obviously time-consuming, and that she herself prefers the south of France.

I feel very honoured to have been chosen as a confidant, but where does the friendship go from here? It is a little scary. Luckily, Ethel has recently inveighed against the use of *passim* in indexes as being old-fashioned, so in the first and immediate instance I was able to steer the conversation, after a slightly awkward transition, onto this. We always used to have *passim*. However, I suppose we must move with the times. It's true it does have a slightly dated look to it. In fact, *passim* is *passé*.

I drew the straw for tidying the kitchen and filled the bin full of paper plates and crumbs, like the loaves and fishes.

Later in the afternoon Ethel sent me a regal email begging me to be discreet about her revelations, saying that although she had enjoyed our chat, with 'a family like mine' she didn't necessarily want everyone else to know about it, particularly the other members of the House Editorial team who were 'always trying to trick personal information' out of her.

Later: The police notified me that they have finally removed the boarding from Hugo's front door and have kindly gone above and beyond and had the door replaced as well, chargeable to Hugo, which he ought to be able to get back from his insurance.

Saturday 16 March

Armed with yellow gloves, face mask, cleaning stuff and bin-bags, I duly went to tidy out The Prisoner's abode while he's still inside. Oh dear. A sorry state it's in and it will take more than one visit to get it straight. It's not just mess resulting from where the police charged in all those months ago, distressing and appalling though it is to see the overturned bookcases, the clothes and papers dumped out of drawers, and the rest of the ransacking. Sadly there was long-standing disarray previous to all this. In short, it's a tip. Got through the door at least, and aired the place which smelt distinctly dank, and tidied out the kitchen as an absolute priority. Glad I brought along a galvanised metal scourer, or a steel scrubber, depending on what you want to call it (though the latter term conjures up a traditionally female person of hard and sparkling proportions) as the counter tops were thick with grime, dust and crumbs, so I scrubbed away until they were nice and bright and shiny-clean again. Quite satisfying to pour lemon bleach down the sink and think of it eating away all the accumulated germs. Looked for the radio so I could at least listen to Radio 3 to cheer things up a little, but it was buried somewhere beneath the moraine of coats, books, magazines and other debris. Not a hope of sourcing Hugo's clothes as access to the wardrobe was blocked, too.

Texted Hugo: 'Not as bad as anticipated: no evidence of major infestation, but very untidy!' and he texted back, 'Could you find my copy of John Dee's *Five Books of Mystery*.' I was quite cross and texted back, 'No I could not, the place is in such a mess that the whereabouts of anything is mystery enough.'

Sunday 17 March

Received text: 'Imperative you find the Dee as I need it to put a spell on Sam, he's making my life hell.'

I was sorry to hear that relations with Sam had soured, especially as it seemed to indicate less chance than ever of getting the book of prayers, but by then my fingers were literally worked to the bone and I had no more strength to reply.

Monday 18 March

Gerard left Philip Midwinter's manuscript *Wounded* in a taxi. Just when Drusilla had finally succeeded in getting the pages put in some sort of order! It's unlikely that anyone thought of scanning it in, and I would lay money there is no e-back-up. I don't know what Gerard was doing with it anyway, it's Drusilla's book. Some other old Oxford connection, I suppose. The good monsignor spent seven years in his study looking out on the old monastery pear orchard writing that one with the quill and ink he inherited from his own venerable father. (Actually, I believe his writing implement of choice is an electric typewriter.)

Ursula has made efforts to trace the taxi, without avail.

Tuesday 19 March

Ursula said that Ethel did tell her to photocopy Philip Midwinter's manuscript but that she got distracted by other things and forgot. Oh dear. Sounds like that's seven years of Monsignor Philip's writing life gone up in smoke.

Gerard highly distressed at his own absent-mindedness and shut himself away in his office again.

Wednesday 20 March

Editorial board, postponed from yesterday due to the uproar with Monsignor Philip's book. Drusilla gave Gerard what for. He said, '*Mea culpa*, dear lady, *mea culpa* entirely. I am in sackcloth and ashes,' – I noticed his shirt and stock were indeed unloosened as visible sign of penance and he looked rather pale – 'and I promise you we'll get it back if I have to rewrite it myself word by word.'

Such disarming humility by no means disarmed Drusilla.

As an attempt at distraction, Gerard reported on Bishop Molly's progress with her manuscript, which isn't much because she has been busy tracking the nine-year-old daughter of her best friend, who was kidnapped and taken secretly abroad by the friend's ex-husband. I hadn't realised Bishop Molly was in MI6 before taking orders. It's even whispered that she is still involved. However that may be, she has been flying off to various destinations in search of this child, who has now – 'you'll all be glad to know' – been found. This slightly downbeat tale left an odd taste in my mouth. I mean, Molly's great, but she doesn't hesitate to involve herself in the seedier side of life. Drusilla also unimpressed and said Molly's first duty was to her book and to us. 'Otherwise we won't be around to provide all these lovely advances. You have to take care of the goose if you want the golden eggs.'

On the positive side, *Rewyrding Britain* got through easily. I think everyone was glad to have something new to focus on. Rang up Nigel Rookhope to tell him and he was delighted. He readily agreed to cut it by half, and said he'd keep the other half for his blog. He seems a genuinely nice chap.

Thursday 21 March

Taxi driver turned up with Philip Midwinter's MS, which he said was a load of tosh. He was closeted with Gerard for two hours having a deep theological argument. Gerard emerged black beneath the eyes. He had to give him £30 from the petty cash to go away (though as we know Gerard himself is not short of spare change). As the last of the altercation petered out down the library steps, I nipped into Gerard's office and got hold of the MS and made three copies (with bated breath lest the photocopier swallow and mangle it but fortunately it was working for once) and gave one to Ethel for safekeeping. Whatever quirks House Ed may have, I do know that once a manuscript is ensconced in their office, it won't go astray. Another copy for Drusilla, and the other one left with Gerard.

Doubtless as a reaction to all this, Gerard let off steam with a spate of health and safety memos.

From: Gerard Delamare Sent: 21 March 14.58 To: ALL@HQ
Subject: FIRE SAFETY

I want to draw your attention to the need for CONSTANT MONITORING to ensure that escape routes are kept clear.
The FRONT STEPS to the library are a PRIORITY in this respect, along with the EMERGENCY CHUTES (currently stored in the post room) for sliding down said steps in case of sudden evacuation. Additionally, the existence of an alternative escape route via the SECRET DOOR at the back of the library was HIGHLIGHTED in the last issue of the fire evacuation notice, and we plan to carry out an EMERGENCY EVACUATION via this route shortly.

Very kindly yours,

Gerard Delamere, Publisher
The House of Marvellous Books
Wayfarers & Wilderness – our award-winning nature list
Sailing through Storms – transcendence through crisis

Don't judge each day by the harvest you reap but by the seeds that you plant

—Robert Louis Stevenson

The smallest act of kindness is worth more than the grandest intention

—Oscar Wilde

The thought of us all whizzing down the steps in chutes sounds fun. I never knew the secret door at the back of the library was usable. I wonder where it leads to. Another domain? It ought to. A door onto the street would be rather boring. A secret passage would do, one that interconnects with several other tunnels throughout London and eventually comes out on the other side of the river. There ought to be something, in this vast warren.

Sales meeting in the afternoon. Bit of a reality check. My American buy-in *Trunk Call*, by Phoenix David Lorenzo, the story of a tree surgeon buried in a tree in Arkansas, and other burial myths, has not taken off – it has sold forty-two copies so far since its publication in January. Roland said he'd give it another three months before remaindering. Tried to dissuade him but he said it was no use anyone protesting, he was the Immoveable Object. Oh dear. Another wasted opportunity. Directly due to my lack of energy and initiative, and not looking for more authentic authors. I whispered as much to Drusilla who responded kindly, 'Well, also due to the advance, of course. You have to take what you can get for £700.' Even Fay's Christmas special, *A Child in a Manger and a Night Full of Stars,* did relatively poorly – 273 copies. Trouble is, no one knows what a manger is these days. Actually, I'm not quite sure myself.

Fay was quite pragmatic and said she accepted that children's literature was dying. She said that the *Twinkle, Twinkle* list should probably be laid to rest. She, however, doesn't have so much to worry about as her main list, *Wayfarers and Wilderness,* scoops in authors like fishes from the sea, while even her poetry list, *Antler Bones*, is full of stellar hits. Dafydd ap Dafydd alone has some 80,000 followers, all guaranteed to buy *Lays from a Shepherd's Hut* once it's out, and Fay is already planning a sequel to be called *Twiglets: Poems written sleeping under trees.* Drusilla protested that that kind of thing is so much easier if you're a man, i.e., sleeping out in the open, and that she would like to see a book on wild sleeping by a woman. Roland said we'd all be sleeping under trees if sales didn't pick up soon.

I was innerly preoccupied with anxieties about them possibly deciding to lay my own *Earth* list to rest as well, so didn't partake in the argument.

Friday 22 March
Gerard continues to worry away at our health and safety. He sent round a questionnaire asking us to rate our comfort and safety at our desks.

Saturday 23 March
Saw a film of Parsifal which lasted four and a half hours where Parsifal turned into a woman. Didn't think it quite worked.

Monday 25 March
Disaster with the Belfast conference. Frantic phone calls from the reps. Ursula was supposed to have sent the boxes of books for it two weeks ago. Patient questioning eventually revealed that they were, in fact, en route to Africa.

'No, I can't remember where,' sobbed Ursula, when someone ventured to hint that Africa was a big place.

Tuesday 26 March
Ursula still in the doghouse. She seems incapable of putting her mind to the question of where the missing books might have gone within Africa and, when pressed, just wails, 'Ask the Post Office!'

Wednesday 27 March
Drusilla tottered from the Fisher Room at lunchtime looking battered after a morning interviewing for a new publicity officer, as we haven't had one since our last, Sally Rather, left in October. Drusilla complained bitterly about Gerard landing her with his responsibilities, and even more bitterly about the quality of the candidates. She said, 'Dear God! They get worse every year! This

last lot were particularly bad. I could hardly get a word out of any of them. Usually they've got plenty to say for themselves, at least. I wonder what we did wrong?'

It wasn't until the end of the day that the mystery was solved, as the last candidate pattered thankfully down the steps. It transpired that Ursula, greeting the candidates at reception, had told each one that the governing body works in mysterious ways, and might wait for the inspiration of the Holy Spirit before deciding to accept or reject someone. You just can't begin to guess what Ursula will do next. I don't know how we're ever going to get rid of her.

Thursday 28 March

Gerard has gone to some urgent meeting with the governing body. An ominous silence hangs over the place. Moriarty seems very uneasy and keeps sidling up to me and all but tripping me up in the kitchen. I checked his automatic food dispenser and it's okay. He should really be out there dealing with the office mice, but he can obviously sense something we can't. What does it all mean?

Friday 29 March

A bad omen. Ursula has had all 5,000 copies of our bestselling *I Messaged God at Bedtime* pulped by mistake. Truly a bit of a disaster as we need every penny at the moment. Alas, it's becoming all too apparent that Ursula can't see the computer screen properly. She simply hit the wrong book in the spreadsheet, missing by one line the intended target, *Prayers by Candlelight,* which is of course woefully old-fashioned and whose sales have been dwindling steadily since 1997. Candles are merely seen as a health and safety hazard these days.

Drusilla was distraught. 'My little children's book of nature meditations and prayers, selling so nicely – gone at the touch of a button!'

Fay said, 'I thought Ursula was a bit quiet. But at least it proves that the warehouse can be competent when they want to be. They pulped the wrong book most efficiently.' She thought a moment, then added, 'Not meaning to be unkind or discriminatory, but I would have thought that working eyesight was the first requisite for a job in most publishing that doesn't deal in Braille and audio.'

Drusilla, with admirable restraint, advised Ursula not to wait but to have her cataract op done as soon as possible.

Gerard sent an urgent email round demanding the return of the personality test questionnaires by the end of the day, as he is off drilling sugar beet and planting the potato crop next week. Fay helped me with mine, saying she knew me better than I knew myself. Drusilla still refusing to do hers.

Later: It never rains but it pours! My father arrived unexpectedly in London this afternoon! Arranged to meet him for lunch tomorrow.

Saturday 30 March

Duly lunched with my father at his club. He had veal kidneys followed by treacle sponge pudding and custard. I had steak and *pommes de terre dauphinoise* followed by caramel cream. I told him the lilacs weren't out yet, due to the rather inclement early spring weather we've been experiencing. He nodded but gave no explanation for his visit beyond saying he always found the French countryside a little trying at this time of year after a winter of mud, wet and wind. He asked how business was with an interest quite unlike him.

'Got any contingency plans?'

'In case of what, exactly?'

'Oh well, you know... things aren't always as solid as they seem. That library of yours, for example.'

'Well, not mine exactly, I'm not sure I'd want to be personally responsible for an upkeep of half a million a year, haha!'

I wonder has he heard anything on that grapevine of his. For someone living in the depths of rural France, he seems to have an uncanny ability to keep abreast of City rumours.

He added, 'The problem with Gerard Delamere's approach is that it leaves the company open to wholesale takeover by profit or plunder merchants looking for easy pickings. They say that Krukinov & Krukinov's shares have gone up quite a bit lately, further to their interest in acquiring London premises.'

I've been listening to this kind of financial talk all my life. I said, 'Really? It's all fine as far as I know.'

He said, 'Well, keep me posted, won't you. I may do a little investigation now I'm here.'

As usual with my father, not really sure what he means. Of course, I know his main reason for visiting London is to manage his stocks and shares, but I don't see how that relates to us at the House. When I asked him, however, he just shook his head and muttered something, more in perplexity than denial. I said I would wait until I heard something definite before taking any action. Left me with a slightly uneasy feeling, I must say. Sadly he isn't in a position to make any offer of support if things did go wrong. Not that I'd want to take anything from him, of course.

Sunday 31 March
Palm Sunday

To the St John Passion at Brompton Oratory. A wonderful Evangelist – such a demanding role – though Pilate always tugs at me the most. After all, we're all Pilate at some point, aren't we?

Monday 1 April

Our annual change of publicity officer. (No one under thirty gets paid enough to make it worth staying here for more than a year.) He's called Fingal St Dunstan, twenty-four, from Edinburgh, and is supposed to be the hottest thing in publishing. As usual with the new boy, people seem to be pinning an inordinate amount of faith on him as the one to rescue the sinking ship. Apart from Fay of course who said suspiciously, 'Well, that was quick! He was only interviewed last Wednesday, wasn't he? How come he's available so soon? Shouldn't he be giving notice somewhere or something?'

Drusilla said loftily, 'The governing body have signed and sealed it.'

'Even more worrying,' said Fay. 'They're hardly renowned for their choice of the right person. It's going to take more than a clever press officer to rescue us. What about Gerard?'

'Gerard gave me carte blanche,' said Drusilla even more loftily.

'That's not what I heard,' said Fay. 'I was told our new boy was headhunted by the governing body as a wunderkind and that Gerard sent him to you with orders to take him on.'

Being an expert at this kind of research, Fay has already found out that Fingal was going to be a countertenor specialising in Baroque music, but opted for the world of books instead. 'Well, let's not judge. It's a hard road, being a professional musician,' she said. 'Apparently he's had a luminous and incandescent career as a bookshop manager. No doubt we will hear the full story all in good time.'

In Gerard's absence, she appointed herself to keep a special eye on him.

Fingal St Dunstan aroused instant suspicion in me by his big, baby blue eyes, and his air of exaggerated, wilful guilelessness. Very tall, with a loud, burry voice and, unfortunately for my sensitive nose, the sort who puts on cheap aftershave after not having showered for three days. He has just left a lover called Conor. It is all round Design how he tore up Conor's passport and put it in the wastepaper bin as he was leaving their flat in Edinburgh. The important things always get round first.

A strange story in the *Daily Mail* that royal displeasure has been expressed at the prospect of us being taken over by Russian bookbinders! The Queen being the library patron I suppose has the right to express an opinion about what is going on, but she sounds much better informed than we are – or misinformed. Even

Fay could make nothing of it, though adding tartly, 'If she's that concerned, she might be interested to know that a million or so pounds from the royal purse would help us out!' Told Fay about my father's visit and his slightly odd remarks. To my surprise she was quite sympathetic. She looked at me quite kindly for her, but just said, 'We're in the hand of the Lord, Mortimer.'

An email arrived from Gerard marked high importance which Drusilla and I rushed to read, expecting an explanation of the *Daily Mail* story, or at least an official welcome to our latest new boy Fingal. However, it was merely a ferocious memo about first aid, in which Drusilla – who's done a two-day course – plays a key role.

'Drusilla should be summoned IMMEDIATELY if someone is taken ill or injured. She will render such assistance as may be possible. If the illness/injuries are deemed to be serious or life-threatening, an ambulance may be called. If Drusilla is not here, a senior manager should assess the situation and take appropriate action AT ONCE.'

I said to Drusilla, 'One thing is clear: if you're not here, we all die.'

Drusilla said, 'You have a small window of opportunity for survival, then, given my invariable routine of being in the office as little as possible.'

We discussed the *DM* article. Drusilla said that St Columba was patron saint of bookbinders, which might interest Sr Evangeline, but didn't get us far.

Ursula spotted a very dusty volume that had slipped beneath some floorboards at the end of the library, beneath the Chaucer window. She made me come and pry up one of the boards where it was loose and by clever use of the kitchen tongs we were able to extricate it. Alas it was a slim volume of scurrilous Victorian drawings, the nature of which dismayed Ursula. 'Oh dear,' she said, and dropped it back under the floorboards before rushing off.

Evening: Got a phone call from my father at St Pancras, just about to return to France. He said he'd sold all his shares in the House. Didn't know he had any. So that's what he came over for!

All that talk about lilacs! How secretive some people are. Made me rather anxious, I must say. I pressed him for further details but he refused to explain further. 'Just an instinct,' he said, adding, 'Do – er – look round at other jobs if you have a moment, won't you, Mortimer.'

Not very helpful, I must say.

Au contraire, on the bright side, I am making good progress with Proust. Just starting Book 2, *À l'ombre des jeunes filles en fleurs*, or *Within a Budding Grove*. Nice to have as an escape for stressful times like this.

Tuesday 2 April

My birthday. I always feel grateful that I just missed being an April Fool – my mother held on and wouldn't push until two minutes past midnight. Good for her! Brought in various cakes – chocolate, carrot and coffee. People very grateful, not to say glutted, with the glazed, cake-high glint in their eyes although sadly due to Lenten restrictions I couldn't join them. A bore that my birthday so often falls in Lent. Made sure to bring in some olives and other savouries which I shared with Toya of Design, who was also observing Lent. She was most appreciative.

Drama with Ursula later in the afternoon, obviously influenced by Gerard's email of yesterday. She is so suggestible. I was just talking to Ethel about the editing of Ivan's *The Natural Kindness Manual*, when I gradually became aware of an ongoing quacking coming from floor level where Ursula, half-hidden by a desk, was lying full length on her back, explaining at great length to Drusilla as honorary first aider that she felt faint and unwell. She must be desperate if she regards Drusilla as a source of medical or maternal succour. Drusilla just sat on the desk swinging her legs, and kept saying in a bored kind of way, 'Get up, you must be feeling better by now.'

Ethel and her other satellites needless to say ignored the incident and calmly proceeded with their work. Ethel merely raised her eyebrows slightly on asking me whether I favoured a light or a medium edit for Ivan's book, as I'd inadvertently omitted to note it on the handover form. Ursula was still on the floor when I left fifteen minutes later.

Fingal St-Whatsit has been spending his time peripatetically as he 'gets to know everyone'. At the moment I'd say he is an absence yet a presence, in that his office is never occupied, but his voice is always floating along the corridors in varying degrees of loudness, depending on where he is. Wherever he is, though, he can be heard throughout the entire building. I've never met anyone with such a penetrating voice, a buzzing, vibrating tone that goes right through one's head. The musical world has had a sad loss; he would have made an excellent singer, I'm sure. Let's hope Fay doesn't take it into her head to complain about him next.

Later: Uncle Albany called to wish me a happy birthday. It was warming to hear his voice. He said, 'Tried you earlier but you didn't pick up. Hope you're having a good one, Mortimer.'

I told him about my father's visit.

'Oh, Justin was over, was he? Must've been something special to bring him to London. Oh, your birthday, of course.'

I said, 'I fear not. I think he came to warn me about the precarious state of things at work and to sort out his investments accordingly.'

'Well, you know you're always welcome to a bed here, Mortimer, if worst comes to worst. Any time.'

I was touched and grateful, and said so, while devoutly hoping it would never come to that.

'Come down soon anyway, we'll give you a Gallhampton Gap special for your birthday.'

I very much appreciated the intent, and said so, although with some slight heartsink at the thought of what the treat itself might entail.

Spent an enjoyable if slightly lonely evening listening to a special broadcast of the Bach John Passion from the Concertgebouw, accompanied by a smoked salmon sandwich and some wine.

Wednesday 3 April

Gerard is back! He went looking for Fingal 'to welcome him properly to the House', but Fingal had popped out for breakfast. You can tell when he's in as a kind of hum pervades the building, unless he's there in full voice beside you, when it's like a burring drill going into your head. This morning all was quiet for around two hours. Gerard came looking for him twice more. I wonder is Fingal going to be as useful as everyone hoped.

We asked Gerard about the royal rumours, and whether it was true that the Queen is said to be 'none too pleased' at 'what is happening', but all he said was that we must cut advances to the minimum. Given that we pay strictly nominal advances anyway, this is going to make us really popular. Fay said, 'Does this mean that authors are going to have to do books for free?'

The only answer to this was, of course, a deprecating laugh.

He added that sadly the personality tests had been less helpful than anticipated in assessing our future creative possibilities, despite having been suggested by friends as being 'fail-proof at weeding out the sheep from the goats'.

'What friends?' said Fay.

Somehow, without anyone being able to say how the transition was effected, Gerard's response moved seamlessly on to how the sparrow, passer domesticus, whose bond with humans goes back some 11,000 years, seems to be making a comeback in London, sightings having risen by 10 per cent.

There can't be anything too serious going on, because, judging from the stream of emails and memos that issue from him, Gerard is devoting all his time and energy to drawing up a disaster contingency plan that will satisfy the minutely rapacious desires of the UK health and safety officers; indeed, he seems to have entered their imaginative world with a vengeance and is now obsessed by scenarios of disaster. What happens if the sales reps get blown up in their cars? If reception catches fire and Ursula is immolated in walls of flame? If Fay's scarf gets caught in the photocopier and she gets sucked in to her doom, never to appear again? Gerard sees dangers lurking everywhere; a vivid and fiery imagination that surely could be put to better use. I sure hope the brain fever hasn't left any lingering after-effects.

However that may be, the results are impressive. Fay has seen the draft document. There are three pages on the dishwasher alone. Even Ethel came out shaking after the latest meeting this afternoon, which lasted three hours, and is said to be 'very near the edge.' The next step will be 'testing the plan', whatever that means.

Holy Week always a bit of a spiritual trial, in my experience. One has to look out for things coming in from left field. Received a command to call Sister Evangeline today. I don't know why she's latched onto me. I suppose one editor is much the same as another to nuns, just as one nun is much the same as another to the lay person. But as Fay was out for the afternoon, Gerard told me I'd better take the call. Sr E was only allowed to speak for half an hour between 6pm and 6.30pm, which meant me staying late, to my annoyance. I mean, you can't have it both ways. Either you're a recluse and live in your cell alone like a good anchorite, or you're a media nun and mix with the world on the world's terms and the world's hours. I was wondering if she might be inspired to speak about the odd rumours going round about the House. But to my relief it was nothing to do with that, merely that the Lord had hinted to her that maybe it was time she wrote another book.

Some crumb of comfort amid the mayhem – Ursula has taken advantage of Fingal's arrival to make a firm appointment for her first cataract op, saying she feels she can leave the ship in safe hands now, as Fingal has been tasked with all her jobs as well as his own, and should go through them like a hot knife through butter. It's probably too late for the boxes of books wandering round Africa somewhere, and certainly too late for Drusilla's poor little pulped *I Messaged God at Bedtime*, but hopefully he will be able to prevent further disaster.

Thursday 4 April
Maundy Thursday

Fire alarm went off today just as everyone was tucking into second slices of cake, which were reluctantly abandoned as the building was evacuated, or in some cases taken outside. According to Gerard's masterly planning, we all accumulated by the recycling site opposite the building and watched the fire engine draw up while Gerard stood chuckling and rubbing his hands. It's the first time I've seen him look truly animated since his return from his illness; the exercise obviously had a great recuperative impact, as good as convalescence by the seaside, bath chairs, bathing, beef tea and spoonfuls of Guinness. The fire brigade, on the other hand, looked well pissed off; as we were watching them stomp into the building, I heard hoarse breathing in my ear and saw that Ursula had finally managed to make it out from behind reception; by her own unimpeded bipedal locomotion, it had taken her twelve minutes to get out from behind the desk, down the library steps and across the road. She could have been burnt to a crisp by then. She said she'd been cutting her fringe in the Ladies and hadn't heard the alarm. No one noticed she was missing, of course, despite much officious ticking-off of names on clipboards. She offered the information that the fire brigade were 'used to it.' 'They know us, we've got a very sensitive alarm system. They've been known to come out to us twice on the same day. Luckily they're just round the corner. I'll take them round a bit of cake later.'

She diagnosed mis-use of the toaster by Drusilla, who, it seems, with her usual unhappy relationship with machines, only has to touch it to set the fire alarm off.

Ethel's mood not improved by this further interruption to her work. She went back in and sent round one of her scary emails warning us that if we don't stick to our deadlines and hand over manuscripts on time, together with the required full five print-outs of each MS, she will refuse to handle latecomers. 'All wailing and gnashing of teeth will go unregarded and be fruitless,' she concluded. Help! I know for a fact that my November title *Healing Sea, Healing Self* isn't going to make it.

If Ethel stuck to her word, of course, we would publish nothing.

Told Fay about Sister Evangeline's call and hinted that the good sister seemed a bit needy in terms of attention from her editor, but she just rolled her eyes and said, 'What will her new book be about?' I said, 'I don't know, she didn't say.'

She said, 'Didn't you ask? Mortimer, you are hopeless!' which I thought was pretty poor gratitude in return for fending her star author. On the other hand, she is taking Chauncey Rivers off my hands so I suppose I can't grumble too much.

An urban myth already developing that Ursula, duly taking a red velvet cake to the fire brigade, was whisked off at top speed in an engine due to them having to rush off on a shout, and her not being able to get out in time, but I don't believe this. It's surely just flamboyant fantasy on her part.

5 April
Good Friday

6 April
Easter Saturday
Mother's birthday. So strange that I still remember it, after all these years, when so much else has been forgotten. Thirty years! Thirty years since she died! Sun and clouds. Showers. My father, or rather Jacqueline, emailed me some pics of the first barbecue of the season at the campsite. They look a jolly and cheerful crew, I must say. Several bottles of wine in evidence. However, I don't think there'd be enough intellectual stimulus for me in that kind of life.

7 April
Easter Sunday
Mooched around Wimbledon. Bought myself an Easter egg. Took it home and ate it. Read Proust. I've been neglecting him shamefully of late. Nice fresh breezy weather.

8 April
Easter Monday
Uncle Albany came up for a taste of metropolitan life, although it meant missing the Easter egg hunt on Scrapsgate Bay. But as he said, 'You can't have it all, Mortimer, I learned that long ago.' Instead we did our usual trip to the British Museum to look at the mummies. They certainly are very imposing. Uncle Albany said as usual, 'Wouldn't like to be alone with them at night!' It's the unhallowed frisson of necrophiliac voyeurism that's the lure, I think – the feeling of desecration, that one is seeing something not meant to be seen, people's private funeral arrangements. Plus the slight possibility that one might pick up a curse along the way, if one catches a mummy's eye at the wrong moment, of course.

Then we went for lunch in Soho. Albany, having won £9 in the Grand National on a horse called *Semper Idem* (what a coincidence! Must tell Drusilla!), insisted on paying, to which I agreed the more readily in the hope of it sufficing as a b-day celebration, thus getting me out of a treat in Gallhampton Gap.

Tuesday 9 April
Uproar. The toaster has been banned on health and safety grounds! This just isn't on! From time immemorial, when one arrived here in the early morning, the silent corridors and empty library would be permeated by wafts of toast. One might catch a glimpse of Ursula taking Gerard a tray with a jug of milky tea and a silver mug to his office. All the good ladies in cardigans who

commute in from Surrey and Herts, who've kept Accounts and Production and Sales and Marketing afloat for so many years, would be quietly regaling themselves in the kitchen, with their slices of wholewheat toast and Tiptree marmalade before settling to another day's honest, lightly paid toil. Banning the toaster is like banning the spirit of the place. A bad omen. Drusilla, proud and pallid, disdained all knowledge of the toaster and said she never had breakfast, it was a bad habit. She managed to make it sound as if having a toaster at all was a fairly severe moral weakness on everyone else's part.

She's in a bad mood because the Vatican are being fairly unhelpful about co-operating with the debt collector over the money they owe us, and highly evasive with regard to organising a face-to-face meeting in Rome to discuss.

After all this everyone scurried off in a great hurry and when I enquired where they were all going, it transpired that it's London Book Fair this week! First I've heard of it! I mean, I know it's primarily a rights fair, but you think they'd keep us commissioning editors in the loop and maybe even offer us the odd ticket!

I said, 'No one mentioned it to me,' to which Fay said sharply, 'There's something called the internet, Mortimer, which lets people know what's going on.'

I must have still looked a bit blank because she went on, 'Where do you think Sales and Marketing have got to? They've been setting up since first thing this morning. Did you not notice that the meetings ended early today? That's to give us all time to get over to Kensington. Do wake up and join us in this world from time to time, Mortimer.'

Felt justly rebuked. I must admit I was so distracted by the toaster episode and all it implied – how our freedoms can be eroded at one swift stroke – that I didn't actually pay much attention to who was in and who wasn't. I offered to go and help at the stand but this was, rather rudely I thought, refused by all and sundry.

Anyway, it turns out I can't go in any case, as we only bought three tickets between us, all of which are fully accounted for.

Sometimes I feel that publishing is a club of which I am not a member.

When everyone had gone off to LBF and I was making my solitary way upstairs with my 11am coffee, Ursula came scampering and quivering to meet me in her pleated polka dot skirt with a frightened face:

'What's happened, oh, what's happened?'

Seeing no one around when she arrived, she had come to the natural conclusion that a) the company had closed down overnight; b) that something too dreadful for words had happened and we had all been killed by some unknown entity or unforeseen event; and c) that Ethel, who was also absent, was dead. Of course, she wasn't to know that Ethel had called to say she was running late as she was dealing with a pigeon down her chimney, but it was irritating all the same.

However, Ursula cheered up once she knew we were, in fact, all still alive, and began telling me how she had heard the first cuckoo on her way to the station this morning. Poor Ursula. I actually felt quite sorry for her as she wiped a tear away and did a rather quavering imitation of the bird's call.

Wednesday 10 April

Felt in need of some recreation, so went round to see Ethel and commiserate with her about the intrusive pigeon. She said that the man from the pest control turned out to be terrified of birds and ran away as soon as he heard it fluttering in the chimney, so she put a towel round her hand and somehow managed to extricate the bird herself, wrap it in the towel, and release it safely into the street. She said drily, 'It managed to pick the one and only day so far all year when I'd baked a sponge cake and got soot and mess all over it.' We had a long conversation about the conspiracy theory that pigeons are really government-controlled drones used to surveil citizens. They have a little microphone going down their ear canal and a tiny camera in their eye...

Thursday 11 April
Watching the sales with an eagle eye (or maybe I should say a pigeon eye!) *Rewild Your Body* up to seventy three, and *Trunk Call* to ninety! Yay! I'll show them yet!

Continuing the avian theme of the past few days...

Of doves and pigeons:

From: Ursula Woodrow Sent: 7 April 11.33 To: ALL@HQ
Subject: Easter Columba Cake

An excess 'Easter Columba cake' was discovered yesterday. Easter Columba cake = a lighter version of a panettone, very nice toasted, but equally good not. It may conjure up visions in some of you of St Columba wandering along the shore and his crane, crumpled and bedraggled from the storm, coming to land at his feet, etc etc.

From: Ethel Tula Gutierrez Sent: 7 April 11.47 To: ALL@HQ
Subject: Easter COLOMBA Cake

Actually, it's **Colomba** cake, not Columba – the Italian for dove. Colomba di Pasqua is an Italian Easter cake, traditionally baked in the shape of a dove, etc etc.

Ran into Gerard in reception and asked him how he was getting on, meaning of course London Book Fair. He paused, looked at the ground, then said, 'Very emotional. Very emotional.'

'Oh really?'

I know people get het up about publishing and books, but this seemed a trifle out of the ordinary.

'Oh dear me, yes.'

Began to suspect it wasn't LBF he was talking about.

'I've been to several funerals and never, etc etc.'

I then realised he was, indeed, dressed entirely in black, with a plain white shirt and black yeoman's stock round his neck, and wearing a black hat. Well, I'm very sorry for his loss, whatever it is, but am none the wiser as to what's going on. Sometimes I wonder if it's worth even trying to keep up with the outside world at all, if people are so tight with information, and won't say what's going on.

Friday 12 April

Everyone back from LBF. Fay and Drusilla in a bad mood. It seems that Gerard, when not attending funerals, spent most of his time closeted with some overseas publisher in secret meetings – at least, he hasn't divulged the content to any of us, thus proving I am right to complain about his solipsistic ways.

Fay said, 'Does the name Krukinov & Krukinov mean anything to you?'

'No… or does it ring a faint bell? …No. Does it to you?'

'No,' she said. 'But I'd be quite interested to know more about the strange company of that name that Gerard was meeting at LBF. He was most mysterious about them.'

On the funeral theme, a rumour is going round that Fingal previously worked as an embalmer. He says he's ambidextrous, and has trouble putting a letter in an envelope, so there was much speculation as to how he might have managed with the more esoteric manipulations that must be required in the funeral parlour.

All this mortality countered by Ursula sowing seeds in our yard at the back, intent on new life, striding about purposefully round the little quad with its arches, urns and meagre flower beds. A statue of St Peter also regarded her benignly, clutching a large key, as if about to hand it to her in approval of her horticultural activities. Ursula told me she does this every spring in every nook and cranny she can find in London as part of her guerrilla gardening. I watched her stalking stiffly about, like a scarecrow come to life, or van Gogh's Sower, some weird, ancient emblem of fertility, casting the seeds from the bag with a long arm in that age-old gesture.

Saturday 13 April
The police have sent me a list of the missing and stolen books thought to have been purloined by Hugo, to refer to as I go through his flat.

Sunday 14 April
To Hugo's, setting an alarm on my phone for a strict two hours. Gathered the first load of stolen books to send back to where they rightfully belong. In this lovely spring weather, it seemed a sin and a shame to be indoors. Thought about going on pilgrimage, and how folks long to be on the move in April, as Chaucer said.

Monday 15 April
Fay on the case. She investigated the Krukinovs and said that not only did they not have a stand at LBF – not even a little table upstairs with the agents – but there was no reference to them at all in the list of attendees. Worryingly little on Google, too, but she said they describe themselves as world digitalisation experts. When tackled about all this, Gerard said they were a group of wealthy Russian intellectuals with high ideals about information sharing and muttered something about meeting them for an informal chat about how they could best help us. Do hope Gerard hasn't fallen for any clever marketing ploys that are going to cost us a fortune.

Fingal took up official residence today, setting up a small shrine on his desk: a picture of Our Lady, a black rosary, two blue candles and a phylactery of a tiny bag of yellow pollen, a small quartz crystal and four feathers of eagle-down. I hope we are not going to start finding out odd things about Fingal now. I said nothing, however, beyond introducing him to my own totem, the bear that sits on my desk, Parsifal, with Hug on one foot, and Me on the other.

Ursula told me that while everyone was at LBF, Ivan Skrulewski came in and threw a tantrum in reception, saying that he would 'bloody well take his books Elsewhere' if we weren't careful. It seems that we have been 'totally unacceptable' in the way we have been treating him, and that he has Another Publisher lined up. Hope it's Calling Crane – that would serve them right for poaching our authors! I'm kind of sorry I missed the scene – I was just taking a turn round the park, although Ursula was probably the best person he could have chosen for a display of this kind, being infinitely unembarrassable.

Fay in a state because she couldn't find her footstool, a private, near-sacred totem that, according to her, supports her back. Seems she was kept awake last night by anxiety-induced insomnia and spinal discomfort – and went round hissing, 'Sit thou on my right hand, till I make thine enemies thy footstool!' (Psalm 110:1.)

Tuesday 16 April

Fingal shows signs of being drawn into our cake culture, in the form of some chocolate orange shortbread he handed round the kitchen this morning.

'There you go, folks – enjoy!'

I understand that Fingal is not short of a bob or two, in fact, he is actually a Scottish laird who lives, when at home, in a Scottish castle. Or so he told Gerard, although of course Gerard, like Ursula, is infinitely suggestible and may have misinterpreted him. I sampled a morsel of shortbread as a courtesy, as it looked dreadfully rich, especially first thing in the morning. I then wished I hadn't as Fingal took advantage to treat me to a spiel about his weekend which seemed to take almost as long as the weekend did. There was a lot about clubbing and Conor. Charming as it all sounded, couldn't help thinking that work ought to take precedence, but it is hard to be churlish when your mouth is full of chocolate orange crumbs.

To help him get over his recent tantrum, invited Ivan Skrulewski to come in as my lead author to meet Fingal and discuss publicity for *Nature and the Golden Rule*. This backfired slightly. Not only did he take an instant and obvious dislike to Fingal, he also tripped over a stray telephone wire and nearly went sprawling. If he will wear a long black cloak he has only himself to blame, but he didn't see it like this.

'Don't you people have any health and safety awareness?' he bawled, clasping at the nearest support, which happened to be some piles of books on Fingal's desks. They toppled, too, of course. 'Paying damages for broken bones sounds like the last thing you lot need at this stage of your business life. Where's Gerard?'

It's very unfortunate that he is a personal friend of Gerard's. Luckily I was able to say, truthfully, that Gerard was immersed in an important project – on health and safety as it happened – and had given strict orders not to be disturbed.

'And meanwhile the house is falling down around him,' said Ivan. 'Gerard always was notorious for his ostrich syndrome.'

I explained that health and safety had in fact been taking up rather a lot of Gerard's time lately. Actually, now I think about it, I haven't actually seen Gerard since last week. The door is firmly closed to his holy of holies with its red velvet throne, ancient portraits, mahogany desk etc. I suppose he is still in there, alive.

We all helped pick up the books that Prof Skrulewski had scattered, but not before he had spotted the name of one of his arch-rivals on one of them. '*The Urban Ecologist's Mid-Life Crisis*, eh?' he snorted, and, with some vestiges of returning good humour, 'Tomer Levine must be well past mid-life by now, I'd have thought,' and I managed to escort the irate professor out without further mishap.

Unfortunately, or maybe fortunately, his tumble drew our attention to the fact that the towers of books on Fingal's desk are all the review copies from the last few months, waiting to be sent out to the press. In fact, they've been waiting for some time now; none of them seem to have shifted at all since he joined us apart from the ones I sent out the other day. Fingal himself seemed to vanish around the same time as Ivan, so we couldn't tackle him about it. Instead, I went out and got some lemon and chocolate chip cookies and handed them round to cheer everyone up.

Wednesday 17 April
Ursula back from her cataract op, in dark glasses, useless for all practical work purposes, as she has been forbidden to look at a computer until the other eye is done, which won't be for six weeks. Needless to say there was some gruesome complication involved but I managed to get out of hearing about it.

Gerard is still shut up in his office, presumably beavering away at the disaster plan. From the memos that emerge from his fastness, he seems obsessed by tripping, falling, slipping, cutting, slicing, strangling, spiking, suffocation and immolation, but with a particular emphasis on sprays. Any spray in use is to be subjected to minute inspection, the spray glue used by Design coming under special scrutiny for some reason. Possibly this relates to some submerged fear of papacy, given Toya's tendency to Rome. We have received several impassioned memos begging us to be careful – proving beyond doubt that Gerard's ability to write is not totally extinct – dealing with the terrifying possibilities of spray being misdirected into the eyes or up the nostrils, rather than the object for which it was intended. Drusilla, raising an eyebrow, said, 'Isn't that the kind of thing one learns when one is four?'

Fay said, 'Mark my words, something is up. I know Gerard of old, he only works like this while he's trying to avoid something. I want to know what he's not putting into the memos.'

Ethel, who grumbled that health and safety has already taken eight and a quarter hours this week, broke the news that the air freshener sprays in the loos don't match health and safety requirements. I had already noted, to my discomfiture, that any sprays are now regularly removed from the loos by some officious person. There was a grim silence before Fay said, 'And replaced, I hope?'

'Oh yes, we'll be getting the proper kind,' said Ethel gloomily. 'Anyone here ever got high on Tippex?'

Thursday 18 April
Footstool turned up in Fingal's office. Fay not amused. Fingal should not presume on his new boy status.

Friday 19 April
Drusilla making interminable calls in loud and mellifluous Italian next door, clearly in negotiations with some special author, at least, she sounded almost reverential at times, for Drusilla. '*Sì, vostra eminenza... Eccellenza reverendissima...*'

Found it rather distracting as my Italian is just tantalisingly below comprehension level, although I got the impression she was planning a jaunt to Rome, so went and sat in Gerard's office as he was out. Inspired by Drusilla's possible future travel, I worked on my somewhat neglected Brendan novel, thinking about the quest for meaning as much as the destination.

*

Seeker on that crowded ocean, where are you going, wither are you bound? The ubiquitous query. I belong in the place of my departure, says Odysseus, and I belong in the place that is my destination. Odysseus sought home; could Brendan have said what he was seeking? These days we go in search of solitude, silence, nature, the wild; in those days, they would have said spiritual displacement, God. We all need a continuum along which to travel; without context, the quest is not possible...

*

Saturday 20 April

To Hugo's. Did a lot of cleaning. Got right down to the bed which has been sitting there with the same sheets for around eight months, and quite possibly unchanged for a further six months before that. Sheets went straight into a black bin-bag. Was finally able to get some clothes for him.

Sunday 21 April

More clearing of the prisoner's flat. Do hope he's duly grateful. Started sorting the books, of which there seem to be thousands. Basically, there are two piles – stolen, and not stolen. How am I ever going to return all the stolen ones to the libraries?

With quite some relief, went to the Brahms Requiem at the South Bank to relax.

Monday 22 April

Busy morning. Parcelled up two pairs of trousers and two jumpers for Hugo in the post room in the intervals of sorting out twenty-four publicity packages. Fay came in with some letters and said, 'I thought Fingal had done those!' (The press packs, obviously, not the trousers.)

I said, 'Well, as these have been sitting on Fingal's desk since he arrived, and he's off sick today, I thought I'd better lend a hand.'

Her face fell. 'Since he arrived?'

''Fraid so,' I said. 'They've now become seriously overdue, of course, as they're all from last autumn.'

'But Fingal should have sent them out the minute he arrived. It was the first thing on the handover form.'

'Yes, the urgency was stressed to him. And these are just the tip of the iceberg. There are plenty more waiting to go. I'm just doing the November ones because Drusilla is fretting about her autumn titles so much.'

'Do you think it's due to him being ambidextrous and not being able to put a letter in an envelope and all that?'

I was feeling unsympathetic and said, 'I fear the problem has deeper roots than that, although if that were the case he should never have applied for the job in the first place.'

Tuesday 23 April

Editorial board. Fay and Drusilla had a humungous row about *Entities and Encounters after Inhalation of Hallucinogenic Drugs.*

'Please tell me this title is going to change,' said Drusilla suavely, glancing round at the captive audience that was the editorial board.

'Of course it will change, Drusilla. It's a working title.'

'Working rather too hard if you ask me. People will think we're taking the micky.'

Alas, things descended from there. Drusilla seemed really riled, instead of indulging in the pleasant stimulus that a row with Fay usually produced. I think the Vatican are still being difficult about the debt collector. She was uncharacteristically testy even with me, suddenly rounding on me and asking, 'When *is* that prison prayers synopsis coming in?'

'It's in hand. Hugo and his warder are working on it together.'

'Well, tell them to get it in by the end of the month or the deal's off!'

Duly bit the bullet and texted Hugo, 'How is Sam getting on with that synopsis?' and Hugo texted back, 'Sam wears white socks every day, has an Alsatian called Mufti, and penalises fist fights with razor blades between the knuckles. Am thinking of writing a short story about him myself.'

As it's obvious we are getting nowhere there, felt I should do what I could and went and watered Gerard's plant again while he was at lunch, and removed all the dead leaves, repenting of my hard-heartedness in that direction.

As if picking up the disharmonious vibes, Ursula and Ethel had one of their discussions about Hell by the photocopier, as to whether a few might be saved, or if Satan had us all marked for wholesale damnation. Their voices resounded along the landing and corridors. Fay emerged and marched into Gerard's office and shut the door firmly. I could tell she'd gone in to beg for Ursula to be sacked again. The theme was taken up by Fingal, who asked in an equally loud voice if anyone here had ever been to Hell. When everyone looked doubtful, and started shaking their heads, he revealed that it was a new club.

St George's Day. Uncle Albany rang and said it had been wild in Gallhampton Gap.

Wednesday 24 April

Fay has lost her initial enthusiasm for Fingal. She came into my office to talk to me about a *globus hystericus* in her throat that was bothering her every time she swallowed, and asked in a stage whisper, had I noticed that Fingal has developed a habit of sidling up when there was any interesting conversation going on? She said she was beginning to find him really quite irritating and intrusive, but as Fay finds most people irritating and intrusive I took little notice of this. She was in a particularly bad mood as Fingal still hasn't handed over the footstool despite her repeated requests for it, so that she was forced to go into his office and retrieve it bodily when he wasn't there.

'Fingal manages to be very distracting without actually doing anything,' Fay continued in her hissing whisper. 'He just wafts around. His attention is spread over the place instead of being focused on his work. And he's so needy! You hear this, "Hem," in the background and suddenly he's there, standing over you, wanting attention. He makes you look quite good, Mortimer!'

Drusilla heard of course over the partition, and leapt to my defence, coming in and saying, 'Mortimer always looks good and is good, too, he's one of the best editors I know,' which I understood to be an apology for her sharp words of yesterday. She added that yes, she was beginning to doubt that Fingal was quite the publicity officer we needed right now, mainly because he was hardly ever in his office.

Perhaps as a warm-up for her proposed trip to Rome, she sent for Ursula to give a progress report on her search of the attics. I left her sitting there like a wily old Pope herself, eyes veiled but searching as she questioned Ursula in the vain hope of extracting a single clue as to where the Daybreak Manuscript could possibly be.

Thursday 25 April

Rather annoyed that Fingal has somehow managed to take Moriarty away from me. He thinks it's cool to be seen sitting feet up at your desk with a big fluffy cat in your lap, and spends the day taking selfies of himself and the cat to post on our Twitter account. 'Poor Moriarty!' he said in his obnoxious drawl, chucking the cat under the chin. 'Yew've never had a trew friend before!' My blood boils. And as for Moriarty himself – well. How fickle can you get!

Friday 26 April

Went into Fingal's office and discovered the secret of his success with Moriarty – a packet of cat treats, sealed with a big paperclip. Talk about sly!

Got a distraught letter from a library in Cologne asking if I could look for a certain rare seventeenth-century volume, *De Mulieribus Extinctis*, and return it to them if possible. Somehow the word has got round that I am Hugo's friend, legal executor and general minder. I blame the *Daily Mail* as usual. No one had heard of me before they decided to give the trial so much coverage. The tie-pin knife, in particular, used to razor out maps and illustrations, seemed to fascinate them. Indeed, like the police, the media gave it far more than its due.

Saturday 27 April
Went out and bought a superior quality of cat treats with which to woo Moriarty back.

Sunday 28 April
Big lurch of the stomach today. I was idly flicking through the *Mail on Sunday* when I saw an article on Sister Evangeline and her work on *Columba and the Crane*. A pic of a smiling Sister E holding out bread to a fairly keen looking crane. A long quote from Rosie Beal, saying how pleased she was to have secured Sister E for her award-winning publishing house. Not a single mention of us.

Monday 29 April
Hah! Moriarty definitely prefers my salmon surprises to Fingal's cod liver nibbles! So there!

A neat little booklet on safety was waiting on my desk for me to start the week with, called *Lifting and Moving Things*. It pictured a man in a helmet, protective gloves, safety goggles and a smug expression pushing a trolley on which was loaded a long box, like a tipped-up coffin. Inside, things were less happy, and showed the unfortunates who had not followed the correct procedures as shown in this booklet, and who were now suffering the consequences – strains and sprains, fractures, wounds, and hernias. The first page was a display of four faces showing four basic human emotions: fear, surprise, nausea and pain, like Guillaume-Benjamin-Amand Duchenne's photographs of neurological experiments, subjects' faces contorted from the electrical impulses shot through their heads. It all seemed a far cry from our sedentary life stuck in front of the computer, when our total lifting is usually confined to raising a cup of coffee to our lips. I showed Fay, who had already flung her copy into the bin thinking it was junk mail. 'Lots of information on lifting sacks, barrels, drums and kegs, I see,' she drawled. 'Very useful, I'm sure.'

I *think* everyone's been so busy with their own concerns they haven't yet noticed yesterday's piece in the *MoS* on Sister E.

Tuesday 30 April

Editorial board. Discussed a proposal for a book on the spiritual life of bees, *Song of the Humble Bee*. Fay accepted it. Now she will have her hands full. Asked for his views on publicity, Fingal said he had no doubt it would create a bit of a buzz, but for some reason we found this less funny than he obviously did.

In fact, Fingal is definitely beginning to irritate us a bit. He just never stops talking, in his helicopter voice, mostly about his ex, Conor, who has followed him down to London from Edinburgh. So it's Conor this and Conor that, not made more appealing by the fact that Conor sounds dour in the extreme, hating London, theatres, cinema and books about equally. I said, 'They don't sound very compatible.'

Drusilla agreed, rather worriedly. 'Less Conor, more work, I'd say.'

She said she ran into a bookshop manager who favoured her with a more in-depth character analysis of Fingal. He said he had only one thing against Fingal: that he's economical with the truth. Strange. I wonder how this manifests. He looks so guileless with his big blue eyes and fresh complexion. However, as Drusilla says, nothing is proven yet and it's only a general statement, not a specific accusation, so we have no means of knowing if it's true. However, it has to be admitted that despite our high hopes, Fingal doesn't quite seem to be settling into office life. He really treats the place like a giant bookshop and spends the day striding up and down the corridors and library, talking to every stray person he can, as if buttonholing a customer, going through all the books, and ignoring his desk altogether. I know nothing more tiring than people who talk at their audience in this way.

Spent the lunch hour holding everyone in thrall – in thrill, I might say – about the name Mortimer whose etymology I do find absolutely fascinating. As it was raining hard outside, people had taken refuge downstairs in the ancient comfy armchairs, so I seized my chance, like the Ancient Mariner. I do think in many ways I would have made a good academic and lecturer.

'Originally the family name on my mother's side, the name Mortimer goes back some three centuries, when after various marriages and intermarriages it morphed into a recognised first name for the sons of the family. As I expect many of you know, Mortimer means dead sea in Old French: *mort*, dead, *mer*, sea. We do, however, also have links with a village in the Seine-Maritime called Mortemer-sur-Eaulne, from which issued one of our more illustrious ancestors, the Norman knight Hue de Mortemer, who fought in the crusades. In the Middle Ages, the Mortimers were a powerful magnate family or dynasty of Marcher Lords in the Welsh Marches...'

I'm sorry to say that people stopped listening long before I had finished. In fact when I paused to draw breath, and looked more closely, they were either lolled back into the armchairs fast asleep, or on their phones. But whom else can I talk to?

Wednesday 1 May

Dear Publisher

My name is Floresta La Bomba, I'm a ex-scort girl here in Buenos Aires. Last year, I released a book called *Diário de Floresta* (Floresta's Diary). It became a great success. My book was in the main bestsellers lists in my country.

In the text I explain how I became a scort girl, the problems with my family, and the relation with my twelve years old daughter. Besides, I tell about how I get my diploma as a Nurse. And I describe many of my moments with the 5000 clients I had during the five years in this job.

I worked in Buenos Aires south, putting creative advertisings in the newspapers of my city, selling my qualities – just me or with another scort girl.

My publisher has just sold the rights for Portugal and Italy, and I'd like to see the book published in your country, too.

I look forward to receiving your reply, telling about your interest.

Best regards

Floresta

Wouldn't mind being in Buenos Aires right now, actually. Some crumbling old colonial house, cream paint cracking, overgrown with greenery, with the shade of Borges tapping his way along the corridor.

Thursday 2 May

Nightmare lunch with a body language expert. Another one palmed off on me by Gerard, from his *Sailing through Storms* transpersonal crisis list. Dr Daniel Abelman has written tomes about body language in frozen trauma and how the slightest flick of an eyelid means that you want to go to bed with the other person, or murder them or whatever, so I spent most of the lunch sitting frozen to the chair myself for fear of making an incriminating movement, and confined myself to finger food – luckily it was a tapas bar – so as to involve the minimum of movement transferring edibles from plate to mouth. Although I have to say Dan looked the least judgemental of people. He was casual in the extreme. Sitting back in his loose baggy trousers, with his longish white woolly hair and his hookah slung on the table for after the meal, he looked like an old sixties roadie manhandling the drums for some minor rock band. We talked about his work in progress, *Moving and Shaking: Unlocking tissue memory in frozen trauma.* I had the awkward job of explaining to him that chapter 13, *Smiling*, which dealt mainly with the putting on and off of condoms, would have to be cut. Gerard told me that Dan had 'taken body language to the limit.' Why can't Gerard do his own dirty work? Dan's been his author for twenty years, after all. All very draining. On the positive side, it was a square meal, always welcome on a junior editor's salary. And at least Dan doesn't pick his teeth at the end of the meal, as Ivan Skrulewski does.

For some reason we got on to body language in criminals, Dan remarking, 'I don't suppose you ever come across suchlike etc etc.'

I was of course able to correct him and said, 'On the contrary, I have a friend currently in Wandsworth prison for serious fraud and aggravated theft.'

Dan was visibly shocked. He said, 'That is indeed a serious charge – very serious.'

I explained about Hugo's sad case. I said, 'As in so many cases, it was all due to his relationship with his difficult mother,' and Dan perked up no end. As with many psychologists of his type, he was at once interested by the combination of potential discrimination and a lame duck, which appealed deeply to his protective instincts.

'Unjust,' he said, shaking his head with quite some relish. 'Unjust.'

He got quite keen about it all and said he would try and visit Hugo himself and make an informal assessment. Anyway, the topic kept us happy until the end of lunch, and I even felt myself relaxing into a normal sitting position and able to order some fork foods such as *arroz con pollo, fabada* and other nourishing dishes.

I suppose I shouldn't have been surprised (though I was, and, just a little, hurt) when, later that afternoon, Gerard told me that Dan had rung him to complain about the proposed cuts to his book, saying he was 'shocked – shocked' and that I was 'fierce – fierce.'

'Oh,' I remarked. 'That doesn't fit my conception of myself. What did you say?'

Gerard stroked his side whiskers and laughed. 'I said, "Of course, that's why I pay him."'

Cheek!

I'm sure it's not true, that I am fierce.

I said, 'Well, some action had to be taken, given that the entire MS read like a pulling manual.'

'Hah! Indeed!' said Gerard. 'Such things may go down well at Calling Crane, but not here. It's up to us to set the standards for the industry.'

I had a flash of inspiration and said, 'Maybe we should try and get Dan together with the Brazilian "scort girl", haha!' and we roared, and Gerard said, 'Now, that really would be a book worth writing!'

Thanks to this man-to-man talk, I am now landed with the entire MS to edit – all 140,000 words of it.

Friday 3 May

Had a chat with our esteemed sales director, Roland, taking leave of the mother ship before heading up north again on his rounds. He told me there was a rumour – widely believed – that Ivan Skrulewski's books are all written by his students. He also told me the story about us being taken over by Russian bookbinders, in the news a while ago, has percolated round all the bookshops and given them a good laugh.

'How are you getting on with young Fingal?' he said. 'The word is he's running a business on eBay.'

'What, from here?'

'Oh yes, very definitely from here. I've just been into the post room to collect my mail, and there are several odd-looking parcels arrived for him.'

I wonder if Fingal could be a spy. He certainly gives the impression of working for someone else. Meanwhile he has a cold and everyone knows about it as he spends much of his time blowing his nose like one sounding the trumpet, usually just outside my office while I'm on the phone – all too audible due to the lack of roof and acoustics, of course.

Our caretaker, Juan, who is a highly qualified Bolivian pharmacist, forced into his job by political exile and parochial UK laws that won't allow him to practise here, sent round an end of week recipe for baking *huminta*, or cornbread. It takes two tins of sweetcorn, anise seeds and chilli powder among other things. Might try it.

Saturday 4 May

Tried baking Juan's *huminta* as a weekend relaxation. After one mouthful, took it straight to the geese at the lake in the park. Their cries and screams of gratitude, or greed, resounded in my ears as I walked away.

Thought about waterbirds on my solitary and silent walk home. Might add a chapter on this in my Brendan book. There is a certain cult of birds among the *peregrini*, the storm-blown fragility and elegance of Columba and his wind-tossed crane, the humbler waddlings of Cuthbert's ducks, their sheeny fragility able to go on water, land and air, their mysterious trumpetings into the unknown...

Sunday 5 May

Hugo very tiresome with texts and calls. He's now requesting me to put his flat on the market for him to raise some cash for when he comes out in five years and eight months' time. Hope he's developed some gratitude by then. It's never enough, is my feeling. Was going to go round to his flat and continue sorting, but I'm not going to now, due to his demanding attitude. Switched my phone off for the day at around 3pm.

Monday 6 May
Bank holiday

Read Wordsworth's Prelude as I've never really got to grips with it before and thought it would be a good antidote to Proust *pour maintenant*. I thought it was rather sad the way he kept addressing Coleridge, who had long since gone. Reminded me somewhat of

Hugo and myself. After another twenty-two texts, have blocked him on my phone. (Hugo that is, not Coleridge of course!)

Tuesday 7 May

Ursula found some books and came rushing to Drusilla and me with them: *Verum Pulchrarum Silvarum*, 1590, *De Floribus Arcadiae,* 1580, *Tulipa Duc van Tol Splendida*, 1601, which had all been hidden away in the great wooden globe in the library, which opens into two halves. She also found a half-bottle of brandy in there.

'Clever of Ursula,' said Drusilla. 'I'd never have thought of looking there myself.'

Alas, I had no trouble recognising them from the list of Hugo's stolen books with which I have been entrusted. Besides, he'd used them all in his last wonderfully fluent piece he wrote about the seventeenth-century tulip craze in the Netherlands, together with the beautiful botanical drawings: the flaming yellow, the delicate, twining green, the striped red flares.

We told Gerard so he could notify the police. He said, 'Hah! A definite case of *Now sleeps the crimson petal, now the white*!'

Sadly, Ursula went to dust the globe before closing it again, and to put the brandy in the first aid cupboard. I went to communicate with the librarians of Amsterdam and Bruges.

Also with Hugo. Unblocked his number swiftly. 'How dare you dump your shameful stash of stolen goods on us! Making us into receivers of stolen goods! It's abominable!'

He texted back, 'I wondered where I'd put those! Thanks for finding!'

Wednesday 8 May

Drusilla making increasingly annoyed noises about Fingal not doing the work she has set him. She complains that he is 'away with the fairies' most of the time and seems to have great difficulty remembering what she's asked him to do. I said, 'Have you considered the possibility that he's a spy?' and she said, 'A spy! What will you dream up next, Mortimer! Spies have to be intelligent and cunning, don't they?'

I said I rather thought Fingal was both and that his volatile, absent-minded exterior was just a façade to pull the wool over everyone's eyes, but Drusilla said crossly, 'I never heard such nonsense,' and went storming down the corridor to shake him personally by the scruff of the neck for not arranging any publicity whatsoever for Philip Midwinter's March title *The Books of Alexandria and Other Lost Libraries*, which together with recent events is threatening to unseat the friendship of half a century.

Went to try out my spy theory on Fay. She was marginally more sympathetic but said she thought spies had to keep a totally clean and empty desk which disqualified Fingal straightaway.

Gerard sent us all a memo saying we must inform our managers before we use our mobile phone chargers as they won't have been assessed with the rest of the electrical equipment and could therefore pose a risk to our general safety. The email was couched in the most urgent terms. Apart from the fact that I don't know who my manager is – we don't really deal in such concepts at the House – I found this uncharacteristically intrusive from Gerard, normally so hands-off, to say the least. We all agreed that next April Fool's Day we would bring in all manner of electrical implements – curling tongs, toasters, hairdryers – and plug them all in. As it was, the offices were ringing all afternoon with ironic requests from one or the other asking loudly if they might plug their charger in. The corridors seemed to resound with the mocking echoes even as I left to go home.

A glass coffee table arrived for Fingal today. It was standing in reception as I departed.

Thursday 9 May
Emergency meeting of the editorial board to find out why we have just one book for next January. No one could offer any convincing explanation or indeed any explanation whatsoever. Gerard was uncharacteristically antsy and said we needed to find out as the governing body are demanding to see a valid spread of proposals to pass on to some external publishing consultancy he's hired to help us.

We went round the table, none too hopefully. I said *What Trees Talk About When They Talk About Love* was in. Gerard said he was doing his best to extract Bishop Molly's book from her, but that she took a lunch a chapter, and that they were on chapter two at the moment. Drusilla talked about a manuscript she's been waiting fourteen years for, like one in a fairy tale. Fortunately, however, it's about ancient man's first ventures across the African seas, so it's not as if the topic is going to change that much. It's the last of a three-book deal signed a long time ago with her dear old friend and eminent historian Philip Midwinter (the first two being *The Lost Libraries of Alexandria*, and *Wounded*.) I'm sure *Island Hopping with Homo Erectus – Rafts and axes from Africa to Europe* will be a big hit when we do get the MS.

Fay was the only one with any fire in her belly; she said, 'Looks like it's time for a spot of creative commissioning,' and reeled off five proposals on the spot that the authors were currently unaware of, but which she could probably coerce them into producing. Diary, I hate to admit it, but Fay carries the list.

In addition to the glass coffee table, Fingal now has a man's bike and a long mirror propped by his desk, tripping everyone up who comes in. When tackled about them, he says they are 'going.' Meanwhile, rumour has it that Fingal's been to several job interviews in his frequent absences, one of them for some overseas publisher whose name I can't recall. Probably some little press on some remote island off the Norwegian coast who grow their hair long, work as smallholders, grow their own vegetables and print their own books with vegetable dye.

On this homely note, Fay has been banned from opening her tinned pilchards in the kitchen, due to the unearthly stink. Also due to the fact that Moriarty has got trapped in the bin a few times, rummaging for the tin.

Friday 10 May

Went in to Drusilla to report formally on my progress with Proust, as it's been a while and I've been feeling a bit guilty that I haven't finished it yet. I said I was bowled over by its splendid heartlessness – that wonderfully outrageous monster of egotism M. de Charlus and the chilly egotism of the Narrator which for me reached its apotheosis in describing the death of his grandmother, but bored to tears by all the 'obsession'. Nothing so tedious as pathological jealousy.

I said, after a ten-minute report, 'So I've just got to the end of volume 5, *La Prisonnière*. I know it's taken ages. Hope you don't think I'm slacking!'

'Oh, you *have* done well!' said Drusilla. 'I never got beyond the first volume and a quarter!'

Felt ever so slightly betrayed by this.

Dr Dan Abelman rang and said he'd been in to see Hugo. He gave me his considered professional opinion. 'He's completely bonkers. I can't do anything for him.'

Blissfully quiet. Ethel has gone back to Texas on business for two weeks, and Ursula is having her other cataract op done, which means we are publishing no books.

Saturday 11 May

Devoted the day to Proust, as one must if one is to make progress. Ploughing through volume 6, *Albertine disparue*. Wearisome beyond endurance, as Dickens said of Wilkie Collins's *Moonstone*.

The truth is that the shine has worn off without the feeling of Drusilla's companionship along the way. It's lonely work, reading Proust without her.

Sunday 12 May

Secret plans are afoot for Uncle Albany's eightieth birthday party in July. Auntie Juls told me in the strictest secrecy. Hope I can remember not to mention it to him.

Finished volume 6. In my very humble opinion, Proust should have had an editor.

Monday 13 May

Drusilla had a birthday over the weekend. I said I would take her out to lunch on the strength of it. She said, 'All right, but don't tell anyone else, will you,' and of course I assured her I wouldn't.

We went to Neel's. Neel was sitting sullenly at one of his own tables in his white overalls and hat and ignored us for ten minutes but once this was over, got up, scowled at us, and cooked us the most delicious prawn curry. Love of cuisine struggles with a deep, instinctive aversion to the customer at Neel's. Grumpy and resentful service, plates banged down, requests for glasses of water ignored, waiters scuttling off crossly. 'Absolutely no social skills whatsoever,' as Drusilla put it, with uncharacteristic understatement. 'Perhaps they're just shy. But the food! This is the only place I can eat rice that's up to my standards!'

We discussed Proust. She agreed with me that he would have benefitted from working with someone who would not have allowed him to have his head – someone very like herself, presumably. 'That's the disadvantage of self-publishing, you see,' she said. 'There's no one to hold you in check.' We had a glass of wine each and toasted Marcel and Drusilla with equal reverence and solemnity.

When we got back, Drusilla announced to Sales and Marketing, clustered in reception, 'Hey, I've just had an important birthday!

I'm seventy-five!' Roland, Harold, Oupie and Noreen all clustered round for hugs, graciously accepted by Drusilla. Fay came down the stairs at that point and she, too, was included in the confidence as Drusilla sang out, 'I'm seventy-five, I'm seventy-five! Three-quarters of a century!' adding, 'Mortimer and I will take you out to lunch, too, next week!'

Rather miffed. So much for Drusilla's special confidence in me. She only had one glass of wine, though I seem to remember she once told me that her limit is actually half a glass, owing to the way she metabolises alcohol.

Tuesday 14 May

Meanwhile, Fingal's making everyone's life a misery with his own form of noise pollution. His voice, a never-ending, rasping drone, goes right through you; an ongoing vibration that seems to permeate the old stones of this building to the core. Fay asked Gerard plaintively, 'Can't you do anything, Gerard?' I think Gerard is too used to Fay asking him to sack people; at any rate, he just shook his head sadly and muttered something about the governing body.

My only comfort is that Drusilla, who is pretty acute at these matters, predicts that he will be gone by June at the latest.

If only he would wash. He smells as if he lives in an old granny's cupboard. Oh, the misery of office life.

Wednesday 15 May

Fingal has been made fire marshal, unwisely I would have thought. This afternoon there was a sudden quiet, and he was found asleep on the folding camp bed that health and safety regulations require us to keep, having gone to inspect the stock of medical supplies. Moriarty was contentedly asleep on top of him and they made a sweet picture – Fay duly took it on her phone – but not one conducive to business. On being woken, Fingal struggled up, yawned, stretched, then sallied forth to give a full report on our medical stocks. 'They have almost no little practical things like plasters for a paper cut on your finger, say, but are really good on things like giant slings for when you break your arm.'

Thought so. You might just as well make Moriarty first aid officer for the mice.

Thursday 16 May
St Brendan Feast Day/Ascension Day
Drusilla much happier as she's working on her contacts in the Vatican to see whether she might forgive their debt in exchange for signing a promising new writer – the Pope. At least, she seems to have found some ingenious way of weaving this into her increasingly complicated and convoluted negotiations. I warned her about the dangers of getting too embroiled with Rome but she is enjoying herself so much I didn't have the heart to say too much.

Fingal is now known to the bookshops as the one who wears lambswool jumpers, according to the latest report from Roland. Not sure of the significance of this but it sounds ominous, as if sentence has been passed by the tribe, finally and irrevocably; like one of those long names they give you in Africa which sum up your life, character and achievements in a sentence – man who runs away from elephants – or something to that effect.

Fay has her own theories about Fingal and why he spends all his time talking, rather than working, based on those blasted personality tests Gerard sent round. 'The trouble with Fingal,' she said, 'is that his feet don't touch the ground, he's too scared of not experiencing all life has to offer and *au fond* he's also scared of not being able to provide for himself.'

I said I thought he was merely in the wrong job and should go back to the bookshops, but Fay continued, 'Fingal is a rare, genuinely anti-social person, someone not meant to mix with humankind; a one-off.'

How infuriating – I'd die for a lighthouse on a remote island. No one ever thinks of me and my needs. Just because I quietly get on with my work and don't make a fuss, I'm completely ignored. What about *my* need for privacy and solitude? No one gets my essence. My life is a constant invasion by crowds, from the obscene cattle tubes, to my tiny flat surrounded by neighbours, to my open-roof office like a prison cell, where everyone can hear everything you say. Why should Fingal be gifted with the status of hermit when it's me that's reclusive by nature, just with no opportunity to express it? So unfair.

Drusilla, informed of these various theories about Fingal, wrinkled her nose and said cheerfully, 'Nonsense, he just doesn't like work.'

Oh dear, we do need someone's hand on the helm. Drusilla is a power in the land, but let's face it, why should she shoulder the entire business and clear up Gerard's mess? It's not like the Pope who, however burdened, does at least have several people to help him, a whole city in fact.

The really annoying thing is that all this is distracting me from my important work *On the Wave with St Brendan*. Set to accordingly, inspired by the balmy days and approaching mid-summer.

*

Brendan the Navigator set sail towards the summer solstice. What summer seas sighing, what blue dawns, the sea reflecting pink from the cloud streamers above. Mirages shimmering on the waves, castles crumbling in the clouds, ships dissolving on the horizon. Ithaca. The marvellous journey, as Cavafy calls it. The many summer mornings when we enter harbours for the first time, the fine silks and pearls we purchase at markets along the way, the adventures we face that we will not encounter unless we bring them along inside our own souls. No one meets the one-eyed giant on the white and dusty road, no one sees the wild sea god in front, rising hoary and dripping from the barnacled waves, unless his or her soul has already set the monster up ahead...

*

Maybe too many summers in there? I quite like the repeated triple effect, though, the way Shakespeare repeats 'royal' three times in Cleopatra's dying scene in *Anthony and Cleopatra*.

Where is all this leading? I confess I don't know. Perhaps the best journeys are circular.

Friday 17 May

Feel I need a break from the machinations of my colleagues, so called Uncle Albany to see if he was up for a visit.

Saturday 18 May

To Gallhampton Gap. Although he describes it as modest, I'd forgotten how huge Albany's flat is compared to mine. You could fit my studio flat into his front hall – it's a room in itself, lined with books from ceiling to floor and complete with writing desk and lamp in the alcove. Then the massive living room, broken into two cosy alcoves by folding French doors, plus three big bedrooms, including his four-poster bed with mustard-gold drapes and (distant) sea view. Albany said, 'You could have the same, too, if you wanted, Mortimer. Very affordable down here. Why not move down? Plenty of Londoners do, you know.'

Must admit, for a moment I was tempted.

Sunday 19 May

Slept well in Albany's comfortable spare room. Was glad to forget all about work. We went for a walk along the East Cliff. It would appear that Coleridge, Dickens and Wilkie Collins, those indefatigable peripatetics of the south coast, passed this way, too, as there was a trail of blue plaques on the rather seedy fronts of a row of Regency flats. Most of the doors looked as if they hadn't been opened, much less re-painted, since Victorian times.

Monday 20 May

I've been here ten years and I still don't understand Fay. I met her in the kitchen first thing, dressed up to the nines in a pink silk velvet skirt and black velvet jacket with a pink silk rose pinned on it, and a little pink and black fascinator set neatly on her black hair.

I said jovially, 'Where are you off to, Buckingham Palace?'

'Sales conference! We've got to go in twenty minutes!'

Fay swished off, clutching a sheaf of typewritten notes that she's spent the last week rehearsing, aloud, in the privacy of her office. I'd wondered what she was doing; I thought she was rehearsing Lady Macbeth. I know she has been quite involved in the local Battersea theatricals at times. Rushed to print out all my advance information sheets, but the printer seized up and they are now stuck somewhere in transit between my computer and the old machine, wheezing on the landing.

Drusilla had forgotten, too, and was happily having black coffee and a flap of Turkish bread and apricot jam for breakfast, but Fay scooped us both relentlessly up and off we went. In the tube Fay lectured us about Freud and memory but Drusilla, a serial sales conference amnesiac, said, 'I'll forget what I want to forget,' and I agreed I had no need to be reminded of the language of forgetting, Liverpool Street was mnemonic enough. We just missed one train and had to wait half an hour for the next.

'We'll be late,' fretted Fay. 'All your fault, Mortimer, faffing around! And where's Fingal?'

'I don't see what all the fuss is about,' said Drusilla. 'The reps could have come to us if they really wanted to see us.'

'It's up to us to set a good example! The commissioning editors are the last people who should be late!'

Naturally I thought of the three latecomers on St Brendan's expedition, the extra monks who turned up for the voyage after time and were thus marked as unlucky. One got left behind, one died and one went down to Hell. They were an unmitigated nuisance in other ways, too. They increased the crew from a comfortable fourteen to seventeen, they sank the boat into the water with their extra weight, they had had nowhere to sit and had to crouch on the spare oxhides, they made inroads on the provisions, making the forty days supply more like thirty-three. In short, the three supernumeraries upset not just Brendan's sacred numbers, but the equilibrium of the entire voyage.

Brendan foresaw their fate when they arrived at the quayside but accommodated them anyway. Why? Why imperil his fragile craft and his quest with three extra, unwanted men? Why not just send them away, tell them the boat was full? He knew, doubtless, that no journey proceeds directly from A to B, but via the twisted paths of God. We cannot cross the sea in a straight line but must take bends and waves, troughs and peaks. Hence the latecomers were part of the journey, slowing it down and sending it off course while they completed their individual destinies. Only when the additional persons were no longer on board could the voyage be completed.

With such musings as these did I shut my ears to the chatter of my own travelling companions as we ploughed through the wastes of north London and into the rural devastation beyond. At last we arrived at the dreary little station and climbed into a taxi smelling of nicotine which chugged off to the aged conference centre, Short Falls. An eighteenth-century hall set in acres of countryside; it should be scenic but for some reason is always like a wet Monday morning. I swear it has its own weather. Grounds saturated by constant rain, white paint peeling, shabby dark-green armchairs, beige walls, food of the least sympathetic kind, travesties of meat pies and mashed potatoes, undrinkable mud for coffee. I don't know how they manage to make God's good ingredients inedible, though, Fay, excusing them, said they were 'under a lot of pressure.' Although, being seasoned editors, we had used the spare half hour at Liverpool Street to load up with cappuccino, prawn sandwiches and hummus wraps. Thus we entered the foyer with its smell of stale school lunches, and on to the conference hall, where Roland and his knights were waiting for us, faces full of sombre intent.

Tuesday 21 May

Got in to find the printer had not only recovered overnight but had printed 200 copies of each of my ten AIs (Advanced Information sheets). What a criminal waste of paper! Went to Gerard with a very strong case for its retirement.

Drusilla in trouble again due to her inability to cope with technology. The reps complained at the conference yesterday that they haven't seen any details of her books and have no paperwork to take on their travels. Though she has actually commissioned thirteen books so far this year, there are only official records for one. Not knowing how to create a new document, she overwrites every single one – contract, book description, advance information sheet, back cover copy, and all – so that she only ever has one file, for her most recent book. Thank goodness she carries round all the details in that capacious brain of hers, but what would happen if she were run over by a bus? Drusilla said to me plaintively, 'I'm always getting told off lately, have you noticed? Sometimes I wonder if it's a hint to me to think about retiring. The problem is that at seventy-five I feel exactly the same as at fifty-five, or even forty-five. The good thing is that I can use the advantages of maturity in my dealings with the Vatican.'

Editorial board. Discussed ways to get Fingal to do his job. The tall piles of review copies are still on his desk – seven months' worth now – the press waits in vain, and Drusilla and Fay are becoming highly restive. Gerard has set Fingal four things to do by next Monday. He said, 'Hopefully, by then we will have a clearer picture of the level of diligence and capability etc etc.' This turned into a monologue about due diligence, and the responsibility of companies to ensure the welfare of their personnel in times of transition and change. No idea what he's talking about.

Fay said she would tackle Fingal. She said she would find some way of motivating him.

Ursula back from her second cataract op, in dark glasses, and full of loud and displeasing descriptions of loose vitreous jelly, whatever that may be.

Wednesday 22 May

Drusilla finally off to Rome to see the Vatican. Fay and I waved her off with many good wishes at lunchtime, although the minute she was out of sight, Fay said, 'Poor Drusilla. I fear she's wasting her precious energy on a wild goose chase.'

'Oh, Fay.'

'Oh, I'm not against it or anything. I'll believe in her old Book if it turns up. But life's too short to go looking.'

Fingal has gone to the Newcastle conference, which explains his absence at our own sales conference on Monday, so we have a few days' blissful quiet.

Thursday 23 May

Engineer in again for the photocopier/printer. His visits seem to be almost daily, as befits a terminal case. He estimated that the old machine had printed one million sheets approximately and was in his opinion well overdue for retirement. 'You should handle her carefully, you know,' he added, rising and laying a hand on the well-used lid. I told him that Ethel frequently sent round emails recommending best care of the Old Lady of the Landing, and how we should treat this venerable machine with tender consideration etc. but that I entirely failed to share her concern and was of the school that favours a good boot up the rear instead.

Friday 24 May

Great excitement. Bishop Molly has made an appointment to come and read us the first chapter of her book on Monday!

Nice quiet day. I didn't notice Fingal was still away until 4pm when Fay came round asking if anyone had seen him.

Saturday 25 May

Reluctantly to Hugo's flat. Removed more books to send back to various libraries next week. Called the police to see if they could provide any support with all this, but they were completely unhelpful and said they didn't do books.

Sunday 26 May

Pentecost/Whit Sunday

Treated myself to a delightful walk in Richmond Park. Cake and coffee at a café. Refreshment for body and soul.

Monday 27 May

Whit Monday

Drusilla came into my office this morning, all chuckles.

'Tell me I've been clever,' she said, taking a seat on the spare chair.

'Oh, what happened? Were the Vatican amenable?'

'Yes, very.' Drusilla lowered her voice. 'Well, as you know, ostensibly I set out to harangue them about the debt they owe us, or rather, to negotiate the best terms. Anyway, while I was there, I thought, wouldn't it be a good idea if I could interest them in the purchase of the Daybreak Manuscript. So I did that.'

She paused.

'Oh, goodness. I would say that counts as clever, yes. Most definitely.'

'First I sounded them out in a general kind of way to see if they might be interested in buying the Daybreak Manuscript to add to the Vatican's Secret Archive – or, to give it its proper name, Vatican Apostolic Archive, secret being used in the sense *Archivum Secretum Vaticanum*, secreted or private a better translation of the Latin.'

She paused impressively.

'They seemed quite receptive to that. Didn't say much but didn't tell me to shut up either. There was no need to big the Book up – they knew all about it. So then I put it to them that they might like to work the £1 million debt they owe us into an offer for the Book – a kind of discount if you like.'

'Oh, very good!'

'Naturally, they want to see the Book. But they could hardly expect me to travel with it and just pull it out of my pocket, could they? It all adds to the mystique if it's not actually there. I let them think it was locked up in a safe in one of our own secret vaults, below the library. I did also suggest that his Holiness might like to give us an option on his memoirs, which I understand are in progress. But I didn't want to push things too far, not on a first visit. Now, not a word to anyone.'

'Of course not.'

'And I'm not going to say too much more myself for now. I don't want to jinx it.'

Bishop Molly didn't turn up. She was last seen speeding off to comfort a friend whose husband had set fire to all her possessions – clothes, photos, everything. What speedy livers these women seem to be, always in the fast lane. It would be splendid if Molly could put all this into her book.

Fay, taxed with my thoughts on this, said, 'We must do the best we can with the material we have, we're all flawed human beings.' Which fatalistic approach – apart from being completely untypical of Fay – is surely not the way to do business.

Tuesday 28 May

Fresh disaster with Fingal, back from the Newcastle conference. Came down for my 11am coffee to find most of the office in a twitter around seven boxes of books returned to us from the conference, standing in reception, all very roughly packed and looking well man-handled. The seven had been returned most meticulously to us here at HQ, though clearly marked for return to the warehouse in Middlesbrough, while the eighth, containing the till, all details of the £11,000-plus worth of transactions, and details of everyone's credit cards, and various other valuables, has disappeared totally. Fingal, who should never have let it out of his sight, was quite resolutely complacent about it, as if not personally implicated at all and merely witnessing some slightly daffy action of someone else's and chased it up on the phone with mild tolerance and a tinge of contempt. Meanwhile the warehouse, in their usual inimitable style, have marked the £11,000 down as returns, thus making us £11,000 in debt rather than in profit.

Wednesday 29 May

Fingal has lost his expenses float. That's around £1,000. Very odd.

Thursday 30 May

Fingal ensconced with Gerard all this morning, trying to sort out the float business. Doesn't sound good.

Friday 31 May

Gerard asked me to be acting health and safety officer as no one else wants to do it. I said, 'I thought Fingal was doing it,' and Gerard said, 'No, he's only fire officer and for various reasons we can't ask him to take on anything else at the moment.' I said unguardedly, 'Does that mean he's in the process of being sacked?' but needless to say that got me nowhere – Gerard just so beautifully didn't hear, as Henry James would have said, and merely thanked me profusely for taking health and safety on. I had hopes of more when he hesitated and drew breath, but he just patted me on the shoulder and said, 'Never make sudden movements, dear boy. Inexperienced shooters sometimes fire the first shot, then turn for advice from fellow shooters. A big NO.'

Later, he sent another anxious directive begging us all to be sure to cut *away* from ourselves when opening post with a knife. Many unkind jokes about machetes, bodies swinging from the ceiling, etc. In my new role, I must speak to Gerard more about all this. Surely it's unhealthy to be working in a box with no natural light?

Ethel has been going round all week clutching cans of spray and regarding them with a perplexed look. She has been tasked with assessing the spray risk to all personnel for the disaster recovery plan, which by now must be reaching mammoth proportions.

Fingal gone back to Newcastle in search of the missing box, so we have a few more days' welcome peace. I was almost glad to see Ursula in the kitchen, she seems quite benign now in comparison. It's awful when a work colleague gets under one's skin. I'd be happy never to see Fingal again.

Saturday 1 June

Glad to reach the weekend. Turned with some relief away from real life and to my Brendan novel, which like all good journeys is making slow, erratic progress…

*

Brendan's was a wild and turbulent pilgrimage. Unlike Cavafy's voyage to his Ithaca, it was undiluted by the luxuries of travel, the silks and leisurely pauses, the mythic beings of an ancient civilisation. A journey of greased oxhides stretched over bare ash wood, extra hides and rancid butter for repairs. Brendan's was like a shot of pure salt water shot through with blue and sun, twists of wind, the fleeting white curve of a seagull, the bareness of wet rock in a strange place. He created his own mythology as he went, islands and strange beasts springing up from the waves to meet him…

*

Longed to discuss all this with someone and texted Hugo to see if he was up for a chat. Despite his peccadilloes, Hugo is the one person who understands why I would bother to keep a logbook from a sinking ship...

Sunday 2 June

Hugo in a bad mood and texted back that I was a prisoner of language. It turns out he still bears a grudge against me for not finding his John Dee. I jocularly suggested that Dee himself had magicked it away to another dimension. Like Prospero, for whom he was the model, John Dee could command the winds and rouse the waves of the sea. For someone who raised a storm to defeat the Spanish Armada, making a book vanish and re-appear would be no trouble. I said, '*The Tempest* is full of secret magic allusions. I can send you that. Or maybe Sam's got a copy, he seems quite keen on books?'

He replied, 'Don't talk to me about Sam. Can you at least lay your hands on *De Heptarchia Mystica* instead?'

I repied, 'Forget the grimoires, they only lead to trouble. In any case, don't think Dee intended Enochian magick for vulgar personal revenge, *De Hept* a guidebook for summoning angels, not spells.'

He texted back, 'An angel would do – preferably a bad one.'

I said, 'Surely life more comfortable without conjuring spirits?? You don't know what forces you are unleashing! Suppose you get a malevolent djinn?!'

Was struck by a brilliant afterthought. 'Dr Dee is on Gutenberg. Why not download onto your phone? Like one of his own magical rites, calling down words out of the ether!!'

Silence for an hour. Then Hugo texted, 'As you're so useless, will try something out of Macbeth from memory. That at least uses genuine witches' spells.'

The words of Solomon sprang to mind. 'It is an honour for a man to cease from strife; But every fool will be meddling' (Proverbs 20:3). Was tempted to send this on to Hugo. However, by then I was making my dinner – fish finger sandwich and trot-a-mouse tea – and felt I could only live in so many worlds at once, so I let him have last word.

Monday 3 June

Fingal has had to return to Scotland because his father has had a heart attack. Handy that he was in Newcastle at the time as it made the journey so much shorter, of course. Well, I'm very sorry to rejoice because of someone else's misfortune, but it is lovely to have our old quiet back again. And, thank goodness, the vital eighth box has been found – sitting by the gents' toilets at the conference centre, unmarked, with not so much as an address label or sticker.

Lovely weather. As Ursula was in a benign and easy mood, I got the key to the so-called secret garden off her, a heavy, ornate iron one, just like St Peter's, as Ursula said. ('Not that I would dream of comparing myself etc etc'.) As I made my way down the road, I thought how lucky we were to have entry to this bit of quintessential London, one of those green communal squares with gated iron railings, winding paths and trees sweeping the ground. I don't know why we call it the secret garden, though, as it's shared with all the other inhabitants of the square.

I slipped into the dappled shade and sat there happily on my favourite bench with my egg and cress sandwiches and salt and vinegar crisps, listening to the summer sigh of the planes across the sky and inhaling London: dust, lime, traffic, the scent of home. Then Fay and Drusilla turned up. Not that I wasn't pleased to see them, but once they had sat down and got out their lunchboxes with chickpeas, free-range boiled eggs, rocket, tomatoes and balsamic vinegar, and started a cheery conversation about EU rights, I found the previous mood irrecoverable.

Tuesday 4 June

Disaster! When Fay and Gerard examined the box from the Newcastle conference, which arrived this morning, the entire £11,730.40 was missing! Fay and Gerard very haggard. They took the box apart and went through it with a toothcomb. Eventually they found details of the credit card transactions squashed between the pages of a copy of *How to Make a Thousand Objects out of a Tree*. This was a huge relief of course but the cash is still missing – around £1,500. Gerard said he didn't like to call Fingal because of the parlous state of his father's health at which Fay suddenly said, 'But his father died when he was eight! He told me. Why didn't I remember before!'

No one doubted the veracity of her word, known as she is to be deadly accurate in all gossip and hearsay. She and Gerard rang Fingal several times, but there was no answer.

Update from Molly. She'd set aside today to come in and read chapter 1 again, but instead sent an email asking us all to contribute to a collection of clothes, toiletries, make-up etc for her badly abused friend, who lost all in a fire-setting incident by her husband, now under lock and key, quite rightly so. She is size 14 and likes Ghost, apparently.

Wednesday 5 June

Strange day. Gerard came bustling in to talk to me about doppelgangers at 7.45am – early morning seems to be the only window for any interpersonal transactions with him – and said, 'Do you know, the other day I was in Bond Street, and I nearly tapped someone on the shoulder thinking it was you and realised just in time it was someone completely different.' Given that he hardly ever says hello even within the purlieus of the building (at most it's a distant, if beneficent nod, a tap on the shoulder being a rare intimacy) I thought it was odd of him to regret an opportunity of greeting me elsewhere. Before I knew it, we were on to Borges and *el otro*, the other, who sat next to him on a bench in the zoological garden in Oxford and told him things he couldn't otherwise have known. So is it that we are all really the same, driven by the same fundamental drives and with the same secret wishes? That there is in fact no difference between any of us? I must say, being told I have a double is one of my least favourite things. It seems to rob me of any individuality. What's the point of being me, if any number of people could pass for me, or be confused with me? It makes me feel that with my best efforts I could disappear without being missed at all.

Sister Evangeline called to say that having thought about it, she feels called to do a book on sleep, inspired by G.K. Chesterton, who calls sleep the ultimate act of faith. Bit of a disappointment as she is known as a solitary, not a sleeper.

Text from Hugo. Seems the spell backfired and he is now being moved to a prison somewhere near Nottingham – which rather precludes visiting, luckily for me. It also means he will shed Sam, at least for a while, to my profound relief. Later, Sam himself also texted, saying he'd be in touch about the book soon. Phew. We all know what that means.

Thursday 6 June

Joy! Fingal has been sacked! Or has resigned with the full agreement of Gerard, not sure which. Either way, he's not coming back. The word is that he's starting his own bookshop on the Isle of Mull. Drusilla, Fay and I agreed we didn't care where he went or what he did so long as it was far from us, and we went out for coffee and cake to celebrate.

Sales and Marketing left in confusion by Fingal's departure – or, rather, the mess he left behind him. They are not answering his phone because it's just too horrible and are all hiding behind his voicemail. Roland got permission to look at Fingal's email, but it transpires that he deleted all his sent messages when he left, which makes it difficult to pick up his tracks.

Thank God he's gone. At least he can't cause us any more trouble.

Friday 7 June

We seem to be weirdly low on stock in the warehouse. Many complaints from the trade that we are failing to fulfil orders for the spring titles. Because the information came from the warehouse itself, no one believed it at first. Gerard just said, 'I expect their system's down,' and went back to reading *Private Eye*. Fay, too, refused to take it seriously, saying, 'The warehouse just can't count,' while Drusilla was equally light-hearted, saying, 'Well, if someone has been purloining the stock, you'd need a jolly lot of space to store it all, wouldn't you, such as a Scottish castle, eh?' when they both stopped laughing and looked at each other.

'It's worth checking,' said Drusilla.

'It's worth checking,' said Fay. Together they rushed into Gerard's office and within ten minutes the rumour was all round the place that Fingal has been siphoning books out of the warehouse to his own private premises for re-sale. For once Gerard rose to the occasion.

'Well now,' he said, pulling at his side whiskers. 'Let's hope that Fingal does better with them than we do.'

This discord seemed to permeate the building as when I went to get a print-out of the edited *The Natural Kindness Manual* I found the printer had broken down again. I had heard a rumour that there was a paper jam, but the reality was even worse as I found the machine lying on the floor in several pieces, the engineer lying prone in their midst while examining the underneath, as if like Hugo and his spells he himself had been struck down by the powers he had summoned.

Sunday 9 June
Texted Hugo to see how he was settling in to his new prison to which he replied. 'Not good. They've offered me an NVQ in bricklaying or plumbing, I can take my choice.'

Monday 10 June
Hah! Gerard asked Roland, currently in the North, to go and call on Fingal. Bet Fingal didn't factor that in. Roland, thus sent as an instrument of justice, arrived at Fingal's Edinburgh apartment at the same time as the Scottish police. He said it was packed with boxes of books. This shatters the castle myth, by the way; Roland said that Fingal's flat is actually quite small.

Fingal himself is thought to have fled the country.

I don't know. I feel as if some intruder had got in with an axe in the night and hacked another hole in the keel of our ship. The books are, of course, insured against theft, storm, fire and most Acts of God, but how two-faced can you get? Disloyalty, treachery, betrayal – they're the worst.

The photocopier died today, finally. Someone covered it with a big green sheet of baize.

Tuesday 11 June
Blissful quiet has returned, thank God. Books all said to be out of Fingal's flat and being conveyed back to their rightful places.

Gerard says we should draw a line and move on.

Had to go down to Accounts with the advance on delivery for Ivan Skrulewski's *The Natural Kindness Manual*, which I'd unaccountably forgotten. Chief accountant Charlene received it without enthusiasm. She looked a shade weary. I asked her how she was. She said she was in the middle of calculating the annual royalties.

'Oh dear,' I said. 'That is a job.'

'Yeah, brings you down when most of it is in deficit. By the way, Mortimer, now you mention him, where *are* all Professor Skrulewski's contracts?'

A cold trickle went down my spine.

'Don't you have them?'

'I've got paper versions of 1983 and 1985, that's all. Where are all the others? There's nothing on the system. How are we supposed to calculate what he's due – guess?'

I thought it was a bit of an academic conversation given that the standard contract hasn't changed at all over the years – nor, much, the sales – but sensed that this was not the moment to mention this.

'I'll go and look for them.'

'Well, hurry up! Royalties wait for no man! I'm sure we had this conversation last year… You know, Mortimer, I'm not even sure we've got enough in the kitty to pay what we do owe him. It'll be tight, I can tell you that.'

I waited to hear more, but Charlene seemed disinclined to unburden herself further, and her face grew increasingly grim and furrowed as she continued to work her way through the royalties spreadsheet.

Wednesday 12 June

A general time of new beginnings. We have a massive, brand new photocopier cum printer which looks equipped to fly to the moon and back. It adds a definite frisson to the landing area: not a very nice one. In fact, I'd say that this is a malign being if ever there was one, squatting there like an imp of darkness. This was confirmed by my first encounter with it, where it swiftly showed its real colours and, as a demonstration of its speed-printing capabilities, churned up the manuscript of *Wilderness Therapy for Wellbeing*, and then jammed for two hours. Everyone crowded round offering advice as if to a casualty, removing pages which had been madly ironed into hot folds, torn half-pages, and infinitesimal scraps of paper from every conceivable nook and cranny of its hot, metallic being. Fay even ran off for her tweezers as it would not function again until every single shred of paper had been removed and kept flashing urgent messages at us as to where the next was hidden, in ever more inaccessible folds of metal. When finally back in action, it spat the MS out in chunks of ten pages, each shot through with staples. I then spent a further twenty minutes unpicking all the staples, pricking my thumb several times in the process, until all 368 pages were running consecutively in due order. It seemed better to do that than risk another run-in. And I didn't want to waste paper, though the photocopier itself seems to have no qualms about this, indeed no ecological conscience whatsoever.

When I complained to Gerard that it didn't seem to like me, he said, 'I don't think it likes any of us much.' Apparently it wrecked *Those Are Pearls*, a slim volume of Gerard's own poems, this morning.

'Definitely not an influence for good so far,' said Gerard in his most toffish way, thumb in lapel. 'Maybe I should have the bishop come in and exorcise it,' which I thought was going a bit far, even in jest.

Thursday 13 June

Bishop Molly seen kicking the photocopier first thing this morning. She popped in to photocopy some agendas for an urgent meeting about her contracts with Gerard and the other trustees, which were too top secret to allow into the hands of Ursula. She must have regretted it bitterly as again it took the combined efforts of about eight people to prise the remnants of her agenda from the photocopier, after which various details of the secret meeting were in several pairs of hands, and, more importantly, under several pairs of eyes. I think Fay must have seen a different scrap of paper to the one I did as she is looking very grave and troubled but won't say what about. I am sure she is wrestling with her conscience, as to whether she should tell us what she managed to see. But I suppose our chances of sharing it are slim. If Fay thinks she has right on her side, she will carry the secret to the grave, much as her human side would love to share it. Drusilla said, 'I wonder who's paying for all this, given our current parlous condition?'

After her meeting, Molly returned to crack a bottle of champagne over the new photocopier. I thought she hit it rather hard. Fay muttered darkly, 'Trust her to turn up for the party. Where's the work, I'd like to know!' It's true that, never averse to a glass of champagne, Molly was off again as soon as it was quaffed, with a wave of the hand, saying she was going back home to her desk to beaver on with the book, so that Drusilla and Fay were baulked of their obvious intent to descend on her and shake a progress report out of her.

I wonder is the new machine fitted with spy cameras. There's definitely something a bit funny about it.

From: Gerard Delamere Sent: 13 June 17.27 To: ALL@HQ
Subject: New photocopier

I am intending to provide some training on the photocopier. This would involve the basic functions as well as how to change the tonner etc. The idea is to ensure that as well as using the machine we use it in a safe manner.

I would like to get some idea of numbers of interested parties. If you are interested can you please let me know.

Very kindly yours,

Gerard Delamere, Publisher
The House of Marvellous Books
Wayfarers & Wilderness – our award-winning nature list
Sailing through Storms – transcendence through crisis

Don't judge each day by the harvest you reap but by the seeds that you plant

—Robert Louis Stevenson

The smallest act of kindness is worth more than the grandest intention

—Oscar Wilde

Can't wait. I'll be first on the list. Interesting that Gerard also sounds distinctly nervous of the photocopier.

Needless to say, Ethel emailed all round to say that 'toner' was the correct spelling, not 'tonner.'

Friday 14 June

Ursula's birthday. As she doesn't know the real date, she chose the Queen's official one which means that it varies from year to year, tracking the second Saturday in June. As reigning Marks & Sparks queen, she brought in brownies, coffee cake and lemon bakewell tarts for the traditional afternoon tea, and we took the opportunity to raise a glass to our royal patron. The celebration slightly quelled by a rapidly circulating rumour that we are moving to an industrial park in the North, near the warehouse in Middlesbrough.

Given permission to go home early after this, alas, she ended the week by managing to get herself trapped on an empty train bound for the Chingford sidings, her progress punctuated by frantic mobile phone calls to Ethel as she was swept into a tunnel and on to her fate. Like St Brendan on his journey from God knows how to God knows where, she was driven far from home, the gales and tides of fortune pulling her on to her unknown destination. It seems that she just hopped back on the train because she thought she'd left her bag on it, when the doors closed and the train took off and she was now on the empty train progressing through the Tottenham marshes at a steady forty-five miles an hour... Ethel told her to walk through the train to the front and rap on the wall to the driver.

Ethel in a good mood, perhaps softened up by Ursula's mishaps. In a moment of rare light-heartedness, she suggested the new photocopiers be christened Gog and Magog, after the ancient giants who guarded London. It was my first intimation that there were two of them! But apparently the other one is a colour photocopier and quite harmless, as no one can get the code for it – it's a closely guarded secret known only to Design.

Sister Evangeline has called several times over the last few days, fortuitously missing me each time. Every time I called her back she was in silence for the day and couldn't be disturbed. In the end I emailed her asking if she cared to state what she wanted by email. Finally, she replied. It was only to say she hadn't done the sleep synopsis, and would it be all right to have an eight-week deadline for it. Eight weeks to do one or two A4 pages? And why couldn't she just have emailed me that in the first place?

Saturday 15 June

I wonder, would I get sacked if I took a vow of silence?

Sunday 16 June

Still toying with the vow of silence idea. It must be very restful. And if other people can disrupt and delay work with it, why not I? Think of Brendan's island of the monks of Ailbe, who eat magic loaves, don't age and maintain complete silence. After all, employers have a duty to respect the scruples of those they employ. Indeed, given that we do so much by email, would it matter? Would anyone even notice? Ivan and Sister Evangeline are about the only ones who use the phone anyway.

Actually spent an all but silent day as I saw no one, apart from saying hello, thank you and goodbye to Ahmed in the corner shop when I dropped by for milk and the Sunday papers.

Monday 17 June
Decided I would go ahead with the vow of silence. Leaving my flat was easy. So was the commute in. However, Ivan Skrulewski had left an urgent message at 7.30am for me to call him as soon as I got in, which I did at 8.20am. I said as little as possible – easy enough as he did all the talking. He ranted and raved about how he wouldn't go ahead with publication of *Nature and the Golden Rule* unless it carried a coloured photograph of his good self on the back cover. This despite the fact that we are just about to go to print. Also, despite the fact that he's published numerous titles with us, without worrying about this. I thought of parading past Gerard's office with this information on a placard, or slipping a letter under his office door, or at least emailing him, but regretfully decided that silence had to be broken in the interests of urgency, so went to see him in person. Gerard sighed and said, 'Thought it was something like that. I heard he'd called. Sounds to me like someone has been talking to him. He's very easily influenced, you know.'

I said that Ivan had never really seemed to give that impression.

'No,' said Gerard. 'No, I know. He veils it very well. English isn't his first language, of course.'

'No?'

'No. He's rather sensitive about it. Hence his tendency to make a bit of a fuss. He's done very well for himself. Very well indeed, really, all things considered. Started from quite poor circumstances in Palmers Green.'

Gerard heaved another sigh and said, 'Well, if it's a deal-breaker, we'd better agree, I suppose.'

This speedy agreement made me very uneasy. Gerard gave the distinct impression of having other things on his mind than my lead author. However, this reminded me I still needed to find all of Ivan's missing contracts. I started with the obvious place, the royalties cupboard. For once I hit lucky. There they all were, filed under P for Professor. Ursula again. Took them all in a small box to Charlene who rolled her eyes and said, 'Has no one ever heard of scanning in this place?' Promised faithfully to do the job myself once she had finished with them all.

The photocopier still hasn't settled down into its new abode. It jammed three times while printing Fay's manuscript *Sacred Stones, Shining Water.* That's the nearest I've seen Fay come to normal uncontrolled human rage.

Tuesday 18 June
Fay said she knows Middlesbrough, our destined change of address, as she visited once and vowed never to return and hence would not be among those making the move. She sat down then and there and drafted her letter of resignation.

Wednesday 19 June
In my capacity as acting health and safety officer, went to check out how Moriarty was performing in his role of holy terror to the mice. Has to be admitted he conveyed an impression of quite some laxity lounging in the basement. The armchairs down there are pretty comfy. In fact, I joined him with a cup of tea and a cherry scone, and we both dozed off peacefully for three-quarters of an hour…

*

Moriarty, the Gaelic Ó Muircheartaigh, 'navigator' or 'seaworthy', muir meaning sea (cognate to the Latin mare, 'sea') and ceardach, skilled. Ship's cat, legendary feline seafarer, a sensitive, a stowaway of first proportion, Moriarty has weathered so many storms with us, despatched so many mice. Did Brendan have a ship's cat? A maritime mascot with sea-green eyes, leaving a trail of his own special atmosphere, a whiff of the ocean, something tarry and briny and exciting…

*

Thursday 20 June

The rumour about moving to the North turns out to be false. Gerard, presented with Fay's resignation, raised an eyebrow and said, 'Middlesbrough? Where's that?'

He then tore her letter across and dropped it in the bin, saying loftily, 'My dear young lady, we're not going there, and you're not going anywhere. We need you here.'

Glad about that. It would I suppose have been sad in its way to lose Fay, but more, highly tedious to leave London. No, life outside this library seems unthinkable. I just can't see the House flourishing anywhere else.

Bishop Molly reported to have given her entire advance to charity after the Lord prompted her to. Drusilla getting legal advice on its return.

Friday 21 June

Summer solstice

Oh dear, what a week. Gerard fell off a stepladder at home yesterday! He is absolutely the most accident-prone person I know. He was in his own library – a converted dovecote in his grounds – going up to a high shelf in quest of *Wildlife in the Wake of the Hanseatic League*, a 1920s account of birds and animals along the trade routes of the south Baltic and North Sea coasts that he thought we might rejig into a new publication, when his foot slipped. Alas, he landed on his posterior extremity, as he might say; very painful, I gather. While everyone was sincerely sympathetic, there's little doubt that this news fair brightened our day.

'How about a nice curry at Neel's?' said Drusilla, and we all sailed merrily out and gorged on bitingly hot prawn curry and the most delicious biryani rice and lovely, hot, puffy, charred-black-in-spots naan bread, dipping it into the delicious buttery lentil dahl.

Drusilla said, 'Gerard simply can't keep out of trouble, why is that, do you think? Some kind of complex? The personality of the accident-prone has always interested me. Do you think there's a book in it, accident-prone personages in history, like Alfred and the cakes, say? You don't attract that much trouble without unconsciously willing it.'

Saturday 22 June
Quiet day. Caught up with shopping, laundry etc.

Ought to go book sorting at Hugo's tomorrow. It's been a while.

Sunday 23 June
Too nice to bury myself in more dusty antiquarian books. Went to Kew Gardens and walked around and then just sat in the shade of the pagoda. Delightful.

Monday 24 June

From: Ursula Woodrow Sent: 24 June 8.15 To: ALL@HQ
Subject: *Please be kind* list

This week **please be kind** to:

- Gerard Delamere recovering from an unfortunate domestic accident.
- Bishop Molly Roper for inspiration for her book.
- Sister Evangeline ditto.
- The House in its current difficulties.
- Anatole and Alexander Krukinov, to help them have the wisdom to direct it.

Ursula

Ursula Woodrow, editorial assistant
The House of Marvellous Books
Wayfarers and Wilderness, our award-winning nature list

We've long regarded the *Please be kind* list as an infallible source of gossip and news but who exactly are these Krukinovs? What difficulties? What is going on? I think something has been revealed to the kindness list or at least to Gerard that is hidden from the eyes of the rest of us. We all agreed that it was time for a word with Gerard about this on his return, but an urgent email from Gerard working from home to ALL@HQ pinged into our boxes, asking us to delete the kind thoughts list immediately, as certain individuals/causes had been inappropriately listed. We were promised a new one shortly.

Tuesday 25 June

Gerard in, moving rather stiffly but otherwise whole. Of course no one dared mention the subject of his unfortunate tumble. Maybe he'll explain further once he's got over the shock. Fay did, however, quiz him about the mysterious mentions of the Krukinovs in the kindness list.

In his most reassuring way, Gerard said there was nothing to worry about, yet. He said he was sure we'd understand that he was not at liberty to speak further, and that we would know more when the time was ripe.

'I hope I – er – may be able to send out another email in a day or two,' he said in his best Oxbridge manner, a compound of sweetness, light, authority and complete untrustworthiness. And with that we had perforce to be content.

Sister Evangeline sent in her synopsis for *Sister Night: Sacred Sleep and the Forest of Dreams*, finally. She seems to have no idea of earthly time whatsoever! Alas, it is 8,900 words long and absolute rubbish.

Wednesday 26 June

I scanned the re-jigged kindness list and was interested to see that the references to difficulties and the Krukinovs had been taken out. All very unsatisfactory.

Thursday 27 June

Editorial board, postponed from Tuesday due to Gerard's accident. I entered the Fisher Room to an unusual silence. There was a stranger seated at the table. Moreover, he had taken the throne. I think the last time someone sat in that was when we had a visit from the Archbishop of Canterbury. The visitor was clearly unaware of his presumption. He was short and stocky in his navy suit, probably in his late forties, with a *brosse* of receding fair hair, athletic shoulders and a slight smile of covert, private irony. High cheekbones, a tired air and sad, blue, byzantine eyes with a downward tilt added to this impression. He surveyed us as we came in and took our accustomed seats.

'Hello,' said Drusilla, and was palpably about to introduce herself and launch enquiries when Gerard came in.

'Good morning, good morning. Everyone introduced? Good, then let's get stuck straight in. —Fay.'

Drusilla opened her mouth but Fay was already off, presenting *Mythic Myopia: Making the mysteries visible*. Drusilla, distracted from our visitor, or, more likely, playing up to a new audience, responded with a twenty-minute talk about her first boss the great editorial manager Tip, even more formidable than she herself, and how she never missed a comma or a full stop in forty years on the *Encyclopaedia Britannica* or whatever it was. It went on and on and Fay was getting increasingly restive until at last she broke out, 'But I don't understand, Drusilla: what has Tip to do with this book?'

'Oh,' said Drusilla, and, with an air of explaining everything, and a nod to the stranger, 'it's the sort of book Tip would not have liked.'

The meeting went its merry way. But to my relief, they were all very supportive about turning down Sister Evangeline's proposal.

'What does she know about sleep?' said Fay, leafing through the many pages, adding, 'I'm glad it's your problem, not mine.'

I said, 'What do you mean, it's my problem?'

'Why wouldn't she tackle solitude?' asked Gerard, as if it was my fault. 'I mean, she's known as an anchoress. *Sister Solitude* would be the perfect follow-up to *Sister Shepherdess*. I just don't think *Sister Night* works.'

I said, 'I did try to persuade her. Like other writers, she would appear to have a predilection for topics that aren't her métier.'

'You weren't strong enough with her, that's the problem,' said Drusilla. 'These *religieuses* need a firm hand.'

'You tackle her then!' I said. 'Maybe she's got a complex about male superiority. She may respond better to a woman.'

Gerard cut across the squabbling. 'No, no, it's not that. She must be under contract to someone else. Wasn't she tied up with Calling Crane a while back?'

A hush fell. It was generally felt he had hit upon the truth. The stranger looked along his chiselled cheekbones from one to the other of us. Gerard sat frowning and pulling at his side whiskers for a few moments.

'Go back to her and ask her if she'd do silence.'

'I think she's already done it. Wasn't her *God's Soundless Footfall* a bestseller a few years ago? With Calling Crane, as it happens?'

'No matter. We can rejig it to look different. Calling Crane are more commercial than we are anyway, you must know that by now, Mortimer. Different market, different readership. Start thinking of titles... *Sailing after Silence*? No, that sounds more like Molly... Might even suggest it to her,' and, with a glance at our observer, 'she'd be good for 40,000 copies, I'm sure.'

'I don't think we can afford to contract Molly again right now,' said Fay, with restraint. 'But Sister Evangeline can do it anyway. It's about time we started training her more intensively to take over from Molly.'

'She hasn't got a boat,' said Drusilla.

Gerard waved this away. 'Let's have a look at the five-year sales. *How to Talk so Plants Will Listen,* Matthew Creedy and Nathan Cramp. That was a *succès d'estime*, I fear... yes, thought so... *The Tree Vigilantes of East London*... hm... 2,300 copies.

Peregrinations with the Peregrini... that was another Creedy & Cramp, wasn't it...? *Wolf Ghost: Hauntological revenants and lost species,* life sales 784... *The Black Cat in the Playground: Mythical manifestations of our time*... *To Holy Island by Campervan,* life sales 1,403... hm, thought Lindisfarne didn't have campervan facilities...' (Gerard is always right about this type of arcane fact.) '...*Home is where the Hygge is*... yes, well, we'll have a go anyway. Make an offer to Sister Evangeline after this meeting, Mortimer. We can't afford to let these media nuns go.'

'A recluse is always good publicity,' said Fay.

'It acts as a vicarious pilgrimage for the readers,' agreed Gerard. 'We can use that nice pic of her with her veil lifting and her habit flapping in the wind.'

'Yes, but I—' I began, but Gerard cut across impatiently.

'It's a no-brainer, Mortimer, as we say in the trade. What does it matter if it's the same book in disguise? It's my convinced theory that authors only ever have one book in them anyway.'

'So cynical!' said Fay. 'How can you be so cynical, Gerard?'

'That is publishing, my dear young lady.'

'You're a disgrace to the industry!'

'Nonsense! I—'

'If I could just interject a moment,' I said. 'I'm not objecting to the book per se. What I don't understand is how I'm suddenly landed with Sister Evangeline in the first place. I thought she was Fay's author.'

'No way,' said Fay swiftly.

'But she's a straightforward spiritual author.'

'Leave out the straightforward,' said Fay. 'She's never been my author, Mortimer. You're the one who encouraged her.'

I was flabbergasted. 'Encouraged her? Me? Drusilla?'

'Not me,' said Drusilla. 'I've got my hands full with the Pope and *The Gift of Despair*.'

'Yes,' said Fay. 'And Dr Chauncey Rivers is a full-time job, as you well know, Mortimer.'

I made one last attempt.

'Come on, Fay. She writes about islands a lot, you know. How about *No Nun is an Island*?'

'You can have the Pope if you want, too,' said Drusilla.

The observer had lost his air of inward, enigmatic irony and was frowning in open bewilderment.

'I don't want either Sister Evangeline or the Pope, thank you very much! I've got sufficient of my own complexes to deal with, without taking on those of others!'

'There you go, Mortimer,' said Gerard. 'All yours. I'm sure we all appreciate your scruples very much. Don't worry, I think the good Sister has a soft spot for you.'

I was left speechless.

'Well,' said Fay, as we all converged in the kitchen after the meeting. 'Who was the inscrutable stranger?'

'Didn't have much to say for himself,' agreed Drusilla.

It was generally agreed that Gerard owed us some sort of explanation.

While we were in the kitchen, Fay had a word with me. She said on no account ever to drive with Sister Evangeline. She said Sister E had given her a lift back to London after an event at Durham Cathedral one night, taking a short cut through the wilds of County Durham and speeding down the middle of the black country lanes at 70 miles an hour. When Fay protested, and begged her at least to keep to the left, Sister E said that it was, 'All right, because we'll see the lights coming towards us.' Fay concluded, 'Now that she's your author, Mortimer, I thought you ought to know.'

Friday 28 June

Drusilla, Fay and I went to see Gerard. He welcomed us warmly into his kingly office. Fay grilled him about the mysterious mentions of the Krukinovs and the silent stranger in yesterday's meeting. Gerard said the time had come to call in outside help. Fay said, 'But that's not the point. Why are we not being told what's happening?'

In his most reassuring way, Gerard said there was nothing to worry about, yet. He said, 'As soon as I am at liberty to speak, you'll be the first to know. I hope I may be able to send out another email in a day or two.'

Then he gave us a long talk all about the wildlife that can be seen from his office window – jays, magpies, sparrows, swallows, starlings and even the occasional fox – and then moved on to badgers and his childhood baling hay in rural Gloucestershire. He gave a gripping description of coming face to face with a badger raised on its hind legs, baring its fangs at him from a corner of a barn, and how he didn't stay to argue. With his long, greying side whiskers, grey hair and hunched brown-tweed back, he was quite convincing in his imitation, snarling with yellowed fangs and hands curled into realistic claws while he tiptoed menacingly round the room. Taking the hint, neither did we stay, and fled none the wiser.

Apart from that, the only excitement was trying to find a copy of *Country Walks for Phobic Folk: Overcoming the fear of open spaces* for a reader unable to leave the house to buy it. Ursula came flapping in from reception, having taken a call from the disgruntled would-be purchaser.

'Well, I can understand she might have difficulties getting to the bookshop, but what about Amazon?' I said.

Ursula looked puzzled. 'They're listing it as unavailable for some reason. I'll have to check the consignment. We appear to have run out of copies, too. At least, I can't find any in the stacks and no one seems to have any on their desks.'

It wasn't until lunchtime that we discovered that the reason we had no copies was that the book had never actually got printed, despite publication having officially been in February. The printer with the long-suffering patience of his kind was, in fact, still waiting for us to give him the go-ahead to press the button. This does explain why the authors have been complaining they hadn't had their gratis yet, although that rather makes them sound like horses waiting for their oats. On the whole I think it's amazing how patient people can be. I'm sure I wouldn't have waited so long for my six free copies.

I shall have to have words with Scarlett Blyth in Production, who should have tackled this long ago.

Saturday 29 June

Very hot. Quick flit to The Gap to see Albany. He was neat and summery in his light suit and straw boater as always, but said he was a bit tired and didn't want to do our usual walk along the prom so we sat on a bench and had an ice cream. He said, 'How's work?' and I said, 'Same old same old. Nothing ever happens there,' and we sat in companionable silence, eating our vanilla cones.

Sunday 30 June

Albany persuaded me to stay over. To breakfast *chez* Patti, in her steel and chrome kitchen beneath a huge black and white photo of Patti herself in her (very Dolly Parton-like) prime with the advice, *Free-range egg me, can't be put into any recipe.*

After that Patti took her lab Rinser out, and Albany and I went round to his flat and unearthed a couple of old deckchairs and sat in the garden and had a gin and tonic or two while he read me out selections from his autobiography. Albany looked ten years younger at the end of it.

Felt quite sad to leave him at the end of the day.

Monday 1 July

Back to work, revived and refreshed, to find two men with clipboards making an inventory of the library; at least, they were going round the shelves, pulling out books and making notes. I asked Ursula who they were. She said, 'The Lord knows. Gerard asked me to let them in and give them carte blanche. It's probably something to do with the insurance.'

She thought a moment and added, 'They don't seem to speak much English. I expect we're using a foreign company because it's cheaper.'

Then, seeing Drusilla pass, she called after her, 'Oh, Drusilla! Molly called! She can't make the eleventh for the Vatican after all, can you rearrange?'

Drusilla came scurrying back to the post room. 'Sssh!'

'Oh yes,' said Ursula in her clarion tones. 'Sorry, I forgot it was all to be a deadly dark secret,' and in her sibilant whisper, 'Anyway, she's got something else on, I can't remember what. Something on the Essex coast. Apologies.'

'Bother,' said Drusilla. 'I was kind of relying on her. For all her faults, Molly does know how to drive a hard bargain.'

'I'll come with you,' I suggested.

'Oh, Mortimer, I wish you could, but they wouldn't approve of a single woman travelling with a single man, unless you were a man of the cloth. Even at my age,' with a satisfied sigh.

Tuesday 2 July

Remembered to ask Production to tell the printer to press the button for our long-delayed *Country Walks for Phobic Folk*. He was not very accommodating, and said he wouldn't have a slot for three weeks now. Hope our reader can hang on that long! Scarlett Blyth not very amenable either. Tried to have words with her about the delay but she merely shrugged and said it was my own fault, and that she had other things on her mind.

Wednesday 3 July

Used the post room to send the latest batch of Hugo's books back to the libraries where they rightfully belong, in Dublin, Munich and Madrid. I'm sorry to take liberties with work facilities, but I get so tired waiting in the post office queues while everyone takes out a mortgage and tells their life histories, and it's SO expensive.

Thursday 4 July

Disaster with *What Trees Talk About When They Talk About Love*! Production 'forgot' to tick the box that tells the printer to produce a laminated or glossy cover, rather than a matt one. You would have thought this was automated by now, given that every single one of our books has to be laminated, as the book trade won't deal in covers that will be thumb-marked as soon as picked up. Result – 2,300 copies that we have to pulp.

Production spent the day sitting outside on the steps of the library in the form of Scarlett Blyth, who made the mistake. Scarlett has been known to have been unhappy here for some time, and much more interested in some gruesome, convoluted database system she is concocting in her spare time called Nemesis. Such weird hobbies people have. At 4pm when it began to rain I took pity on her and went out with an umbrella and persuaded her to return to her desk. No one had noticed she had been missing, of course.

Friday 5 July

Tree Talk authors cutting up rough. Understandable. I've assured them reprinting is taking place as we speak. To make matters worse, the printer delivered all 2,300 copies here by mistake, instead of to the warehouse in Middlesbrough, and Ursula unpacked all seventy-six boxes over the library floor before I discovered this. There must be a hex on this darned book. Scarlett is off with stress – I suspect, working on her horrible computer program, Nemesis. Well, if it keeps her happy and out of further mischief. It's highly unlikely to affect me.

Saturday 6 July
Sat in bed and read Agatha Christie. I've got to have a break from Proust. Ate toast, with butter and Marmite, and then with peanut butter and blackcurrant jam. Didn't really get out of PJs.

Sunday 7 July
Worked on Brendan. I feel my poor book has suffered as a result of Hugo's depravations on my time.

*

Shipwreck. That final grounding, a sudden crunch against the rocks, a sickening tearing and splintering, and that last, fatal uprush of water...

*

Monday 8 July
Not a harmonious day. I should have been warned when I opened the overseas rights cupboard in the stacks first thing, only to have a ton or so of foreign editions descend on my head and scatter themselves over the floor. I do wish Rights would tidy up after themselves. Surely we don't require eight copies of the Taiwan edition of *A Return to Earth Closets*. Asked Ursula to go through it and tidy up. She seized on the chance to go through another cupboard.

Tuesday 9 July
Molly in like the breath of heaven and called all the ladies together for an impromptu meeting in the basement. Fay came in to me afterwards – the first time I've ever seen her in tears.

'Naturally we were expecting to hear a clarion call to solidarity, a revelation about what's going on, or at least a rousing prayer meeting for the future of her book and the house,' she sobbed. 'Instead of which, what did she pull out of her briefcase but a handful of thongs!'

'Um... I'm not too sure what they are?'

'Items of intimate female attire, Mortimer. In black silk, though some were red or yellow. All primary colours apart from girly pink or hot fuchsia, no subtle shades of blue or silver or grey. She said she was doing some market research for a friend of hers who's starting a business selling designer thongs. "Any opinions, girls? Would you pay £64 each for one of these? Be honest, now."' Fay gulped again and applied a handkerchief to her eyes. 'The prospects for the House are hopeless. Molly will never write that book. She's conquered the flesh and the Devil, but she's too enamoured of the world. She's in thrall to frivolity.'

Wednesday 10 July

Ivan Skrulewski's row with House Ed still rumbling on. His email said: 'After a rather long and somewhat irritating working day yesterday, I returned to my flat to find Ethel's email. She has done it again!!!! An absolutely unreasonable deadline!!!! Does she imagine that I sit at my computer day in day out awaiting her emails so that I can give an instant response? I was incandescent with anger.

'I am not going to communicate further with Ethel, any future emails she sends I will not even open, in order to spare my blood pressure.

'When I have had a chance to properly consider the proofreader's questions I will forward my response to *you*, Mortimer.'

Thursday 11 July

Drusilla gone to Rome. She says you have to get up early and take the 5.30am flight because in July and August the Vatican closes at midday and doesn't re-open, thus making an early start imperative if you want to get any business done.

'What do they do the rest of the afternoon?'

Drusilla shrugged. 'Pray? The world has to be kept going somehow.'

Hoorah! Some good news amidst all the mayhem. The *Tree Talk* authors have agreed to buy 1,800 copies at cost price between them! – as they can't bear the thought of wasting so many trees – leaving us with a mere 250 which I'm sure we can squirrel away in the stacks. Ursula and I packed them all back into their boxes this morning – thirty boxes for each author. I myself personally saw all sixty boxes off onto the 4.30pm van and waved them goodbye with a light heart. Farewell, *Tree Talk*!

Scarlett hasn't returned to work after this debacle; in fact she's given in her notice and has a doctor's note to say she needn't return before this expires. I noticed that the messages on her leaving card were rather brief.

Spent the afternoon in the stacks, accompanied by an interested Moriarty, hiding away the last 250 copies of *Tree Talk*. Had to stop him sharpening his claws on a nice tempting pile of them. Have to say they took up rather more room than I'd anticipated. Luckily the shelves in the old cupboards are deep and voluminous, so I was able to double-pack them behind other worthy offerings on wilderness and wildlife, bird flights, seasonal shifts, seashells, sheep, islands, night skies, ancient myths and modern-day legends. Forests of books, in fact. Strange to spend time down there. The sound of the London traffic was hushed and it took little effort to imagine authors long dead and gone whispering from behind the files. I could hear only too well what they were saying: *What happened to my sales? What happened to my sales?* At one point I got quite a fright, as I distinctly heard some books tumbling to the ground, but when I went to see, everything was on the shelves and all was quiet. Doubtless just Moriarty prowling around. Such ghostly fancies apart, it gave me a feeling of great satisfaction finally to tidy away all traces of the ill-fated *What Trees Talk*

About When They Talk About Love. So that's that out of the way, thank God!

Friday 12 July

Drusilla back from Rome negotiating with the Vatican. She looked weary and said she hadn't made as much progress as she would have liked. The cardinals are being rather challenging and asking her what proof she has that the Book exists. She says she hasn't got anything to show them, but neither have they anything to show her.

She said, 'I told them it's all a question of faith, not proof.'

I said, 'What about the vellum scrap?'

'I'm keeping that up my sleeve for the time being. I want to get a little bit closer to the Pope before I produce that.'

Been quite a stressful week so I gladly joined the others for an after-work drink at the Lady Luck. Had a long talk with Fay about the best way to propose, should the occasion ever arise. She said the thing to do was to be masterful. She kindly let me practise on her and I proposed forty times in forty different ways. Fay, a stickler for perfection as ever, kept suggesting I try it just once more.

Monday 15 July

Rumours that Gerard was mugged over the weekend, by irate booksellers, or, in another version, by some eastern European heavy who mistook him for someone else. But in the depths of rural Gloucestershire? Of course, farming is full of accidents, indeed I believe it's the UK's deadliest industry, and there's no reason why Gerard shouldn't have sustained one in his day to day life without any question of mugging.

Told Drusilla about my coup in getting rid of *What Trees Talk About When They Talk About Love*. She admitted she thought it clever. Hah! Looking forward to a quiet week now!

Tuesday 16 July

From: Mair Jones Sent: 16 July 07.58 To: Mortimer Blakeley-Smith Subject: *What Trees Talk About When They Talk About Love*

Dear Mortimer,

Sorry to be a nuisance, but Phoebe received her 900 copies of the book last week but I have never received the 900 I agreed to buy. I wonder whether you ever got my email asking for the books? If not, can I still get any?

Best wishes – Mair

Aaaaargh! What do the English do in such a case? Run amok, beat the walls with their fists and heads, then compose another polite email. Spent the rest of the day trying to track the wretched books. You'd think 900 books would be hard to misplace, yet they seem to have vanished into thin air…

Gerard arrived looking dignified with one black eye and a bandage round his head. Naturally no one dreamed of asking him for details, and we all just got on with it and ignored his dressings and injuries in the best British way.

Editorial board. In these troubled times, Gerard suggested we leave an empty chair for Elijah, in hope that inspiration and guidance would come to us. Unfortunately, I think Elijah must have been occupied elsewhere, as Fay and Drusilla had a dreadful row about Dr Chauncey Rivers's new book (the sequel to his *Encounters*, which Fay snapped up months ago) *Waiting for You: Edges, empty landscapes, and the eerie in England, Scotland and Wales*. On the face of it an innocuous book enough until it transpired that Fay wanted to start an entire list for her new author, to be called *Blue Marble*, after the 1972 image of

Earth taken by the Apollo 17 crew. I draw a veil over Drusilla's objections to this favouritism.

Not one of our more successful editorial board meetings.

Drusilla and I went out and had lunch in the secret garden, and a long discussion about whether Fay was losing her own marbles or was merely overly influenced by an author who was tall, Gaelic and rather personable.

Wednesday 17 July

Thank God! *Tree Talk* turned up! Mair emailed to say that all thirty boxes of books were sitting in front of her door when she got home; in fact, it was some time before she could gain access to her flat as they formed a neat tower blocking the entrance.

Phew! Thank God that's over!

Thursday 18 July

> From: Mair Jones Sent: 18 July 15.50 To: Mortimer Blakeley-Smith Subject: Re: What Trees Talk About When They Talk About Love
>
> Dear Mortimer,
>
> Sorry to be a bother but, if it's not too late, I have just heard from one of the contributors that he would love a publisher's copy. He is Charles Fonblanque, Gatehouse Cottage, Eryl Hall, St Asaph, Denbighshire. Our book seems to have given you lots of headaches so please don't bother about this if it is a problem as I can send him a copy of course! It would just be more of a thrill for him to get it direct from the publisher.
>
> With best wishes – Mair

Grrrrrr!

I have developed a nervous cough, which is very irritating. I was hardly aware of it until Fay pointed it out, somewhat crossly. She's on tenterhooks as Molly promised to deliver three chapters tomorrow.

Can't wait for my holiday, booked as usual to avoid the annual royalties fall-out, when the authors discover that their advances are all still earning out.

Friday 19 July

Alas, no Molly. One of her friends went into labour unexpectedly – she didn't even know she was pregnant, in fact – and Molly had to deliver the baby in her bathroom, so no chapters from her. I was struck by the way Molly seems to take it all in her stride, and to know exactly the right thing to do in such dramatic circumstances. Fay came scurrying out of her office and let off steam in mine for twenty minutes about how she didn't think Molly was serious about this book.

'I don't think she quite appreciates that without it, we could go to the wall,' she said. 'I suspect she hasn't written one word of it yet.'

''Course she hasn't! She won't write it!' came Drusilla's voice over the partition and she joined us. 'You'd better get busy, Fay.'

The truth is, Fay is highly talented at re-writing, or even simply writing inadequate or non-existent manuscripts into bestsellers, or at least into existence. Fay said she was busy channelling *Stepping Stones to Home*, via the islands of the Hebrides, Orkneys, Shetlands, Fair Isle, then Iceland, Greenland to Nova Scotia, written by a learned nature writer with almost no English, but would put Molly next on the list.

Absolute silence from the *Tree Talk* authors. Presumably they have now discovered just how much room 900 copies each take up in their respective living rooms, garages and halls.

My cough still going. Fay said, 'For goodness sake, Mortimer, haven't you got any cough sweets? It sounds like the bark of a seal: an attention-seeking seal.'

Very glad it's my holiday. I left at 4pm, as Charlene and Shannon were sending the royalties out on the evening van. I looked at the bundles of white envelopes all neatly stacked in piles in the post room and fled. They can just get along without me.

Saturday 20 July
Off to The Gap for Uncle Albany's eightieth, hoorah! He sat there looking pleased with all the attention, if a bit bemused, with that slightly cross, lost look that has won him so many female protectors, and said to me in a low voice, 'Didn't we just go through all this for my seventieth?' Generations of family swarmed down to the village hall, a severe outpost of Gallhampton, which Patti, Auntie Juls and Carol had decorated with bunting. I accepted gratefully Auntie Juls's offer of an early glass of champagne when I arrived. Things hotted up rapidly once all the aunts had had a glass or two and Juls and Carol took the opportunity to announce their engagement and forthcoming wedding next March. Albany said to me, 'Sit next to me, Mortimer, we two boys of the family must stick together.'

I said, 'I want a do like this for my fortieth,' but Albany shook his head and said, 'Don't think I'll be there for that one.'

'Oh come now. You must. It wouldn't be a party without you.'

He shook his head again. 'Got such a feeling I'm not going to make it. All this' – he waved a hand at the drunken aunts and chattering cousins – 'all feels more like a farewell to me. A send-off. Know what I mean?'

I protested, but there was something valedictory about it, it's true. I thought of Bede, whose swallow flies in at one end of the vast banqueting hall and then out again at the other end into the dark and stormy night. Or is it a sparrow? Swallow sounds so much better, I think. The mood was broken by Auntie Juls, who shouted, 'Mortimer! Get Albany! It's time for his pills! Put your hand up his shirt for his wallet, he can't reach it himself,' but I felt unable to take this liberty – the pill wallet was on a string round his neck – and in the general bustle of scolding aunts, the moment passed…

I rather wanted to walk back to the hotel and think about it all at the end of the evening, but as the only two routes were along a busy dual carriageway or through MOD property, was persuaded to wait my turn for a taxi with the others.

As it was a special occasion I'd booked in with the others into a posh hotel on the front with sea views but Auntie Juls was in the room next to me and snored all night. Wish I'd stuck to the old B&B.

Sunday 21 July
Big family breakfast at the cliff-top café. People distinctly jaded. Auntie Juls had smuggled in eight bottles of Prosecco and when these were surreptitiously distributed – I don't think the place has a licence - things began to look more cheerful. Auntie Juls gave her famous rendition of *Edelweiss*, with Carol accompanying her on the guitar. It was enough to bring tears to the eyes of a strong man. I have to admit I cried.

Nice to wind down after all that with an afternoon walk along Scrapsgate Bay. The sea was a beautiful green flecked with white, and, by some strange coincidence, I did see a seal! Must tell Fay. Uncle Albany and I were just strolling along the front when he grasped my arm and pointed out to sea. The seal, which was quite large, was swimming along all by itself and kept pausing to look round in the most human way. We kept pace with it for quite some time. I wondered was it curious about us here on the littoral and what we get up to.

Albany said, 'I could write a poem about that, Mortimer. In fact I already have. I'll look it out for you. It's called, *Selkies not made for land life*.'

We stood looking out to the horizon where, far off, a fishing trawler with its flags and trail of seagulls was making for port. I thought of Brendan and his coracle and longed likewise to take off into the blue unknown. To be away from all the dreary actuality of the land; to have just salt, lapping water and the occasional wing of a gull. I thought of the Irish poet-monks of medieval times, enlivening their manuscripts with scribbles in the margins about the cold, fresh wind and the sun glinting on the sea. I thought of my own novel, painstakingly chugging along like Brendan's own little curragh boat.

'Yes,' said Albany as we strolled along the sea wall where dried, black seaweed bubbles made popping noises under our feet. '*Yes,* I never wanted to be anywhere else but here. This is the place for me.'

We walked back in the early evening and got two cones of chips from the Scrapsgate Bay Fish Factory with loads of salt and vinegar and two big pickled onions. The brine ran down our chins as we bit into them and savoured the indefinable, silvery, piquant tang of chip-shop onions.

Monday 22 July

My God! I'm seal-haunted! I met a selkie! Behind the bar of the Old Pavilion on the beach, the pavilion-turned-assembly-rooms-turned-nightclub-turned-casino-turned-pub. Eyes of blue water, hair black and smooth round her head. Name of Nieve, variant of Niamh, daughter of the god of the sea. How can such a being be working, living and breathing here? Hasn't anyone else seen her, noticed her? She seems to have emerged wet from the waves, fresh with the freshness of fresh water, and unspoken to by human kind. I see her dancing by moonlight while her precious skin lies in a bundle beneath the rocks, and water worlds glimmer in her eyes.

Tuesday 23 July

Spent the morning in the Old Pavilion. Their policy of coffee refill made this easy, if slightly hard on the bladder. At lunchtime plucked up my courage and asked Nieve if she cared to go for a walk once she came off duty. She said yes!!!

Albany said he knew Nieve. He said she was a minx and tended to short-change customers unless carefully watched.

Wednesday 24 July
I seem to have entered another dimension. I was walking along the prom hand in hand with Nieve when, out of the blue, there was a fluttering of feathers and a flock of green parakeets went flying past us, almost through us, they were so close. In a moment or so they were perching on the branches of a nearby tree like heavy fruit. Nieve was laughing at my surprise. She said parakeets were as common as seagulls here. A magical moment. On impulse, begged Nieve to marry me. She laughed and said, sure, some day.

I'm engaged! I'm engaged! I'm engaged!

Thursday 25 July
Got drunk with Albany. Broke the news of my engagement and he smiled and said he hoped I'd be very happy. Later, went for a walk alone beneath the starry summer sky, beside the gently shushing summer waves. Rang Drusilla and told her all about Nieve. She said she was glad it had come to me at last. When I rang off I saw it was 2.13am. Oh dear.

Friday 26 July
I have no words to tell what has happened. Went down to see my betrothed and there, lying on the sand, in the shelter of the Old Pavilion turned pub, saw Nieve intertwined with – no, no, it doesn't bear thinking about. Felt as though someone had kicked me in the stomach.

Rushed back and packed and left early, forgoing the last day of my holiday.

Albany talked to me all the way to the station about the vicissitudes of love and how no girl was ever really worth it, but I hardly took any of it in.

Saturday 27 July

Got home to find Fay had kindly posted me a spare ticket she had for the Proms tonight but was too upset to go and therefore missed the St Matthew Passion, to my intense annoyance. Called Uncle Albany. He said, 'If I had a quid for the number of times I'd been rejected, Mortimer, I'd be a millionaire.'

For once I found his stance unhelpful, especially as it's palpably untrue – when was the last time he was rejected? I said, 'Yes, but it's not a million times, it's happened to me once and that's more than enough. It's my individual tragedy.'

He said, 'Mortimer, it just wasn't meant to be.'

I'm sorry to say I put the phone down at that point and went out for a long walk.

Later I called him back to apologise and he said not to worry, he knew just how I felt. He said it happened to us all at some point.

Sunday 28 July

Decided I couldn't let myself go to the dogs, so baked a big Victoria sponge to take into work as a post-holiday gesture, then went out and picked blackberries on Wimbledon Common. There were tons of them. I was at it for hours, with pricked, stained fingers and black fingernails. Does no one pick blackberries any more? I guess they're all too busy buying fashionable blueberries from the supermarket.

A neighbour pushed a note through my door at home saying there is a bees' nest in the eaves, and to keep my window closed until our local apiarists Maybee could be got in to deal with it.

Monday 29 July

To HQ. Got back to find a packet of cough sweets on my desk. That's very kind of someone.

I was unpacking my holiday offerings in the kitchen when Drusilla breezed in.

'Refreshed and revived?'

'No, not really. My marriage proposal was a fiasco.'

'Oh dear. So you're not an engaged man?'

'Not just at present, no.'

Drusilla, never one to waste sympathy, said briskly, 'Well, I think Gerard's got something to say to us, so maybe that will cheer you up.'

Sure enough, Gerard gathered us all round him, like a mother hen with so many chicks as he fondly put it, and gave us a longish talk – as Fay said, 'Without rhyme or reason.' He started off by saying how eccentric it is to run a publishing business from the premises of a library. Then he said the time had come to tell us more about the governing body's latest plan to work with a group of wealthy Russian intellectuals on their idealistic dream of an international network of digital libraries, so that knowledge was freely available to all. With our own dear library just to hand, we were the perfect partners to help promote this noble scheme and save the House.

'And what do they get out of it?' said Drusilla. 'The idealistic Russians, that is?'

'What do you mean, dear lady?'

'There seems to be something missing from the story. I can't put my finger quite on what. But I fail to see why a group of Russian intellectuals would want to work with us gratis, no matter how idealistic.'

Gerard said stiffly that the story was complete.

Naturally, it took no time at all for the talk to transmute into a discussion on bee-keeping – I think some parallel between this year's shortage of bees and our own worker writers – in which I found an unexpected interest.

'A swarm of bees has nested in the eaves of my flat,' I announced. 'I had a good look out of the window and so far I haven't seen a single bee.'

'Yes,' said Gerard, who, truth to tell, is much more at his ease with this type of conversation than the managerial kind and, furthermore, will respond in a civilised way ad infinitum to almost anything so long as it's addressed to him in the right accent. 'Experienced beekeepers say that after the first three or four stings it doesn't hurt as much, as your body starts handling it differently – in fact I understand it's almost a pleasant sensation – quite a buzz, as one might say. I'm thinking of getting a few hives myself this summer. I've got room for them in the south meadow.'

Normality restored, we discussed for a while how bees could count (up to four or five, it appears, as, like dolphins and humans, they can grasp the concept of nothing or zero) and asked Fay how *The Song of the Humble Bee* was going. She said that due to the author changing the brief quite significantly she was changing the title to *How Are We Going to Tell Them? A Beekeeper Writes*, drawing on the old tradition of telling the bees any significant family news.

Everyone a tad unsettled. A steady flow of people from office to office the rest of the afternoon asking each other if Gerard's talk about benevolent Russians needed 'interpreting.' Had a long talk with Fay about our employment prospects should the worst happen. She said, 'This is the only job I've ever had in my life where I feel able to be myself.'

I told everyone the saga of walking through the parakeet flock to try and keep their spirits up. Ursula, told to look for fifty budgets that had been lost, heard budgies, and was or pretended to be even more bewildered and confounded than usual. She said, 'Oh but, Mortimer, I confused it in my mind with your tale of the green parakeets!' I don't think the current atmosphere of unrest and unwholesome excitement is good for her.

Flooded with grateful emails for the Victoria sponge, but the bowl of blackberries I spent two hours picking yesterday was completely ignored. I took them all back home with me together with some plastic cups from the water cooler and froze the berries in the cups so as to have a regular supply to eat with my porridge throughout the winter.

What with one thing and another, I was insensibly cheered by the events of the day.

Tuesday 30 July

Molly in. She did the rounds of the offices and came in and sat on my desk eating the last slice of my cake with much *empressement* and asked how things were going. Told her about the Nieve fiasco. She was very comforting and gave me a hug and said, 'If I wasn't on my third marriage, I'd consider you myself, Mortimer. You're a good catch. Handsome, cultivated and rich, and you bake a mean Victoria sponge. One can't have everything.'

'What do you mean?' I said. 'And I'm not rich.'

But she had already jumped off the desk and vanished through the door. Of course I thought of R.S. Thomas's speedy God, always disappearing round corners as we strive in vain to keep up, and all that. All the same. Was pretty darn chuffed at this.

Fay and Drusilla burst into my office demanding, 'Where is she?' and bringing me down from my pleasant daydreams. I said, 'She's just gone. She said that if she wasn't on her third marriage—' but they just scowled at me and rushed off again, thirsting for her blood or, more accurately, her book. Their voices receded excitedly down the corridor. I went out and followed them and leaned over the landing railings to see that Molly had been too quick for them and was already through reception and pattering down the steps and out into the open air.

Sister Evangeline emailed back a fairly grudging agreement to tackle *Sister Silence: Meditations from the field paths and hedgerows*. In fact, she was very rude and said we were a 'publisher of last resort,' but who cares! Anything to please these celebrity nuns! Took it straight to the editorial board as it was, just a print-out of the email and Gerard said, 'Well done, we'll get the contract out straight away!' and slapped me on the back and I felt I had indeed reached the inner circle of commissioning. Drusilla drawled, 'Well done,' and even Fay bared her fangs in what could have been a smile, though she couldn't resist adding, 'I wouldn't be in your shoes, Mortimer!'

Editorial board went on for a long time as we were wondering what Molly could need all that money for – seems she was in to demand more of her advance (or advances) from Gerard. She's now contracted for five books for huge sums, but is always asking for cash up front, in defiance of clause 16, which stipulates payment on delivery of the manuscript, and of clause 27, which states that royalties are paid but once a year. She goes through it like water. After long, deep thought, we concluded it was drugs, bribery or smuggling. I said her boat must be expensive to run and Fay said yes, they'd discounted that as presumably she gets some kind of travel allowance from the church.

'Were we wrong to pin so much faith on her?' said Gerard rather pathetically.

Drusilla said, 'Oh, I don't think we can let her go now. We're in too deep and she owes us too much money.'

Despair descended. Fay, however, then came up with a brilliant idea – that we each write a page of Molly's book, and just keep passing it round until it's finished. We started it off there and then and got five pages done in all (Fay did an extra one) – which really boosted everyone's spirits.

Success breeds success, so I went straight back to my desk, dealt with the annual flow of post-royalty emails from authors complaining about their sales, and then set about re-tackling the pest problem with renewed energy, following a close encounter in the Gents this morning. Yes, another chance to spread my writing wings with an ALL@HQ mouse email! Thought I might do it as a conversation between Moriarty and the Mouse, in the form of rhyming couplets, but it all proved too tricky, so after two hours on various drafts, I just decided to keep it to a nice normal mouse memo – though, I flatter myself, with a spring in its step.

From: Mortimer Blakeley-Smith Sent: 30 July 15.57 To: ALL@HQ
Subject: The Mouse Is Dead: Mourn the Mouse!

Dear All

The mouse is dead – one of them anyway, but we can't of course assume he was the only one! *Au contraire* in fact, as Rat Off Pest Control assure me that for every mouse sighted, there are a horde who are much more shy – or wise? The corpse of this bolder specimen has been disposed of and Rat Off have been advised.

As I'm sure you're aware, this is a huge library, and Moriarty, persistent as he is in patrolling the corridors and placing the smaller inhabitants under mouse arrest, can't be expected to do all the work himself. The library mice are a persistent and impudent race themselves.

So, in view of these recently observed renewed sightings of the Mouse, remember:

- Please do not leave food out on your desk (you might just as well write the Mouse a lunch invitation).
- Put away your crockery quickly after lunch (so the Mouse can't use them, haha!).
- Check your work area before leaving each day to make sure there is nothing which might attract mice (like a nice juicy read).

At the moment we are mourning an individual specimen; let us do our best to keep him in single numbers.

Cheers,
Mortimer

Mortimer Blakeley-Smith, junior editor
The House of Marvellous Books
Arriving in Ithaca, not yet home

I think it was quite a well-worded email. Short, punchy, and to the point – that's the kind of thing that strikes a chord. If only the mice could read, I'd have the library cleared of them in no time.

From: Fay Meredith Sent: 30 July 16.57 To: Mortimer Blakeley-Smith
Cc: ALL@HQ
Subject: Re: Mouse – gender

Dear Mortimer,

We also can't assume the mouse was male – you refer to it as 'he'. Maybe it was a she?

Fay
Fay Meredith, Senior Editor
The House of Marvellous Books
Wayfarers and Wanderers | *Antler Bones* | *Blue Marble*

From: Ursula Woodrow Sent: 30 July 17.15 To: Mortimer Blakeley-Smith
Cc: ALL@HQ
Subject: Re: Mouse – slaughter of the innocents

Dear Mortimer,

You appear to think it acceptable that mice with the rest of their lives before them are suddenly cut short in the full flower of their youth. Pests have to be disposed of, I do understand that, but the cavalier way in which you dispense life and death to these poor little furry innocents is really rather offensive. Please, next time, can we have some sensitivity when you write to us about dealing with the inevitable, instead of this cheerful, nay, even brassy tone?

Just a little more respect for beings who didn't ask to be born, and who know no better than to patter round the library upon which they thought they depended for protection.

Thank you,
Ursula
Ursula Woodrow, editorial assistant
The House of Marvellous Books
Wayfarers and Wilderness, our award-winning nature list

Gerard, too, was roused to slight animation by all this, not alas by the writing but by the subject matter. He came in to my office and said, 'It's a well-known fact that you mustn't ever make eye contact with rats, or you'll never get rid of them. Once you look at them directly, that's it. They'll never leave.'

'How terrifying!' I said.

'Yes, and they always seem to know what you're thinking. Very cunning, the way rats evade poison and traps.'

I asked him how he knew all this and he said it was his childhood in rural Gloucester, where they held an annual ratting party in the barn with men and spades and blood and terriers.

Sometimes I wonder if this childhood in Gloucester stuff is all a fantasy, picked up from reading too much Housman and Seamus Heaney (although that's Shropshire and Ireland respectively, of course).

I said, 'I hope you're not spinning me some tall *tales*, haha!' and he laughed and said, 'Hah! That's the least of my worries, dear boy. I think I can *rat*ify everything I say!'

We parted with much laughter. I suppose I should have pressed him for details on what was bothering him but I didn't want to spoil the moment.

On reflection, re Molly, I think being married to a bishop would be a little high octane for me, but it's nice to have had the thought. One of those little 'maybes' that gives life its magic.

Wednesday 31 July

Talking of maybes, Maybee arrived and cleared out the eaves first thing this morning.

A distinct theme of bees around this summer. By some weird coincidence, Ethel herself had to leave early to go to A&E with an allergic bee-sting which had swelled her thumb to twice its normal proportions and looked like a large and nasty burn.

As if in sympathy, Ursula has developed a slight but perceptible swelling on her head, just above the hairline. She insisted on pushing up her fringe and showing me – she wanted me to feel it but I declined, as politely as possible. It certainly doesn't look right, even on Ursula. I advised her to see her doctor.

Thursday 1 August

Annual summer outing with Fay. She's off to North Wales again tonight for the weekend to check up on Dafydd ap Dafydd and to make sure that *Lays from a Shepherd's Hut* is on track. Some disquieting rumours lately about him upping sticks and moving to Mallorca. Don't blame him really. She says she's going to lure him to stay with a proposal for *Deer Scat: Poetic droppings from an earth elder.* We went to the V&A and saw an exhibition of tiaras, over 200 of them. Very pretty I'm sure, although my private feelings are that once you've seen one tiara, you've seen them all. Fay, however, was entranced, and after two hours looking at them all, bought herself a reproduction of Queen Victoria's 1840 sapphire and diamond coronet, because, 'You never know.' Then finally we sat down and had a most welcome cup of tea and a scone. I asked Fay if she'd never considered marrying. She said that, while she had in fact received proposals from both Dafydd ap Dafydd of shepherd's hut fame and Dr Chauncey Rivers of demonic possession fame, no, she was wedded to her work, but had once long ago been engaged to a Welsh hill farmer called Eddie Edwards, but the combination of two cultures, urban and rural, hadn't worked, and he had in fact died soon after the breaking of their engagement, casting a long shadowy pall of sad romance over her to this day. It had, however, left her with the spiritual gift of empathy, which was why she was able to run a list of scintillating bestsellers, drawn from the marrow of her adoring authors.

Quite a successful outing, if slightly tiring.

Wouldn't whisper it to anyone else, Diary, but sometimes I wonder if Fay isn't slightly older and lonelier than she lets on.

Prior to leaving for the harvest, Gerard called me into his office to ask me to take over a book on urban psychogeography and spiritual crisis as a matter of urgency for his *Sailing Through Storms* list.

'I do have an author who's willing to have a go, Luna Seabrook-Shore. In fact, she's written the book. *Soul in the city: Urban psychogeography and spiritual emergence*. I wondered if you could maybe have a chat with her.'

'Yes, of course. What's the problem exactly?'

'Well, she's taken a dislike to psychogeography as an expression of capitalism. She's refusing to use the word psychogeography at all in the writing of the book and doesn't want it in the title either.'

'Which rather militates against its eventual publication?'

'Yes, it makes for evident difficulties. I mean, I do see her point. She feels that psychogeography has become politicised and is an expression of power that reinvents capitalism and its systems as an alien force indifferent to human welfare.'

'I see.'

'No doubt she's right, but it certainly makes it hard to publish a book on the subject if you can't mention it *at all*.'

'Yes, I can see it's not easy.'

Gerard sighed. 'She's not an easy lady, I'm afraid.'

Friday 2 August
Luna Seabrook-Shore came in to discuss psychogeography. Not sure we struck up an instant rapport. Long blonde hair she kept tossing around, slightly bulging eyes shadowed with grey, and an overall air of haunted intensity. We discussed a title for a couple of hours. We nearly got there with *Burger Joints, Car Parks and Traffic Lights - Urban Psychogeography and Liminal Spaces*.

Our discussion was accompanied by much relentless cheerful singing and humming from Ursula, going through the ancient shelves just outside.

Lord of all hopefulness,
Lord of all joy.

She seemed to be everywhere today, up and down the corridors all day, like a species establishing its boundaries, only she uses sound rather than scent. I'm sure her penetrating hum will resound for evermore in the stone and brick of this ancient library and will still be sounding years after we have all moved on. When I came out, she was sorting contracts from the huge old cupboard, sitting cross-legged with her plait pinned untidily round her head. She was watched by Moriarty, sprawling on a pile of old, yellowed documents and looking very much at ease, not to say distinctly unprofessional as I ushered our visiting author out. 'No luck yet, I'm afraid, Mortimer,' Ursula whispered loudly. 'But don't give up the ship!'

I opened my mouth to protest, but the sheer hopelessness of it all overcame me so I just got rid of Luna S-S and went into the kitchen and had a cup of tea and the last piece of carrot cake left over from the singer's own offering of earlier in the week.

Whose trust, ever childlike, no cares can destroy...

Saturday 3 August
Damn and blast. Still got Ursula's voice going round my head.

Be there at our waking and give us, we pray…

Sunday 4 August
Hugo texted and officially offered me the job of surrogate mother which I'm pleased to say I turned down.

Monday 5 August
Silly season story about us in the *Daily Mail* again today, about the House of Marvellous Books being the helpless pawn of a Russian supergroup of internet pirates which is culling assets from traditional academic libraries and putting them out of business. Drusilla and I read it and she said, 'I must get my skates on. Gerard will beat me to it if I'm not careful. He'll go and sign some secret agreement with these sharks and then we really will be up the creek.'

I agreed it was a timely and salutary kick up the behind in terms of alerting us to our fate, even if not strictly and literally true, but by the time I'd finished speaking, Drusilla had already grabbed her bag and left.

Tuesday 6 August
Gerard still away harvesting, so I sat in his office with the windows open, inhaling the atmospheric plume of traffic rising on the summer air. Imagined myself as Lawrence Durrell writing the Alexandria Quartet, in that sultry city far from London, with a dozen genders and the motorbikes throbbing and men in long white robes and red fez and pipes and all that. Shame he let alcohol and vanity muddy the water so much. That could have been such a great book.

Went to see Ethel to see if she'd dealt with Ivan Skrulewski. She said coolly, but with a glint in her eye, 'Yes, I got back to him. I told him we're not the customer services department at Marks and Spencer's. I also told him that he's wise – given that our procedures irritate him so much – to make this his last book for us. I hope I did the right thing, Mortimer.'

I said, 'Oh yes, absolutely!' and then realised that she'd sacked my star author. Take away Skrulewski's sales, and there is no Earth list, really. Luckily Ivan isn't the type to take any notice of a dismissal like this, it's all routine backchat as far as he's concerned.

Wednesday 7 August
Sat in the secret garden and read Proust.

Thursday 8 August
Drusilla back from another trip to Rome. Have to admit, I didn't even know she'd gone this time. It's all moving too fast for me. Molly had been booked to accompany her but had had to cancel due to a family emergency, so Drusilla had taken Monsignor Philip instead, as hopefully being a benign influence on the papal powers that be. 'Never again,' she said. 'Absolute nightmare. Far too hot. Philip nearly wasn't allowed on the plane. They thought he was dying.'

She was very vexed. 'Having finally managed by the grace of God and much hard work to get an appointment to see the Pope, Philip ruined it all.'

It turned out the Pope was in hospital and, as a woman wasn't allowed into his room, Philip had gone in instead to represent Drusilla, but had forgotten what they had come about and had fallen asleep sitting by the holy bedside.

Drusilla said she did understand Philip getting sleepy as the early start was hard on the most seasoned travellers, but even so, it was hard to see all your plans collapse at the last moment.

I said, 'All this to-ing and fro-ing with Rome does seem like a lot of trouble, even for the Daybreak Manuscript. Did you never think of selling to the British Library?'

'Yes, I've got an offer from them which I'm using to drive the Vatican price up further. They have more money, you see.'

Friday 9 August
Ivan Skrulewski emailed me that he wants Ethel to come to the launch of *Nature and the Golden Rule* because he 'enjoys making her laugh.' Meanwhile Ethel is still seething with rage at him for ignoring all her copy-editing queries.

Hugo's b-day next week. Must think of something. Turns out he isn't allowed a Kindle.

Saturday 10 August
Asked Hugo for prison-friendly present suggestions. He suggested a Bible as being a veritable library of books.

Sunday 11 August
Hugo texted again to say be sure to get a King James Version, so he could mark up the secret occult symbols that Dr Dee revealed to the team who wrote the book for publication in 1611. He said Dee, that Elizabethan master of intrigue and deception, and Enochian black magician of the highest standing, was the hidden hand in the KJV and had filled it with references to Luciferian Masonic lodges and secret messages of the Illuminati, which Hugo wants to explore for an article he's been asked to do by a literary journal that still has faith in him.

Monday 12 August
Ethel very unwell with a self-diagnosed bleeding duodenal ulcer. She confided in me as we were getting our morning coffees in the kitchen, looking distinctly pallid.

'I have a bit of medical knowledge so I suspected what was happening and rang NHS direct, and took myself down to A&E

on Sunday night, and they confirmed my diagnosis,' she said in her calm, stoic way.

I was quite shocked. I said, 'I'm sure you shouldn't be in work, why don't you go home? I'd be very happy to accompany you.'

She smiled faintly and said, 'Thanks, Mortimer. I appreciate it. Unfortunately there's far too much work here.'

'But you can't work when you're ill.'

'I'm all right,' she said doggedly. 'Might as well be here as sitting at home.'

Poor singletons! Poor House! It makes my own heart bleed! I watched her go slowly up the stairs, a lone figure against the hordes. I thought her shoulders looked distinctly thinner. Maybe she overdid it with Ivan Skrulewski.

Tuesday 13 August

Drusilla came in looking unexpectedly chuffed. 'The Pope took quite a liking to Philip,' she said. 'He found him soothing company. He can come again, in fact. I've just got time to book him a ticket before my next visit on Thursday.'

Wednesday 14 August

Received another ominous email from Ivan Skrulewski about a review of *Nature and the Golden Rule* (now finally in print) which, alas, picked up on an index that is totally out of sync with the book.

'I note the comment about the index, presumably this is an error on my part unless pagination changed at some point,' he wrote acidly. 'I must confess the index question is one of my reservations about the House's policy, given their relatively modest payments, to ask authors to either produce their own index or else pay for the privilege does seem a penny-pinching and, as the present review implies, counter-productive approach.'

One of my reservations! I wouldn't dare ask what the others might be! He couldn't possibly have as many reservations as I have!

Didn't show this to Ethel. We don't want to lose her.

Thursday 15 August
Hugo's Bible arrived but was ripped apart by over-zealous warders looking for drugs. Utterly furious. Put in a complaint to the prison authorities at once.

Friday 16 August
Read Proust in the secret garden. A suitable backdrop, with its overhanging trees and bushes, its scent of lime trees, and its general air of neglect and forgotten time.

Monday 19 August
Philip Midwinter in disgrace again. Drusilla back from Rome looking distinctly drawn.

'Give him an inch,' she said wearily. 'There mustn't be too many more of these trips. I had to go, of course, and as Philip and the Pope got on so well the last time, I thought it couldn't do any harm to bring him again, but I'm approaching my limit.'

She said that while she'd had a nice early night with a glass of wine and some Derrida, Monsignor Philip had played poker with some of the Italian cardinals all night, the prize being Bishop Molly and the rights to all her books, and, unfortunately, the Vatican had won.

'What, they won Molly?'

'Yes.'

'And all her books? Even the ones she hasn't written?'

'Yes, all the contracted ones.'

I said, 'So our lead author now belongs to Rome?'

'Technically, yes, I'm afraid so.'

'Does she know?'

'No. No, not yet.'

There was silence for a few moments.

I said, 'If Molly had come with you as she ought to have done, this would never have happened.'

Drusilla shook her head sadly. 'Those cardinals are an artful lot. Molly would have had them for breakfast. Poor Philip was no match for them.'

'And the vellum scrap?'

Drusilla shook her head firmly. 'I'm not showing it to anyone but the Pope.'

She's now considering a trip to France, to sound out the Taizé community near the Swiss borders about a possible purchase instead. They're not as rich as the Vatican of course, but she hopes they might prove more *sympathique*.

It was impossible that this be kept from Fay, but she merely shook her head and said, 'Poor Drusilla. She's wearing herself out over that Daybreak Manuscript. I'm sure it did exist in some form or another once, but people should know when to give up.'

Tuesday 20 August

Drusilla texted first thing to say she was on the Eurostar, destination Lyon, on a much-needed holiday.

Sales and Marketing are refusing to work with Luna Seabrook-Shore on the grounds that she has scary eyes. She's arranged the launch of *Ghosts of Place* (working title) in the House of Commons, which some parliamentary secretary was rash enough to suggest to her and is demanding forty-eight bottles of wine for it, for an estimated attendance of eighty people! Forty-eight! We only provide twelve for Molly at the best of times! Luckily, Gerard would only ever contribute the usual £50 towards it in any case.

Took her out to lunch to try and break the news that the book was not going to happen. I'm sure it would all have gone better had I not chosen squid ink pasta, so that I ended up baring black fangs at the unsuspecting author and wasn't able to get the requisite words out to tell her the book was off...

Emailed Ivan Skrulewski to ask what he thought of doing a book on urban psychogeography. 'Wouldn't touch it with a bargepole,' was the good professor's immediate response.

Decided to put psychogeography on the back burner.

Wednesday 21 August

Prison chaplain wrote back and said the prison was well equipped with Bibles so I mustn't worry about the spiritual welfare of my friend, despite his undesirable habit of writing in all the Bibles he came across. I wrote back and said it was his literary welfare I was concerned about, as he had been commissioned to write a piece on the occultising of popular arts and entertainment of the period through the people's new holy book, aka the King James Bible, and the plays of Shakespeare, but that all the Bibles he had access to had been so simplified in terms of language as to be virtually stripped of meaning.

Several missed calls from Luna Seabrook-Shore. I must speak plainly to her before things go any further, yet I feel like the proverbial rabbit in the headlights.

Thursday 22 August

Luna Seabrook-Shore has changed the venue of her launch (presumably the House of Commons was unavailable for her chosen date) to a bookshop in Fulham and wants 800 copies of her book to be available on the night – ten for each of the eighty people who said they'd turn up. Fortunately, Dorian the bookshop manager put his foot down and will only allow 100 books on the premises – still double what we'd usually have.

How do I to get through to this author and make her understand that we are unable to publish her book?

Friday 23 August

Gerard to the rescue! He popped in looking hale and sunburnt and said I could have £50 to commission a reader's report from Ivan Skrulewski as our resident expert in psychogeography to say Luna Seabrook-Shore's book won't do. Then we can cancel the contract with a light heart. After some thought, Gerard decided that Luna S-S could keep the advance, which means sadly we are £350 poorer off. Gerard brushed this aside and said it was a cheap lesson.

Told him about House Ed and the fracas with Skrulewski. He gave a dry smile and admitted that he used to sack Ivan once a year himself when dealing with him directly as a young and sprightly junior editor.

Saturday 24 August

Hugo texted, very excited about a short story he's writing. It's called *The Enchanted*, which is prison slang for prisoners on the 'Enhanced Privilege Level'. It's all written in prison slang, which will be a useful expansion of his style, I guess.

This reminded me there are still a few stolen books in his flat, so I determined to bite the bullet and do the last of the sorting.

Sunday 25 August

To Hugo's. Packed up the last of the stolen books and brought them home ready to be sent off. Texted Hugo this and hinted he might like to consider reimbursing me, if not for all this time and trouble, at least for the postage.

Monday 26 August

Bank holiday

No reply from Hugo. Worked on Brendan.

Tuesday 27 August

Back to it. First drop of fool's gold leaves in the park.

A difficult time with Ursula at the moment; that is, even more difficult than usual. She was put on reception as the place where she could cause least trouble, but we just cannot get her to take messages. She says things like, 'Someone rang for you, she sounded like she might have been a friend of yours.' Scatty she has always been but this is something new. Fay found her today lying with her head pillowed on her arm, eyes closed, while the switchboard flashed and the phones rang all around her. Fay said she was a liability rather than an asset even in the simplest job in the business. She said, 'We do require people to be awake as a minimal requirement for work.' I said that Ursula might have sleeping beauty syndrome, but Fay flashed back that the beauty bit of it might be slightly lacking. Should have seen that one coming.

Wednesday 28 August

Hugo becoming very tiresome about his prison slang and keeps sending me texts in it – twenty-two today! A typical one went: 'My kanga (kangaroo=screw) says the pie and liquor (vicar) is coming to see me on orders from the vanilla fudge (judge). FTS!' (Fuck the system, his invariable sign-off at the moment.)

I mean, I totally get that there are topics he is unable to discuss with the other prisoners but it sometimes seems to me that his mental processes are being coarsened by prison life. Finally, I texted back, 'Cockney slang is dying, and being replaced by terms such as "reem", "sick" and "bait".'

That shut him up.

Thursday 29 August

Got an angry call on my mobile from Sister Evangeline saying she'd been trying to get through via reception for half a precious hour and that she didn't expect to have to call me on my mobile,

Satan's implement, except in an emergency. I explained about our recent problem with Ursula's somnolence, possibly caused by the persisting warm temperatures. Sister Evangeline said that Ursula wasn't worth the space she took up in the reception seat and she couldn't understand why we retained her. Interesting to see the Ursula effect operating on outsiders as well.

All a bit of a nuisance as Ursula should be preparing for our annual garden party, where we all consume a cake baked in the shape of a book. Fay snorted with impatience and said she'd do it herself and got it all organised with ten minutes' intensive delegating.

Friday 30 August

Garden party postponed from today to Monday. Even Fay couldn't pick up all the pieces in time.

Saturday 31 August

Hugo has abandoned his prison slang writing due to the inherent limitations in vocabulary and has reverted to something more in his usual style called *Prospero's Library* which is actually mostly about Coleridge the Mage, Master of Words, and his magical island of opium dependency and creativity, and our responsibility to use words carefully and to treat them as living, powerful entities.

Later: Hugo called and said he had lost his touch and that his writing confidence had gone completely, and would I help him with his piece.

Sunday 1 September

Spent the day re-working *Prospero's Library*. I told Hugo he places too much emphasis on words as powerful entities. Asking for a cup of tea, for example, is not always a magical act. Sometimes words are just words.

Monday 2 September

Annual garden party in the secret garden. A sudden end of summer feel to it all. The lengthening afternoon shadows, the fragrant scent of hot tea, the delicious egg and cress sandwiches, all combined to create a mood of gentle melancholy. There was a huge cake, the making of which Fay had cannily entrusted to Charlene in Accounts, by far the best baker of us all. It was stupendous. Charlene had worked night and day to create a medieval manuscript with gold lettering on light blue icing. Extremely clever. No one wanted to break into it and only after several photos had been taken, with and without smiling people, did we allow ourselves to consume a slice, or rather several slices.

Drusilla turned up for the last hour, with a backpack, just back from two weeks living rough in France. She had a wonderful time camping in the ruins of a remote farmhouse in the Pyrenees with friends, where they threw buckets of cold water over each other for showers and foraged in deserted orchards for golden little Mirabelle plums. She did call in at the Taizé community on her way back but mainly as a precaution and a back-up, as she says she's so embroiled with the Vatican now. She said she had a lovely restful time waxing the wood floors for the nuns in return for her lodging and listening to the chanting in the chapel by moonlight after she had finished work.

There does seem to be something slightly amiss with Ursula, who went quietly to sleep on a bench in a corner, with a plate of cake sliding off her lap. She hadn't even taken a single bite.

Tuesday 3 September

Whatever next! Gerard was arrested on suspicion of terrorism today!! He was walking past Parliament on his way to Lambeth Palace, in his best bib and tucker – ivory silk stock, linen jacket and boater, walking stick with silver swan's head – when he and some other passersby were whisked into a police van for questioning. When asked where he was going he said, truthfully, 'To see Bishop

Molly Roper in Lambeth Palace.' To which the copper said, 'Yes, you're the third one this morning,' and made a formal arrest.

Fay managed by some miracle to get hold of Molly and together they went down to Scotland Yard to vouch for Gerard. After a bit of faffing around – Molly was apparently pretty formidable in her purple – Gerard was duly released, making an appearance just in time for tea. Someone had the tact and forethought to get in some lemon buttercream sponge, which he received very gratefully, and sank down in his armchair, wiping his forehead with his big ivory silk handkerchief. About his arrest and imprisonment in the paddy van, however, he said absolutely nothing, of course.

Is there really any such thing as bad luck or do we attract such events by some inner vibration of the heart? Is some kind of karma involved? And is Gerard's bad luck contagious? Is he the one we should throw overboard, the Jonah in our midst? Will we, like sailors of old, have to tie his hands, attach a weight to him, and slide him into the sea?

We have been working fast and furiously on Molly's book but, as might be anticipated, Fay has taken over the project as she says she can't bear the sudden changes of style every page.

Wednesday 4 September

Rumours that Fingal was spotted serving at Foyles St Pancras by the Eurostar terminal – which makes it sound much more glamorous than just running a bookshop in a train station. Gerard promptly set out to see, as Fingal still owes us quite a lot of money one way and another.

Thursday 5 September

Gerard reported that he just missed Fingal – he left Foyles last week to take a rather grand-sounding job with some overseas company. Foyles told Gerard that if he caught up with Fingal, they'd be very interested to have a word with him, too.

Friday 6 September

Ursula asleep on reception *again*. Drusilla very disapproving of the whole situation, which caused her to miss a long-awaited call from the Vatican. She'd been hoping this would be the decision on making an offer for the Daybreak Manuscript. Usurping Gerard's nominal authority, she took over as receptionist this afternoon so as, she said, to maintain some semblance of discipline in the place, dismissing Ursula to the first-floor contracts cupboard where she could keep out of mischief filing. I found her up there, crying, as well she might over the faded sheets from 1973 with their manifold crossings out and writings over in faded blue fountain pen, and amendments clipped on with rusting staples. She said, 'Oh Mortimer, I'm so sorry to be a nuisance but I just know there's something dreadfully the matter with me.'

I said, 'Nonsense!' in my most hearty way and sat down beside her on the floor and told her all about the Nieve saga and my broken heart to cheer her up. She sat up and wiped her eyes and listened, then said, 'The Lord gives, and the Lord takes, Mortimer, we just have to put up with it and be grateful. It's just that I've been through all these cupboards so many times now…'

'Don't give up the ship,' I suggested.

'Fight till she sinks,' she sniffed.

Then she sighed and said, 'I always feel funny this time of year, it's something to do with the end of summer and going back to school.'

Saturday 7 September

Finished *Prospero's Library* this evening. I was quite pleased with it. Hugo grumbled at the changes but actually thanked me for my help and said I had got him out of a real hole as his editor had already extended his deadline three times.

Sunday 8 September

Change in the weather. London has lost its early autumn gold and gone grey and misty, become a cosiness of plane trees dripping in the rain, their roots bulging the pavements, dank brown leaves glued to pavements, basement church cafés with Formica tables and sliced white ham sandwiches, red carpet and dimly lit chandeliers in great halls glimpsed through magnificently closed doorways…

Monday 9 September

Gerard has recommended that Ursula see her doctor about her periodic sleepiness. He thinks she might have narcolepsy. I hope not or she will undoubtedly want me to publish a book on it.

We have the auditors in this week, so the place is full of quiet people in suits. Quite a different atmosphere. Almost like moving to another job.

Tuesday 10 September

Got a strange email from Gerard asking me why I often seemed to use green paper for my author contracts, and what were the criteria that made me decide to use green instead of blue, and if I knew when this practice started and stopped? Very odd. I went and checked the files and, to be sure, some contracts were indeed on light green paper, and some on light blue, but in my memory this was only due to whatever paper happened to be to hand in the stationery cupboard. I emailed back that my only criteria was that there be sixteen clean pages of consistent colour to print out the two copies, or twenty-four in the case of a third copy for an agent or co-author.

I suppose it's part of the audit. Even coloured paper is costly these days.

Wednesday 11 September

Bit worried about Ethel. She told me she's writing a novel about vampires in which the main character keeps a scimitar in the airing cupboard. Went along accordingly to check she was all right. She said she didn't like the auditors coming in, she found them rude and disruptive, asking all sorts of invasive questions about her and her method of working.

'They never used to be like this,' she said, looking quite upset. 'They're a new lot and I'm not at all sure I care for the change. I do wish Gerard wouldn't land us with his clever ideas, although to be fair I do think he had his arm twisted by these Krukinovs.'

I said, 'Them again! I thought they were consultants, not auditors?'

She said, 'I don't care who or what they are, I just want them off my back if I'm to get the autumn typescripts out in time. I should be looking at January, not still wrestling with September and October. It's a real headache.'

Apparently, she meant this literally and even asked me if I had any paracetamol.

Of course this was never going to be a straightforward transaction. I said, 'Well, I do, but health and safety regulations being what they are, I'm not allowed to give you any, as you know. How about if I do the time-honoured trick of putting them down on the desk and then you can just pick them up if you fancy it.'

Accordingly I trotted back to my office, retrieved the packet, and laid it down on Ethel's desk. She picked the pack up, examined it closely as if proofreading, then announced, 'It's out of date.'

How she or indeed anyone could even read the tiny lettering stamped into the pack is beyond me. I was flabbergasted. She must have microscopes for eyes. I duly trooped back to my office and got another pack. This time Ethel condescended to take a couple.

Told Fay all this in case she wanted to go and look after her sister woman but she looked at me scornfully and said, 'Gerard is but a tool of the Krukinovs these days, surely you must know that, Mortimer,' and marched off.

Thursday 12 September

Hah! Fay's turn to be in a tizz today over her to-do lists, of which she has four, colour-coded depending on importance. I said to her, 'The sun and moon rise and set, the tides ebb and flow, the leaves blossom and flourish, and wither and perish, without the mandates of late-stage capitalism,' and walked off feeling quite satisfied with the exchange. For once I got the better of Fay!

Friday 13 September

It's not just Fay – we are all being colour-coded! Gerard came round hotfoot at 8.30am to ask why I hadn't filled in the questionnaire he sent, designed, it would seem, to elicit whether we were red, blue, green, or I forget the other one, which would give valuable insights into our psychological weaknesses and strengths. I said I hadn't received any such email. Gerard looked somewhat embarrassed but said that it wasn't voluntary, unfortunately I did have to fill it in as the governing body were waiting to see it and I was late, one of the last along with Drusilla. Then I couldn't find the blasted email. Eventually it turned up in my spam. Drusilla said she had trouble filling in her questionnaire as her techie skills weren't up to the multiple choice test, and it wouldn't save and kept returning her to the beginning. 'I thought colour profiling went out in the eighties, anyway,' she said. So, after I'd done mine, I went through hers with her. It all took ages. Hope the results are worth it. Gerard clearly has a bit of an issue with colour. Or is it the auditors? Maybe I should send them Havelock Ellis's 1987 paper *The Colour Sense in Literature*, on the imagery used by Shakespeare, Chaucer, Coleridge, Poe and Rossetti among others. Hahaha!

Hopefully analysing our shades of character in this way will stop us splashing out on any more large capital expenses. Although Gerard says the new photocopier has already saved us £121 in operating costs. I found it whirring and beeping, and clearly overheating with a sense of its own importance, so turned it off to let it cool down for a while. Forgot to turn it back on, a fact only brought home to me by the sound of Fay cursing on the landing as the reason for the non-appearance of her latest MS became apparent.

Talking of cutting-edge, whizz-kid technology, there is an absurd rumour going round that we have bought Scarlett Blyth's revolutionary new system, Nemesis! When I think of all that dysfunctional acting out with *What Trees Talk About When They Talk About Love*, and how much she cost us with a print run we nearly had to pulp, I don't think so!

Saturday 14 September

Emboldened by his success with *Prospero's Library*, Hugo's now asking me to help him with a book proposal, about his life as a thief, to be called *Book Klept, Book Kept.* What a bloody naff title. He'll never sell that.

Sunday 15 September

Had a dream about Lucifer, Son of the Morning. I saw him clearly with his darkened, anguished face circling the rooftops of London and crying, 'I've been looking for a home for so long, circling round, looking for whom I may devour.'

Monday 16 September

Oh God, it's true. Scarlett Blyth's new system was installed over the weekend! We came in to new computers which looked as if they could fly to the moon amid screens of unrecognisable icons all flashing *Nemesis* at us. Gerard and the governing body never were hot on communication, but this really is the limit! No one tells us anything, it's all landed on us without warning. And surely we ought to have some training? The assumption seems to be that we just pick it up. Not sure I'm going to be able to cope with this. I shall miss my old banger horribly. Primitive it may have been but it did the job. Drusilla, too, not at all impressed and said she'd been working with stone and chisel too long to change.

Managed to avoid the issue by the simple expedient of not using my computer all day.

Tuesday 17 September

All work frozen while everyone wrestles with Nemesis. Fay says she is getting the hang of it. But the rest of us are stuck. Ursula in tears all morning and went home at lunchtime with another headache. The worst thing about it, as far as she's concerned, is that it has finally put the Fees book to rest, replacing the big, shabby book she knew and loved with an incomprehensible screen of a million functions and choices. 'It's the end of an era,' she sobbed. 'It really is Nemesis. Even if Accounts were always on at me for not filling the Fees book in right.'

'The Fees book should have been electronic years ago,' snapped Fay, as Ursula's distraught form disappeared down the library steps. 'In this day and age! Just another example of how Ursula has held us back.'

'Gerard, to give him his due, has always been opposed to too much innovation. Besides, it must have cost an absolute bomb.'

Fay said, 'Didn't you read the *Please be kind* list this week? The Krukinovs donated Nemesis to us.'

I said, 'What a strange thing for auditors to do.'

'I thought they were Gerard's expensive consultants? Anyway, Nemesis is here. I just wonder what other data it's hoovering up while it gets to grips with our complete publications catalogue.'

The expressions coming from Drusilla over the partition indicative of equal frustration and surely not suited to the lips of a dignified widow.

'Nemesis! Beelzebub, more likely!'

Apparently Scarlett has been able to buy a house in London on the proceeds of her Nemesis sale. Don't want to give in to the sin of *invidia* or envy but it does make me feel rather cross. At least half its creation was done in work time, and probably with the assistance of the Evil One. Actually, the word is going round that Scarlett sold her soul to the Devil for the secret of the system. Told Drusilla, who said, 'I hope she fries.'

Later, to my horror, I heard Drusilla quietly crying over the partition. I didn't dare investigate for a while. I have my limits. But in the end I went in of course and she sobbed, 'Oh Mortimer, I've lost all my books with this wretched new system. Manuscripts, contracts, proposals, ideas. The whole lot's vanished.'

I didn't know what to say. I laid an arm round her shoulders and said, 'Don't worry, we'll get them back.'

It sounded lame even to my ears. It was terrible. Drusilla can conquer America, the Vatican and the East End of London, but Nemesis has vanquished her completely.

A distinct atmosphere of unease. Ethel said, 'Gerard should be more careful about what spiritual influences he allows into the building. It's my belief that once Satan infiltrates, he can be remarkably hard to dislodge.'

Wednesday 18 September

Gerard has had a revelation! If you take every fifth hieroglyph in the Voynich manuscript, it gives the clue to the secret code, which reveals the messages embedded in the text. Actually, it isn't even a revelation, as Ivan Skrulewski told him this. Everyone knows he was only pulling Gerard's leg, but Gerard pasted a big Do Not Disturb notice on his office door and spent the morning trying to work it out. He emerged at lunchtime saying that it represented a breakthrough in cryptography studies. Drusilla laughed and said, 'Oldest chestnut in the book,' but no one had the heart to go in and tell him it was all as old as the hills.

Fay said that this was all defensive behaviour so he wouldn't have to take in the reality of Nemesis, with which he can't get to grips either. So far Fay is the only one who has managed to get any data onto this pernicious system.

Not doing too well myself, in fact ended up in a bit of a faff as I somehow managed to wipe out all information on my next year's titles. So much for Nemesis. It's a code as hard to crack as the Voynich. Don't think I'll bother with it again. I can switch the computer on, and I can get onto my email, so will just work like that for the time being. After all, most of the job is parrying authors' expectations by email. The new system also means I can't work the printer on my desk any more but have to run downstairs to ghastly Gog and Magog on the landing. How our freedoms are eroded, subtly, one by one.

Drusilla has gone back to handwriting her proposals. She says it saves time and trouble.

Later: Drusilla and I both in big trouble for not using the new system. Gerard came round and asked us why we had no data on it. He said, 'It isn't that I'm bothered myself, but our kind friends the Krukinovs are coming in tomorrow to inspect their princely gift and it would be nice for them if they could see it actually in use.'

Thursday 19 September

A sudden tube and bus strike disrupted London today. All work was suspended and we gathered round in the kitchen and brought out the gingernuts. It wasn't until we had had two cups of tea and most of the packet eaten that we noticed that Gerard had gone, his office dark and his coat vanished.

Drusilla went to inspect the empty office and came back with a funny light in her eye, saying, 'Isn't he supposed to be last off the ship or something?'

We all went back to making plans about walking home, and who could sleep on whose sofas. This all meant that the mysterious Krukinovs didn't come in, and we could safely abandon Nemesis for the day.

'Reprieve,' said Drusilla. She gave her toothy, gracious grin, a gleam in her eye, buttoned her jacket, and set off to walk home to

East London. She offered me a bed for the night but I gratefully refused and said I had already made other plans.

Diary, don't tell anyone, but I was able to fulfil a long-held wish to sleep on the premises. I don't know why, but I've always wanted to do this. Went over the road for a toothbrush and was all set. I was quite comfy on the camp bed with the first aid blankets and Moriarty draped snugly over my feet. Someone had left an adzuki and edamame bean salad in the fridge, along with an avocado and a potato, which made a highly adequate repast, and I was able to have a good wash in the Gents first thing in the morning.

The library at night was marvellous – not that I haven't seen it in the dark before on winter morns and evenings – but being there alone all night was different. The sense of privacy and space! And the huge rafters towering into the darkness were soothing and reassuring. I did hear a little rustling which suggested that once again Moriarty hadn't quite been doing his job, and there were other odd, unaccounted noises – distant creaks and footsteps stopping and starting – but I put all this down to a trick of the acoustics and my own ghostly expectations. The muzzy white round of the moon was visible through the stained-glass window and the distant traffic sounded like the plane trees rustling in the wind. Slightly eerie but comforting. The glow of the security lighting in the flooring reminded me of nightlights as a child and my nursery, and my mother coming to tuck me in. Slept well.

Friday 20 September

Fay took me to one side today and said not to worry but she thought we had an intruder in the library. There were indisputable signs of someone having slept on the premises as a toothbrush and a teddy bear had been left on the bed in the first aid cupboard.

Damn, damn, damn! Can one have no privacy in this life?

Saturday 21 September

To Gallhampton Gap for the harvest festival; looking forward to the balmy mix of salt air and the scent of hay, and wandering round the fair with its fudge stalls, pumpkins, chrysanthemums and piles of glowing apples. Read my horoscope on the train: Aries – creative Aries, in fact. It said my colour is hunter green so maybe the colour profile made a mistake!

Matters magickal quite the order of the day, as I got there to find that Albany and Patti were manning a bric-a-brac stall at the psychic fair which always forms part of such events. Alas, it rained, so it took place in that bastion of art and culture, the Smugglers Inn. Some odd-looking people sitting at the little tables. Patti whisked me in to see the star of the show, Madame Claire Voyant, a large lady in a turban who was doing cut-price readings at £10. She said orange was my colour, the symbol of warmth, passion and energy! Clearly I make more of an impression here than in London! Then she went on about betrayal and back-stabbing at work, and to be careful whom I trusted. Hahaha!

None of it makes sense outside of Gallhampton Gap.

Sunday 22 September

Hugo texted and phoned numerous times about me helping him do the synopsis for his bloody book. Could really do without it. However, the quickest way to get rid of him was just to do it, so tidied it up and gave him lots of useful tips. *Book Klept* forsooth!

Monday 23 September

Colour profile results in. They're a joy. We all, every single one of us, turned out blue. Apart from Drusilla, who was red. Drusilla said, 'What is the significance of blue, pray?'

'The colour of introspection and quiet, intellectual affairs.'

Drusilla said, 'Well, surprise, surprise, in a publisher! I could have told Gerard that, without him spending all that money.'

Ethel greatly disapproved of the whole affair as being the first step down the path to divination. Fay said it was more likely to be the first step down the path to sacking. 'You have to be so careful how you fill these things in.'

Tuesday 24 September

Furore with Drusilla and Fay. The spring catalogue, due to go to press today, has had to be put on hold because Ursula re-wrote the blurbs for all the titles, carefully leaving out the key points for each one. She said she thought it read ever so much better without all those bullet points. It's not the worst thing she's ever done but for some reason it broke my dear colleagues.

'If only they'd sack her!' they cried in unison.

'It's so *stressful*!' said Fay. 'I've got to do my titles all over again now!'

'She makes three times the work,' agreed Drusilla. 'And so obstinate with it! She's a complete waste of time and money!'

'She'll never be gone,' said Fay in despair, and Drusilla said at the same time, 'I'll have retired and she'll still be here, sabotaging things.'

Unfortunately, Ethel backed Ursula up, with the steady face of one who knows she is in the wrong but has gone too far to backtrack. She said that space in the catalogue was at a premium and that leaving out the bullet points was a key factor in making the copy shorter. Bosh!

A funny old atmosphere. For once, Drusilla and Fay both seemed thoroughly dispirited. I went out and got a nice lemon Swiss roll at lunchtime and we sat in the secret garden beneath the mellowing leaves consuming it and fantasising about an Ursula-free office. Told them all about the psychogeography saga while we were at it, and Drusilla said, 'Psychogeography's so hard to sell. I wouldn't bother if I were you. It's not as if it's going to help anyone. The author sounds like a handful, too,' and Fay said, 'Don't get embroiled. We care for you, Mortimer, we don't want to see you disappear into that morass,' and then they both said in unison, 'Just walk away,' at which I was really very touched. There *is* a softer side to the commissioning editors, let people say what they will.

I told them about Ethel being in a bad mood due to the auditors being in, and we agreed that Gerard should at least bring them round and introduce them, as having strangers in for so long was affecting the ambience.

Fay said, 'Surely they should have finished by now?'

Drusilla said, 'It's like having rats in the building. You can't see them but you know they're there.'

I said, 'Ethel's seen them. They've had the temerity to ask her questions about her working methods.'

Drusilla said, 'Bad news. Any chance they may recommend the removal of Ursula as a total drain on the company while they're at it?' Fay said, 'Accounts have gone rather quiet, which is strange. They do hate it when the auditors come in. Unless they know something we don't.'

Wednesday 25 September

From: Gerard Delamare Sent: 25 September 7.38 To: ALL@HQ
Subject: Weekly *Please be Kind* list – ADDENDUM – SAD NEWS OF REDUNDANCY

Dear All

Please add to the *Please Be Kind* list for this week Ursula Woodrow, whose role with us has come to an end.

Very kindly yours,

Gerard Delamere, Publisher
The House of Marvellous Books
Wayfarers & Wilderness – our award-winning nature list

Sailing through Storms – transcendence through crisis

Don't judge each day by the harvest you reap but by the seeds that you plant

—Robert Louis Stevenson

The smallest act of kindness is worth more than the grandest intention

—Oscar Wilde

Good Lord!!! After twenty-seven years, the House has finally acted! What on earth could have caused this sudden surge of energy?

It's a strange thing when you get your wish granted. It needed to happen; indeed, is long overdue. Ursula is exactly is the kind of person we can afford to lose. All the same. After so many years of provocation and inefficiency, why now? She was due to retire in a couple of years anyway. Why bother?

Ethel was devastated. She said that Ursula was her right-hand man – I'd never thought of Ursula in that light before – because of her encyclopaedic general knowledge and eagle eye at proof stage. Even Drusilla, now that her desire had been achieved, seemed a little shocked. Looking rather guilty and quelled, she said, 'Oh dear, I hope I didn't influence this decision in any way. I hate to think of another human creature being made unhappy.'

I, too, feel a bit funny. Despite our long, contortionate history, Ursula is I suppose harmless enough and, more to the point, will find it hard to get employment in the outside world. She's the kind of person who has always gone to the House for refuge. She is one of the women in cardigans for whom the House has been their life, and they seem to be showing very little compunction about getting rid of her.

Fay expressed no relief at Ursula's imminent departure, only scorn at the decision: 'What will they save? They barely pay her a living wage as it is.'

It crossed my mind that they achieved a certain dismantling. I don't know where this thought came from, nor who They might be, but for a moment I thought I caught a glimpse of some far-reaching intent with regard to the House. Said as much to Fay but she just tossed her head and said, 'We all know we should have lost Ursula years ago.'

I was slightly shocked at this lack of sentimentality and said, 'Can we not muster a little compassion for her? I mean, she's always lived for the House.'

'Yes, I know. That's rather the point, isn't it?' said Fay, and flounced away. Her heavy tread could be heard irregularly thud-thudding down the corridor back to her office. For one supposedly an athlete in her youth, she does walk with a distinct lurch.

I think redundancy etiquette dictates that employees be escorted off the premises after clearing their desk under supervision, but of course that was not going to happen here. It was an awful morning. Ursula with her red eyes kept breaking into stifled sobs over her desk, and could be heard all over the building, with its wonderful acoustics. From the far end of the library, Chaucer and his pilgrims in the stained-glass windows seemed to be looking down in mute sympathy.

We'll just have to wait for a further explanation from Gerard. Doubtless he'll be sending round a more official email shortly which will make it all clearer.

From: Gerard Delamare Sent: 25 September 14.05 To: ALL@HQ
Subject: HEALTH AND SAFETY – PROTECTING THE ENVIRONMENT

Dear All,

We're all well aware of our policy on the use of paper from sustainable forests for the books, and the need to think before we print. I want to take this opportunity to remind you of a few of

the more salient points with regard to saving the environment:
Recycle EVERYTHING
Re-use envelopes (put a label over the address and re-use)
MAKE SURE THAT:
Cans, tins, bottles and jars are put in the appropriate bins
RECYCLE clothes, shoes, any excess first aid blankets – there is a charity bin at our fire evacuation point
ETC ETC
Gerard Delamere, Publisher
The House of Marvellous Books
Wayfarers & Wilderness – our award-winning nature list
Sailing through Storms – transcendence through crisis

Don't judge each day by the harvest you reap but by the seeds that you plant

—Robert Louis Stevenson

The smallest act of kindness is worth more than the grandest intention

—Oscar Wilde

This set off an earnest discussion about how many blankets there could be on the premises. I said I rather thought there were one or two in the first aid supplies, which reminded us that no one has replaced Fingal as fire marshal.

When I checked my pigeon hole, I found the entire directive printed out and fourteen individual copies to everyone (including Ursula) on a thick file of yellow paper.

Thursday 26 September

Hahaha! We had a break-in last night and all our new computers have been stolen!! Just big, sad gaps on the desks to greet us when we got in. Hooray!

Drusilla also expressed glee. 'Serve them right,' she said, though declining to expand further on who They might be, or why They might deserve such a fate.

When asked what we were going to do, a rather haggard-looking Gerard muttered something about the insurance taking care of it.

He called in an IT consultant to re-install the old computers, which have all been sitting in a corner of the post room. It was a joy to see people struggling up the stairs with their old machines happily clasped to their bosoms.

Odd day. I guess word got round about the break-in. Received several phone calls from literary agents commiserating with us for the difficult time we were going through. Jon Grisi of Batten & Leech sounded quite concerned. He said, 'Are you sure you want to go with the Krukinovs? They've got quite a reputation as asset-strippers, you know,' and rang off before I could tell him that the place had already been stripped.

Rosie Beal from Calling Crane also called. 'What's all this about you being bailed out by a load of corporate raiders?'

I said, 'Well, we have had a raid of sorts, is that what you mean?'

'I mean those Russian chancers Gerard's got you embroiled with, the ones who run those pirate digital libraries. Three times bankrupt, with no publishing experience. Convicted of phoenixing more than once.'

'What is that?' I said, dreading some indecency.

'Ripping off the assets of a company but not the debts, forming a new company with them, and closing the old company down. I'm not saying it's a bad thing to buy up and impose efficiency measures on underperforming companies, but it's got to be done without sharp practice. Who knows, if Gerard had offered the House on the open market in the proper way, we might have been interested. As it is, I advise you as a friend, Mortimer, to go and shake the living daylights out of Gerard until he tells you the truth.'

Went and told Gerard all this and he said, 'Sharp practice? Takes one to know one. Rosie can talk. I wouldn't sell to her in a million years.'

Drusilla still away, so told Fay all this and we agreed it was time we got the full story. Fay said she would tackle Gerard alone. She said she would lie in wait for him very early tomorrow, from around 7am onwards. He has to come in via reception – unless he penetrates via the secret door at the back of the library. Fay said the early start was no hardship for her, she gets up at 5am every day anyway for three hours of meditation with scented candles 'otherwise it's just all work.'

In view of all this, my heart started thudding when Gerard himself called me into his office and said, 'It's been brought to my attention that we are lacking an important safety official. Would you like to help this House out and take over from Fingal as fire marshal for the building, dear boy?'

Acquiesced at once of course! I get to wear a dinky little hi-vis waistcoat. Sent a selfie to Hugo to this effect at once, as Gerard had it all ready to hand over there and then.

'What did he say?' hissed Fay, pouncing on me in the corridor. I was saved from replying by Hugo, ringing up with a load of stuff about jobsworthy, hi-vis Britain and our pernicious safety culture.

It was only as I reached my office that I realised I should have used my new role to extract information from Gerard about the Krukinovs. Damn! Will I never learn?

Covers meeting. With my new-found confidence instilled by my status as fire chief, I boldly said I thought the cover of *Rewyrding Britain* was very twee. It shows a small barred aperture leading onto a road winding up into hills and wide open spaces, and I said all it needed was a dwarf trudging up to be fit for *The Hobbit*. Much banter, but as no one was up to confronting Design, we approved it. Fay rather spoilt the mood by telling me to take my high-vis jacket off at meetings – she would – but my spirits refused to be dampened.

Friday 27 September

Fay tackled Gerard. He did penetrate via the secret back door so she missed the moment of his entrance, as she was waiting for him in reception, but her sharp ears soon picked up the sounds of his arrival. She waylaid Ursula in the corridor, who was ignoring her redundancy for the time being and bringing Gerard's tea up as usual in his stag's head pewter mug at 7.30am to the strains of *Immortal, Invisible,* floating down the corridor. Fay took the tray off her and brought it in herself, banging it down and spilling, she told us later sarcastically, half the precious liquid. Coming in just before 8am, I caught the sounds of raised voices from Gerard's office and tiptoed along the corridor to listen as the tempo heightened but all I heard was Gerard's final salvo of, 'Don't you speak to me like that, young lady!' I saw the door beginning to open and nipped smartly back into my office before Fay flounced out and went storming by. Didn't dare go and investigate further, but told Drusilla when she came in. She said, 'Well, it's something for Fay still to be called young lady, I suppose. I should think she would be grateful for that at least.'

Anyway, surprise surprise, Fay said that, after a lot of flannel, Gerard revealed absolutely nothing.

Ursula's leaving do in the afternoon. So soon! Talk about hustling someone out of the door! We all gathered in the kitchen at the sacred hour, 3pm, where we have shared cake so many times, and Ursula in her long, olive cardigan, and gold-rimmed glasses and untidy plait looked round and said, 'How quickly life changes. I can't believe I'm not going to be seeing all this ever again.'

Gerard was in a good mood, i.e. teetering between tears and determined high spirits, indeed, before you could take your first mouthful of Victoria sponge he was onto doppelgangers again.

'There was a time,' he announced, 'when I used to visit Oxford quite frequently, seeing authors there, and I noticed that whenever I walked down a particular section of the High, people would say hello to me – several people, as a matter of fact. I've since wondered if perchance I resembled a well-known local character. The other explanation of course is that I have a doppelganger in Oxford.'

Gerard certainly makes his double sound a lot more interesting than mine. I merely look like anyone else, whereas his doppelganger clearly bears a close resemblance to a distinguished don. Why do some people have to bag all the glamorous possibilities, leaving the rest of us to our drab lives? However, Gerard is always easier to deal with if you enter his world, so I said, 'Perhaps if you were to go back now, Gerard, you would find you had a room there, and students waiting for a tutorial.'

That naturally got us on to Borges meeting his younger self again, and Graham Greene's Other Man living his life for him, and Henry James meeting the man he would have become had he stayed in America, and right through until the sad time when the farewell speeches began. Diary, I have a strange premonition that these will not be the last I hear at the House this year.

Gerard made his usual leaving speech, a long and fulsome affair, all about what a brick Ursula had always been and a truly marvellous employee, how she'd always got in at 7.30am ready to make him that first welcome cup of tea, commuting in from deepest Bracknell or High Wycombe or wherever it is, through wind, ice and snow in her twenty-seven years with the House, always there, always to be depended upon. It went on and on and everyone was getting uncomfortable, when Charlene from Accounts suddenly heaved her immense embonpoint up and out like a Wagnerian soprano and shouted out from the back through a mouthful of sponge, 'If she's that bloody wonderful, why are you getting rid of her?'

There was a gasp and a gust of laughter, and Gerard went white, then red.

'I'm afraid,' he said, in a strangled voice, 'circumstances beyond my control...'

Gerard actually removed the handkerchief from his top pocket, unfolded it and wiped his eyes.

'I think I'll leave it there,' he said. 'Ursula, farewell.'

And he went up and gave her a big hug, tickling her face with his grey side whiskers, like an amiable badger. It was a quiet cake session after that, though it was only when all the chocolate cream sponge was gone that anyone felt truly delicate about continuing to stuff themselves in the face of such evident distress.

Saturday 28 September
What a week.

Ordered myself a cap off Amazon saying 'Chief' to wear in my capacity as fire chief.

Sunday 29 September
I don't believe this! I asked Hugo did he have a publisher in mind for his book, just out of politeness really, and he said, 'Can't remember what their name is but I was approached by some woman called Rosie Steel who runs a cranes business in East London.'

I begin to see why the others hate Calling Crane so much.

Monday 30 September
We had to call the police to break into Ethel's flat today. She didn't attend Ursula's leaving do, hasn't turned up for work since last Wednesday, has sent no message, and has been totally incommunicado, not answering her landline or mobile phone. In short, the system has ground to a halt while the manuscripts on her desk are piling up alarmingly. A lot of discussion about who should go round to her home. In the end we despatched Drusilla in her capacity as first aider and as the one nearest her heart (assuming she has one), who finally made contact just after the police arrived, reporting back to us that Ethel was 'fine, but in a strange place in her head.' Fay said, 'This is what happens when

you do the work of five people for ten years. It's a lesson to us all, that we're human and fallible,' – somehow she managed to exclude herself from this – and Drusilla looked guilty and said, 'Oh Lord, I suppose I should stop bunking off at lunchtime every day but how would that help Ethel, if she's determined to take it all onto her own shoulders?' We consulted Gerard, who said he would offer her two weeks' compassionate leave. I await developments. If Ethel stops work, that really is the ship sunk.

Tuesday 1 October

From: Ursula Woodrow Sent: 1 October 6.07 To: ALL@HQ
Subject: Volunteer work

Hullo Folks,

As I was sitting at home in the dumpy depths of misery, I had a brainwave – I can still come in, whether the House pays me or not. In short, I can be a volunteer!! Quite apart from my redundancy payment, the decease of poor Mama left me surprisingly well off, I found out from our sweet old family solicitor Quintus Pashley last week. Furthermore, I do have quite a generous pension to look forward to thanks to the good old government (hip-hip-hoorah for our dear leaders!) So, this is just to let you know that if you see a familiar figure flitting around in the corridors and halls, don't think you're seeing a ghost – it really will be me, Ursula!

Meanwhile, thank you so much for all your lovely signatures on my leaving card which mean a very great deal to me, and for the treasured leaving gifts of personalised pillow and inflatable Scrabble game – what comfort for chilly autumn nights! I also loved the flowers, though saddened to think they were murdered by humans to make other humans happy.

See you soon!
Ursula

Drusilla said, 'Oh Lord. I'm not sure I should have been so free with my sympathy now. More scorn from Fay. 'She was practically a volunteer anyway, they paid her so little.'

'But at least she can go on looking for the Daybreak Manuscript,' said Drusilla. 'At this stage, when it's such a race against time, we need all the help we can get, no matter the form in which the Lord thinks fit to send it.'

'She won't find that old book. You're in desperate straits, Drusilla, if you're relying on that.'

'You never know. God moves in mysterious ways.'

I felt the strange sinking of the heart that occurs when change is halted, yet a certain sneaking sense of comfort at the same time. So hard it is to shift the status quo.

From: Professor Ivan Skrulewski Sent: 1 October 13 33 To: Mortimer Blakeley-Smith
Subject: Proofs – *The Natural Kindness Manual*

I have now had a chance to look at the proofreader's queries. I must confess I find nearly all of these either bizarre or irrelevant but attach my comments. As I say, I am very happy to discuss, but would be very unhappy to see virtually any of the suggested changes implemented.

All good wishes,
Ivan

Nemesis may come and go, libraries may scatter and burn, people be made redundant and die, but some things truly never change.

Wednesday 2 October
Another autumn, leaves falling on the London streets. I always associate this time of year with preparing for the Frankfurt Book Fair, and indeed, despite our recent woes, Gerard is making plans to go ahead to Frankfurt as usual, to be followed out by the sales team. They say that setting up at Frankfurt with Gerard is an experience to be remembered.

Ethel back in, having evidently declined to take advantage of the proffered two-week compassionate leave. She made very little reference to her absence beyond saying it was an 'aberration.' I had a perfectly normal talk with her early this morning, and a friendly exchange of flapjacks, though now I think about it, there was a touch of hysteria in her refusal of my offering of a ginger cookie.

Accounts have got wind of the cancelled *Urban Psychogeography* contract and are pursuing me like avenging furies for the return of the advance. I've tried to explain that we're writing it off, but they won't listen. Why don't they pick on someone their own size? Like Molly, who must owe us hundreds of thousands of pounds by now. What are they bothering about a paltry £350 for?

Thursday 3 October
Drusilla says the reason Accounts are in a bad mood is that they've had several worrying calls from the shops and wholesalers wanting to know what's going on with their orders. These Krukinov people have paused our financial outgoings and are refusing to pay several of our bills unless they can be sure that the customers are worthy, which is causing us great embarrassment in the trade. Fay said, 'I suspect it's much more likely that they simply don't have the cash,' and Drusilla agreed but said, 'Insolvent or divine scourges of the industry, either way it's worrying.' They're said to be sitting on a rather large pile of orders.

Email to everyone from Ethel. I rushed to open it, expecting some explanation for her recent strange behaviour:

From: Ethel Gutierrez Sent: 3 October 8.46 To: ALL@HQ
Subject: Gog & Magog

Gog & Magog, our new photocopiers, were left on overnight. If you are the last to leave in the evening, please make sure that they are turned off. Like any *genius loci*, Gog & Magog need propitiation, not provocation. We can't expect their protective powers if we don't treat them right.

At the moment, these are young, green household deities who have yet to grow into their role – petulant adolescents who don't do what you ask them to. It would be dreadful if, through lack of sleep, they also started to jam our documents in revenge, as did our previous machine, the late, lamented Old Lady of the Landing, and if they were to fail to protect us in other areas, too. Don't forget, Satan effects an entry in many strange and unexpected ways.

Sincerely,
Ethel
Ethel Tula Gutierrez, editorial manager
Editorial Manager
The House of Marvellous Books
Wayfarers & Wilderness – our award-winning nature list

Friday 4 October
Ursula started her voluntary work for us today. She's barely had a break between her paid and unpaid work – just a scant week walking the St Cuthbert's Way in Northumberland, from which she returned with hazelnut and stem ginger shortbread. This was graciously received by Ethel, who seems to have made a good and complete recovery from her 'aberration.' Indeed, it seems to have had a humanising effect as she has been proving to be something of a biscuit queen herself, coming in with her own home-baked,

most delectable chocolate chunk shortbread. She was pleased to see Ursula back, and a long, ceremonious exchange of cookies took place between them in the kitchen, after which they went up the stairs side by side as usual, arguing about where the soul of Lazarus hung out during the three days he was dead, and whether he qualified for Hell, limbo, purgatory or Heaven.

Gerard has offered me an extension of my fire watching duties, so that in my capacity as fire chief I am managing to be both deputy senior fire marshal *and* a mere fire marshal at the same time. Hoorah!

Saturday 5 October

Had two glasses of red wine, listened to the Matthew Passion and wished for company.

Sunday 6 October

Woke early, 6.30am, to a sliver of moon and the first light just starting to show some streaks of grey cloud. The morning full of birds gently calling and cawing, a grand soft morning, as my Irish ancestors might have said. I wonder what happens to them all later, the birds I mean. They just seem to vanish from the sky.

Worked on Brendan. If I live in a world of my own, as everyone says, why not have something to show for it? Hope it's not too vain, but pretty proud I'm up to 22,000 words now! Took the train down to Gallhampton Gap to get into the mood by the coast and arranged to meet Uncle Albany later. Then spent the afternoon making notes at my old haunt, the Pavilion. Shades of Nieve (she wasn't there). How much work have I done since the happy, deluded summer? Sat outside as it was quite mild, at a table overlooking the beach. A fine view of Scrapsgate Bay at dusk. Watched the ferry coming in as darkness gathered, a town of lights. The water grew quite black, with just a few pinpricks of light winking from the odd boat or lighthouse on the coast of France. Thought about being lost at sea...

*

No sooner had Brendan set out than he was blown off course, with stormy seas and high winds. For fifteen days his crew tossed and heaved, weary days of long, sliding waves, of land glimpsed between the billows only to recede and disappear in a mist of spray. Cold salt water trickled down their faces and stung their eyes. Their arms and legs throbbed from the days of rowing; their garments were heavy with wet. Eventually they were blown onto an island that appeared to be empty. Imagine the boat driving onto the sand, then staggering out, cramped and trembling with exhaustion, and walking up to land with invisible eyes upon you.

Getting lost is not so much an essential part of the journey; it is the journey. The whole point of the navigatio is being blown off course, of rowing in an unknown direction. We all need that feeling of having made a grave, irretrievable mistake, of being hopelessly at sea, on the trackless waves. Exile is the pre-requisite for home, getting lost the precursor to finding the way…

*

Was quite pleased with this. Called in on Albany about 7pm and we went for a drink at the Smugglers Inn. The fire was lit in the basement and leapt and crackled in orange flames, and the lamps shone out to wayfarers from all the nooks and crannies of this vast old coaching inn. We sat by the fire in the big armchairs and I read Albany what I had just written. Then he read me the latest from his autobiography. A happy evening.

Monday 7 October

To HQ. Everyone frantic with last-minute preparations for Frankfurt. Much running up and down the corridors and fervid phone calls.

Drusilla managed to lose her plane tickets, but fortunately found them again in a drawer of her desk. Fay said, 'I can't understand why in this day and age, Drusilla, you don't have them on your phone,' and Drusilla said loftily, 'Because I only have a brick phone as a matter of choice. If the Pope can get through to me on this, so can everyone else.'

She's going to be unbearable now.

Ran into Gerard in the kitchen. He seemed even more highly strung and overwrought than usual. I noticed his eyes were quite red.

'Look after the ship for me, dear boy, while I'm gone, won't you,' he said to me. I said, 'Of course,' and he seized my hand, wrung it, and thanked me fervently.

Hope he's okay.

Accounts still in a two and eight, due to the fact that all activity at the warehouse has now been frozen, leaving the booksellers high and dry and rather restive. Seems like we now owe them a small fortune in unfulfilled orders. Accounts very vocal. Everyone too busy to listen to their woes.

Sister Evangeline added to the mayhem by ringing up and offering to take the books down to Frankfurt in her campervan, having heard a rumour that we were in trouble of some kind. She said that as a publicity stunt she was happy to preach from the campervan window, as from the cell of an anchorite, about silence and solitude. She took quite some convincing that we had already made the usual arrangements with the warehouse for the transfer of the books.

I was feeling quite light-hearted once I'd got rid of Sister E, and as I'm not involved in Frankfurt, (being a mere commissioning editor rather than one of the magic circle of Sales and Marketing) I took advantage to wander round and have a chat with House Ed about the etymology of my name.

'If you go far back enough, Blakeley is Irish – northern Irish, I believe, though some say the Scottish borders, from the Anglo-Saxon Blæcleah – blæc 'black', 'dark' and leah 'woodland clearing'. The hamlet of Blackley was mentioned in the Domesday Book…'

Later: Finally! Everyone off to Frankfurt. Now for some peace and quiet.

Wednesday 8 October

We have been taken over!!! This House is now officially owned by Krukinov & Krukinov!!! Apparently, this has been going on since April and no one has told me!! Not a single word! Just SO typical. I saw it in *The Bookseller* on the tube in and couldn't repress a gasp and an exclamation. A quote from Gerard about making a fresh start with partners untrammelled by the traditional shibboleths of publishing, who would see things with a business eye, their lack of experience in publishing a strength rather than the reverse.

Then an email from Gerard confirmed it, couched in official Gerardese saying it would 'make absolutely no difference,' and that he 'hoped, trusted and prayed that we are acting for the best.' Words to sink one's heart. No wonder his eyes were red-rimmed! The deal has clearly gone through, otherwise it wouldn't be in *The Bookseller*, so The Kruks must have done the key thing and put up the moolah, though this was of course couched more decorously in Gerard's memo, which referred to 'financial saviours.' No one can retaliate or query further in person as Gerard will now be incommunicado, as he always turns his phone off for Frankfurt.

I managed to get hold of Fay, who was still at Gatwick, going out slightly later, due to the fact that she has to travel alone. Fay crushing with me for my ignorance. 'You must have been blind as a bat not to have noticed what was going on. What do you think the stories in the *Daily Mail* were all about? And all those secret meetings with Gerard and the governing body? Have you no insight at all?'

Fay added that it was the beginning of the end and that the only thing left for us all to do was start looking for other jobs, except that there was no other job for her, as hers was a unique niche in the publishing world.

Called Drusilla, already at Frankfurt, and was lucky enough to catch her just as she was setting off for her first appointment of the day with Penguin New York. Drusilla said the term 'financial saviours' was inaccurate as she knew for a fact that not only had the business been transferred for nil consideration but that the Krukinovs, far from investing in us, hadn't actually paid for the new photocopiers or the Nemesis system, and, are not only still sitting on that huge pile of orders, but also owe us £63,000 for book orders themselves as they have been ordering quite lavishly for shipment to Moscow.

'Too late,' she kept saying. 'Gerard beat me to it. I had the Pope all lined up. The Vatican were quite ready to pay a fabulous sum for the Book,' then, lowering her voice and saying she'd better go as people were looking at her as if she were mad.

Scoured the building for someone else to discuss this with. Met Charlene in the kitchen. She said, 'Yeah well, you know, Mortimer, it's been tough, working full-time with two kids all these years. You know, you keep going, take a day off here and half a day there, and you get through. I did hope we could have lasted long enough to see my girls through school and uni. They're fifteen and seventeen now. If only we could have held on that little bit longer.'

Ethel was distraught. She said, 'I blame myself. With all my business experience back home, I should have spotted that all that so-called auditing was really sneaky due diligence for the sale. If only I hadn't been so distracted by *Rewyrding Britain*.'

Found Toya in Design and said to her, 'Looks like we have a new beginning. From Russia with dosh, eh?'

She said, 'Good luck with that one,' and carried on packing up her swatches and stylus and camera and graphite pencils and sketchbook, adorned with, I couldn't help noticing, many small drawings of naked men. She said she was going straight back to Catalunya to live with her mother in the family home in the Catalan Pyrenees.

I offered to help her carry her stuff to reception. Duly wheeled her chair out, hung about with bags of all kinds. Was relieved when her boyfriend turned up with his van.

Thursday 10 October

Utter chaos. Because Gerard has his phone off, messages have to go through some tortuous route, which unfortunately involved Ursula. Via these forked paths, it gradually emerged that Gerard and Ursula had between them somehow failed to order the books to go from the warehouse to Frankfurt. I suppose the Krukinovs freezing all warehouse activity hasn't helped. The warehouse proved to be their usual unhelpful selves, saying the earliest they could get them there would be Sunday, when the fair ends.

Rang and asked Sister Evangeline could we take her up on her campervan offer after all. She said she'd be delighted, adding with a coy giggle, 'Shall I pick you up from work or home, Mortimer?'

I was speechless with horror. The merriness of nuns pushes the boundaries of the subversive sometimes. Then my innate self-preservation instinct kicked in and I said, 'It's really sweet of you to think of it. But I'm afraid it would be against Gerard's orders for me to come to Frankfurt as well. There must be someone here to man the ship in his absence.'

This call to male authority did the trick, and Sister Evangeline reluctantly subsided. Fay messaged and said could Sister E bring her nasal spray, which she'd left on her desk.

Packed up what books we had in the office – fortunately we had all the press copies as no one had, of course, got round to sending them out – so that six neat boxes were waiting when the campervan screeched to a halt outside. Sister E in the best of spirits. She stopped for a quick coffee and two slices of angel cake – her last sustenance before Dover (she doesn't trust Le Shuttle as she can't swim) – and then was gone, saying that if God cleared a path she should be there by around 8.30pm. Felt rather guilty as I waved her off and watched her charging through the London traffic, giving no quarter. It's a long trip for a solitary lady, but then, solitude is what she's all about.

Some fifteen minutes later I had just settled at my desk with a coffee and the last slice of angel cake, when my phone went off and it was Sister E again on her own handpiece of Satan. 'Moriarty's come with me,' she said. 'He must have smuggled himself into the van while we were loading up. He just appeared now, on the passenger seat. I'm in Mayfair, I don't want to turn back. Could he come with me? I'll buy him a burger at McDonalds Dover.'

I said, 'He hasn't got a passport.'

'Oh, I'll just hide him for customs. They never stop nuns.'

Much opprobrium against Gerard who, it is widely felt, should be here, sorting things out, not in Frankfurt.

Finally the usual Frankfurt hush descended and the few of us left behind all went our different ways, popping to Oxford Street to buy our winter coats, meet our friends for coffee, etc.

Friday 11 October

Drusilla rang me first thing and asked had Molly by any chance been in touch, as she was supposed to be at Frankfurt today as star author, to talk about *Sailing with the Angels* and her other books, and hadn't shown yet.

'I'm afraid I haven't heard from her,' I said.

'She's abandoned ship,' came Drusilla's far-off voice.

'I'll try and find out where she is,' I said.

'That's no earthly use to us now,' said Drusilla. 'I don't give a monkey's where she is. She should be here.'

'Oh dear.'

'It's all Gerard's fault. She said she'd go if he went with the Krukinovs. I wish I hadn't told her about them now, except I was trying to convince her to support me a bit more in terms of getting the Vatican to buy the book.'

'What a bloody nuisance.'

'It's not a nuisance, it's a disaster.'

'But what about the governing body? How could they have allowed all this to happen?'

'Ah, yes, exactly. I told them until I was blue in the face, not to touch the Krukinovs with a bargepole. They wouldn't listen either.'

She rang off. I sat for a moment. Then I went back to reading the news online. It didn't take long for Molly's whereabouts to surface – she was opening a new gallery on *HMS Caroline*, Belfast, en route to New England to visit a friend and admire the fall tints. There was an impressive picture of her saluting, wearing a sailor's cap. Well, it's a worthy cause and I'm sure they deserve all the celebrity promotion they can get.

Didn't dare pass this news on to Drusilla. She'll find out soon enough.

Saturday 12 October

Quite a relief to reach the weekend. Long letter from Hugo, addressed to My Guardian Angel. A most pathetic missive all about his lost freedom. 'The days when you and I used to talk Dr Johnson and Boswell by the hour over a pint in the Bird and Baby seem long ago now,' he wrote wistfully, though I was a shade embarrassed by this reminder of my undergraduate days. Have to confess that Hugo seems increasingly far away these days.

Sunday 13 October

The pangs of conscience smote me with regard to Hugo, so I buckled to and replied to his letter, c/o HMP Lowdham Grange, and gave him a full account of the latest worrying passages at work.

Monday 14 October

Had my own brush with the fates this morning in the Gents, when I found myself standing side by side with the mysterious attendee at our editorial board. Glancing at me sideways, he said slowly, 'You don't publish any books on Shakespeare, do you? Macbeth? Richard III?'

'No,' I said. 'I'm afraid we don't. Oh, hang on. Actually, we did do *Wolves and Wild Thyme: The natural world in Shakespeare* – quite good on where to spot violets and other wild flowers around Britain today. Was that what you meant?'

'Maybe. Maybe,' he said, adding, 'I do love old books!' and I left him slowly and methodically washing his hands.

It wasn't until I was halfway up the stairs that I realised this must be one of the Krukinovs. I thought he had a slight lilt but couldn't quite place it as Russian at the time. The son, I should say, rather than the father.

Tuesday 15 October

Everyone back in. I asked Drusilla how the fair had been and she said it had been shambolic, retrieved only by her own and Fay's considerable gift of the gab. I said, 'What about Sister Evangeline?' and she shook her head, beyond speech.

Very quiet. Everyone in, except Toya of course, who messaged me in some distress, asking me to please send on a picture of her white kitten Oscar, propped up on her computer, which she'd unaccountably forgotten to take with her.

Roland was in, here for a couple of days before his next stint up north. He said Frankfurt had been salvaged only by the grim tenacity of himself and his sales team.

Wednesday 16 October

Some much-needed good news – the Vatican will let Drusilla off the poker win (whereby they effectively own Molly) if she gives them the Hebrew rights to all Molly's books.

'Lucky they're still available,' she said. 'I knew there was a reason they didn't sell at Frankfurt.'

I had a thought and said, 'Surely this is all obviated by the fact that neither Philip nor the Vatican actually have any legal control over Molly's rights? Her contracts are with us, not them.'

'I wish the Vatican would see it like that,' said Drusilla. 'Cardinal what's-his-name in particular, you know, the one who's tipped to become next— Well, I'd better not say too much, but he's the most slippery person I've ever had to deal with.'

Thursday 17 October

How bizarre – we have all been given a literature aptitude test to complete. It started with a multiple choice test asking us to choose between Ernest Hemingway, Jack London, Tolstoy, Dostoevsky and Turgenev, and then went on to Shakespeare, asking us to compare and contrast the characters of Macbeth and Richard III in a two-page essay. What a weird way to go about appraising the company finances. In all my years in publishing, no one has ever thought to query me about my literary suitability. Said as much to Fay who said, 'I think it's because the colour personality test results came out too similar. Didn't really give them any idea of who to fire.'

'By them, you mean the Krukinovs?'

'Yes. But let's look on the bright side. At least they seem interested in books!'

Friday 18 October

The Krukinovs have arranged for Gerard to go on a promotional trip to Alaska with Molly in her boat, the *Fair Weather Friend!* It takes an effort to visualise Gerard fronting the spray in his tweeds, cap, walking stick and inflatable life jacket. Fall sailing recommendations from the Vancouver Sailing Club, which we looked up with some alacrity, also recommend a knife with serrated blade and marlinspike. Surely it's against health and safety regulations and not to be recommended with someone as accident-prone as Gerard.

Fay said, 'He'd do anything to get away from reality.'

An escape undoubtedly, but one hardly suited to his temperament, given the bishop's gung-ho personality and notorious disdain of safety. Some slight comfort that Molly says the weather 'should be all right.'

Saturday 19 October

I have been served with a noise abatement order! This is like serving a noise abatement order on Mole in *Wind in the Willows*! I'm a perfect stranger to the place, always out at work or at concerts. Unless of course I have a secret poltergeist, or someone gets into my apartment and creates a racket unbeknownst to me, leaving just before I return.

Went out for the day – quietly. Must admit I pressed my ear to my front door on my return. But all was silent.

Monday 21 October

Told Drusilla about the noise abatement order. She said I was too old to have a poltergeist, which tends to be the prerogative of adolescent females. I must have looked rather hurt because she went on, softening things with her cronish charm, 'I don't seem to have seen you for weeks,' adding, 'I need to talk to you about Fay, I'm slightly worried about her. I don't think the Krukinov infiltration has been good for her.'

I said, 'They certainly seem to be causing everyone a good deal of stress. I can't decide between Tolstoy and Dostoevsky.'

Fay generally agreed to be in a state; at least, I heard, 'Oh, I'm going to run away and never come back,' followed by the sound of her office door firmly shutting. Not entirely reassuring, given that our commissioning strength really rests on Fay. Heaven help us if she ever did leave. I went to see if I could help. Fay looked pale. She said she was going to carry on reading a manuscript called *Gone with the Wings* – not a bad title for Gerard's escapade with Molly, actually – before rejecting it.

'It's going to take me the rest of the day as it is,' she said, glaring at me as if it were my fault.

Drusilla, hovering in the corridor, heard this and said, as I closed the door, 'This must be stress-induced behaviour. Isn't it rather mad to spend all day reading a manuscript you're going to reject?'

I said, 'I think we have other criteria than sanity at the moment, don't we?'

Decided to sit – quietly – by myself in the secret garden to get away from it all and to admire the autumn tints on this fine day, but it transpires that the big old iron key has been replaced with an electronic key fob as one of the improvements being introduced by these Krukinovs. I couldn't make it work and so remained locked out from Paradise, looking through the railings in deep frustration. When I went back and complained, Ursula said the trick is to hold it four inches away while pressing and holding down the button on the fob until you hear two bleeps, while simultaneously keeping on turning the lock until the bolt opens. I said, 'Of course, simplicity itself. Why didn't I think of that?' and Ursula looked very sad and said, 'I know, Mortimer, I know. The best is behind us, it's all downhill now.'

Tuesday 22 October

What was our horror to see on the news today that Molly's boat has been caught in a storm in the Gulf of Alaska, and all contact lost! Molly managed to send out a brief message as the storm struck, but nothing has been heard since. All work was instantly suspended and we descended on the kitchen and put the kettle on. Someone had brought in some iced lemon cake so I swiftly cut and distributed slices, then Ethel raced in bearing two boxes of her precious chocolate chunk shortbread and unwrapped them with shaking hands.

'Lost at sea! It may be meat and drink to Molly, but it's just not Gerard's cup of tea,' said Fay, tears in her eyes. 'It'll kill him. I shall hold the Krukinovs personally responsible for his murder.'

For one normally so scathing about our beloved captain, she certainly was showing emotion. She got out a handkerchief, like a dainty miniature of Gerard's own, and applied it to her eyes.

'They'll make land, trust Molly for that,' said Drusilla. 'I've never seen anyone so fond of her own skin,' adding with a certain relish, 'a bit of wild living off the terrain never hurt anyone.'

I said, 'Well, I could certainly see you dismembering a penguin with a penknife and chopping ice into bricks for an igloo, but I'm not sure about Gerard. He's more of an armchair explorer when it comes to the search for wilderness and its meanings.'

'No, no,' keened Fay. 'That's not the sort of accommodation to suit Gerard. He wants his nice cosy farmhouse, a scalding hot bath straight from the geyser, and his own armchair and slippers.'

I agreed with her. The thought of the good bishop directing Gerard to dig a trench downwind in the packed snow doesn't bear thinking about.

I said, 'Poor Gerard, he does seem to have such terrible bad luck.'

'They'll freeze,' said Ursula anxiously, 'and be embalmed in the ice. Like those explorers, you know, Captain Scott and his team on the Ross Ice Shelf. Buried under fifty-five foot of snow and their frozen corpses being slowly moved by glaciers to the water's edge towards McMurdo Sound.'

Drusilla said, 'Nonsense, first snowfall isn't until November.'

At that moment the phone rang and Ursula ran for the switchboard, then called me over. I snatched it up but it was only the *Rewild Your Body* author Melissa Todd wanting to talk about her son, in his first term at Oxford, who was refusing to read her own cool book and spent all his time in his room browsing through Spenser's *Faerie Queene* or discussing *The Dream of the Rood* with his mates.

'I can't help feeling rejected. Never mind, I'm working on a book which I hope will sell.'

'What's that?'

'Bedtime stories for dogs.'

Newsflash, 11pm: Gerard and Bishop Molly have been rescued, pretty cold but well, somewhere near Alaska. She was a little over-optimistic about the weather, it transpires. Her boat quite severely damaged. No more details.

I suppose this can't be intentional, but it certainly had the effect of distracting everyone's thoughts from the takeover.

Wednesday 23 October

Ethel is definitely not all steel. I found her comforting Ursula who was crying with headache this morning. Oh dear. Ursula had managed to get her fringe all wet and blubbered and kept pushing it back off her forehead with her hand. A pathetic sight. We advised her very strongly to go to her doctor – she didn't go on Gerard's advice previously because she was too scared and was convinced she wouldn't get an appointment. I went and got her a blueberry muffin from the kitchen but she couldn't eat it, so Ethel bundled her into her duffel coat like an overgrown child and hauled her off to A&E down the road.

Thursday 24 October

More calls from the bookshops. The pile of unmet orders has now risen alarmingly. Accounts are having a collective nervous breakdown. I went in to see them and Shannon and Charlene were drinking gin and playing cards.

Friday 25 October

Long talk with Hugo today about werewolves. He rang just as I was getting my coffee and said they were demonised throughout history as projections of moralised mental disorder, notably in the fifteenth century.

Hugo said, 'Johann Vincenti's 1475 *Liber de adversus magicas artes*, Book of Hostile Magical Arts, of which I procured a copy in Cologne, has a chapter on werewolves. Even back then, it was the same old prejudice – difference and mental illness stigmatised.'

His voice came excitedly from whichever cell he was incarcerated in – I've rather lost touch – and I, too, got quite absorbed by the topic and walked up and down the corridor as we discussed the finer points of medieval lycanthropy, and the notorious German werewolf Peter Stubbe, executed in 1589, and Borges, who wrote an early story for a Spanish newspaper on the topic, *el Lobisón,* the werewolf legend being popular among Argentinian cowboys. 'After all,' Hugo kept saying. 'After all, Beowulf does mean bee-wolf.'

Later Ethel sent me an email asking if I could kindly keep my private phone calls confined to my office as her team had been rather distracted by my conversation with Hugo, erudite though it undoubtedly was. I went round to House Ed.

Ethel said, in her best regal manner, 'I know Desk Ed are traditionally a bit of a nuisance to the commissioning editors, and I am sorry you have to put up with Ursula,' – here I felt a terrible pang of guilt about my mean and uncharitable ways – 'but might I suggest we all adjust ourselves to the reality of what actually is, especially at this time, and treat each other with the professional consideration and courtesy that we all deserve, instead of regarding each other as encumbrances that have to be borne with?'

Then she added more naturally, 'Sorry, Mortimer, I'm actually quite worried about Ursula at the moment. What with the awful headaches she's been having, and all the usual work stress, plus everything else that's going on, it's making me a bit more short-fused than usual.'

I gratefully seized on this new turn of conversation and asked how Ursula had got on at A&E, with a renewed pang of remorse at not having asked before.

'They checked her over,' said Ethel, 'but as she's always had migraine they weren't too concerned once they'd made sure she didn't have meningitis and hadn't had a stroke. Anyway, she agreed to take a few days off to see if she feels better.'

She added that they were going to do a scan but Ursula became hysterical and got into her coat saying over her dead body, so they discharged her without a clear diagnosis, advising her to go to her GP. This she did, and was put on antidepressants.

'So what with all that and then these interfering Russians poking their noses in everywhere, and cutting my budget for freelancers, not to mention the fact that I'm still waiting for Fay to finish writing Molly's *Sailing with the Angels*, I have been a bit pressed. I do apologise.'

I said, 'Of course, that's quite all right, I can only sympathise, and I'm sorry for causing any upset, let me know what I can do to help. Have you any idea who these Krukinovs might actually be?'

'No, not at all. My private theory for what it's worth is that they're Russian billionaires looking to launder money in the UK via the House.'

She smiled as she said it, however, and I took it for a light-hearted dismissal and escaped, leaving the burdened queen of House Editorial to bear her towers of manuscripts alone.

Saturday 26 October

My landlady came round to discuss the noise abatement order. Turns out my neighbour downstairs doesn't like my habit of conducting to Radio 3 first thing in the morning and stomping in time to the music. Well, what a killjoy.

Sunday 27 October

A silent Sunday. Thought about Sister Evangeline and Brendan and wondered if silence in general was really worth it. From my experience, it seems to make people quite bad-tempered.

Monday 28 October

Heave has won the BBC religious book of the year award! This is really quite an achievement for a book that never existed! Apparently Ursula submitted it. It just shows how much stronger myth is than fact in the media. Fay apoplectic. She hasn't been off the phone all day. I told her that the media's role is to provide us with a discourse, not news, and a bullying, aggressive discourse at that. I don't know if she took this *bon mot* in, as she merely snorted and snatched up the phone again.

Gerard is back. He made an appearance around 4pm, looking terribly haggard. He really didn't look well, all pale and white and grey. When someone asked him if he'd been surviving on a diet of ice and penguin flesh, he smiled wanly and muttered something about beer and tins of corned beef. No one dared ask him any more, and such is his oyster capacity that I suppose we never will know more. The story ends there. We tried to cheer him up by telling him about the award for *Heave*.

Tuesday 29 October

Fay emerged wild-eyed from her office, saying she'd finished writing Bishop Molly's book *Sailing with the Angels* and sent it straight over to Ethel for immediate processing. Drusilla said, 'Well done,' in her dry, spare way, but Fay held up a hand and said she had no time for congratulations, she had to go and stand over Design now to make sure they prioritised the cover and didn't try on any funny stuff with cherry blossom or kittens or anything, as she wanted something strong and modern in purple and lime green. I only hope there's someone there for her to stand over.

Wednesday 30 October

Ursula back from her few days off sick, behaving a bit strangely – I mean, more than usual. She's always been a tad exhibitionist but she now seems to be losing her inhibitions even further. Maybe the takeover's upset her more than she lets on. She brought a copy of *Playboy* in, if you please! – because it had a picture – 'quite discreet' – of some actress who reminded her of Princess Anne. Brightly, she displayed the double-page spread.

'Tasteful enough, isn't it, Mortimer? Dark cloak, pearls, and just enough leg to show that she's human?'

To my horror I recognised our author Luna Seabrook-Shore! I said, 'I didn't know she was an actress.'

'Maybe actress is too generous a term,' conceded Ursula. 'But don't you think the resemblance to the dear princess is rather striking?'

'Well, not really,' I said, profoundly ill at ease. 'It might be faintly reminiscent, but personally I wouldn't pursue that one. You don't want to end up in the Tower. The death penalty for treason was technically only abolished in 1998, you know. It's still early days, historically speaking. I wouldn't take any chances.'

I hope I succeeded in conveying my disapproval, albeit in a jesting manner, but sadly I think Ursula was just pleased at the attention. It makes me wonder. How much do we really know about Ursula? She speaks of her absorbing hobby – miniature Alpine gardens – but how does she really spend the rest of the week when not volunteering here? There are times when I find her almost sinister, or at least a little spooky. Gerard, who by some strange process of osmosis had got wind of the story, agreed.

'Spooky is the word. I took the – er – offending magazine off her. Really, I felt quite like a headmaster. I had to tell her it wasn't appropriate material to be showing round at work, especially here.'

'Indeed, no. Supposing our star author visited?'

'Molly? Hah! It would be water off a duck's back! It's the trade I worry about. I don't think the bookshops would be amused. Our name is mud enough as it is.'

'Can you really not get rid of her?'

He sighed. 'Honestly, we've done our best. I fear it will take an Act of God.'

It was only when he'd vanished down the corridor again that I realised I had missed a chance to worm any more out of him about the latest on the bookshops and the Krukinovs. Honestly, Ursula is a menace. Such a distraction. As I hesitated, all was lost. By the time I reached his office, he'd gone for the day.

I have the strangest feeling that Satan is among us, but invisible.

Retreated from the world and took refuge in my Brendan novel. Somehow I've amassed 33,000 words. Not bad!

*

Brendan landed on an island where angels who fell with Satan turned into birds and sang, white-feathered creatures whose voices were heard ringing out clear in the lonely places. An unearthly calling more than song, a crying that formed a circle round the globe, of searing pain close to eerie joy: the song of the universe calling to itself.

Brendan's music was the jangle of the wind through the sails, the whistling through the coracle skins. He heard strange screamings on the sea-winds. Plainchant, too, was heard coming over the waves, a hallucination born of solitude, or maybe real singing, reflected to him like a mirage, a Fata Morgana of sound on the horizon, penetrating round wind corners and through rays of light bent by layers of different air temperatures. Certainly that ocean was full of boatloads of monks, chanting in time to the pull of the oars. Maybe their voices are travelling still across space and time...

*

Thursday 31 October

Some very odd news indeed about Gerard. Apparently someone broke into his private study at home last night and stole all his poetry. Every last handwritten sheet of it. Very mysterious as nothing else was taken and, well, there seems to be absolutely no motive as far as anyone can see. Certainly it's safe to say there's no pressing literary inducement. Who on earth would do such a thing? It must be someone known to us, as the hallmark of Gerard's poetry is not so much that it has failed to find a wider audience, as that it is an esoteric gift reserved for the select few *intimes*. Is it some kind of revenge? Does someone want to blackmail Gerard into paying for its return? Do I get a glimpse of strange movements in the deeps? Rather troubling.

Poor Gerard is devastated. It was, of course, his only copy. Fay was heard muttering, or rather her lips could be seen shaping the words – for even she was not brave enough to voice them quite aloud – why in heaven's name didn't he get it photocopied or put in the bank if it meant so much to him? 'Did he learn nothing from Philip Midwinter?' Then everything went deathly quiet for the morning until we all agreed, via email and in whispers, to go out for lunch.

Fay then went to see if she could administer any comfort, followed by a bevy of anxious lookers-on, but as Gerard refused to answer his door, we all slunk off, leaving instructions with Ursula to try and get a cup of sweet tea down him.

As with all mishaps of Gerard's, however, it seemed to have a distinctly cathartic effect. Sad that someone else's misfortune should have this result, but once again, as we surged out of the building and down the steps, there was a distinct lightening of the atmosphere, a feeling of relief, as if the worst had now happened. I said that Gerard definitely seems to be taking on the role of scape-goat, previously held by Ursula in a more minor capacity.

Drusilla, taking advantage of a captive audience, seized her chance as soon as we were seated in Neel's and explained that scapegoat, first use 1530, 'goat sent into the wilderness on the Day of Atonement, symbolic bearer of the sins of the people,' was coined by Tyndale from scape + goat to translate Latin *caper emissarius*, itself a translation in Vulgate of Hebrew *azazel* (Lev. xvi:8,10,26), which was read as *ez ozel* – 'goat that departs' – though some argue that this is the proper name of a devil or demon in Jewish mythology (sometimes identified with the Canaanite deity Aziz).

Talking of animals useful and otherwise, Moriarty is in disgrace for bringing me one of Fay's pilchards and draping its mashed-up remains over my shoes. Fay in disgrace likewise. She's been told countless times about her blooming pilchards she eats straight from the tin for lunch – she was banned from bringing them in not that long ago. Was not happy to be followed home by three cats and to be lunged at by every passing dog.

Of course, one has to expect some upheaval, it's Halloween, All Hallows, Samhain, a day of tricksy spirits being out and about. Agent Jon Grisi sent me an American book of origami haunted houses to consider as a buy-in, even though he knows full well we don't do illustrated books or stationery. I spent quite a while trying to puzzle out how they would get the ghost into each little paper house. It seemed like a rational query at the time. Sometimes I wonder how my mind works. Maybe I've simply read too much M. R. James and H. P. Lovecraft.

Friday 1 November
All Saints
Sister Evangeline has called several times, fortuitously missing me each time. Bit the bullet and called her back just before home-time, as a kind of penance for the day. It is All Saints after all, when the veil between the worlds is thinnest and the souls of the dead come visiting. I did so hope she might be in silence but no, she picked up all bright and chipper and we were on to poetry in no time, and my own vocation manqué as a *poète maudit*. She said the island was at the heart of every journey, from the Odyssey to Atlantis, and that to find artistic success we each need to create our own island. She talked about Day of the Dead and *Under the Volcano*, and how Lowry had effectively created his own island with alcohol, although its deadening insularity militated against the readability of his book. Not to be outdone, I said that *Ithaca* was Cavafy's version of Baudelaire's *The Voyage* and Rimbaud's

Drunken Boat, albeit in a tone of wry, sad, ironic acceptance rather than rebellion. Sister Evangeline said she had no time for Baudelaire. She said Rimbaud only interested her when he had his leg cut off and began to repent. Verlaine she just thought a nasty bit of work, unstable and unkind to his wife and far too free with kitchen knives.

I asked whom she did like and she said, 'Gerard Manley Hopkins, the Master, no doubt about it. There isn't anyone else.'

Then she asked what I liked and I said, 'Well, my real speciality is twentieth-century literature, but my abandoned thesis was *The Garden in Literature 1375 to 1674*, from the otherworldly garden in *Pearl*, to Marvell, Milton, and a bit of Vaughan and Traherne.'

'What happened to it?' demanded Sister Evangeline, with the blunt curiosity of those who live apart from the world. 'Why did you abandon it?'

'Oh well, it's a long story... things didn't work out... It was really one disaster after another, until I was lucky enough to find my present job here.'

There was a short silence in which I wondered if Sister E might be praying for me. I tried to tell her about the company takeover, to see if she could provide any spiritual succour, but she started off again, about God's garden and the importance of dormancy at this time of year.

We were on the phone for almost two hours. So much for silence.

Uncle Albany FaceTimed me, all fired up in his Halloween fancy dress as Banquo's Ghost and armed with a bucketful of sweets for the local trick or treaters. Tried to tell him about the disaster with the Krukinovs but he was too into his role, so beyond saying (misquoting slightly), 'Thou hast it all now, and I fear, played most foully for't... O treachery!' he didn't really seem to take it in. Up until last year, Albany would lie in a coffin outside the front door awaiting his small visitors, rising with groans and shrieks and bursts of demoniacal laughter to greet them, but this has sadly been discontinued by Patti.

Saturday 2 November
All Souls
Dashed out and bought a copy of the eminent magazine where *Call Me Prospero* is published. What a disappointment! Big byline for Hugo, but nothing for me! Hugo didn't credit me at all! I was gutted.

It's just more of the same: take, take, take.

Monday 4 November
The Krukinovs have come up with an annual plan of eighty-two objectives. We need but one, surely: to sell more books. It was in our pigeon holes today, made of thick, shiny paper with many glossy illustrations, thus proving that Gerard is not the only one who knows how to waste money on expensive stationery. I wonder when we are going to meet these Kruk people properly. I don't think our previous two encounters really qualify as a formal introduction.

Bishop Molly is capitalising on her disaster with Gerard to contract another book, *Melting Wax: On the Wing with Icarus*. Gerard said to be none too happy with this, as he fears he will end up starring as the Icarus figure.

Tuesday 5 November
Drusilla seems to have smoothed out Monsignor Philip's gaffe with the Vatican; in fact, she has turned the tables on the awkward cardinal and has commissioned him to do a book on thrushes in Rome, on which he is an expert.

'It was a near call,' she admitted. 'What's good as well is that I let him think he's using me.'

'I think you've done brilliantly,' I said.

'Every author has their chink of vanity. I also whetted their appetite by hinting about the half-page of vellum.'

'So will you show it to them now?'

'Still hanging on for the Pope. I'm going to ask for it to be considered as a relic, which would push up the price of the Book substantially. They won't accept it as one, of course, as it's not skin or bone of anyone saintly, but I'm taking the tack that the Book was written by a saint and so the scrap may at least have miraculous powers. That should also boost the value. All this hoo-hah with the cardinals has put me terribly behind in my negotiations. Although I shouldn't wonder if that was their intention.'

Wednesday 6 November
Read through the eighty-two objectives suggested in the annual plan and realised that only two apply to my list. Should I be worried?

Ursula asleep on reception *again*! I do suspect that she's genuinely unwell. She looks rather heavy about the eyes even when awake, and still has this weird swelling on her forehead. Tried to persuade her to return to her doctor, but she was obstinate so went round to see Ethel and she nodded and said she would attend to it.

Thursday 7 November
Damn! Sister Evangeline has sent me two huge carrier bags full of medlars from the convent garden! This means I now have to spend all this weekend making them into jelly. I do vaguely remember mentioning that I know how to make medlar jelly while discussing divine and poetical gardens, but I never dreamed I was letting myself in for this. The bags have been sitting downstairs behind the desk in reception collecting fruit flies all week as Ursula forgot to give them to me – Sister Evangeline gave them to Monsignor Humberto Sanchez de Cima to bring in as he was coming into town on Sunday to preach one of his star sermons at Westminster Cathedral. The two bags certainly weighed very heavy. How these nuns do boss people around. Of course it's all in line with the emphasis on humility in monsignors but even so. Had I known I would certainly have met him there and saved him the trouble of lugging all that fruit into the office. When I mentioned this to Ursula, however, she said, 'No worries, he was coming in anyway to see Drusilla.'

Goodness. I hadn't really taken in she was negotiating *that* high up. Italian cardinals seem different somehow, so much further away.

I thought this might raise Fay's spirits as a funny little anecdote, so went into her office bearing one bag to show her.

Raising it with some difficulty – it must have weighed at least 10–12lbs – I said triumphantly, 'This must be the only place in London where someone has carrier bags full of medlars under their desk.'

Fay seemed bursting to say something, and after a pregnant pause, exclaimed, 'No one in London even knows what a medlar *is*!'

I was mildly surprised at this, as surely everyone knows that a medlar is a cross between a pear and a quince, or do I mean an apple and a rosehip, but Fay collapsed into laughter and continued, 'Honestly, this place! Where does Gerard get them from!'

I thought that was pretty rich, coming from her, indeed, I was surprised and slightly offended that she should even begin to consider me unconventional, when she is so palpably eccentric herself. However, I was glad to have provided some light relief in the midst of all our anxieties.

Bumped into Gerard in the corridor and showed him the bag, too. He said, 'Hah! Told you Sister Evangeline had taken a shine to you.'

He went into his office and shut the door. I stood there, burdened by medlars, their aged, brown smell rising, poised between ripeness and decay, and realised I had once again missed my chance with him. Went up to his office door, slightly hampered by a trail of fruit bumping onto the floor behind me from a hole in the bag, but heard the sound of his voice already on the phone.

Went back to my office and started sorting the two huge bags into four smaller ones, as I couldn't possibly carry all those medlars home at once. Saw that quite a few of the fruits were already bletted and soft and that I must lose no time in transporting them, so left an hour early to try and avoid them being prematurely squashed to jam on the tube.

Friday 8 November

Ursula off sick once more after Ethel forced her to go to her GP again about her headaches and sleepiness and went with her to tell him that the antidepressants wouldn't do. It then transpired that Ursula hadn't taken any of them. She's been referred to a neurologist and signed off work for two weeks.

Drusilla said, 'Thank God for that. Ursula well was a sore trial, but Ursula sick was quite unmanageable. Hopefully she'll be signed off for a nice long time.'

Nevertheless she said she would call in on her on the way home. That's Drusilla. She's all talk.

Saturday 9 November

Spent the day making medlar jelly. How fortunate that I saved all my glass jars from the past year instead of taking them to recycling! Somehow I must have known. Had to buy quite a lot of sugar, though. Ahmed in the corner shop looked at me strangely as I returned for the third lot and muttered something about being cleaned out, so I trotted on to the supermarket – a bit further on, and four packs of sugar rather heavy to carry, but it's a one-off, I shan't have to do this again. The jelly turned out a lovely autumnal orange. I had brought some sticky address labels from work and felt really quite proud as I affixed them to the full jars with their wonderful translucent contents. Quite a feat – nineteen jars in all! Weather turned very cold. Went for a walk round Wimbledon Park; the lake glittered with many silver lights and the birds glinted in the air like pieces of flying silver paper. Thought of Brendan's angels, singing like white birds from the bushes. Couldn't get the sweet burn of sugar out of my nostrils.

Sunday 10 November

To Gallhampton Gap for Remembrance Sunday. The Last Post at the crossroads in the high street with a handful of others, a lone trumpeter and the vicar, his surplice clinging to him in the wind and rain.

Monday 11 November

Sister Evangeline has been banned from driving for speeding! She accumulated sixteen points on her licence over the last year or so, but they kept letting her off because of being a nun. Sister E now reduced to public transport. Refusing to let this cramp her style, she promptly commandeered a bus pass belonging to one of the more elderly sisters, being herself too young for the privilege by some years. The older sister didn't really want to give it to her, she said. No bus driver has challenged her yet. She rang to tell me all this at 8.30am from her cell, where she has been placed as a disciplinary measure by the Mother Superior after they finally caught up with her. She managed to smuggle her mobile phone in, keeping it literally up her sleeve.

'It's a sad thing,' she said, 'when Satan is your only companion. As Walter Scott has it, *As I went down the water side/None but my foe to be my guide*.'

I suggested she use the time to work on her book but, as Design would say, good luck with that one.

Tuesday 12 November

No editorial board because of another directive from the Krukinovs saying that all commissioning is to be put on hold while they are reading the publication proposals for the last year so they can acquaint themselves with all the books in progress and ensure they are in line with the high moral standards they have set themselves. This sounds very conscientious and honourable of them, but it's causing endless trouble with the shops. All the goodwill we've built up over the years is rapidly vanishing downhill as the Ks are still holding on to the money placed for orders without actually sending them the books.

Brought ten jars of medlar jelly in and left them in the kitchen for people. Hopefully a bit of cheer for these troubled times. The rest should last me nicely through the year ahead. After some thought, I sent Sister Evangeline a jar, well-padded with bubble-wrap, and a handwritten card thanking her for her bountiful gift. Hope she isn't in touch again too soon.

Ursula taken into hospital as she suddenly became very poorly.

Later: My God! Hugo has escaped!!! He rang me at 9pm from an unknown location saying he couldn't bear the prospect of another Christmas behind bars as the other prisoners were too drearily conformist in their celebration of this antique pagan ritual. Apparently they had already started putting up the tree. He said it was the last straw. He wouldn't tell me exactly how he did it, but I gather it was something to do with breaking parole or absconding on an outing. He managed to smuggle his passport and some money out and took a ferry from Dover – how he got past Customs in this day and age I do not know but I guess they are maybe not too vigilant about foot passengers leaving the UK. Hugo said he used a spell from John Dee to make himself invisible. 'So that one worked,' he said with satisfaction. He wouldn't say where he was or where he was going so I wouldn't be compromised by the knowledge. Bec, maybe, in Normandy, some little hideaway at the abbey. The monastic library at L'Abbaye Notre-Dame du Bec was always one of his favourite haunts until the Frère Bibliotécaire began to regard him with suspicion. Waited with bated breath for a call from the police or prison authorities, but nothing so far.

Wednesday 13 November

Poor accounts of Ursula, still in hospital, seeing neurologists and having brain scans. They're keeping her in for a few days. We agreed we must get in to see her.

Nine of the ten jelly jars still sitting in the kitchen. Does no one care about good old-fashioned preserves these days?

Sister Evangeline emailed thanking me for her jar, saying it would be much enjoyed by all the sisters, and adding that she was under her superior's orders not to go out or to communicate with the outside world for the next six weeks. Phew.

Several of Fay's books are now off because they don't meet with the approval of the Krukinovs. I can't even begin to describe her feelings. Worryingly short of books for my list myself.

Got a letter from Calais headed, *I call myself Spellbinder.* Pretty much in Hugo's old style. Good to see his mojo coming back with his new-found freedom.

I think I need a holiday.

Thursday 14 November

Email from my old friend, agent Jon Grisi, would we consider a three-book deal by one Professor Ivan Skrulewski – *I Went to the Woods, I Went to the Mountains, I Went to the Ocean.* Emailed back by return, yes. It means crossing swords over the contract with Jon, of course, but anything is better than Sister Evangeline, and at least I know his warrior style. Drusilla told me I was enabling both Ivan Skrulewski and Sister Evangeline, and that I should be much tougher and see them off definitively if I didn't want them to drive me mad between them.

Really feel I could use a break. Spent the afternoon looking at last-minute hols on the internet.

Friday 15 November

Bad news day. Ursula has been diagnosed with a brain tumour. Sadly inoperable.

A very quiet afternoon.

Booked a last-minute flight to Lanzarote for seven nights – half board, quite cheap, though to be honest right now I would pay anything.

Took the nine jars of medlar jelly back home.

Saturday 16 November

Flew out to Arrecife at 2am with hand luggage. Thought about Ursula with quite some guilt in the bleak small hours at the airport. No place more conducive to thoughts of mortality, with its claustrophobic, sterile lighting and looming sense of inevitability. Wish I'd been nicer to her – not to her face, of course, as I sincerely hope I've always been a perfect gentleman. But more charitable in my thoughts.

The moment when you step out into the brilliant warm sunlight after the damp, raw grey of an English November.

Later: Utter bliss to be here. Settled down by the pool, and with seven hours' superiority under my belt had fun watching the latest UK arrivals stumble out into the sunlight and sharp shadows in their dark winter clothes. Why does everyone in London wear black?

Hotel fine if rather permeated by Eurodance hits from the mid-1990s, so that one ends up walking extra quick everywhere. Food adequate. A lot of chips, and slippery yellow-brown flan, ice cream or tinned fruit seem to be the only desserts.

Ventured to swim. Pool freezing. Sea too dangerous; the hotel staff say two people drowned by the rocks just outside last year. Came out blue and shuddering with cold, and took a long while to warm up again, even with a hot chocolate and brandy. Needless to say, I was the only idiot in the water. But at least I can say I've been in.

Sunday 17 November

Delightful day. Blue sea, sunshine and a general, age-old atmosphere of relaxation and holiday. The very silhouettes of the mountains on the horizon seem to embody a profound letting go of care. So still and solid and reassuring. Just lovely to be here, alone and away from everyone. A complete break. Wish I'd booked longer.

Think I will move out here, buy a small flat and forget all about England.

Monday 18 November

My GOD!!! Hugo is here!!! My first thought was I should have brought him out a jar of medlar jelly. Funny how the mind works in a crisis. In a minute or so, however, I had readjusted and it seemed the most natural and logical thing in the world, indeed I felt a fool for not guessing that here in the Costa del Crime would be where he was hiding out. He was standing in front of me in the mini-market – one of those situations where you observe someone vaguely for a few minutes before twigging who it is. But there was no mistaking the nervous twitch of his shoulder or the slight stutter with which he addressed the shop person. He looked better than in England, not tanned exactly but a slightly healthier colour, and wearing long beige shorts and a khaki short-sleeved shirt and black baseball cap and sunglasses. I realised what a long time it was since I'd seen him but he hadn't changed a bit and, after the first exclamations of recognition and greeting, he typically started grumbling about the place. He said he had already been forced to leave Tenerife due to there being too many criminal types there.

Hugo said he hadn't celebrated his birthday all the time he was inside, so off we went to a restaurant for lunch, the sea sparkling blue before us. After a couple of glasses of wine, we happily discarded the personal and recited the medieval gem *Pearl* to each other from memory, each taking it in turn to do a stanza, with the appropriate regional accent of course. Though I flatter myself, I do the late fourteenth-century Midlands twang better than Hugo does. We got quite a long way before breaking down. Then we had some light-hearted banter about ontological vs epistemological knowledge, and how it must all be deemed to be useless without axiology to provide moral grounding and direction. Hugo looked pleased and said he hadn't had a conversation like that with anyone for many a long day.

Tuesday 19 November

Went for a walk with Hugo. Laughed at people going up the hot, wobbly and very unstable mountain by camel. The camels seemed feisty enough, despite being kept in chains in the boiling heat next to piles of their own dung, and kept wandering very near the edges of some high drops. Hugo kept shouting after them, 'Hold on tight!' at which the unfortunate riders gave sickly grins or, more often, shouted abuse back. One man said, 'Just wait till I get off this f-ing camel and I'll come and f-ing kill you,' which made Hugo's day.

On the way back, Hugo and I got chased by a wild dog which was guarding a building site, a huge, yellow, bounding creature. We were just walking back to my hotel at dusk discussing Schopenhauer's blind and insatiable metaphysical will as the force behind the phenomenal world, when it came after us, out of the night. I threw a stone at it and ran, while Hugo, panting at my rear – he's marginally less fit than I am – explained that this was the worst thing I could have done. He said the dog was merely guarding a building site and wasn't chasing us but had just run to one corner of its property and would come no further. Unless baited of course, when it would be very dangerous indeed. Which was why I should not have thrown the stone.

Wednesday 20 November

Hugo and I had a row over dinner about gender fluidity in Shakespeare and how the plays very often ended up with a situation where boys were girls pretending to be boys. Hugo said the best Lear he had ever seen had been an anguished crone. He said, 'What about the Sonnets?' as if that proved everything. 'What about "the one and onlie Mr W. H.?" Answer me that.'

I had no answer.

Then Hugo went on about how the Mr of Mr W. H. proved that he wasn't an aristocrat after all as he wouldn't have been addressed as a mere Mr, and argued that 'onlie begetter' didn't have any double entendres at all but was merely a polite reference to the late Mr William Holme, who probably had the Sonnets sitting on his desk awaiting publication until Will's own publisher himself, Thomas

Thorpe, an old friend of William Holme's from Chester, took them over after William Holme's death, which also explained the dedication's strangely funereal form which has always puzzled researchers.

After that we both got too confused to pursue it any further, especially as we were nearly through our second bottle of wine by then.

Thursday 21 November
Hugo and I went on a camel ride. I pass it over in silence.

Friday 22 November
Went to see César Manrique's house, on my own. I needed a break from Hugo. Not sure I'd want to live amid a flock of volcanic bubbles myself, but I can see how it could be quite nice if you had money enough to make it so.

Saturday 23 November
Where has the time gone? Feel as if I have wasted half my holiday. Went shopping along the strip in the morning and feverishly purchased useless souvenirs. Sat on the beach alone in the afternoon and thought about things.

In the evening, worked on an article with Hugo called *The Great Escape.*

We talked about his career. He said the great thing about stealing is that it often preserves books, sending them into the hands of those who can afford to care for them instead of leaving them to moulder in neglected old libraries, or worse; in fact, most of John Dee's surviving library, which is still turning up, is made up of books that were stolen and taken abroad. Thus they avoided theft, fire and general barbarianism in London.

Sunday 24 November
End of my holiday. Mixed feelings. Hugo asked me to access his bank account in the UK and to bring him out £15,000 in cash,

to avoid transfer and exchange charges. I said I was unable to do that.

I said, 'On no account. In my opinion, it would be a foolhardy and dangerous thing to do, bordering on the criminal, and in any case I can't afford to come out again.'

I was amazed he had that much money, and said so, at which he looked shifty and muttered something about his mother's inheritance.

We talked about holidays being a liminal zone and I felt somewhat perturbed to think of the permanent liminal zone that Hugo's life must be. Felt distinctly sad as I went through Departures at the airport and Hugo waved me goodbye. I thought back over the last few full days. Our row about Shakespeare has already acquired a golden retrospective glow. Yet there's no doubt there is a kind of atavistic, animal relief at setting foot on the gangway to the plane. There is a primitive satisfaction at plumping down in the air-conditioned cool of one's seat. It means safety, home.

Monday 25 November

Back to HQ. No one asked how my holiday had been for the simple reason that no one realised I had been away. The gloom of introspection and self-absorption pervaded the building as people mulled over their wasted lives in true Monday morning style. That old familiar atmosphere from the last ten years. It was particularly strong in the area of House Editorial, where Ethel and her entourage were working in grim, unbroken silence. I hope I was able to bring a little Monday morning cheer to the place, as I did the rounds with my holiday photos and laid out chocolate mini-rolls in the kitchen – from the supermarket alas, as the *Galletas de la Gomera* I had bought for this purpose had unfortunately all got broken in transit.

Slightly cheerless day. Ursula was moved to hospice care while I was away.

Ivan Skrulewski called and told me he was moving to Another Publisher. Being fed up of sales and the way we treat him etc. Although he does this at least twice a year, it gave me a curious sinking feeling this time. There was a certain edge to his voice. I said, 'What about *I Went to the Woods*?' and he said, 'Screw the *Woods*. It's not contracted yet, nor is the *Mountains* nor the *Ocean*. I've told Jon Grisi to hold fire on them. I'm not giving it to you to sell seventy copies of, not in your current condition. Ever heard of rats and a sinking ship?'

With bleak post-holiday clarity, I realised that what Ivan says is true.

Uncle Albany texted me. 'Annual Gallhampton Gap Christmas light switch-on this Sunday. Might you be there?'

Texted back, 'I fear not.' Which might be re-phrased as, 'No fear!'

Tuesday 26 November

A nasty shock. Drusilla came in looking cross and carrying a book which she laid silently on my desk. It was called *Saved, in the Nick of Time! Sins, bins and petitions*, Sam Mungo, published by Calling Crane. For a moment I didn't get it. Then a flood of all too revelatory light broke upon me.

'Why,' I said. 'Why, it's the book of prison prayers! The skunk!'

'Yes,' said Drusilla. 'Of course it's the old story. Calling Crane pay proper advances.'

She surveyed the cover. 'I wouldn't have had a comma in the title after *Saved*.'

'No, certainly not. An exclamation mark, possibly.'

'Possibly.'

We inspected the author bio and photo. Sam, sandy, self-satisfied and snub-nosed, grinned out at us. His short, stocky figure was standing in front of a portcullis in his black trousers and white socks, swinging his keys on a long chain.

'Oh,' said Drusilla. 'Oh, I didn't think he looked like *that*. Somehow I imagined him differently.' She began to laugh. 'Well,

Calling Crane can keep him! Just as well he's published with them really. I don't fancy *him*!'

Leafing through the Calling Crane catalogue, I was pleased to see that Luna Seabrook-Shore had also found a home for *The Place That Dare Not Speak its Name,* due for publication next spring.

Ethel, Drusilla, Fay and I went to see Ursula in the hospice at lunchtime. She looked wasted and was too sedated to talk much – a sight I never thought to see. It was a bit grim, like a robin which had had an accident, still trying to sing. Nice to be out in the open air again.

Wednesday 27 November

Office Christmas lunch. Goodness they do bevy! A lot of red wine disappeared very quickly, and Gerard in his paper crown started cosying up with Charlene of Accounts. His tones could be heard far and wide across the tables. 'You're HOW old? You're NOT. You're NEVER fifty-six! Ah, Charlene, where have the years gone? You don't look a DAY over thirty-five. You make a MUCH BETTER fifty-six than I do! Etc.' It was good to see him behaving more in line with requirements for a traditional publisher. Hopefully he will now drop all his newfangled ideas. He's done nothing lately but make people's lives a misery with his intrusive, childish questionnaires, simplistic psychological appraisals, and labyrinthine computer systems that no one can work. At least the Krukinovs didn't attend the lunch.

Good to see the tribe in festive mode. Roland was sombre as ever in a glittery hat shaped like a helmet coming low over his brow, with the same look of brooding intensity, making him look more like a conquistador of old than ever. He and the rest of the sales team all sat at the same table. They, too, drank a lot and didn't talk to anyone else. Work not possible after that so went Christmas shopping. Blasted ubiquitous Christmas songs in all the shops! My annual bane! If only they would think of some new ones, not the dreadful dreary suicide playlist that's wheeled out every year. I do feel for the poor staff, stuck being tortured by it eight hours a day.

Sales and Marketing put up the Christmas tree in reception. A nice tall presence, exuding welcome.

Thursday 28 November

Another weird article in the *Daily Mail* about us! It says our offices have shut their doors and all the sales staff have been sacked by email! They must have got hold of some disgruntled former employee with a big gob, Fingal perhaps. The article was full of ominous terms about missing millions, huge irregularities and serious misconduct. I went round with it to see Gerard. He was reclined in his armchair with a copy of Tennyson open before him and Moriarty on his lap. I handed him the paper. He looked over the top of his spectacles and smiled benignly and said we should treat with compassion the poor papers who had to make a living and sell copies with such dystopian fantasies. Then he invited me to a sherry and we discussed early loss and blighting in the person of Arthur Hallam, close friend of Tennyson, who died at twenty-two. So much promise gone, literally at a stroke. I thought of Hugo.

Wrapped and despatched my Christmas gifts: a silk tie from Harrods for my father, a book of Mary Oliver's dog poetry for Jacqueline, and ordered the usual Fortnum & Mason hamper to be sent out.

Can't get *Driving Home for Christmas* out of my head from going round the shops yesterday. At least it's one of the most pleasant of that mournful series of dirges. For some reason had a bit of a lump in my throat as I went to bed.

Friday 29 November

The whole of Accounts has been made redundant!!! The word is that there's no need for six accountants now that the Krukinovs have effectively halted all sales, publication proposals and projects in progress. How can this be? No one's said a dickybird about it, Gerard hasn't sent out any emails, there hasn't been a whisper from the governing body. It must be fake news. And yet a strange silence pervades the place. There hasn't been a sound from Accounts today. Not a single voice floating up the stairs. I've been going to the kitchen and loo with eyes lowered for fear of making eye contact with any of them in a chance meeting. Went to discuss it with Ethel, who silenced me by shrugging and saying, 'Well, one could see it coming, but it doesn't make it any easier, does it?'

Felt utterly ashamed to admit I had seen nothing coming whatsoever.

Drusilla said that we would now have to think of a cunning plan to stop any of Accounts applying for Ursula's old job. Fay suggested raising the bar high and asking for a second language, such as Mandarin.

Albany rang and persuaded me to change my mind and come down for the Gallhampton Gap Christmas light switch-on this weekend. He said it was one of his favourite moments of the year. He said the high street switch-on was admittedly a waste of time as it was just an electric blue tree outside the pound shop, but that the harbour one shouldn't be missed, and painted such a glowing picture of the dark basin leaping into magical light, with all the individual boats turning into fairyland, lights strung along the masts and prows, and an unseen brass band striking softly up in the shadows with traditional Christmas carols, that it would have been churlish to have held out further.

Sunday 1 December
First Sunday of Advent

Uncle Albany and I walked down to the harbour at 6.20pm to watch this famous lighting up of the boats. A few vessels were already strung with long golden beads which quivered in the wind, but the harbour walks were dark and deserted and it was bitterly raw and cold. Albany was shivering in his parka.

'I'm sure they said there'd be a band,' he said.

We waited, leaning against the railings onto the black water. 6.30pm came and went. Nothing happened.

Monday 2 December

To HQ. Hardly anyone in. Ethel was at her desk. She said, 'Good morning, Mortimer, have you had a chance to approve the back cover copy of *Planet Self-Sabotage* yet?' and I understood that here at least it was business as usual. I asked her how Ursula was. She said, 'About the same,' and looked away.

Talked to Accounts. Charlene said she has two hobbies; one is an evening class in advanced accounts, the other is an evening class in Mandarin. She told me that the Mandarin class started with seventeen people and is now down to four, three of whom are Chinese. She explained that in Mandarin you don't write in a linear way, across the page, but up and down like noughts and crosses. She added, 'However, that's not going to get me far.'

She said that after twenty-three years with the company, the decision was 'a bit of a sickener,' and that she had fully expected to retire from this job, not to be looking for a new one. 'I've only ever had three jobs in my life, I'm nearer sixty than fifty, you know, and I don't think I'm going to get another job.'

I said, 'Yes, the Krukinovs do seem to have a penchant for getting rid of people who've given their lives to the House. The crime seems to be longevity.'

Charlene said, 'Too right. I can see a lot of people here who are definitely not going to be able to get another job. You take care of yourself, Mortimer.'

Tuesday 3 December

Visited Ursula again after work, as it's just across the park and I happened to be in the area, paying a state visit to Ivan Skrulewski in his consulting rooms to see if we could lure him back to the list. (After a lot of stomping, he agreed to resume work on the synopsis for *I Went to the Woods.*) I thought Ursula's face rather fell when she saw that I was the visitor so brightly announced by the nurse, and I have to say it all felt rather too soon after my last visit, but we both made the best of it and chatted awkwardly for fifteen minutes or so – Ursula was even less easy to talk to than normal as she kept losing the thread of the conversation. Ursula's face was blotchy and grey, her old reddish colour gone, and she kept wrinkling her forehead as if to get rid of her discomfort. A distressing sight.

Then Ethel arrived, to my relief. Ethel seemed imperturbable as ever, and able to keep Ursula in order as of old. I left them discussing whether London might have any secret portals through which it might be possible to penetrate to the kingdom of Heaven, such as the secret tunnels beneath the library. The last I heard as I walked away was Ursula speculating whether one day one might be wheeled down the corridor into another world, melting through the wall into a field of buttercups and daisies with the cuckoo calling.

Wednesday 4 December

Relations with the Krukinovs have broken down. Gerard went to remonstrate with them about the sacking of Accounts. He said he didn't get anywhere.

That weary pilgrim Drusilla off to see the Vatican one last time, bearing the contract for *Songsters of Rome*, *Cantautori di Roma*.

Thursday 5 December

My father sent the usual bottle of Christmas brandy. I rang up and thanked him. Told him about the situation at work.

He said, 'So it's got round to you at last.'

I said, 'What do you mean?'

He said, 'I did try and drop a hint when I came out in spring. Hope you managed to look at other possibilities?'

I made an effort to laugh. 'Well – I, er – I wouldn't really know where to go.'

My father said, 'Well, I wouldn't give the House any undue loyalty, that's for sure.'

I was mid-way through telling him the list of possible actions I'd thought I might take before I realised he had rung off.

Friday 6 December
Christmas card from Gerard in my pigeon hole, handwritten in navy ink with his fountain pen, in his beautiful calligraphy, 'To Mortimer. Thank you for all that you do, and are,' and signed in full, Gerard Woodward Delamere.

Saturday 7 December
Uncle Albany came up to see the lights. We always go to Chelsea as being more pleasant than Oxford Street. Told him about the unsettled situation at work and he made his usual kind offer of a home with him in Gallhampton Gap if need be, and I thanked him. He added, 'It's none of my business of course, but I never could understand why Justin doesn't set you up with a little place of your own in town. I mean, it's not as if he doesn't have the dosh. He's got those two flats in Wimpole Street, hasn't he? What difference would another one make to him? It could be another investment for him.'

Took me a few seconds to work out that Justin was my father. Felt a bit cast down after that. The lights in Sloane Square seemed like magical white orbs meant to be seen only by the rich.

Gave Albany his Christmas present, *Men are from Mars, Women are from Venus*, by John Gray, with which he was delighted.

Sunday 8 December
To Brompton Oratory as is customary at this time of year. A wonderful Messiah, although the chairs are always rather hard at the Oratory. Coffee and mince pies after. I talked to the deputy organist about Handel's linguistic idiosyncrasies in the score,

e.g, 'trone' for 'throne' and 'death' for 'dead', and how he varies between 'maketh' and 'makes' in 'If God be for us'. We put it down to Handel's early copyists rather than the stereotype of Handel acting the part of a rumbustious foreigner. Handel's English was perfectly good.

Walked to the tube in meditative silence, the glorious, divine sounds of Messiah ringing in my ears.

Monday 9 December

Drusilla back. Looks like it really was her last trip to Rome. She finally had her audience with the Pope, who intimated as much, dismissing her with a pat on the shoulder and saying, '*Quod habuit haec fecit – She hath done what she could,*' (Mark 14:8), then telling her to go home and wait with the rest of the world as befitted Advent.

'Mission accomplished, I think. Wesley would be proud of me.'

'Wesley?'

'My late husband.' She paused a moment. 'I showed the Pope the vellum scrap, by the way. I think he was convinced. All I've got to do now is liaise with the Papal Secretary about the price, and I've already got a fairly formidable estimate from Christie's for that.'

And find the Book, of course. But I didn't like to say so just then.

Tuesday 10 December

In quite some contrast to Drusilla's successful negotiations, the workplace mediation person who came in to resolve matters with the Krukinovs (arranged by Gerard) said they are 'deranged and deluded.' Quite a strong statement for one of the leading impartial authorities on workplace relationships.

Wednesday 11 December

Accounts' leaving do today. Has come round mighty quick, and the governing body mighty ready to get rid of its faithful servants, as Pepys might say. Charlene has in fact got another job, and mighty quick as well, actually – she and Shannon are both going to the same shipping company in Docklands, 'where they can be foghorns together,' as Fay unkindly says. We all assembled for cake in the kitchen at 3pm as usual. It seemed odd to say farewell to so many people at once.

'At least we'll have some peace and quiet now,' said Fay, and I agreed, but with an odd pang. Who'd ever have thought I might miss the raucous voices of Shannon and Charlene resounding round the old place?

Gerard made his usual leaving speech, all about Accounts' many virtues, how for year after year they'd stayed late, worked all sorts of ridiculous hours, late into the night and all over weekends, trying to keep a temperamental system afloat, how he always remembered them as being so self-effacing, so kind, so willing to help. All a bit like a funeral in that it didn't seem to bear much resemblance to the individuals concerned at all. Unlike a funeral, however, those concerned were there to give a bit of comeback. I could see Charlene getting redder and redder in the face trying not to say anything, but I could hear her thoughts, loud and clear, and wasn't really surprised when after a particularly fulsome bit of praise, she burst out.

'So you work your bollocks off for twenty-three years, give the company the best years of your life, do overtime and weekends, and what happens? Just when you're thinking of winding down towards retirement, you get the boot.'

There was an awful pause. Gerard looked round at us all, and said, 'I feel it all as much as you do, you know. If not more.'

I did hope he was not going to cry again, but fortunately he remained dry-eyed. Charlene said, 'I know it's not your fault, Gerard,' adding, 'I've been looking into the financial background of these Krukinovs, by the way, and it's quite interesting.'

Shannon said, 'Yes, isn't it! I thought that, too!'

'What do you mean?' said Gerard, paling visibly.

Charlene said, 'Put it this way, Gerard, I feel quite lucky to be getting out now with some money.'

Shannon said, 'Yeah, might be an idea to have a look around, folks. Check out other job possibilities.'

Drusilla said, 'Just what are you referring to exactly, young Charlene, pray?' but Gerard over-rode this, saying, 'Oh well, I'm planning to take early retirement pretty soon and just live off the farm, anyway.'

I didn't like the sound of these dark hints at all. I said, 'Can you be more explicit?'

Charlene shrugged and said, 'The Lord gives, and the Lord takes away.'

Ethel seemed uncharacteristically affected. I caught her eye as we walked past the denuded desks in the basement, and she said, 'I've just about had enough of all this, I need to get out. Fancy a walk, Mortimer?'

We strolled round the park where a few late, rain-washed roses held their fragile cups full of silver drops. Pampas grass waved white in the wind, the last yellow leaves danced on the trees as we ruffled through their fallen brown companions.

Ethel said, 'I don't know about you, but I don't trust these Krukinovs. I know those people, they're corporate wreckers. They just move in, break up the existing structure, sack everybody and sell the business on.'

She spoke with more worldly bitterness than I would have given her credit for. I wondered very much where she got her knowledge from, but there are many things one cannot ask Ethel.

'They're making all the old stalwarts redundant,' she added. 'We're losing our feeling of being a family and becoming just like everywhere else.'

We walked sadly along by the indifferent old roses.

Thursday 12 December

From: Gerard Delamere Sent: 12 December 9.32 To: ALL@HQ
Subject: Weekly *Please be kind* list – Sad Addendum

Please have very kind thoughts towards:
Ursula Woodrow who departed this life early this morning, after an illness gallantly borne for several months.

Very kindly yours,
Gerard

Poor old Ursula. She wasn't quite made for this life, somehow.
The Lyf so short, the craft so long to Lerne,
Th'assay so hard, so sharp the conquerynge…

I went into the kitchen. Ethel was there, pouring a carton of goat's milk down the sink. Gerard came in and said, 'Ursula has gone home for the weekend. I mean, Home,' and burst into tears, fumbling for the famed hanky while I patted him awkwardly on the back. It was all we could do not to join in as he brokenly murmured the C.S. Lewis quote about our birth being important mainly because it opens the portal for our death. Indeed, one or two people did succumb. It was as if we were crying for much more than the passing of Ursula.

What a year it's been for disruption and deaths. And yet, Diary, I feel in my bones there's more to come.

*

Home
By the seventh year of his great voyage, Brendan had given up all hope of getting back home. He lived the exile by sea voyage, the

islands, the temptations, the far-off blue mountains, the dream of arrival. He accepted that he would live among sea monsters and talking birds and mermaids with gross, green-furred faces, among slow-moving tribeswomen who ate whale lard and spoke in chirrups, squeaks and booms like the whales themselves, among little sticks of feathers blown about by the island winds. Brendan had changed too irrevocably to return. His hair was silvering and straggling, his body browned and broken into a thousand pieces by the ocean winds. The burning salt waves had scored lines and crevasses into him, his eyes were remote, always listening for something through the crash of the ocean. Patron saint of sailors and travellers, leader of seafaring monks, the Wanderer, stranger in a strange land. He knew that he would never belong at home again, could never go back to the place of his departure. Home is elsewhere. Return is not an option. You can only turn back if you know where you are going, and where you came from. The only road for the wanderer lies ahead, on the shifting waves...

*

Friday 13 December
Terrible news. Gerard has been run over and killed by a bus on a pedestrian crossing in Islington! If ever a man was unlucky! I can't believe it. I'm trembling as I write. Being run over by a bus is a cliché, a generic euphemism for one's eventual projected demise, not something that's actually supposed to happen. People don't really get run over by buses. Feel all shaky and sick inside. Heard the news at 11am and came home at lunchtime, yet only now at 4pm am I starting to take it in. I frankly feel like vomiting.

Went out for coffee with Drusilla and Fay but it's all a blur.

Later: Opened my father's Armagnac and had a good half-glassful. Found myself noting appreciatively its spicy and peppery notes, with undertones of vanilla and walnut. Then the tragedy overwhelmed me again.

Saturday 14 December

Very poor night. Seemed to spend all night semi-awake and suspended in a kind of trance of shock. Bowels distressingly loose first thing this morning. I had a sweet cup of tea and two rich tea biscuits then checked the news again and there it was, in black and white on the website, along with a picture of a red bus, as if we'd never seen one before. It was a 73, en route for Angel. What's going to become of us?

Later: Can't seem to get my bowels under control. Went out to our friendly local pharmacist, Andreis, and told him all about the shocking event. He prescribed Dioralyte and suggested I contact my GP to discuss counselling. I said I knew how to get counselling if I needed it – I am after all surrounded by healers and wise people at work, although most of the ones I know would be primarily concerned about the impact Gerard's death would have on their book sales – but thanked Andreis anyway. It was just good to talk to someone kindly and impartial outside the situation.

Called my father in France and told him the shocking news. He said, 'Oh dear, very sad. Will that affect your job, too?'

I said, with a trace of annoyance, 'I don't see how.'

He seems to have a bee in his bonnet about my work security. Money, money, money, that's all he thinks about. Called Albany. He knew exactly the right thing to say, a mix of comforting, practical and spiritual, with a reassuring fundament of banality. He said, 'Everything happens for a reason, Mortimer,' and I was consoled, not by the depth of the sentiment but by the sound of his voice.

Sunday 15 December

Took a deep breath and realised that I must draw on my inner Albany, as it were. I reasoned that Gerard must have wanted that way out, must have desired this exit. We all choose our own death, its manner, place and timing. Otherwise it surely couldn't have happened, this mythical demise beneath a bus.

Monday 16 December

To HQ. Everyone still very shocked. We all huddled in the kitchen. Someone brought out the gingernuts as being vaguely medicinal and more respectful than chocolate or anything. The pack was passed round and we munched in scared silence.

'He must have had some profound death wish,' said Drusilla at last, echoing my own thoughts. 'All those near misses.'

Fay said, 'He never got over having his poetry stolen. It broke him.'

I said, 'Then whoever stole it is guilty of murder, or manslaughter at the least. Will we ever find out who it was, I wonder?'

Fay said, 'That may be something we just have to live with. Besides, technically if nothing else, surely the bus driver is guiltier for failing to stop at a pedestrian crossing?'

Another long silence.

'You don't think it was deliberate, do you?' said Ethel.

'Gerard was not suicidal,' said Fay sadly. 'He loved life. He was planning to retire and enjoy his farm.'

They both started crying. Thought it was up to me to start putting things in perspective a bit, so I said, 'I've been looking into this a bit, and it would seem that the first mention of being run over by a bus is in Conrad's novel, *The Secret Agent* in 1907, where he says, '...it was a pure accident; as much an accident as if he had been run over by a bus while crossing the street.'

Dabbing at her eyes with her dainty hanky, Fay said, 'I've been looking into it, too, and it seems it isn't as much of a meaningless cliché as you might think, in fact London Transport have a truly horrific safety record. The figures say there's one death every three weeks involving London buses, or a horrifying total of nearly 2,000 people killed in a five-year period, depending on which source you cite.'

It's true that tragedy makes you give consideration to things that would otherwise never pass through your head. We continued gloomily to munch our ginger biscuits.

Tuesday 17 December

To work. Ethel cleared out Ursula's desk. I hung around offering what moral support I could as she unearthed jars of Marmite, bicycle clips, granola bars, Union Jack flags, pictures of the royal family, a ball of string and a yellow sou'wester hat. We found a collection of some thirty vintage trolls in one drawer, with streams of purple, green and orange hair. They grinned up at us most horribly. Ethel said, 'I guess these must be worth quite a lot of money these days,' and we looked them up on eBay to find that this was indeed the case. However, no one felt quite able to organise the sale just then, so we shut the drawer on the trolls and hoped for the best.

A rumour going round that Gerard was deliberately murdered by Russian agents, put about mainly, as far as I can see, by the *Daily Mail*. Asked Drusilla if she had seen it and she said, 'But there was no need to murder Gerard – he was so accident-prone, all anyone ever had to do was wait.'

Getting just a little bit fed up with the *DM*. I always thought them so on the button, prescient even, rather than taking liberties with the facts.

Wednesday 18 December

More jubilant headlines in the *DM*, saying the library was put up for sale for £27 million yesterday, and was snapped up at once by an Arab prince as a little bauble to make into a nightclub, but withdrawn today due to the fact that the premises are subject to ancient covenants which restrict its use to a place of study and of work.

The prince protested that he would hang the walls with genuine works of art and make a magical garden of the quad and have resident poets and musicians in situ, but in vain. The new governing body are said to favour a plan to make the library into a state-of-the-art, one-stop shop selling beauty services including tattooing, cosmetic skin procedures and nail art. Word is they've found a way round the legal restrictions.

Drusilla wasn't in yet, so rushed round to see Fay with this, but to my dismay, she wasn't there either and her office was cleared out! All the pictures, cushions and books had gone, and her desk was bare. Now I think about it, I haven't seen her since Monday when we were all in the kitchen, grieving Gerard together. Of course, Fay always did have her ear to the ground.

Thursday 19 December

Got in to find a letter from the new governing body requesting us to ignore media rumours and carry on as normal, pending final decisions about the company, left in everyone's pigeon holes – including ones for Gerard and Ursula, which didn't seem very tactful to say the least.

Called my father again to give him this latest update. He was having breakfast, and halfway through his second croissant. He gave a gulp – swallowing nourishment rather than indicating distress – and said sharply, 'Albany's still down in Gallhampton, isn't he? He'd put you up if that governing body of yours do decide to get rid of everyone. You'd have a roof over your head, that's the great thing.'

Tears dimmed my eyes as I put the phone down and gazed round my office. Modest it may have been, but here had I found one of the nooks and crannies of this strange old bank of a city. To leave London! Farewell the secret garden and the scent of the limes, farewell the soft, misty rain round the old squares at twilight, farewell the comforting rumble of the underground, the oblongs of daylight falling in at Kensington, the faint ubiquitous smell of soot and petrichor, oh farewell.

Rang Calling Crane and spoke to Rosie. She was keen to hear all she could about our predicament and the passing of Gerard – she promised to come to the funeral – and said she'd heard a rumour we were moving to Margate. I was able to deny this quite categorically. Then I asked her about jobs. She was quite sympathetic but said she had already taken on Fay; in fact, Fay was already in situ, working at her new desk as we spoke, and that there was no room for any more new employees at the moment.

She said, 'If it changes, you'll be the first to hear,' adding, 'interesting to compare both your versions of events.'

I should have known. I expect Fay was on to her weeks ago.

Friday 20 December

To work early, at 7.30am. Started to sort through the dusty old hardbacks on my shelves, which included worthy early tomes on the discovery of vitamins, putting some into carrier bags to take to the Oxfam down the road. The futility of such proceedings struck me around 10am and I ceased my travails. Went round to see House Editorial but no one was there either. There, too, were great gaps on the shelves where the chunky big dictionaries used to stand, and the desks were bare and impersonal, cleared of all the photos, cuddly toys and healthful snacks that used to clutter them. It dawned on me that I was the only person in the building. Everyone had abandoned ship.

Then there was a rustling next door and to my joy, Drusilla's high voice called over the partition asking if I was there. She was much more graceful and gracious about it all. She said she would take the opportunity to retire.

She said, 'As it happens, my widow's pension is quite generous, and then I'm pretty busy with my work as a street pastor, which also means there's always a passing stream of company staying at the flat, so I'm never lonely. Then there's the other bits and bobs I have on hand, such as running the food bank in Poplar, volunteering at the homeless shelter, teaching English at the Tower Hamlets migrant centre, governorship of a couple of schools, little things like that. Plus freelance editing of course, I've got two or three old friends asking me for help with their books as it is. Never mind the grandchildren, where an extra pair of hands is always welcome. More than enough to keep my hand in.'

I told her about Fay clearing off to Calling Crane. For the first time since I've known her, Drusilla was at a loss.

'Oh,' she said. 'Oh. What, cleared her office out and gone?'

We went down the corridor and looked again. The winter daylight came streaming bleakly in. A fine layer of dust had settled on the empty desk and shelves.

'Oh,' said Drusilla again. 'Fay told me she didn't know what she was going to do the other day. She made quite a fuss about it.'

Looking at the bare office where so late the books and pictures had been bright, I said, 'I suppose it's a case of every man – or woman – for him or herself.'

Drusilla was silent. Then, 'I suppose so,' rather sadly. 'It's rather salutary, isn't it, to think that a twenty-year-old friendship can mean nothing when personal survival is at stake.'

I was about to query whether she and Fay had, in fact, ever been friends but, seeing her wipe away a tear and mutter something that sounded like, 'So shallow,' realised in time this would have been tactless. Instead I proposed coffee. I said I rather thought there was some chocolate cake in the kitchen.

As we went downstairs, Drusilla said, 'You okay for Christmas, Mortimer?'

Taken aback, I said, 'I – er – haven't given it much thought.'

She said, 'Well, if none of your rich family have invited you yet, you'd better come to me.'

I said, 'I can't possibly do that,' and she said, 'No arguing. Bring a Christmas pudding if you want one, I don't eat the things, and arrive as early as you like. At least I shan't have to worry about *you* being underhand and deceitful, and two-faced, and disloyal,' and so it was settled.

Saturday 21 December

Christmas card from Hugo – well, a postcard of a camel with tinsel round its head and a speech-bubble saying, 'Oh camel ye faithful!' Put this straight into the bin.

Gerard's proverbial and untimely demise made the obits; there was some mention of him as a bit of a litterateur but, sad to say, he probably owed his coverage more to his unhappy end than to his literary prowess. No one mentioned the lost poems. Or poor Ursula.

Damn and blast Hugo! Would I go round to his flat and check the boiler isn't leaking again, as tends to happen in cold weather. I responded fairly grumpily, 'All right, but it will have to wait until tomorrow.'

Sunday 22 December

Albany rather hurt as usual by my decision not to join him in Gallhampton Gap for Christmas. Didn't tell him about work in case he offers me a home again. Promised to go down for New Year even if I have to dress up as Elvis Presley himself to do so.

Didn't bother to put up the tree. It hardly seems worth it this year.

Forgot to go round to Hugo's.

Monday 23 December

To work. The place very quiet. Took the opportunity to finish Proust, stretched out full length on one of the sofas downstairs. The basement suitably atmospheric, with its saggy armchairs, old books and sense of forgotten time, its odd bumps and bangs and rustlings. Once or twice I even thought I heard the sliding open of files and drawers, and I could imagine the shade of poor old

Ursula, still looking for the Book, and Gerard's ghost wafting around, sad at being deprived of all those spring sowings and harvests to come. Felt rather sad myself by the time I finally lumbered to the end of volume 7, *Le Temps Retrouvé*, with all the stuff about old age usurping one's time surprisingly and unexpectedly. It left me with a decided feeling of impotent hurry. I must get on with some writing and finish my Brendan book before it's too late. Nevertheless, hastened back up the stairs and into Drusilla's office, exclaiming, 'I've finished Proust! I've finished Proust!'

She said, 'Well done, you're a man in a million.'

Said I'd take her out for a nice tea at Liberty's to celebrate and said she'd prefer a McDonald's if I didn't mind, she didn't want to be a drain on my purse, and we'd never get a booking anyway this time of year, and I said it was all the same to me, so we strolled down to McDonalds Baker Street and gorged ourselves for around £3.30 each. Drusilla said she felt her Christmas had now begun and the best bit of it all was she no longer had to read Proust, I had done it for her.

Tuesday 24 December

Another weird report in the news that a posse of booksellers has stormed the House and gutted the basement of its bookly contents, taking all the latest publications in a bid to make good the monies owing to them. Like Jesus overthrowing the tables in the Temple, (Matthew 21:12–13) they overthrew all the bookcases, and unlike Jesus took all the stock. Rumours that someone was hurt in the process. No time to go in and check this in person.

Update: two people were hurt, a father and son who were found on the premises, said to be unconnected with the book trade. They were arrested on suspicion of breaking and entering and intent to cause wilful damage and taken to hospital, where they gave the slip to their warders and carers both and vanished into thin air.

Wednesday 25 December
Christmas Day
To Drusilla's for the day. I expected it to be overrun with quiversful of cheerful grandchildren but she said they were all coming tomorrow and the day after in stages, as she could no longer face full-on family Christmases. I was surprised at this first sign of *faiblesse* in her. Took her a paperback representation of the Book of Kells as her Christmas gift, at which she was absolutely thrilled. She kept saying, 'No one told me you could buy this kind of thing, I didn't know it existed. It really is marvellous. Clever you! Where did you find it?' It rather broke the mystique to admit I got it off Amazon. Told her what my father had said about leaving London. She was very kind and offered me a home with her for as long as I needed it. She said, 'In theory of course your father should offer to help you out but I can see that's not going to happen, so if you do find you're having difficulty with the rent...'

I was terribly touched and said so. Of course, there's no way I could take her up on it, but it was very warming to have the offer. You certainly find out who your friends are in times like this. We discussed the storming of the library. Drusilla agreed it was shocking but doubted that it would do the booksellers much good if one took into account the usual sales pattern of our books. She said, 'We have to face it, publishing is dead. You and I are well out of it. However, we owe the booksellers a debt of gratitude for getting rid of the Krukinovs. They say they caught them just about to set fire to the library.'

'No! An insurance scam!'

'Looks like it. Anyway, the booksellers gave them a good duffing up and sent them on their way. They said that taking our stock was one thing but vandalising the library quite another.'

'Hoorah for the booksellers!'

We both raised our glasses.

'To the shops.'

Drusilla added that one business which is doing well out of us at the moment is the funeral trade. Gerard's reliquaries will be on 11 January, with Butterworth's *The Banks of Green Willow*; Ursula's, complete with *Lord of All Hopefulness*, not until 1 February for some reason, even though she predeceased him by a day. Drusilla said that Ethel had arranged both before departing finally to Texas where she has long had 'an understanding' – or even an arranged marriage of some kind – with a distant cousin who is a fellow tycoon. Ethel says she's through with publishing, too. *Guide me Lord, the storm has ended.*

'The Krukinovs left the business in a dreadful state, practically bankrupt,' went on Drusilla. 'Do you know how much they were paying themselves each month for managing the business? Thousands siphoned off into a Swiss account, and unpaid bills everywhere. They never even paid for Nemesis, though luckily we had it on a trial period only which expired when the computers were stolen. Shouldn't be surprised if they were behind that, too. Looks like what's left may have to be sold at auction to pay all the debts off, unless a miracle happens.'

'Oh, Drusilla. After all your work selling the Daybreak Manuscript to Rome.'

Drusilla got up and went to check the turkey in the oven. She pulled off a piece of kitchen roll and blew her nose.

'Yes,' she said. 'It's rather annoying.'

'Where did the Ks go?'

'Fled to Switzerland, or Argentina, I can't remember. Somewhere they can safely plead bankruptcy.'

'You know, it's funny to say so, but I quite liked the younger Krukinov, the son. He didn't say much, but he knew something about literature.'

'The one at the meeting, the youngish blonde one? Yes, I know what you mean. He had a certain enigmatic charm.'

Thursday 26 December
Boxing Day
Well, what do you know! The governing body has offered me Gerard's job!! I got an email first thing this morning! At a slightly diminished salary, it's true, i.e. less than Gerard was getting, I know for a fact. Still, bit more than I'm getting now. All very exciting, anyway. Felt terribly flattered to have been selected, until I rang Drusilla and told her the news. She and Fay had both turned the job down. The sad truth is that I was last on the list. Fate comes a day late, as they say. If only it's not *too* late. Why do I get my dream just as the House is faced with ruin and closure, and I'll be saddled with all the blame?

Friday 27 December
Emailed the trustees back that I would consider my options, as so many at the House have done before me. Don't want to look too eager!

Saturday 28 December
Remembered with an awful pang that I hadn't gone to check Hugo's boiler. It completely slipped my mind. Must do it tomorrow without fail. Suppose the place is two feet deep in water?

Sunday 29 December
To Hugo's. The boiler was fine, but as I looked round his bleak little place, still only half-cleared, I felt a crash of utter exhaustion. Everything that's been going on – the final debacle at work, the Krukinovs, Gerard, Ursula, Fay leaving, Drusilla retiring, the job offer, Hugo himself – all seemed to rise up and overwhelm me. Accordingly I swept a pile of books off an armchair and sunk down into it and went to sleep for an hour, still in my coat. When I woke up, a book on Marilyn Monroe was staring up at me from atop the pile on the floor. Still half-asleep, shivering a little in the dankness of the flat, I was warmed by her smile which seemed to come straight

from some inner sunshine, and pulled it dazedly up to look into for a little recreation while I came to properly. But as I opened it, my heart sank as I realised that inside, cunningly disguised by the cover, was yet another of Hugo's blasted antiquarian thefts. A smallish book, leather binding reasonably intact, pages rather tattered at the edges, but clearly vellum, marked down the centre here and there by a faint, raised impression where the bones of the animal had been. The title page was missing, so I couldn't check it against Hugo's list. The rest looked all right. Plenty of decorative embellishments. Lavish use of decorated capital letters intertwined with peacocks and unicorns, fishes and owls. A delightful illustration of a daisy caught my eye, a real 'day's eye' with particularly fresh verdigris or green. Insular script and nice use of diminuendo, with the letters decreasing in size across the page. Clearly it was precious enough to be taken care of. Some library docket was stuck between the pages which might give a clue to its origins. I ran my eye down the last page or so and caught something about Anathema, scribbled in the margin. For no real reason, I had a flash of Ursula, saying, 'Don't give up the ship.' Half-asleep still, I rose to make a cup of tea, putting the book in my pocket, to have a proper look at some future time. Hopefully there would be enough clues in its provenance so that I could return it to its rightful owner.

Damn and blast Hugo. Really, one too many. But if I don't look after this poor book, nobody else will.

Monday 30 December

The governing body emailed back saying they were pleased that I was interested in the job, and to take as long as I liked to consider before they advertised the post externally on Thursday. I asked whether I could go back and inspect my new domain, as I may call it, before deciding whether formally to accept the job. Not that I haven't seen the place before, of course, but I simply felt unable to go ahead without another look. They replied that the library was still locked up from Christmas and Juan our caretaker not back yet, but that I was welcome to let myself in via the secret back entrance, to the basement, the key to which is hidden in the statue of St Peter in the back yard. I never realised that the key he clutches in his right hand is a real one.

Slightly unnerving, all this corresponding with faceless entities and powers that be. I wonder why wouldn't the governing body just arrange to meet me there? Maybe they don't exist, after all...

Bishop Molly called me on my mobile, grieved beyond measure at Gerard's demise – always such a generous friend – and very much concerned at our predicament. She promised to write the book of books to get us out of it and we agreed to meet at HQ to discuss it tomorrow. Diary, it's a positive sign!

Tuesday 31 December

To HQ. A cold, dark dawn. Found the key all right, but as I took it from its hiding place I got the sudden feeling I was being watched. An agent of the Krukinovs perhaps, some burly, balding tough with raincoat and umbrella, spying on me from behind a tree on the other side of the road. Or maybe it was the statue of Saint Peter, eyeing me to make sure I was the right keeper of the key, and I might feel the saintly hand of stone come down on my head if I failed to pass muster, or my intent was perceived to be unworthy. Unnerving thoughts, and my hand shook slightly as I put the key in the lock. The small door of old wood unlocked quite easily, leading straight into the basement, and I closed it swiftly behind me and went in, into the hush.

Already, the place was laid waste. The old ramshackle working bustle was a thing of the past. All was silent, empty. The books were gone from the stacks, and the gutted bookcases were shoved roughly to one side. The place was bare, desolate, a dwelling-place for dragons, an astonishment, and an hissing (Jeremiah 51:37.) I hurried back up to reception, where the Christmas tree stood dropping needles, with a faint, spent whiff of pine, and then through the panelled door into the library.

It was beyond the bounds of imagination that I had ever worked here. I stood a moment looking down the central aisle, where the last shadows of night formed a chiaroscuro with the floor lights (I was unable to find the main switches). I was profoundly grateful for the superstitious awe that had kept the booksellers from touching it, protected as it was by ancient laws all these centuries. The shelves were intact and dusty, as ever. As I turned away to go upstairs, out of the corner of my eye I thought I saw a figure cross swiftly from left to right, as if making for the kitchen. Molly had arrived!

I had brought some lemon drizzle cake with me so I ran into the kitchen, calling, 'Hello! Molly, I'm here!'

But there was no one there. Swiftly I unwrapped the cake, put the kettle on, and went out to look, calling again. She couldn't have gone far.

Silence met me as I went round the dark interior of the library again, from alcove to alcove where the armchairs sat silent and empty. Then my phone pinged. It was a text from Molly saying she'd got caught up and couldn't make it; profoundest apologies. I stared at the phone in my hand for some moments, aghast.

After a minute or two, I pulled myself together and went to see if anyone else was around. But I didn't really expect to find anyone, and nor did I. Like Babylon, the place was, truly, without an inhabitant. The figure I thought I had glimpsed was not Bishop Molly, nor any of my colleagues, nor a ghost, but a confabulation of the lonely. I was alone.

Went back into the kitchen, made coffee, and ate a slice of lemon cake, thoughtfully. It was odd to be there, without Fay and Drusilla scolding, and Molly flitting in and out like a sunbeam, and poor Ursula trying to press her goat's milk onto me, and Ethel glowering and Gerard with his side whiskers, walking sticks and poetry. But, with the exception of Drusilla, they had all vanished, truncated by fate or by human whim, relationships as shallow and ephemeral as puffballs on the wind. They had all, every one of them, gone their own way, without consulting me. It was as if I had never known them. Albany lived in a parallel universe; my own father was terminally selfish and remote; Fay had betrayed us. And now Molly had let me down.

As for Moriarty. Who once had come to meet me, brushing softly round my legs, gave me no welcome. His automatic feed dispenser had been left well-stocked by Juan our caretaker, but I couldn't find him anywhere. Even the cat had fled the sinking ship.

I went back into the vast ark of the library. With the beams soaring and criss-crossing above me, it was as if I were living upside down, in this ship that had now gone down irretrievably. I walked on through the library. From somewhere above in the upper galleries, I thought I heard a soft humming of *Abide with Me*. There was a faint smell of toast. It was all unchanged. And yet I knew Satan was coming. I could feel his rumble on the air. God would hang him spinning from the ceiling, a skinless humanoid with dark eyes of anguish and boundless energy confined in his wingless shoulders. For centuries he would hang there, feet unable to touch the ground. Long after I had passed on, he would still be there, staring out into the darkness and deep into himself. The library would be broken up, the passing of an old world that would never come again, our history lost, for the history of libraries is the history of power; in medieval Europe, the monasteries had literacy and land at a time when most people didn't. I thought of our lives as editors, like so many Prosperos, magicians on our islands, making books appear and disappear, stewards of our own libraries. I thought of other private libraries and their guardians, the desert libraries of Chinguetti, Mauritania, the Bibliothèque al Habott crumbling into sand with its rolls of fragile parchment. Only the infinite library dreamed into being by Borges, which manifested as the internet, was untouchable, our cosmic consciousness, flowing through the ether. Was it wrong to have dreamed of universal digitalisation?

I wandered over to the stained-glass window which the wintry sun, just rising, was transforming into rich hues, and looked up to where Chaucer and his merry folk were jogging gently along on their eternal ride. *The lyf so short, the craft so long to Lerne.*

'I've done my best,' I said aloud.

I went upstairs, my steps echoing. The corridors seemed thronged with reproachful ghosts. It was strange to think we had ever spent our days here; that this had until so recently been a living, working establishment. On the landing, the photocopier beeped at me faintly as I passed; I turned it off and watched the green button die. One old enemy the less, anyway. As I passed down the corridor, the office doors stood open, giving glimpses of the emptiness within, although Gerard's was all too full of chaos, books and papers strewn everywhere. It was clear that this had received the main brunt of the booksellers' attention. I went in. The *ficus benjamina* was a dry husk of its former glossy self. I poured some water on it all the same and the plant soaked it thirstily up. Maybe there was a spark of life left in it yet. Then I thought I heard a door slam downstairs and found myself listening for footfalls along the corridor. But there was silence, and the faint whistling of the wind.

Sitting down at Gerard's desk, I surveyed the devastation. The drawers had all been wrenched open and their contents scattered over the desk. Cavafy's *Complete Poems* lay there, tossed open at 'The God Forsakes Antony'. The December copy of *Essential Smallholding* still in its plastic wrapper, was full of sage advice. ('*A murder of crows: How to protect your lambs from foe crows…*') Automatically, I began to tidy up, sorting magazines and books in little piles: Cavafy, farming, rejections. I gathered up some folios in Gerard's beautiful handwriting and shuffled them together. The title page emerged: *Marvels,* by Gerard Woodward Delamere. It struck a faint chord. Slowly I realised that I was looking at the book of missing poems. So this was where it had been all this time! Not stolen, but lost in the vastness of his own incompetence. I glanced through it. The MS appeared to be complete. I found a paper clip and secured the pages. Some vague, dim apprehension of a possible future project began to form in me. Bit of a liberty perhaps, but if it *could* make March or April, while Gerard's memory was still fresh?

I stopped, appalled at my own temerity in leaping so soon into a dead man's shoes, and was about to go, but my eye was caught by one of the poems. I began to read more closely.

'Why,' I exclaimed aloud. 'Why, this isn't bad!'

'What are you reading that's so good?' came a voice from the doorway.

'Drusilla! I thought I was the only one here.'

Drusilla came in, looking apologetic. 'Oh well, you know, I was bored at home. Besides, I really ought to tidy out my office. So what is it that's caught your fancy?'

I held up Gerard's folios.

'Oh, so you found it! Well done! If only he'd published it earlier. I did try and persuade him, oh, years ago. I always had an instinct it might do rather well with the rural nostalgia brigade, you know, a kind of second Housman, only of course he was so embroiled with Molly he couldn't think straight.'

'Embroiled with Molly?'

'Oh, surely you knew about that. He was absolutely smitten, poor man. Why else would he have been giving her all those advances? She was far too urbane and sophisticated for him, of course, but that only fed the flame. Fed his poetry, too, I daresay. Congratulations on your new job, by the way.'

'How did you know I'd accepted? I haven't really made up my mind yet.'

'*Daily Mail*,' said Drusilla succinctly.

I bowed to fate. Clearly, there was no turning back now.

Drusilla continued, 'They're full of you today, how you've vowed to save this fine old publishing house along with the library, one of the nation's key institutions from the time of Henry Vlll, haunted by Anne Boleyn, etc. and how you've finally found the Daybreak Manuscript, that age-old mystery book of secrets that will make it all good, etc., etc. Nice picture of you, looking really rather noble. And you didn't tell me you were publishing a book on St Brendan with us!' (Here I had a guilty start, like any author who has yet to finish a book.) 'Tipped to be a bestseller, too, so they say. Quite a lot on the governing body and poor governance and questioning how simple country squires like Gerard get to be in charge of such a venerable old house, but they have great faith in the unknown new Mortimer. As they should have. What is all that noise downstairs?'

We went out into the hall and looked down. There was a commotion as several boxes clearly containing books were dumped one by one in the foyer. A black cab was parked outside. With some misgivings, I recognised the same taxi driver as had returned Monsignor Philip's manuscript all those months ago. The other person was Fay, in a red coat and matching beret. The taxi driver was haranguing her as he brought in the last of the boxes.

'You don't want to come back here, lady,' he was saying. 'Bloke here knows nothing about books.'

We watched as Fay paid him off and came storming up the stairs.

'Happy new year,' said Drusilla. 'How's life at Calling Crane?'

'Impossible. Literally a sweatshop. That woman's mad. All she thinks about is world dominion.'

'Ah,' said Drusilla. 'Thought it mightn't last.'

'And the editorial manager makes Ethel look like a pussycat. I can't possibly work there. My instinct for what to commission is being totally ruined by the stress.'

'Never mind,' said Drusilla. 'Look at what Mortimer's got here! Isn't he clever!'

We showed her Gerard's manuscript. Fay leafed through it once, twice, raised her eyebrows.

'Hm. Full of typos, I see,' she said. 'Typical Gerard. It might just make April if everyone pulls together, though.'

'Just what I was thinking,' said Drusilla. 'It does need a good trawl through, I agree. I wonder if Ethel might be bored by now of being an oil princess, lounging by a swimming pool in Texas without any errors to correct?'

'Let's photocopy this first and foremost,' said Fay, shuffling the pages. 'If nothing else, we can learn from our mistakes. Who turned this off?' glancing at me accusingly with unerring instinct as she switched the photocopier back on.

Drusilla said, 'But how are we going to pay for it? Not much left in the kitty now, you know.'

Fay was putting the MS through its paces on the photocopier, face sharp and intent as a fox. Drusilla was frowning in thought. I dug my hands into my pockets. My left hand met something solid. I pulled it out.

'What's that?' said Drusilla without much interest.

'Oh, just another of Hugo's old books. Well, not his exactly. I came across it in his flat and now I have to find out where it comes from...'

But Drusilla was not listening. She snatched the book from my hands.

'...you know, make an effort to track down the library he stole it from...'

Drusilla was examining the book. 'Don't think you'll have to look far,' she said. There was a strange note in her voice.

She turned to the second to last page. 'Look,' she said, the same slightly strangled note in her voice. By now Fay, her attention caught, was also gazing at the book as the last of Gerard's manuscript fell in neat folds from the photocopier.

'What?' she said. 'Don't tell me after all... Are the initials there?'

'Yes, and the little black boat.'

We all looked at the intertwined initials next to the tiny painting of the black boat.

'Oh,' I said. 'You recognise the provenance?'

'Oh look, and the curse,' said Drusilla happily, turning back a page and pointing to the marginalia scribbled in Latin. 'So it does exist after all! I thought it was just part of the Book's mythology. Cursed be he who steals this book from its rightful place, may he perish, *fiat fiat*, amen! Well, I hope some poor soul isn't really paying for this, or that the curse lifts now we've got it back.'

The library slip fluttered from the Book. I picked it up.

'Why, it's one of ours!' I said.

'Mortimer, you're hopeless,' said Fay. 'If you hadn't just been appointed editorial director... Can't you see?'

I took the book back into Gerard's office for more light, and we all clustered by the window. The sun was rising properly now, bathing the room in a gentle golden glow. And, as I turned the pages and felt the subtle, undeniable bounce of vellum, I did see. It was as if another sunrise of luminous clouds was disentangling itself slowly, from pages that were stirring into life after centuries of sleep. There were the bands of orange and gold, the pillars and far-off mountains, the waterfalls and streams. As I leafed through, more came into focus: the mythical beasts and plants of iridescent green, the gorgeous, sinuous gargoyles in blue and red, the kindly, ironic sages, the white herons rising, the intricate, elaborate peacock wings in patterns and colours of all kinds. Above all, there were the words, beautiful firm strokes of black and gold, letters of wisdom as clear and new now as when they were written all those centuries ago.

'It's the Book,' I said.

I sat down, in Gerard's chair. It was as if the finding of Gerard's poems had been a dress rehearsal for this, just as sleep is a dress rehearsal for death. Dazedly I saw Drusilla fumble in her bag and produce the scrap of vellum. She placed it on the torn title page and the apple tree was rounded out and completed and the torn letters of gold were reunited: *De Aurora*.

'The Daybreak Manuscript,' she said.

I placed the open Book on the desk. There was silence for a minute. Was it my imagination, or did it seem to give off a faint, indefinable scent, from very far away and very long ago?

Suddenly Moriarty appeared around the door, stalked unhurriedly over, and leapt on to my lap, purring. At the feel of his light weight and warmth, I felt a profound, irrational surge of relief. Life was suddenly the right way up again.

'Where have you *been* all this time?' I said.

'You've just missed a very important event, Moriarty,' said Fay.

He leapt up onto the desk and sniffed the Book, placing his paws on the page.

'Ah-ah,' said Drusilla. 'No cats' paws on the Book.'

I held him aloft gently, and pushed the Book further away, out of his reach. Drusilla caught it up.

Acknowledgements

I am very grateful to the team at Fairlight Books for their enthusiasm and patience, including Daniela Ferrante my editor, Mo Fillmore, Laura Shanahan, Sarah Shaw, Rebecca Blackmore-Dawes and Lizzie Vascenko. A special thanks to publisher Louise Boland for her support and for her particular contribution to this book.

FIONA VIGO MARSHALL

Find Me Falling

She bought a house where you can hear the sea, murmuring on the edge of consciousness...

Bonnie, a traumatised concert pianist, finds refuge at the edge of England, in a cliff-top house haunted by memories and broken dreams.

When Dominic, a road sweeper who is visited by neurological hauntings of his own, gives Bonnie a ring he finds on the street, elemental forces are unleashed that neither is able to control.

'The evocation of the eerie alternate realities that are just a few misfiring neurones away for us all stays with the reader long after the last page is turned'
—Dr Sallie Baxendale, Consultant Neuropsychologist, Department of Clinical & Experimental Epilepsy, Institute of Neurology, UCL

RICHARD SMYTH

The Woodcock

In 1920s England, the coastal town of Gravely is finally enjoying a fragile peace after the Great War. Jon Lowell, a naturalist who writes articles on the flora and fauna of the shoreline, and his wife Harriet lead a simple life, basking in their love for each other and enjoying the company of Jon's visiting old school friend David. But when an American whaler arrives in town with his beautiful red-haired daughters, boasting of his plans to build a pier and pleasure grounds a half-mile out to sea, unexpected tensions and temptations arise.

As secrets multiply, Harriet, Jon and David must each ask themselves, what price is to be paid for pleasure?

'The bleakness of the coast, the mist, the shifting nature of the sands all speak of contingency, brutality, deception'
—Alice Jolly, *TLS*

'Smyth's evocation of place and nature ... is imbued with a compelling sense of closely observed realism'
—Alexander Larman, *Literary Review*

SOPHIE VAN LLEWYN

Bottled Goods

When Alina's brother-in-law defects to the West, she and her husband become persons of interest to the secret services, causing both of their careers to come grinding to a halt. As the strain takes its toll on their marriage, Alina turns to her aunt for help – the wife of a communist leader, and a secret practitioner of the old folk ways.

Set in 1970s communist Romania, this novella-in-flash draws upon magic realism to weave a tale of everyday troubles that can't be put down.

'It is a story to savour, to smile at, to rage against and to weep over'
—Zoe Gilbert, author of *FOLK*

'Sophie van Llewyn has brought light into an era which cast a long shadow'
—Joanna Campbell, author of *Tying Down the Lion*

ALAN CLARK

Valhalla

May of Teck, only daughter of a noble family fallen from grace, has been selected to marry the troublesome Prince Eddy, heir to the British throne. Submitting to the wishes of Queen Victoria and under pressure from her family, young May agrees. But just as a spark of love and devotion arises between the young couple, Prince Eddy dies of influenza. To her horror, May discovers she is instead to be married to the brother, Georgie, a cold and domineering man. But what can she do?

From the author of *The Prince of Mirrors* comes this gripping account of the life of Queen Mary, one of the most formidable queens of Britain.

'This novel took me by surprise. Clark takes an iconic and forbidding figure and transforms her into a passionate, loving and damaged woman. It's a very moving tale he tells'
—Simon Russell Beale

'This is a heart-breaking tale and no mistake. A beautiful and lyrical tale told with deft brilliance'
—John Sessions